To Chris,

Full Circle

Contemporary Fiction/Western Romance/Adult Content

Full Circle

Book Two

of

The Belanger Creek Ranch Series

Gloria Antypowich

Gloria Antypowich

Copyright@ 2014 by Gloria Antypowich
Canadian Copyright Number:
Library and Archives Canada Cataloguing
(Book II of the Belanger Creek Ranch series)
Originally published under title: You can run...
Issued in print and electronic formats.
ISBN-13: 978-1511555258
ISBN-10: 1511555254

All rights reserved. No part of this book may be reproduced or transmitted in any form or by any means, electronic or mechanical, including photocopying, recording, or by any information storage and retrieval system, without permission in writing from the copyright owner.

This is a work of fiction. Names, characters, places and incidents either are the product of the author's imagination or are used fictitiously, and any resemblance to any actual persons, living or dead, events, or locales is entirely coincidental.

Published by Gloria Antypowich

I. Title. II. Title: Antypowich, Gloria, 1943-. You can run...

PS8601.N878F85 2015
C813'.6 C2014-908489-7
C2014-908490-0

Revised

Full Circle, Book Two of the Belanger Creek Series

ISBN
Softcover: 978-0-9939166-2-5
E-book: 978-0-9939166-3-2

Book Two of the Belanger Creek Ranch Series.

5 stars! Reviewed By Gisela Dixon for Readers' Favorite

Full Circle (The Belanger Creek Ranch Book 2) by Gloria Antypowich is the second book in the Belanger Ranch romance novel series. This book revolves around the relationship between Shauna Lee Holt and Brad Johnson. Frank and Colt Thompson, who were introduced in Book 1 of the series, still play a part in this novel, but not as the central characters. Full Circle is about the life and past of Shauna Lee that makes her go from one man to another without being able to achieve emotional intimacy. However, things start to change when she renews a relationship with Brad Johnson. Brad is genuinely interested in Shawna Lee, and is not ready to settle for anything less than a real relationship. However, their relationship is rocky as Shawna deals with the hurt and trauma in her past. Whether the couple are able to overcome the odds and lay the demons to rest forms the plot of this book.

Full Circle (The Belanger Creek Ranch Book 2) by Gloria Antypowich is an entertaining read, although at times I found it hard to keep track of all of the characters in the book. However, as I read more and the characters became more familiar, I was able to enjoy the story more. I liked the character of Shauna Lee as a strong, self-reliant person who, despite undergoing severe difficulties in her life and past trauma including death, is a fighter. Shauna and Brad seem to complement each other well. The Belanger Series keeps getting more interesting and I am looking forward to more books in the series.

***

5 stars! Reviewed By Mamta Madhavan for Readers' Favorite

Full Circle (The Belanger Creek Ranch Book 2) by Gloria Antypowich is a love story dedicated to all those who have gone through painful experiences and have faced betrayal, wrath, and also unconditional love while being in their relationships. Shauna Lee Holt has left her past behind and worked hard to reach where she is today. She owns Swift Current Accounting and Bookkeeping Services. Though she is known for her accountancy skills in business circles, no one knows about her personal life and her pain. Brad

Johnson, who has moved to Swift Current to set up his company, is attracted to Shauna Lee Holt. As their love story progresses, there are a lot of other things that get in the way to shake their relationship. It's a story of unconditional love, betrayal and passion, which portrays the nuances of human relationships.

The characters in the story are portrayed so well that they seem real and readers can connect with them. This love story has its complications and does not come that easily. The challenges that Brad Johnson and Shauna Lee face in their respective lives and their personal experiences give the plot many dimensions. It's a compelling read and the author's style of writing is elegant and simple but very effective. The narration is detailed, making the scenes visual to readers. What makes the read interesting is that the plot has love, betrayal, passion, denial, hatred, and anger all woven together to make it an undeniably engrossing love story. A love story readers will definitely enjoy reading.

***

5 stars! Reviewed By Rabia Tanveer for Readers' Favorite

In Full Circle by Gloria Antypowich, Shauna Lee Holt will have to decide whether to let the past win or her future prevail. When Shauna was eighteen years old, something really tragic happened in her life. Instead of curling into a ball and letting misery take over, Shauna worked her butt off. Right after graduation, she saved every single penny she could. She didn't take a relaxing breath until the day she purchased Swift Current Accounting and Bookkeeping Services. Now she is one of the best accountants. But even now, she never lets anyone near her heart. A wild romp in bed is the only intimacy she allows herself.

Brad Johnson owns Windspeer Energy and is totally in love with Shauna. But he wants everything from her. The woman is a constant dilemma, but he wants to know her and make her see how good life can be with the right partner. He has no idea what secrets she hides in her closet. And when her past is revealed, he is terrified because he knows that he can do nothing about it. It is Shauna who will have to fight her past and step into the future and love him. But is she capable of that?

Full Circle by Gloria Antypowich was very endearing. At first glance I felt that the story was going to be filled with clichés, but Gloria surprised me and I'm really glad about that. Shauna is a very powerful woman and I really loved that about her. Also, I really enjoyed the fact that her characters are middle aged, meaning that they are relatable and real! Great job. Another 5 star novel!

Reviewers note to Author:
I have to tell you, you are an amazing writer. You have put me in a state of frenzy. I'm crazily reading your books. I love them!

TABEL OF CONTENTS

DEDICATION	12
OTHER BOOKS	13
ACKNOWLEDGEMENTS	14
CHAPTER ONE	17
CHAPTER TWO	28
CHAPTER THREE	39
CHAPTER FOUR	54
CHAPTER FIVE	69
CHAPTER SIX	89
CHAPTER SEVEN	109
CHAPTER EIGHT	123
CHAPTER NINE	134
CHAPTER TEN	147
CHAPTER ELEVEN	159
CHAPTER TWELVE	176
CHAPTER THIRTEEN	188
CHAPTER FOURTEEN	209
CHAPTER FIFTEEN	215
CHAPTER SIXTEEN	241
CHAPTER SEVENTEEN	253

CHAPTER EIGHTEEN	271
CHAPTER NINETEEN	286
CHAPTER TWENTY	298
CHAPTER TWENTY ONE	316
CHAPTER TWENTY TWO	332
CHAPTER TWENTY THREE	338
CHAPTER TWENTY FOUR	345
CHAPTER TWENTY FIVE	356
CHAPTER TWENTY SIX	363
AUTHORS NOTES	372
BOOK THREE CHAPTER ONE	374
BOOK THREE CHAPTER TWO	386
BOOK THREE CHAPTER THREE	393
ABOUT THE AUTHOR	401

DEDICATION

To all who have endured painful experiences in life:

"Cry. Forgive. Learn. Move on. Let your tears water the seeds of your future happiness." - *Steve Maraboli*

"When we think we have been hurt by someone in the past, we build up defenses to protect ourselves from being hurt in the future. So the fearful past causes a fearful future and the past and future become one. We cannot love when we feel fear.... When we release the fearful past and forgive everyone, we will experience total love and oneness with all."
— *Gerald G. Jampolsky*

OTHER BOOKS
by Gloria Antypowich:

The Second Time Around, Book One of the Belanger Creek Ranch Series

The Hand of Fate, Book Three, of the Belanger Creek Ranch Series

Second Chances, Book Four, of the Belanger Creek Ranch Series

ACKNOWLEDGEMENTS

I want to express heartfelt appreciation to the following people who read and reread this manuscript, edited it and seeing it through fresh eyes, have made unbiased suggestions: Monicka Gregory, Sharron Hynes, Darlene Bell, Diane Maureen Pleasance, Cathy Hoy, and Donna Wassenaar Rezansoff. There were times when I struggled; this project would have been much more difficult without your support. You are all very special to me.

Monicka Gregory is a Social Media maven. She is the owner Bizz~Linkzz Social Media Services. She also has a successful web page of her own; Kids Goals at http://kidsgoals.com/

Sharron Hynes is a longtime friend, who is very creative in her own right. She designs and sells beautiful all-occasion cards and business cards. She is a musician and singer. She and her husband, Mel, sing and play with their band the Kootenay Legends. Their CD's are enjoyed by many people around the world.

I also want to say a big Thank You to Steve Caresser and the team at ePrintedBooks-

(http://eprintedbooks.com/)

Steve Caresser and I have worked together before, and I appreciate the quality of work that he produces. It is a pleasure to work with him again. ePintedBbooks offers a wide range of author services, as well as a virtual bookstore. Steve is also the author of five books. I have read *the Sacred Crow, What Every Married Woman Needs, and Five Gallon Bucket.* He has produced several audible poems and he is in the process creating "The Whole World News" Reality is what you make it. Steve and Jason Sinner are the newscasters for this production.

*Jason Sinner i*s a talented copy editor and proofreader at ePrintedBooks and I had the privilege of working with him on one of my husband's book before he edited this series.

Laura Wright LaRoche, at LLPix Designs, (http://llpix.com/) designed the covers for the Belanger Creek Ranch Series. She was a pleasure to work with. I'm convinced she can do anything—that she has magic in her fingers! I also discovered that Laura is an author and her creative imagination shines in that field too. I have read both *Black Woods* and *Black Woods Revealed.* They have touch of paranormal, along with mystery and horror. I thoroughly enjoyed them and the image of the "beast" lingered with me for days! *Broken Soul* is on my Kindle, waiting to be read. Her books are available on Amazon.com.

I also want to thank Jen Blood for evaluating the four book series in the first draft. She gave me terrific input, suggestions, and encouragement. Since then, she has established a successful editing service (http://jenblood.net/adian-enterprises/) and has become a bestselling author. It was a once in a lifetime opportunity for me and I would never be so fortunate now. (I cannot claim that she is a close friend) I am a big fan of her writing, and I have read all of the books in the *Erin Solomon Pentalogy.* Look for them on Amazon!

And last, but not least, my husband Lloyd Antypowich (a prolific author who has published six books at this time: *A Hunting We Did Go, From Moccasins to Cowboy Boots, Horns and Hair of the High Country, A Chip off the Old Block, Louisiana Man and Grasshopper McLain and Gotleep the Frog*; also my children and their spouses, my grandchildren and the great-grandchildren that I'm blessed to have—I love you all. I appreciate the times you have encouraged me, ragged on me for spending too many hours sitting at the computer and asked when the books were going to be published –after two years, you must have wondered if it would ever happen

CHAPTER ONE

Shauna Lee Holt stared out the window in her office. A knot of frustration formed in her gut. She sighed as she looked back at her desk, her eyes resting on the folder in front of her. *Thompson Holdings: Belanger Creek Ranch and Cantaur Farms.* She flicked a loose staple with her long, brightly colored fingernail, then absently tapped the keys on her computer keyboard.

COLT THOMPSON — the name popped up on her screen. She stared at the door he had just exited. "Why did I let him go so easily?"

But, she knew why. When he had asked her to marry him four years ago, neither one of them had professed to be in love and there were no unrealistic, romantic notions. They were mature adults... friends, companions. He came from an esteemed family in the area. He was good looking and treated her with respect, was a great dinner companion and someone to go to high profile events with. They had vacationed in Mexico once, even though he was totally out of his element.

And… he was great in bed.

Yeah – he was great in bed! She pushed her chair back and stood up, scooped up the file on her desk and carried it down the hall to the junior accountant that the client had been assigned to.

Then she walked back to her office and grabbed her jacket. Stopping at the reception desk, she told Christina Holmes that she was leaving early. As she pushed through the door, she took out her cell phone and quickly dialed a familiar number. She smiled when the deep, masculine voice answered. She knew he had read his call display when he said, "Hi sexy, how about dinner tonight?"

"Why did it take you so long to ask? I'm available, willing and ready!"

Josh Kendall laughed. "Alright sweet cheeks, but if you're available, willing and ready, I'm definitely going to need some nourishment first. We could grab a bite at The Steakhouse on George Street. Then we can head on over to your place."

She gave a throaty laugh. "That works for me; I'll meet you there."

Shauna Lee pulled up in front of the restaurant and parked. She surveyed the parking lot but didn't see Josh's car. She hesitated for a minute, running her fingers through her blonde hair which was cut in a curly shoulder length bob. She looked in the rearview mirror and big, blue eyes reflected back at her. They were her most notable feature, wide and luxuriously fringed with sweeping dark lashes that she had inherited from her mother.

A quick glance showed that her mascara and subtle application of eyeshadow were still in place. She took a slim stick out of her purse and applied fresh lipstick. Josh still hadn't shown up, so she decided to go inside and get a table and order a glass of wine for herself while she waited.

She picked a table against the wall, midway down the dining room. After ordering a glass of wine, she smoothed her stylish dress and stretched her legs while admiring her high heeled shoes. She sipped the wine and looked around the room.

People were coming and going. She watched them idly. Suddenly, she heard a familiar laugh and was suddenly alert. Colt had come into the dining room with another man; someone she didn't recognize. Her heart leaped. What was he doing there? She thought he would have been back in his happy home by now. He had left her office an hour and a half ago. He hadn't said anything about staying in town.

She watched him intently, willing him to look at her. There was a time when he would have instantly been aware of her, but today he sat down at a table, absorbed in conversation with his companion.

Irrationally, she felt slighted. If she went to the washroom, she could go past his table. She got up and walked by, tossing her hair and swaying her hips. He didn't notice her. Neither did his companion.

She went into the ladies' room, fluffed her hair and retouched her lipstick. Then she sashayed out and up to his table. She feigned surprise when she stopped by him. "Colt," she purred. "You didn't mention that you would be in town tonight."

He looked up at her, surprised. "Shauna Lee, I didn't expect to see you here." He didn't ask her to join them or indicate that she was would be welcome.

"I thought you'd be home by now."

He motioned to his companion. "We're going to an agriculture seminar at the Best Western tonight. Have you two met?"

They shook their heads, so Colt introduced them. "Shauna Lee Holt, this is Brad Johnson. Brad has set up a business here in Swift Current. He owns Windspeer Turbines. He's giving a presentation about small wind energy generated turbines at tonight's seminar."

He looked at his companion. "Shauna Lee owns Swift Current Accounting and Bookkeeping Services. Her firm has looked after our accounting needs for years."

She looked at Colt's companion: tall, well-toned, dark brown hair, gray eyes. He was a long legged, good-looking guy wearing blue jeans, a soft shirt, a western cut denim jacket and cowboy boots. His cowboy hat lay on the table. He was definitely a real country boy.

She gave him an intimate smile and she didn't miss the spark of interest that flashed in his eyes. "How nice to meet you, Brad. Are you new to the area?"

"Yes. I'm from British Columbia; Dawson Creek, to be exact."

"If you need someone to show you around, I'm free and over twenty-one." She flashed him a smile as she reached into her purse for a business card. "My number is on the card. If you need accounting services, my firm is the best." She winked. "And, I'm good company too, aren't I, Colt?"

Colt had been watching the exchange with amusement. Her question startled him. What the hell was she up to? "Oh... yeah... I guess you are."

"Colt," she chided him. "You guess? Have you forgotten already?"

She glanced up when the restaurant door opened and Josh Kendall walked in. He sauntered up to them.

"What's this sweet cheeks? I'm late, and you're checking out the competition already?" He winked at Brad. "You're out of luck this time, buddy. She's mine for tonight." He slid his hand familiarly around her waist, letting it rest on her hip, with his fingers trailing down toward her pelvic bone. "Sorry I'm late, babe. I got hung up at the last minute."

His words sent a flush of anger through her and she felt color rise in her cheeks. Then Josh tightened his arm around her waist and suggestively rubbed against her. She was suddenly embarrassed.

When Josh and Shauna Lee moved away, Brad looked at Colt and raised an eyebrow. Colt just shrugged and the two men resumed the conversation they were having before they'd been interrupted.

Shauna Lee led the way to the table where she had left her glass of wine. They sat down and Josh ordered a drink. While he downed it, he continued a commentary about his anticipation of the night ahead. It was a conversation they had shared before, but tonight it wasn't working for her. Before the waitress came to take their food order, Shauna Lee realized that she had lost her appetite for food, as well as for Josh and the distraction he offered. She had initiated the evening, but it had been a knee-jerk reaction to Colt's indifference to her. Josh was primed and ready for a night of sex, but his words gnawed at her. *He made me sound like a prostitute... or a common whore.* Embarrassment twisted in her stomach. Then anger surged through her. She would show him who was out of luck!

She set her wine glass on the table. "Josh, suddenly I don't feel very good. I'm going to pass on tonight. I'm just not into to it."

He looked at her in surprise. "What do you mean you're not *into it*? You're always into it." Then he laughed. "Are you playing hard to get?"

He reached across the table to caress her hand. He raised an eyebrow as she pulled away. "Come on, sweet cheeks. We both know that you're never hard to get. In fact, I'll bet you're hot and wet right now, and I'm ready to go." He reached for her hand.

"I'm serious, Josh!" She stood up, avoiding his touch. "I shouldn't have called you. I'm going home now, and I'm going alone."

"Like hell you are! You think you can tease me and get away with it? I'll be at your door, right behind you." He stood up and grabbed her arm, trying to pull her with him.

"Josh Kendall." She had raised her voice and heads turned. "Take your hands off me. I said *no*."

His face turned red and he let go of her. He swore as he turned and went to pay his bill. Then he strode outside.

Shauna Lee finished her glass of wine. She looked out the window and saw that Josh was still standing outside, waiting for her. Damn him! She cringed when she saw Colt look at her, and she decided to escape to the washroom. She avoided his table on her way.

Ten minutes later she thought it would be safe to leave, certain that Josh would have left by then. Colt and Brad Johnson were paying at the till when she slipped out the door. She had started toward her car when Josh stepped around the corner of the building.

"Thought you'd ditch me, eh?" He grabbed her arm. "What the hell's gotten into you? I don't appreciate being embarrassed in public."

"And I don't like having you talk about me like I'm a common whore."

"Funny, you never seemed to mind acting like one before. What's got you so high and mighty now?"

"You bastard!" She slapped his face.

Colt and Brad witnessed the scene when they came outside. Colt quickly realized that the situation could get ugly. In an instant, he made a decision and stepped into the angry tableau.

"All right, you two; it's time to cool off." He looked at Josh. "It's none of my business, but she clearly said 'No' when you were in the restaurant. You'd be wise to walk away for now. Both of you need time to rethink things and work out your problems when you're calmer."

Josh's face flushed. "Damned right it's none of your business and aren't you one to talk! How many years did she screw the balls off you?" He laughed harshly. "Why aren't you home with that wife of yours instead of here defending her? Don't tell me you've still got the hots for our Shauna Lee!"

"That's enough!" Colt spoke with steely calm. He reached into his pocket, took out his cell phone and flipped it open. He pushed a button and waited while it rang. Then he spoke.

"I'm calling to report a problem brewing in the parking lot at The Steakhouse on George Street. I'd appreciate it if you would send someone down here to diffuse the situation before it gets out of hand."

He waited for a couple of seconds. "I'm Colt Thompson. Yes, I'll wait here to fill you in and I'll give you a statement."

His hard, green eyes pinned Josh as he closed the phone and put it back in his pocket. "Don't ever question my love and loyalty to my wife. Shauna Lee is my business associate, and I still view her as a friend! That's it, period!

"But I won't stand by and watch any man force himself on a woman. The fact that she and I had a relationship in the past makes no difference now. That is in the past."

They heard a siren blip twice and the flash of red and blue lights could be seen coming down the street. Josh swore violently as he turned to his truck. "You'll pay for calling the cops on me. I know people in high places."

He laughed. "Hell, I know a guy at the cop shop that's screwin' her, too. Good luck, bitch!" He slid into his truck, started the engine and gave Colt 'the finger' as he eased past the patrol car that was pulling into the parking lot.

Shauna Lee covered her face and wished she could disappear. She had been insulted by Josh's attitude and his lack of respect for her. Now she was humiliated. Colt had come to her rescue, but he hadn't defended her honor. In fact, he had left no doubt about where she fit in his life. There were no lingering feelings of attraction there. What a fool she was; and now she had to go through all of this hassle with the police.

Two officers stepped out of the patrol car. Colt stepped toward the one nearest to him. He extended his hand. "Colt Thompson, sir. I made the call." He introduced Shauna Lee and then briefly sketched out what had happened.

Brad Johnson stood back, not wanting to get involved. He was grateful that Colt hadn't drawn him into the situation, even though they were together. He was surprised by this steely, calm side of Colt Thompson. Clearly he was a man who didn't stand for much nonsense. He thought about the way he had made that call, knowing it would involve him in an awkward situation.

His eyes moved to the woman standing by Colt. She was clearly someone from his past; he had left no doubt about that. She was good looking. It would seem that she was pretty hot too. Josh Kendal was probably ten years younger than her, and he had left little doubt that their relationship was all about sex. She was definitely trouble; the kind of woman a smart man would steer clear of.

Colt walked over to Brad. "I'm sorry about this. I have to stick around for a few minutes. Go ahead and get set up. I'll get there as soon as I'm finished here." Brad nodded and walked across the street to the Best Western.

Twenty minutes later, Colt came into the small meeting room, followed by a subdued Shauna Lee. Brad had saved a seat at the front for him and he was surprised when Colt ushered Shauna Lee into it. "The place is packed. I'll find a spot against the wall at the back," he said softly as he stepped away.

Brad scarcely looked at Shauna Lee, but he could sense the tension in her body as she sat next to him. Shauna Lee shifted uncomfortably in her seat, and he couldn't help but notice the way the slim skirt of her dress rode up on her thigh, or the curve of her ankles and the slender length of her legs. She was petite and delicate looking.

He had set up his laptop when he had first arrived, so all he had to do now was turn it on and start his PowerPoint presentation. He fidgeted, waiting for his turn; wanting to get up and move away from her. He was uncomfortably aware of her.

He had been an onlooker in the parking lot, but he couldn't push aside everything that had happened; like the way she had smiled at him when Colt had introduced them. He had recognized the invitation. Then she had baited Colt and that had thrown him. Colt's cool, disinterested response had piqued his interest. Then Josh Kendall had shown up and the whole picture had deteriorated.

Brad gave his presentation about the innovation of wind energy and its potential for use in agriculture. He didn't miss the change in Shauna Lee's demeanor as he spoke. She became alert, with unfeigned interest. She watched the slides and listened to the questions from the audience and paid attention to his answers.

The seminar broke for coffee after he finished and people started circulating around the room. He fielded several questions about his company's wind-energy program. Eventually, he noticed Shauna Lee standing at the edge of the group listening and talking with the others. He noticed the professionalism in her manner and the respect in their demeanor as she conversed with people. She was all business. There was no sign of the coquette he had seen earlier.

He had to wonder. Who was the real Shauna Lee Holt?

After the meeting, Colt joined Brad and helped him pack up his presentation. He looked directly at Brad when they were finished. "I need to ask a favor of you."

"OK."

"The cop said that Shauna Lee shouldn't go home right away. He wanted to have a talk with Josh and tell him to back off, and he was concerned that Josh would show up at her place before he tracked him down.

"I suggested that she come here with me. I told him that I'd make sure she got home all right after the meeting. I hate to ask you, but would you come with me? I'd rather not go there on my own. Do you understand?"

Brad sensed the tension in Colt. "Yeah—I think I do."

"It won't take long. She doesn't live far from here. I just want to make sure that she gets in the house all right. Then I'll bring you back to your pickup and I'll head home to my wife and kids."

**

Shauna Lee sank onto the couch in her living room. Colt had been a perfect gentleman. He'd followed her home in his truck, walked her to the door and made sure she'd gotten safely inside.

She couldn't ignore the emptiness in her gut. What the hell was wrong with her? She couldn't get Colt out of her mind. It was insane. He was married and nauseatingly happy with Frank and had the family he never thought he would have. Even though she'd never seen him exclusively, she and Colt had been 'friends with benefits' for four years before he'd gotten married. She'd watch him change into a wonderful, loving husband and father, and she'd began to regret that she'd let him slip away.

She winced. She had made several subtle advances to him throughout the past year, but he was so involved in his own happiness he hadn't even seemed to notice.

And tonight... she cringed remembering how he had made it very clear to Josh that she was part of his past.

She stood up and walked into her bedroom. She threw her purse on the chair, stripped out of her clothes and went into the bathroom. She turned on the shower and let uncomfortably warm water sluice over her, feeling the burn, wanting to wash away the humiliation that Josh's words had left with her.

She stepped out on the mat and gave herself a brisk rubdown, then quickly blew her hair dry. She didn't look too closely at her reflection in the mirror, unwilling to meet her own eyes.

As she turned to step back into her bedroom, she muttered *Screw him*, as she flipped the switch to turn off the bathroom light.

Her eyes lit on the bed. She laughed with irony. *That's exactly what he planned to be doing; right there on that bed, just like they'd done how many times before?* She felt a flush of disgust. She wasn't certain how many times they had wrinkled the sheets there.

She sat on the edge of the bed, thinking. He'd been a voracious sexual companion. She hadn't asked for love. But he didn't respect her. *What do you mean; you're not into it? You're always into it.* His words played a loop in her mind. *We both know you're never hard to get.*

She cringed remembering his response when she had told him she didn't like having him talk about her like she was a common whore. *Funny, you never seemed to mind acting like one before. What's got you so high and mighty now?*

Anger washed through her, followed by embarrassment. *Hell, I know a guy at the cop shop that's screwin' her, too.* Her breath hitched. He had to have meant Jim Wiley. She had been with him a couple of times. Had they compared notes? Revulsion washed over her.

She buried her face in her hands. "How did I get to this place?" she groaned.

She turned back the covers and shut off the light on her night table. She lay down, pulling the sheets up under her chin. She tried to force the tension out of her body and relax, but her mind would not shut off. She could hear Josh's voice saying, you're *out of luck this time, buddy. She's mine for tonight.*

What had Colt and his friend thought? Not that it really mattered but damn it, it did matter to her. She turned the light back on, then went to her dresser and pulled out a pair of cotton pajamas. Usually, she didn't wear anything to bed, but tonight she felt naked and she needed something; as if the pajamas would cover her humiliation.

She went to the bathroom. She opened the medicine chest and took a sleeping pill, then after a hesitation, swallowed a second one to ensure the oblivion of sleep; a respite from the devil that beleaguered her mind.

CHAPTER TWO

Frank Thompson tiptoed into the nursery to peek at the three-year-old twins who were sleeping soundly in their beds. Selena's dark curls were tousled on her pillow. Her 'blankey' was clutched tightly in her fingers, tucked up under her chin and pulled up against her cheek.

She was a combination of both her mother and father. She had Colt's dark curly hair and Frank's dark brown eyes. Her cupid bow lips were parted softly and a slurp of drool ran out of the corner of her mouth and onto the pillow. She was a wisp of a child; pixie-like, but determined and feisty.

Sam was curled up in the other bed, his back to her, moonlight spilling softly over his sheets. She could hear the slurping sounds he made as he sucked his thumb. He was as sturdy as a linebacker; quiet and unexcitable. He had inherited his mother's auburn hair with the same fiery glints, but his eyes were calm blue ponds like those of his namesake, Frank Samuel Lamonte, his great-grandfather, and the man she had been named after.

Her hand moved to the subtle roundness of her tummy. "I hope you have your daddy's green eyes," she whispered as she turned and eased out of the room silently, closing the door gently behind her.

She went downstairs and into the living room and walked over to the bay window. Pushing aside the ruffle of the gauzy white Priscilla curtain, she looked out past the veranda, her eyes traveling down the tree-lined driveway that lead into the farmyard from the gravel road.

She glanced at her watch, noting that it was nine-thirty. Colt should be getting home any moment. He had gone to Swift Current earlier in the day. He'd had an earlier appointment at the accountants and then later in the evening he was attending a meeting that the district agriculturist was hosting at the Best Western Hotel.

Restless, she wandered over and turned on the electric fireplace, then sank into a deep armchair and watched the artificial flames flicker in the darkness. A few minutes later, she heard the crunch of tires on the driveway.

Colt bounded up the steps onto the veranda and was opening the screen door as Frank opened the inside one to meet him.

"You had a long meeting!" she said with a smile, as she clasped his hand and pulled him inside. She shut the door behind him and he pulled her into a warm embrace.

"Yeah, it was interesting—not just the meeting!" He released her, took off his hat and put it on the rack, and then turned to her.

"What else happened?"

"Oh, Shauna Lee...." He shook his head. "She was at the restaurant where Brad and I went for supper before the meeting. She came by and said hello and made a hit on Brad right off the bat!" He grinned and shook his head. "That woman never changes. Then Josh Kendall came in. He's a young high roller who works in the oil business and he has an office in town. I guess they had arranged to meet there. When he arrived, she was talking to us. He got territorial and let Brad know that she was his for the night.

"I think she was embarrassed by the way he said it. She got pretty red. They went to their table, and I have no idea what happened, but obviously the evening didn't go as planned. They got into a disagreement and she told him 'no' loud enough for the whole restaurant to hear. He was pissed off. He paid his bill and stormed out.

"She stayed at the table until he went outside. She waited a few minutes and then she went to the washroom. I think she was giving him time to get out of there. She must have slipped outside while Brad and I were paying for our meal.

"When we went outside, Josh was still there and they were going at it again. She slapped his face and he grabbed her. It was getting ugly. I thought I could diffuse the situation if I stepped in and got them both to cool off."

He looked at her sheepishly. "It didn't work. He just got uglier and made her sound like the town tramp. Then he got personal, bringing up the fact that she and I had been together in the past and suggesting that I still had a thing for her.

"I set him straight on that score, but his attitude really put me off. I called the cops, and then he was really pissed off. He threw some more insults at Shauna Lee and sped out of the parking lot just as a cop car arrived."

"Colt!"

"He won't be a problem. He was embarrassed as much as anything. I suspect he was planning to spend the night at her place, but she plainly told him 'no' and he was trying to force her into the situation. When the cops came, I told them what I'd seen and they talked to Shauna Lee."

"Where was Brad when all this happened?"

"He stood back and watched the whole mess unfold. After I called the cops, I told him to go set up for the meeting and I'd meet him there when I was finished. He left right away. I'm sure he was relieved."

"I wonder what he thought."

"He didn't comment. But after Shauna Lee talked to the police, they said she should wait for a while before she went home, so they had a chance to track Josh down and warn him to leave her alone.

"I ended up taking her to the meeting with me. After it was over, I asked Brad to come with me, and we followed her when she drove home. I made sure she got into the house and heard her turn the dead bolt. Then I took Brad back to his truck and came home. That's why I'm so late."

He put his arm around her and pulled her back into his embrace, kissing her deeply. "I love you," he whispered. "I can't begin to tell you how much I appreciate having you in my life."

She nibbled on his bottom lip. "Let's go to bed." They turned off the lights as they moved through the house and up the stairs, stopping at the nursery to check on the twins.

"Little angels," Colt whispered as he looked at them, smiling.

She chuckled. "They look like angels when they are sleeping," she whispered. "But sometimes the halo needs a little polishing when they are awake."

He led her into the bedroom, where he began to unbutton her blouse as he kissed the corner of her lips. His fingers gently brushed her skin as they slid down to undo the tiny clasp between her breasts, releasing her bra. His mouth followed the same path, dropping soft feathery kisses all the way down her throat, over her shoulder to where the bra strap had lain, then down along her breast, coming to rest on her full nipple.

She moaned and pushed against him. Three years of marriage and the birth of the twins had not dimmed the fire that his touch stirred in her. The flames leaped hungrily as they helped each other undress. They tumbled on the bed and lost themselves in the ageless ritual of sexual fulfillment.

Exhausted and satiated they dozed, Frank lying in the circle of Colt's arm, her cheek against his chest. An hour later, they stirred and moved to pull back the sheets and get into bed. Colt was quiet.

"What are you thinking?" Frank whispered.

"About how wonderful our life is; you and me, the twins, and in a few months our new baby is arriving." He reached over and rested his hand on her belly. "When I think about where I was stuck before, in my anger and bitterness; all I would have missed if you hadn't come along...."

"That goes for me too, Colt. When you told me what happened with Shauna Lee tonight, I had to feel sorry for her. I wonder if she'll ever find what we have."

"You know, I'm not sure what she's doing these days, but if any of the stuff Josh was rattling off is true, I'm concerned about her. He made it sound like she is pretty promiscuous. When I was with her, she was definite about not wanting to get into a real relationship.

We spent a lot of time together over those four years, but when I asked her to marry me; she wasn't very keen on it. If I hadn't been so insistent, I doubt if she would've agreed."

"What is she running from, Colt? Obviously, it's not sex because she seems to gravitate to that. So what has hurt her so much?"

Colt sighed. "I know her dad was an alcoholic. Shauna Lee had a brother quite a bit younger than her and she worshiped him. He died in an accident on the farm when he was three or four."

Frank groaned. "It makes me sick to think of that. How could any of them deal with it?"

"I think that is part of her problem. It was like the straw that broke the camel's back. From the little she said, her dad just buried himself deeper in the bottle. Her mother slid into depression. Shauna Lee was about thirteen when it happened. She had no support at home.

"Her dad eventually left them and I think her mom died. She moved in with a local guy when she was really young. I don't know if they ever actually got married. I have no idea what happened after that, but eventually she was on her own again. She's got guts. She pulled herself together, finished her education and got her CA."

"I wish she could meet someone she would truly be happy with."

"I doubt if she'll meet that kind of guy doing what she seems to be doing now."

"Do you think it would help if you talked to her, Colt?"

He frowned. "I'd really have to think about that. It bothered me to hear the insinuations that Josh made tonight. That's why I asked Brad to go with me when I followed her back to her place. I don't want to do anything that could be misinterpreted. I don't want to put us at risk."

Frank snuggled close. "I'm not worried about that. We're solid."

The phone rang at six-thirty the next morning. Frank was pouring coffee when Colt answered it. The conversation was brief.

"That was Ollie. He's wondering when we're going to bring the cows and calves in from the lease."

"I want to go with you this year. I'd enjoy a few days in the saddle again!"

Colt frowned. "Will that be okay? You know; for the baby and all?"

"I'm not sick! I'm pregnant. That's the oldest condition in the world and I'm as strong as a horse!" Her smile was radiant. "I was riding range when I was carrying the twins and it didn't hurt me. I've missed being on the roundup the past three years, but I really couldn't go while the twins were so small.

"They're old enough to leave with your mom now if she'll look after them. It would be great if your mom and dad would come out to the ranch and watch them there. Then we could give them a kiss goodnight and tuck them in. What do you think?" Excitement sparkled in her eyes.

Colt thought for a moment. "Ollie would sure be happy to have you there. He still swears you are the best ranch hand he ever had." He reached out and took her hand, pulling her onto his lap. He nuzzled the curve of her neck. "And I'd love to have you with me. We made some wonderful memories out there."

She turned her face to settle her lips on his. Their kiss deepened and she could feel him harden as she rested against him. He shifted and turned her to face him, his hand moving to her breast. Fire leaped in her groin.

"Do we have time?" he whispered. She nodded and he swept her up in his arms and carried her up to their bedroom. They tore off their clothes and fell onto the unmade bed that they had left little more than an hour before.

Fifteen minutes later they lay together, panting and sweaty. Colt ran his fingers through the tips of her hair. "You're still hot, woman!"

"And you're still horny!" she said with a laugh. "We'd better get up and have breakfast. The coffee will be cold and the twins will be up in half an hour. Quickie time is over!"

He sighed. "You're right. While you make breakfast, I'll call Mom and see if they'll come out to the ranch and watch the kids."

Colt was frowning when he came to the kitchen after he'd called his parents. "Mom can't come; she and dad already have plans. She suggested a nanny that one of her friends knows. The woman was an elementary teacher. Her husband died ten years ago and her kids are grown. She retired and the last couple of years she's been a nanny for Mrs. Chapman's daughter. Mom says she comes highly recommended. We could check her out. What do you think?"

"I don't know. We don't know her and the twins don't know her. I'm not sure if..."

"We could meet her and see how we feel about her. If it feels right, we can bring her out here and see how it works with her and the kids. I've been thinking about this for a while... I want to get someone to help you. You handle everything so well, but sometimes I'm just blown away by all you do. I see how much work the twins are, and now with you being pregnant again, I'd like to get someone to give you a hand."

"Colt, I don't need help—"

He laid two fingers across her lips. "I have a selfish motive in this, too. I'd like you to be able to come to a meeting, like the one last night. Or go with me to a horse race when I go, and you could come out to the ranch for a day without having to worry about the twins. You should have a bit of time for yourself. I didn't marry you to keep you barefoot and pregnant. I wanted you to be my companion as well!"

"I... all right, we can check her out. When are you moving cows?"

"Ollie and I decided next week will work best, so we'd better get on this nanny thing right away. I want you to be on the roundup this year."

"Did your mom tell you her name?"

"Ellie Raines. Mom is going to call back with her phone number."

"Does she know if she's available now...?" Her keen senses detected a whimper upstairs. "That's Selena! The kids are awake!" Frank whirled and went flying up the stairs to the nursery. Colt shook his head. She was so in tune with the twins that it amazed him.

He could hear her crooning to their daughter. Selena would be rubbing her eyes with her little fists, her face all scrunched up on the verge of tears, protesting grumpily as she shed the drowsiness of sleep. Sam would be sitting on his bed, calm and wide-eyed. They were as different as night and day.

The phone rang. Colt answered it, ignoring the call display. He didn't recognize the callers' voice.

"Could I speak to Colt Thompson?" a youthful sounding female voice asked.

"Speaking."

"This is Ellie Raines. Connie Chapman talked to your mother this morning. She said you were looking for a babysitter next week."

"We are. Of course, we need to meet you first."

"I could drop by any time today."

"That would be great. Do you know where we live?"

"Connie said you lived on a farm near Cantuar, but I don't know your exact address."

Colt gave her directions and she said she would be there around eleven that morning. Then he bounded up the stairs to tell Frank and the twins.

Ellie Raines was punctual. She drove down the tree-lined driveway and parked her silver colored compact car in front of the older two-story house. She noted how well-kept the house and grounds were. As she stepped out of her car, she looked through the tall trees that formed a dividing line between the lawn around the house and the equipment yard.

She looked with interest at the huge, modern combines parked in front of a large machine shed. Experience told her that harvesting was finished. The weather had been good for harvesting. She noted the large metal grain bins lined up. The little tell-tale piles of grain on the ground in front of each one told her that grain had been augured into them and they were probably all full.

She turned as she heard the house door open. Her eyes met a tall, good-looking man with the greenest eyes she had ever seen. She decided he was probably in his late thirties or early forties. She smiled as she sized him up.

"Hi. I'm Ellie. I was just looking at the combines and the grain bins. My husband and I had a mixed farm near Chitek Lake. Our kids weren't interested in the farm and it was too much for me to handle, so I sold it after he died. But, I've always loved harvest time."

Colt smiled as he watched her walk up the sidewalk. She was dressed in comfortable brown chino slacks and a fresh-looking pink blouse. She was probably about five foot four, pleasantly rounded and motherly looking; not fat, but definitely not thin. He guessed that she was in her early sixties. Her hair was a warm brown with golden highlights and a few threads of silver showing up in the temples, It was cut in a smart style that suited her well. Her eyes were a cool gray; warm, open and friendly. His first instinct was that he liked her. He reached out to shake her hand and invited her in.

"Fran," he called. "Mrs. Raines is here."

He heard her answer from upstairs. "I'll be right there. I'm changing Selena's clothes. She spilled a glass of milk on herself. Will you make a fresh pot of coffee? Oh, and watch where you step by the table. I didn't get the milk all wiped up."

Colt motioned for Ellie to follow him into the kitchen. He pulled some paper towels from the roll and turned toward the table. Ellie reached to take them from his hand. "Let me clean up the spill while you make the coffee. I'm dying for a cup." She smiled as she took the paper towels from his hand and nimbly bent down to wipe up the spill.

Frank and the twins came down the stairs, and smiles of unfeigned delight wreathed Ellie's face. Colt introduced her to Fran and each child in turn. Selena ran to Ellie, open and accepting and Ellie stooped and picked her up. Frank and Colt watched the immediate connection between them and looked at each other with mutual understanding.

Ellie moved slowly toward Sam, speaking to him softly as she knelt down in front of him. She gently stood Selena on the floor beside her, cradling her close to her as she held her hand out to Sam. She spoke to both of the children, letting Sam make the next move. At first he clung firmly to his mother's legs, but he gradually relaxed as Ellie gained his confidence and reached out to touch her fingers.

She looked up at Colt. "Well, daddy, is that cup of coffee ready?" She took both children by the hand and followed

Frank and Colt to the kitchen table. As they drank coffee, Ellie told them she was looking for full-time work and asked them to phone her past employers, particularly the family where she had last worked. She was no longer needed there because the mother had been laid off, but she had been sad to leave. She said she loved working with small children.

She left, giving them time to make a decision and assuring them that she could be available immediately. That evening, after they had checked her references and talked to her former employers, Colt phoned Ellie and confirmed that they wanted to hire her for two weeks. If the five of them worked well together, he assured her there was a good possibility that they would want her to stay on full-time.

She was thrilled and agreed to be there the next day.

"Where is she going to stay?" Frank asked.

"Well, she could stay in the spare room."

Frank wrinkled her nose. "Not enough privacy. That cuts out early morning activities like this morning." She grinned as she arched her eyebrow.

"We can't have that! What else can we do? We don't have anywhere else to put her."

"Could we buy a mobile home; something that's not too big, yet roomy enough for her to be comfortable? Then she would have her own place to stay. She'll have enough space to do whatever she wants, and we'll have our privacy too."

"That is a great idea. We'll have to figure out how to get power and water and sewer hooked up for it right away."

CHAPTER THREE

Shauna Lee struggled to consciousness. Her thinking was fuzzy, still affected by the extra sleeping pill. She stretched out and rolled over onto her back, pushing the covers away from her face. She squinted against the light that streamed in through the bedroom window and then looked at the clock on her night table. "Ten o'clock. Jeez, I simply died!"

She swung her legs off the bed and sat up. Her pajamas were uncomfortably twisted around her slender frame. Her head was still foggy. She rubbed her eyes and yawned, thinking that a cup of coffee would bring her back to the world of the living.

She stood up and wandered into the kitchen. After she had set up the coffee pot, she wandered over to the front window and looked outside. Idly she watched a couple strolling hand and hand down the street, enjoying the beautiful September morning. Another family came into sight; a husband and wife and two small children.

The girl swung on her father's hand. The little boy was

about four years old. He was running ahead, then spinning back and charging toward his mother. He stopped just beyond her reach, eluding her as she smiled and leaned forward to catch him. Then he ran back up the street again, laughing as he went.

Shauna Lee's eyes fastened on the boy. She bit her lip as she watched him. Feelings she had buried twenty-one years ago bubbled to the surface. She shook her head, pushing them away, but she couldn't seem to tear her focus away from the child. Tears filled her eyes, blurring her vision, then escaping down her cheeks. She turned from the window, dashing them away with the back of her hand.

She stumbled to the table and sat on a chair. Sobs racked her body and she cried uncontrollably until she was exhausted and drained. Then she sat, staring out the kitchen window, her emotions numb.

Ben would have been twenty-two now; the son she had loved with all her being and the son whose father, Dave Trutcher, wouldn't accept because he had been born with a physical deformity that revolted him.

Shauna Lee couldn't hold back any longer. She ran to the bathroom and vomited the bitter acid that roiled in her stomach. It burned her throat and lingered sour in her mouth. She hadn't eaten anything since late the afternoon before. The coffee she had made sat in the thermal carafe on the counter.

She was cold and sick. She filled a glass with water and rinsed her mouth, then crawled back into bed and huddled under the sheets, willing her thoughts to go away. Gradually the exhaustion of her emotions claimed her in sleep.

She awakened later in the afternoon. Her watch showed it was four-thirty. Her head hurt and she knew she needed to eat. She went to the kitchen and poured herself a cup of coffee. The carafe had kept it lukewarm. She sipped it mindlessly and opened the fridge to look inside. Nothing looked appetizing. She closed the door, uncertain what she would do. She knew she needed something, but what? She looked like hell and she was definitely was not leaving the house. Pizza? She could order in. She reached for the phone and then hesitated.

In her mind, pizza was meant to be shared. Suddenly she realized that she couldn't think of anyone to share one with. At one time, she would have called Colt. In the years since then... well she'd seldom had lonely weekends. Men like Josh hadn't been hard to find for company.

What the hell had happened this time? It was as if Josh had opened Pandora's Box with his crude remarks and things just kept tumbling out. She had been forced to look at her life, like Scrooge at Christmas time, but she wasn't Scrooge and it wasn't Christmas. However, as it had been for Scrooge, it was difficult for her to accept what her life had become.

She picked up the phone and ordered a pizza. She decided to have a shower while she waited for it to be delivered. She would eat it by herself while she watched TV and escape reality until she got back on track.

Shauna Lee woke up crying at four-thirty on Sunday morning. She had been dreaming about the night Ben had died. The horror of it clung to her as she fought off the cloud of sleep. Dave's rage hung in the room, so real she could feel it.

She lay there thinking about that soul-destroying time in her life. She hadn't told anyone about Ben, not even Colt. What had triggered those memories, making them come to the surface now?

She got up and went to the bathroom. She was still wearing her pajamas from the day before, and they were creased and damp with sweat and tears. Glancing at the clock, she noted that it was only five in the morning.

What day is it? she wondered. She went into the kitchen and turned on the soft light under the microwave that was installed above the stove. Automatically she emptied the thermal coffee carafe and set up a new pot of coffee. She poured herself a bowl of dry cereal, splashed some milk over it and added a sprinkle of sugar.

Full Circle

Then she sat down at the table. She ate mindlessly, purposely pushing her clamoring thoughts aside. It must be Sunday... it'll be another long day to get through. What am I going to do? I can't just sit here and drown in my memories.

She sighed and got up to pour herself a cup of coffee. "Maybe I should go for a drive, but where would I go?" She wandered over to the couch and turned on the TV, but there wasn't much that interested her at six in the morning.

She surfed through the channels and clicked on a program about small wind turbines. She listened with idle interest as the spokesman explained to the interviewer how the new small wind turbines were helping the environment by replacing dirty grid power with free, clean, green, wind-energy that was economical and affordable too.

When he introduced their newest dealer, she became alert. She recognized Brad Johnson. She heard him say, "Years ago the landscape of western Canada was dotted with windmills that were mainly used to pump water out of the ground."

The rich timbre of his voice and the smooth way he delivered his words caught her attention. Its cadence captured her. She watched his expressions and the way he moved his hands as he talked, shifting slightly on his feet from time to time. He was confident and sincere, an earthy, unpretentious, solid individual. She'd been aware of that Friday night, but now she was really struck by it.

She picked up his words again... "and eventually I can see this type of landscape recreated again with our small power-generating wind turbines popping up on farms and ranches across the country. They are highly efficient, require very little maintenance and are simple to install. A truck or a tractor will easily pull the assembled tower into place."

The sound of his voice washed over her. She studied his physique. He was tall; over six feet she was certain. And she'd bet he didn't get those muscles pumping iron in the gym. He probably got them from throwing bales or wrestling calves.

He was wearing blue jeans again, and a western shirt that

accentuated the gray of his eyes. He wasn't wearing a Stetson today, and his rich brown hair was ruffled by the breeze. Did he have cowboy boots on? She watched closely as the camera moved back. "Yes!" she murmured "And nice ones, too. He is a hunk!" She watched him dreamily until the camera shifted away to show a wind turbine being installed.

"And... I'm sure he thinks I'm the town tramp. He probably wouldn't come near me." The reality hit her like a punch.

Discontent washed over her as she surfed through the channels a few more times, then stood up and turned off the TV. She dropped the remote on the coffee table and glanced at her watch again, debating what she should do. It was only eight-thirty. She sighed deeply. "This is going to be a long day. Well, I have laundry to do. That will take up some of my time."

As she gathered her laundry from the hamper in her bedroom, she wondered what had happened to her. Why haven't I made friends? Right now, I wish I had someone to talk to—maybe a girlfriend. But I've never had a real girlfriend, she thought as she dropped a load of whites in the washing machine.

The phone rang as she was closing the lid. She turned the washer on and ran to answer it. Glancing at the call display, she hesitated, trying to recognize the name. It was from the Country Lane Inn in town.

Who the heck? she wondered as she answered. "Hello?"

"Shauna Lee, this is Mitch...."

"Mitch...?" There was a question in the word. Who...?

"Mitch Wagner, from Saskatoon."

"Oh, Mitch. It's been a while. You caught me by surprise."

"I'm in town. I have a meeting tomorrow, but I was wondering if you wanted to get together today. I think the Eliminators Car Club has its show and shine at Riverside Park. We could stop and check it out if you like."

"Hey, I'd love to get together. I'm just sort of kicking

around here on my own!"

"All right, I'll drop over in an hour or so to pick you up. It'll be great to see you again!"

"I'll be waiting," she said with a smile. *Mitch, you're a wish come true. You've rescued me from myself. Thank you! Thank you!* She quickly shut off the washing machine and ran to the bedroom. She opened a dresser drawer and selected a sexy, lacy set of matching panties and bra. She dashed into the bathroom and turned on the shower.

She washed her hair and lathered her body quickly and then reached for her razor and shaved her underarms and legs. As she rinsed off she ran her hands over her skin. Smooth as silk, she thought with a smile.

She blew her hair dry, applied her makeup and added a light spray of seductive perfume. Then she slipped into her bra and panties and checked out the closet to decide what to wear. After some thought, she selected a silky, bayou blue top that closed with a crossover tie and showed a lot of cleavage. It brought out the color of her eyes.

She picked out a pair of stretchy jeans that fit her like a glove and grabbed a long, tweedy blue sweater. She rifled through her sock drawer, grabbed a pair of white ones and then slid her feet into a pair of running shoes. She was ready. She went into the kitchen and tossed her purse and house keys on the table. She poured herself a cup of coffee, just as the doorbell rang.

She had totally slipped into predator mode without even thinking. She waited a minute and then strolled to the door. *Can't appear too eager*, she mused as she opened it. She smiled coyly at the tall blonde man that stood in front of her.

"Mitch, imagine seeing you again!" She stood aside to let him step in, then closed the door behind him. She looked him over from top to bottom, then slid her arms around his neck and pulled him to her.

He smiled as he bent his head to kiss her gently. "It *has* been a long time," he said softly.

She nestled her head against his shoulder. "It has." She slipped her hand into his and led him into the living room, pulling him down onto the couch beside her. Her hand slid to rest on his thigh. "You're looking handsome," she said, smiling into his admiring eyes.

"And you're still gorgeous! You never change. How long has it been; three or four years? What's been going on in your life? I heard once that you were engaged to a farmer. That surprised me!"

"What surprised you; that I was engaged or that I was engaged to a farmer?"

He laughed and raised her hand to his lips, nibbling on her fingers. "Both. I couldn't picture you with a farmer; or for that matter, one guy. You always said you never get married."

She gently pulled her hand away. "And I didn't."

"I heard something to that effect."

She stood up. "So what are we going to do?"

He raised his eyebrows and looked at her quizzically.

"Hey, cool your jets boy! We've got the whole day ahead of us." She playfully punched him in the shoulder. "I at least expect a nice dinner and a good glass of wine," she said, laughing as she walked to the table and picked up her keys and purse.

"It's just that you're looking so...."

"I'm sure I heard you say something about going to the Eliminators Show and Shine." She walked to the door and stood waiting for him. "I thought they usually had that in August."

"There was a change in schedule this year." He grinned as he pushed himself up off the couch and walked over to join her. He pushed the door closed and pulled her against him, kissing her deeply, his tongue slipping into her mouth, dancing with hers.

She could feel the bulge in his crotch as he rubbed against her and fire leaped in her groin. She moaned as he ravaged her mouth. Then he swung the door open, pushing her out in

Full Circle

front of him. "We'll do it your way for now; then we'll do it my way tonight!"

It was a beautiful, fall day and there was a large crowd at the show. Shauna Lee smiled for the first time in two days. She loved looking at the hot rods and old classic cars. She knew a lot of the people there; several of them were her clients. She stopped and chatted with them as she moved through the rows of cars with Mitch.

Mitch met a man he knew and stopped to talk business, so she kept wandering down the line. A hopped-up old truck caught her eye. She wandered closer to look it over. "Sweet!" she said softly as she trailed her finger along the polished grill.

"It's well done," a deep rich voice commented from behind her. Shauna Lee jumped and whirled around, almost losing her balance. She stared into a pair of warm gray eyes that widened in surprise. Brad Johnson was standing there.

Her heart stood still momentarily. "Oh... you... I didn't hear you come up behind me."

She looked so shocked, so defenseless, he couldn't help but smile. He reached out and touched her shoulder in a gesture meant to steady her. "I didn't realize it was you."

She flushed. *Or you probably have gone the other way*, she thought. "Isn't this a cool old truck," she babbled, trying to hide the fact that seeing him had thrown her off balance. She slid a caressing hand along the bright red fender. "It's a 1949 model!"

"It's custom built. These guys rebuild old cars and trucks for a hobby, and it's an expensive one!" He touched his toe against the spokes of the chrome tire rim. "Look at these wheels, and did you notice the chrome stacks behind the cab?" He rubbed his hand along the top edge of the box. "This baby never looked so good; even when it was new."

They fell into step and moved along the line to the next vehicle.

"Oh! I saw you on TV this morning."

He looked puzzled and shook his head.

"Yes; you were being interviewed about the wind turbines."

"Oh, I see." He smiled and her heart missed a beat. "They recorded that last week. So you saw it this morning?"

"I don't know what channel it was on. I was surfing and I happened to hear a guy talking about the wind turbines. And then, there you were. Actually, it was quite interesting. Listening to you today and having seen your presentation the other night, I can see where there is a lot of potential, especially in the outlying areas for farmers and ranchers."

"The potential is incredible, and not just in the rural areas. Hydro isn't as expensive here in Canada, as it is in other parts of the world. The manufacturer is a forward thinking guy and most of his market is overseas now. But hydro costs will eventually go up here, too. Then people will be looking for the opportunity we offer. It's just a matter of time."

"I can see where a few of my clients could be interested in them; especially ranchers and farmers. So many of the smaller places have amalgamated into the larger ones; in some areas you travel miles without seeing an active home site."

Brad looked at her, seeing the intelligent businesswoman he had gotten a glimpse of on Friday night. They stopped and inspected a bright yellow Ford Fairlane. Brad ran his hand along the front fender. "My dad owned one of these fifty years ago."

Conversation flowed easily between them, and neither of them noticed that an hour had passed before Mitch caught up with them. He came up behind Shauna Lee and slid an arm over her shoulder.

"Sorry for leaving you on your own. I ran into a client and I needed to talk to him."

"Not a problem. I ran into Brad. He markets and installs wind turbines. He gave a power-point presentation on them the other night, at a seminar that the DA put on. They are a fascinating concept."

She turned to Brad; she could see the speculation in his

eyes. *Jeez*, she thought fiercely. *What must he be thinking?* "Brad Johnson, this is Mitch Wagner. We've known each other for several years. He's from Saskatoon, but he's in town for a meeting tomorrow, so he looked me up this morning."

The two men shook hands and made small talk for a few seconds before Mitch reached into his pocket for his cell phone. She saw him frown as he turned away and answered. His face blanched. "I'll be right home. No; forget about the meeting. I'll reschedule. You just hang in there! I'm on my way."

He turned to Shauna Lee. "I have to go home."

"Is something wrong?" she asked with genuine concern.

"M- my son, Kyle. He was playing baseball and got nailed in the head with a bat. They're taking him to the hospital right now."

Your son? "How old is he?" she asked, her voice choked.

"Eleven... I've got to go." He looked at Brad. "Look, I'm sorry to do this, but could you give Shauna Lee a lift home?"

"Don't worry about me, Mitch. Just go... your son needs you and you should get home as soon as possible. I'll have no problem catching a ride. I know a lot of people here."

"I'll take her home," Brad said. "Just get on the road, man! I hope your boy is okay."

"Thanks, guys. I'm out of here."

Shauna Lee watched him run through the cars. *That bastard! He's married and has a family. A few hours ago he was trying to get in my pants.*

Brad touched her arm, mistaking the reason for the troubled expression on her face. "All we can do is hope that everything is all right. Getting hit in the head with a baseball bat is rough. It's hard to say how bad it is until the doctors examine him."

"Poor kid." *You have no idea!*

"Look, it's four o'clock. Are you in a hurry to go home?"

"Brad, you don't have to worry about me. I'm a big girl. I can take care of myself."

"Hey, your friend asked me... and honestly," he chuckled as he looked her over from head to foot, "you don't look like a very big girl to me. If you're in a hurry to get home, I'll take you straight there. If you're relaxed about it, we could go have supper somewhere and then I'll take you home."

"Well..."

"Look, we both need to eat sometime. Company with supper would be a nice change for me."

"Well, when you put it that way, I have to admit you're right. We can go anytime you like."

"We could swing by The Steakhouse. What do you think?"

She nodded. They turned and walked back to the parking lot. She felt disappointed when he didn't reach for her hand or curl his arm around her waist and draw her close against his side. It would feel good to snuggle against his shoulder.

The restaurant was busy, but they found a table in the corner where it was a little quieter. Brad asked her what she would like to drink. She opted for red wine; he ordered rum and coke and when their drinks came they slipped into easy conversation.

"How long have you lived in Swift Current?" Brad was looking down at his drink, swirling amber liquid over the ice as he spoke.

"I've been here for thirteen years. After I had got my CA, I came here to work for the previous owner of my business. I worked for him for three years. He had a good clientele, and I'd worked with him long enough to earn their confidence. He wanted to retire so I bought the business from him."

She caught her bottom lip in her teeth and then sighed as she released it. "I had worked hard through the years; in fact, I did little else but work and study." She twirled the stem of her glass between her thumb and index finger. Then she looked up to find him watching her intently. "I'd saved enough to buy the business. He did give me a break though; he was happy to have me take it over. It's done well over the past ten years."

"You can be proud of what you've accomplished. What about your family? Didn't you have support from them?"

"I don't have any family." She decided she needed to shift the conversation away herself. "Now tell me about you? The other night you said you were from B.C.?"

"I'm from Dawson Creek."

"Where is that?"

"More northern; if you drew a line from North Battleford across to Dawson Creek, you would find that they are pretty close in latitude. I took the Wind Turbine Maintenance Program at Northern Lights College and that got my toe in the door. Experience got me here."

The waitress came to take their food order and Brad checked with her to make sure that it was all right before he ordered another drink for each of them.

"So were you born there?"

"Yeah, my dad owns a bulk station in town. He handles diesel, gas, oil and grease. Mom's retired now, but she was a teacher."

"Do you have any brothers or sisters?"

"We're the 'perfect' family; there is two of each of us."

She smiled. "So what did you do for fun? Did you play hockey or football?"

"The truth? Neither one, but I like to watch both. As far as football goes, I'm a Saskatchewan Rough Riders fan now, but it's hard for me if they are playing the B.C. Lions. I still cheer for the Vancouver Canucks when they play hockey, but I like junior league hockey as much as the NHL. They are young and full of piss and vinegar. They usually deliver a good game. Are you a hockey fan?"

Shauna Lee shrugged. "Not really, but I've never actually checked it out. I've seen games on TV in the bar, but I wasn't actually concentrating on them. But, tell me more about you; what do you do for R&R? Somehow, I don't think you're a couch potato."

He grinned. "No; I'm an outdoors guy. I like to hike in the mountains. Dad and I hunted together from the time I was a kid; we used to pack in with horses. We would ride back into the mountains where you seldom saw anyone else. I loved doing that. I also rode bareback in the high school rodeos."

Her eyes sparkled. "Wow! A real cowboy; sexy."

"Don't get carried away. I wasn't big time or anything like that. I loved to ride and I still do. Give me a horse and turn me loose and I'll be happy for days."

"You are Colt's kind of guy; you both like cows and horses."

"I like Colt. I think we have a lot in common."

"So," she said leaning across the table toward him. "Are there any women in your life?"

He raised an eyebrow. "Are you always so direct?"

"Well, you're a good-looking man. I'm just curious."

"How many guys are there in your life?"

She blushed. "Touché."

The waitress brought their meals and they ate in silence.

When he was finished, Brad put his utensils onto the plate and pushed it aside. "Are you ready for coffee?"

"I am stuffed. You could take me home and stop for coffee. It would give me half an hour to digest the steak."

He looked at her for a long moment. Her heart accelerated as she wondered what he was thinking. "If you'd like to do that, we could," he said soberly.

"Sure, let's go. I might even offer you some dessert."

Brad paid for their meal, and then held the door open for her as they exited the restaurant. His hand touched the small of her back when they walked to his truck. His touch sent a hot tightening into her belly and down into the heat of her femininity. He opened the door and helped her up onto her seat in the truck. He was smiling when he got in on his side. "These trucks are so high. It's quite a stretch for a shorty like you to get your little tush up onto the seat."

"Now, a gentleman wouldn't have noticed," she said with

a sexy little giggle.

"I guess I'm not a gentleman then because I did notice."

When they pulled up in front of her house, he got out and came around to open her door so he could help her get out. Shauna Lee felt giddy with anticipation when they walked the sidewalk to her house. She smiled as she opened her front door and stepped inside, standing aside to let him in.

"You can leave those beautiful boots on the mat." She spoke over her shoulder while she moved into the kitchen and tossed her keys and her purse on the table. "Just grab a spot to sit and I'll put on the coffee."

Brad looked around the open kitchen and living room area. It was beautifully decorated, but he noted the lack of personal things. There were no pictures of family or friends and no books: all she had was furniture and a top-of-the-line TV and stereo system.

He eased his long frame down on a kitchen chair. "Nice place."

"It works for me," she said with a warm smile. "Do you want a tour of the rest of the place while the coffee pot does its magic?" She smiled at him, raising an eyebrow. "There is a laundry room, bathroom and a bedroom with a queen-sized bed."

"I just got settled here. Why don't we just sit down and chat until the coffee is ready." It wasn't a rebuff. It struck her as meaning that there would be plenty of time later. As they talked, her eyes registered an unspoken invitation, her inherent sexual essence oozing out.

Brad smiled, accepting the cup of coffee she gave him. Her fingers brushed his softly, lingering with promise. When their cups were drained, he leaned back in his chair and looked at her, his gray eyes cool and intent.

"Shauna Lee, I told you I'm a hunter. I have hunted cougars in the wild. That is where I like to keep them: in the wild, with me doing the stalking."

Her face went scarlet. "Are you calling me a cougar?" she

asked, indignantly.

"I think the description fits you fairly accurately. You're no teenybopper getting her first hormone flushes. If you were looking for a wedding ring, you'd have one. You're successful, and I'm not blind; you're hot.

"I'm not stupid either. You're on the prowl for sex. You've been stalking me all evening. I could take you to that queen-sized bed that you mentioned earlier and do it justice. But I seldom hunt where everyone else has been working the territory."

He stood up. "I enjoyed your company today. I enjoyed having supper with you, but I'm not into playing this game. I'm not willing to be another one of your boy-toys." He walked to the door and opened it.

"I'm sure you don't want my advice, but I'll throw it out there anyway. Figure out who you are before it's too late. You've got a lot more to offer than sex, but you'll never find that out if you keep running from real intimacy. Bed hopping with your 'nothing serious, no strings attached, no risk' attitude is never going get you there. One day, you'll wake up and find yourself old and alone."

He stepped out and closed the door.

She stood immobile for a second, stunned. She grabbed his cup off the table and flung it against the door. It shattered into pieces, but she didn't even flinch. "Who the hell do you think you are, Brad Johnson?" she raged. "A shrink? Well, I don't need one."

She kicked the leg of the chair he'd been sitting on. "I've got news for you. I know just who I am and I've been old and alone since I was eighteen years old."

CHAPTER FOUR

It was seven-thirty in the evening when Colt turned off the main road and followed the long driveway to the ranch house. As they crossed Belanger Creek, his eyes met Frank's in the dim light of the cab and he winked. She reached across the seat to squeeze his hand. They were both remembering the night they had struggled to save the culvert during a heavy rain four years ago when she had been working on the ranch as a ranch hand.

She'd twisted her ankle and Colt had carried her to the truck and then into the house. As much as they had tried to deny it, the sparks flew and a fire ignited. They had made love for the first time that night. Hot and passionate; it was possible the twins had been conceived then — or most certainly the next day.

Colt brought the truck to a halt in front of the old ranch house. "We're here, Ellie."

Colt opened the backdoor on the driver's side and Selena, who was first out of her car seat, scrambled over Sam into her father's arms. He gave her a hug and then stood her on the ground.

Sam was waiting patiently for his father to take him. Colt looked at his son. He was so laid back and mild mannered; a complete opposite of his sister. "Come on little man," he said softly as he lifted him out of the truck and held him in his arms.

Ollie's face was wreathed in smiles. He squatted down to catch Selena as she catapulted into his arms. "Ollie, Ollie!" she yelled as he hugged her. Colt put a squirming Sam down and he followed her.

Colt and Frank were right behind the children. Ollie shook hands with Colt and then enfolded Frank in a big bear hug. "So you're going' ridin' with us this year; I can't tell you how good it will be to have you here, back in the saddle again."

"I'm so excited about it, you can't imagine," Frank exclaimed. She turned back to look at Ellie, who was standing by the front fender on the far side of the truck. She walked back and reached out her hand. "Ellie, this is Ollie Crampton. He's been the ranch foreman for so many years he's a member of the Thompson clan now."

Ollie's attention perked up. "Ollie, this is Ellie Raines. She is our new nanny. She gives me a huge break and keeps the twins in line."

Ollie reached to shake her hand, his eyes gleaming with interest. Ellie didn't seem to notice, but Frank did. *Interesting,* she thought. *There might be snow on the roof, but Ollie's still got a fire in the stove! I've never seen him with that look in his eye before!*

"Come in, come in. Watch your step. There are shadows from the yard light here. Patch is inside too and you'll want to meet him."

"Patch?" Frank queried.

"That's the new ranch-hand, isn't it, Ollie?" Colt asked.

"Yes, he got here a couple of weeks ago. Nice guy. I think he'll work out well."

Everyone followed Ollie into the house. A short, slender, white-haired man was standing at the sink drying dishes. When he turned to look at them, the first thing Frank noticed was the weary lines around his sad, hazel eyes. His smile was friendly and he had the look of a tried and true ranch hand; bowed legs and all.

Ollie motioned to Colt. "Patch, this is Colt Thompson. He owns the ranch. And this is his wife, Frank, and their twins, Selena, and Sam." He turned to Ellie. "And this good looking lady is Ellie Raines. It sounds like she is keeping these two little monkeys in line."

Patch nodded to them all. Colt shook his hand. "I missed your last name, Patch."

Ollie apologized. "Sorry, guys, this is Patch Bergeron. He worked on the Gang Ranch in central British Columbia for fifteen years before he came here."

"I've heard of the Gang Ranch many times," Colt replied. "There's a lot of history there."

"It's nice to meet you all," Patch responded.

Colt turned to Ollie. "It's getting to be bedtime for the kids. Any special room you want to put them in?"

"There are three single beds in the room at the back. Will that work?

Ellie responded quickly. "They'll be fine in twin beds. I'll sleep in the room with them."

Frank shepherded the twins and Ellie to their room and helped everyone get settled. When she came back to the kitchen, she found Colt, Ollie, and Patch talking about the round-up the next day. She went over to stand by Colt.

Ollie looked at them and grinned as he said, "You two can sleep in your old room."

"You mean my old room, don't you?" Frank refuted.

"Yeah, well it was officially your room." He winked at her. "You know I might be old, but I'm not dumb. So I think I'm not far wrong when I say *yours*."

Frank blushed, and Colt slipped his arm around her

shoulder and pulled her against him. "It's about four years too late to deny it, Fran," he said, dropping a light kiss on her cheek. "Come on. It's time to go try that bed out again."

Frank's face went scarlet. "Colt!"

"Get your mind out of the gutter!" He laughed as he turned her around to lead her down the hall. "I simply meant it's late. It's time to go to bed."

As the bedroom door closed behind them, she turned and landed a playful punch on his shoulder. "You're bad!"

He pulled her into his arms and kissed her soundly. "And that's good isn't it?"

He reached for the hem of her tee shirt and slipped it up over her breasts. He leaned in and planted a kiss in the exposed cleavage. "Lift your arms up," he whispered as he bit gently on the nipple that protruded against the lace of her bra.

She squirmed and lifted her arms up. He slid the tee up over her head, pushing it higher, stopping at the elbows as he pushed her against the wall, trapping her there, her arms imprisoned. He leaned against her, nibbling at her lips. He slipped his tongue between them and started a sensuous mating dance with hers.

Fire leaped in both of them. Colt pushed his hardness against her and heat settled in the core of her femininity, leaving her swollen, moist and aching. She jerked her arms down out of the sleeves that had pinned her and slipped her hands between them, her fingers working the button on his jeans open.

He shifted his hips back to allow her room to slide the zipper down. She pushed his jeans as far as she could down over his hips. Then she hooked her fingers into the elastic of his jockey shorts and tugged down. The tee shirt fell out of his grasp to the floor.

His hand moved up to unhook her bra and slipped it off, letting it fall to the floor. His finger deftly undid the button on her jeans, jerked down the zipper and pushed her jeans and panties down in one swoop. He let them fall down to her feet, lifted her up and left them in a pile on the floor.

He carried her to the bed and laid her down, then hurriedly shoved his jeans down and kicked them off as he lowered himself on top of her. There was no need for more foreplay. It had started when they had looked at each other with a knowing smile as they had crossed the bridge over Belanger Creek on the drive in.

The passion of the memories they had made in this house four years ago had simmered just beneath the surface all evening, building the tension that had mounted as it led them to this moment.

Later, he held her close. "This is where it all started," he murmured, kissing her hair as she slid her arm around his waist. "You, me and the twins. Right here in this bed."

She nestled her cheek against his chest. "Yes. Remember that first time?"

"Are you kidding? I'll never forget. I was so out of control, I forgot that I didn't like you! All I could think about was making love to you over and over."

"Yeah," she sighed. "For about 36 hours and then you couldn't get away fast enough." She gave him a little pinch.

"Ouch!" He flinched. "You know that's not fair. I knew how I felt about you, and I knew how much you would mean to me. I was scared to death."

She reached up and laid a finger against his lips, silencing his defense. "I know, I know. I just had to make you grovel a bit now!" She smiled as she snuggled closer. "We have to go to sleep. Tomorrow is going to be a busy day!"

The next morning the sky was clear, the air crisp. Colt went out to check on the horses while Frank slipped down to check in on the twins and Ellie. Selena and Sam were still asleep. Ellie wasn't there, so Frank wandered back to the kitchen.

As she got closer, she could hear the murmur of voices and then laughter. She recognized it was Ollie and Ellie. She walked quietly to the kitchen door and peeked in. To her surprise, Ollie and Ellie were working together, making breakfast. *Interesting — he usually doesn't like to have anyone messing around in his kitchen.*

But he was happy to have company now. They were working side by side, sharing tasks. He asked her to turn the pancakes while he cracked the eggs. Then Ellie made coffee. They were working in close proximity, even brushing each other as they moved around.

Frank was surprised at the ease with which they interacted. "Good morning, you two. I see you are hard at it! I just checked in on the twins. They are still both off in dreamland."

Ellie smiled. "They were played out last night. They may not wake up before you leave." She smiled at Ollie. "I'm going to cook supper tonight so it'll be ready when you all get in."

"That sounds wonderful. It's so nice to come in and find a warm meal waiting." Frank looked at Ollie. "She's a good cook too."

Frank turned as she heard the entry door open. She smiled when she heard Colt speak. She realized that Patch had been out doing chores with him. They came up the steps from the entry, engaged in companionable conversation.

Colt smiled when he saw her. He walked over and slid his hands around the back of her neck, under her collar. She jumped away. "Ohh! Get away from me. Your hands are cold."

Colt looked at her with a grin. He leaned forward to kiss her cheek and whispered; "Now that's not what you told me last night."

She wrinkled her nose as her laughing eyes met his. "That was then," she murmured quietly. She added in a louder voice, "Brrrr... It must be chilly out there."

"There's a bit of frost this morning. It's time to bring those cows in."

Ollie announced that breakfast was ready, and he and Ellie were busy putting the food on the table. Everyone helped themselves to the pancakes, eggs, and bacon while Ellie went to check on the twins. She announced that they were still sleeping when she came back and joined them.

After breakfast, Ellie chased Ollie out of his own kitchen, assuring him that she would clean up the dishes and put the roast in the oven when it was time. He smirked as she ordered him out, but to Frank's amazement he went without an argument.

When Frank and Colt went outside, she chuckled. "Did you notice that she has Ollie eating out of her hand already?"

Colt looked at her and raised an eyebrow. "You're joking?"

"No... Didn't you notice? They were making breakfast together like they'd done it every day for years! And you know how Ollie is about his kitchen."

Colt smirked. "It's got to be something in that house. Look at what happened to you and me." He reached out and took her hand. "It feels good to have you along for the roundup. I've missed you the past four years."

She hugged his arm. "It was a great idea you had about getting a nanny. At first I wasn't sure, but she is so good with the twins and I'm really beginning to appreciate the freedom she gives me."

He led her to the pickup. "We'll catch up with Ollie and Patch. They left with the horses in the trailer just after I came inside. They won't be far ahead of us."

Colt opened the door on the driver's side and motioned for her to get in. She looked at him questioning. "I want my girl to sit close to me." She grinned and slid in, moving over until the gearshift rested between her legs.

He got in and rested his hand on her thigh as he grinned at her. "Do you realize that we've never really done this? We never actually had a courtship. By the time I accepted that I couldn't live without you and found you in Stettler, you were so pregnant..."

"I was huge. And after the twins were born, I had my

hands full. Not much time for anything that couldn't happen between feedings and diaper changes and exhaustion."

He started the truck and backed up so he could turn onto the driveway. They caught up to Ollie and Patch on the road through the Gap. Colt followed them to the corrals where Frank had spent the summer in the travel trailer when she had ridden the range.

He got out of the pickup and helped her put her feet on the ground. She took a few steps and then stood spread-eagled, her arms and legs spread wide. She threw her head back and took a deep breath. "This feels so good. I didn't realize how much I've missed this!"

They unloaded the horses and saddled up, then decided on a plan of attack. Ollie and Patch had driven through the pastures for the past two days, so they had a good idea where the cattle were. They headed out on horseback, traveling familiar trails. Frank was flooded with memories of the summer she had spent riding the range.

Time went quickly with the four of them riding hard. At the end of the day, they had brought over half of the cows and calves in. They arrived back at the ranch after seven. The twins were already in their pajamas waiting for Frank and Colt to come home. The aroma of the meal that was waiting wafted out to greet them when they stepped into the entry.

"It smells like heaven, Ellie," Colt called out. His voice was an instant trigger for the twins who came screaming down the hall. "Daddy, Daddy!"

Ollie stepped around Frank, as she stood watching her happy family hunkered down in the hallway; a tangle of giggles and arms and legs piled on Colt, all squirming in a knot. He walked into the kitchen with a spring in his step. The table was set.

He lifted the lids on the pots on the stove-- mashed potatoes. He sniffed. Not just mashed potatoes; garlic-mashed potatoes. The next pot contained peas and carrots in cream sauce. He also found a pot of rich beef gravy. When he opened the oven, the sight of a beef roast that looked like it was cooked to perfection greeted him.

Ellie was watching with a smile on her face. "Well, does it meet your approval?"

"Humph..." He reached in to pull the roaster pan out and took it over to the cutting board. He lifted the roast out and carved a couple of slices. It was pink and juicy; perfect.

"Damn you, woman!"

Ellie flinched and lost her smile. "What's wrong?"

"You're going to ruin my reputation." He looked at her and grinned. "Everything is perfect. You're too damned good!" He walked over and rested a hand on her shoulder, looking in her eyes. "If you were looking for a job, I'd hire you any day!"

"Knock it off, Ollie," Frank protested. "She's already got a full-time job; I'm pulling rank on you."

Ellie's smile had returned. She preened as she turned to the fridge and took out a salad to put on the table. Ollie had spotted dessert inside before she closed the fridge door.

While they ate, they talked about the day's accomplishment, acknowledging that it would be more difficult the next day. The remaining cattle would be more scattered and take longer to bring in. Colt and Ollie went to the office after supper and talked about shipping dates and when they should haul the calves to market.

Colt stretched out his long legs and leaned back in the chair. "I've been thinking; I was at the seminar that the DA put on ten days ago. A guy named Brad Johnson was there. I'd met him before a couple of times at farm equipment promotional days. He's a nice guy and we hit it off. He sells and installs small wind turbines. I need to look into it further, but I think they have real potential here. I was thinking about putting up two or three, maybe even four. Two right here on the ranch and one at each of the water tanks on the range."

"Don't know anything about them. Just as long as they don't make more work..."

"Brad says they are pretty much maintenance free. I want to discuss it with Fran before—"

"What do you want to discuss with me?" Frank asked when she stepped through the door.

"I've been thinking about putting up some wind turbines here at the ranch. But I wanted to talk it over with you before I did anything definite."

Frank smiled at him. "You've always made those decisions, Colt."

"I know, but now that you have help with the twins and you're not so crazy busy with them all the time, I'd like your input too." He reached out and took her hand, pulling her close to him. "You're an intelligent woman; I want us to make decisions as partners."

She ruffled his hair with her fingers. She looked across at Ollie and words from the past echoed in her mind. *What he needs is someone who cares about the business and is willing to work with him.*

Ollie was playing with a pencil on the desk, acting disinterested, but Frank was sure he was thinking the same thing now, waiting for her response.

"I... I appreciate you wanting my input. So, tell me what you're thinking?"

"I was talking to Ollie about the wind turbines, but right now, I think it's been a long hard day and we need to get to bed. When we go back to the farm, I'll call Brad. I'll have him come out one day and he can go over everything with both of us. Then we'll decide what to do."

He reached out a hand to her. "Help an old man up. I'm sore in places I forgot existed after all that riding today."

Ollie smiled as he watched Frank take both of Colt's hands and tug to help him stand. *True love,* he thought wistfully.

"Good night, Ollie. We'll see you in the morning."

Ollie shut off the light in his office and stood in the hall watching the two of them go to their bedroom. *Somehow, I let that pass me by.* The thought was tinged with regret. He went to the kitchen to have a shot of Jack Daniels before he went to bed.

To his surprise, he found Ellie bustling around at the sink. Warm pleasure flooded through him. "What are you doin', girl? I thought you'd be gone to bed."

She glanced at the clock on the wall. "It's getting that time. Frank helped me clean up and put the twins to bed. Maybe I should have checked with you first..." She hesitated. "But I thought if I made lunch for everyone now, it would simplify things in the morning. Did I step out of line?"

Ollie looked around the room, then back to her. "Don't see no line anywhere that you could have stepped out of."

She threw a tea towel at him.

He caught it in midair and advanced toward her, mischief in his eyes. A lighthearted feeling washed over him, something that he had experienced so long ago he'd forgotten what it was like.

He stopped. His heart did a little flip as he looked into her gray eyes; warm, open and friendly, twinkling with laughter. He wanted to reach for her but pulled himself up short. *Old fool*, he thought. *It's watchin' those two young 'uns puttin' ideas in my head.*

He tossed the tea towel on the counter. "Want to have a nightcap with me?"

"That depends on what you've got."

"I'm having a shot of Jack Daniels. What would you like?"

"Rum and coke?" she asked with a smile.

"It's a done deal." Ollie mixed a drink and handed it to her. "Grab a chair," he said sitting down. "It's been a long day. It must have been long for you, too, doing all that cooking and looking after the kids."

"I had a wonderful day," she said with a smile. "Sam and Selena are great kids. And the cooking... honestly, it felt good to be part of everything going on; sort of like belonging again. I've missed that."

"Do you have any kids?"

"Yes, but they both ended up at the opposite ends of Canada; my son is in Toronto and my daughter is in Vancouver. They are so busy with their own lives that I seldom see them. My husband, Eric, has been gone for ten years, but I still get lonely.

"One thing I have to say—I haven't been at Colt and Frank's for very long, but they treat me like family; they are wonderful." She smiled. "Do you have a family, Ollie?"

"No, I'd been a rolling stone all of my life until I came to work here. Now the Thompsons are my family."

***

Colt and Frank fell into bed, exhausted from the day's ride. Colt spooned Frank and slid his arm around her waist, dropping a kiss on the nape of her neck. They snuggled in silence for a few moments.

Then Frank spoke softly. "Colt, I'm sorry; I haven't been much of a partner as far as the business goes. I know you have a heavy load, but I've been so involved with the twins that I just assumed... I mean, you've done it all for years. Have I disappointed you?"

"Are you kidding? I've felt damned guilty about the load you've been carrying. That's why I wanted a nanny; to give you a break from the kids. And yeah, I want days like today with you. I want to be able to share ideas, without demanding too much of your time. But you have never, ever disappointed me. I'm almost in awe of you."

She turned in his arms and laid her cheek against his chest. "But now we're going to have another baby. I won't be able to just pick up and go with you after it comes."

He kissed her forehead. "That's true, for a couple of years anyway. But it will be easier than it would have been without Ellie's help. Hey! I'm looking forward to having this new little guy... or gal, in our family; possibly another one, sometime later too."

The roundup took three days of hard riding. It took

another three days to haul the cattle from the pasture corrals to the ranch. After the last load on the stock liner had arrived at the ranch, Colt and Frank sat on the top plank of the corrals and looked at the herd.

"They look good, Colt," Frank commented.

"Yes and the prices have been steadily coming up. We should do well this year. We'll have to wean calves and sort for the next couple of days. How are you holding up? You're not used to riding like this. You're not getting overtired or anything? It's not too much for you and the baby is it?"

"I'm tired, but it's a good tired. I have to admit I'm sore; I haven't used some of these muscles for almost four years, but I've loved being back in the saddle again. I love it out here on the ranch."

"Let's go for a short ride. I want to run something past you."

Frank tilted her head and looked at him questioningly. "What are you up to now?"

They swung up into their saddles and Colt led the way up a wide draw to a level plateau just above the ranch buildings. He turned his horse so they could overlook the scene below; the old house, the barns, corrals, the shop. "Nice eh?" he asked.

"Beautiful. What are you thinking? Wind turbines?"

"No, they'd do better at the top of the ridge behind here. Could you imagine a sprawling ranch style house here?"

"You... you mean for ...."

He reached out and took her hand. "For us?"

"But how can we do that? What about the farm? We can't live all the way out here and have you go back to run the farm. We'd be apart most of the time."

"Well, you and I need to talk about this. I love it out here; you love it out here. It's a great place to raise the kids. I can see us having an arena down there by the barns in that open spot. You can teach the kids how to team rope. I might even teach Sam how to bulldog steers."

"Sounds like perfect, but what about the farm?"

Colt swung down from his horse, and Frank joined him. They stood there, reins in hand, side by side, overlooking the view around them. "I've been thinking that we should look for a farm manager. This is the life that both of us love; it's what I want for us and our family. What do you think?"

She smiled up at him. "I'd be here in a heartbeat, even if we lived in the old ranch house. But we can't let the farm go downhill. That's your inheritance, your dad's life work."

He squeezed her shoulders. "No, no. I think I should have Shauna Lee find someone with the right background and credentials to manage the farm. There are guys out there who are very capable.

"In the meantime, we could start looking at house plans, and we could start building the house early next spring. Hopefully, we'll be living out here by this time next year. Imagine it; Christmas here on the ranch! The five of us — make that six with Ellie."

"And Ollie?"

"He'll stay where he is. He's part of the family. But he's in his sixties and he'll need extra help soon, too."

"Can we really do all this? I mean, can we afford to build a house, hire a manager and all that?"

He looked at her with a smile. "I think so hon. Between the ranch and the farm, we've got a good-sized holding. We've done well the past few years, and I've invested with good returns."

"I'm ashamed to admit, I've never really thought about the money. I've been totally involved with the twins and our life."

"And you've never asked for a lot, hon, but Dad and I have worked hard. I don't care about traveling around the world when I'm old. Look at Dad. He worked himself into the ground and now they don't travel much anyway. They hardly even come out to the farm anymore.

"What do they say? Life is a journey, not just the

destination. I want us to *live* our whole life, enjoying what we do as we go; not just marking time until we retire." He kissed her lightly and then smiled. "So, what do you think? Do you like this spot for the house? Or do you want to look at other places?"

"No, I love this. There's shelter from behind, full sun, we can see the creek winding through the field below, and it overlooks the barn and corrals. There are just enough trees around to make it nice." She kicked at the grass with the toe of her boot. "And it's not bad soil for a yard; maybe even a bit of garden. It's perfect!"

"I've been thinking something else, too. If you want to, we could set up a small vet clinic for you. We're way out in the country, but there are ranches and hobby farms around. Word of mouth travels fast. You probably wouldn't want a major surgery facility, but big enough to do emergency stuff. What do you think?"

Frank's eyes were sparkling. "Colt, this sounds too good to be true. It's like a dream world; you and I out here on the ranch with the kids, a new house and a vet clinic too! But let's take it one step at a time, okay? We can start looking at house plans. That sounds like fun, but we have to find a manager for the farm."

She patted her tummy with a smile. "And we have to get this little one on terra firma and give it a year or two to grow before I get into a vet clinic." She turned to hug him. "This is exciting."

CHAPTER FIVE

Shauna Lee looked at her calendar first thing when she got to work on Monday. The day looked pretty slow. She liked it better when she was busy.

She looked out the window, focusing on the street outside. She was thinking about the weekend. She hadn't been able to push Brad's parting words of unsolicited advice away, even though he had infuriated her. *Figure out who you are, Shauna Lee, before it's too late. You've got a lot more to offer than sex, but you'll never find that out if you keep running from real intimacy. Bed hopping — with your 'nothing serious, no strings attached and no risk' attitude, is not going get you there.*

She had spent Friday night at home watching TV. Boring! Saturday she had changed the sheets, done laundry and cleaned house, but the evening had loomed ahead of her like a lonely prison sentence. *To hell with him,* she'd thought. *I'm not sitting here all by myself. I'm going to the bar and I'll see what happens!*

She'd showered, shaved her legs, styled her hair and

dressed in one of her sexiest mini-skirts and a sheer red blouse with a matching silky camisole under it. She'd taken a pair of strappy red high heels from her closet and put them on. No jewelry; she didn't need it. She'd surveyed herself in the mirror and smiled with satisfaction. The outfit was a head turner and she knew it.

She had taken a taxi to the bar. She told herself that she shouldn't be driving home after she'd had a few drinks. But she'd known she wouldn't be coming home alone, and she hadn't. She'd singled out Troy Wilson and he hadn't had a chance. He was a twenty-seven-year-old hottie in town with an oil service crew. She'd flattered him and teased him and by midnight he was practically begging to take her home. Of course, she had surrendered to his charm.

He'd stayed the night and her clean sheets had gotten a good workout. They had grabbed a coffee and toast for breakfast, then spent most of Sunday in bed. He'd been insatiable. He'd taken her out for seafood dinner that evening, then brought her home and once again took her on the wrinkled sheets. He'd left at around eleven o'clock that evening, with her phone number tucked in his wallet, promising that he would call her when he was back in town.

She smiled to herself. There hadn't been any loneliness or boredom. But as she looked back on it, she didn't feel exhilaration either. *That damned Brad! He doesn't know anything about me.* But his words haunted her. *One day you'll wake up and find yourself old and alone.*

She was startled when the phone rang. Christina, her receptionist, was on the line. "Colt Thompson on line two."

"Ok, I've got it." She lifted the receiver with a smile on her lips. "Good morning, Colt."

"Hi, Shauna Lee. Have you got an hour or so later this afternoon?"

"Colt, I always have time for you," she teased. "At the office or at my place?"

He ignored the flirtation. "I can be at the office at about

three-thirty if that's not too late. What time do you close? I could rearrange my schedule, but I've got things I have to take care of this morning and I have an appointment with Brad Johnson at Windspeer at one o'clock. I'd like to connect with him first if it works for you."

"Three-thirty is fine. See you then."

I wonder why he's seeing Brad. She winced, hoping their meeting was strictly about business.

She couldn't help it. Anxiety shadowed her all day as she waited for Colt to come. She was surprised when he walked in with his young son in tow. "So, are you giving Frank a break?"

He tousled the little guy's hair and grinned. "Fran is grocery shopping. She's got Selena with her. I'm showing Sam the ropes early." He sat down and lifted the child onto his lap. "Aren't I, son?" he asked him, pride shining in his eyes.

Shauna Lee's heart curled as thoughts of 'what might have been' threatened to crowd in. *Ben...* She had to force the door closed, but a tear spilled over before she managed to do it. She quickly dashed it away.

Colt was surprised to see the shine of tears in her eyes. He looked at her curiously, wondering why. She smiled. "I'm getting sappy," she said. "It's touching to see you so happy and proud of your family."

"Thanks, Shauna Lee. I couldn't imagine my life without them now."

Shauna Lee swallowed hard. "I hope you never have to, Colt." She knew she had to get the conversation on a different track. "What did you want to see me about today?"

"I wanted you to know that I bought a mobile home this morning. It's a used one, in beautiful shape."

"Why did you buy a mobile home?"

"We've hired a nanny to help Fran with the twins. We're expecting again in May and I want her to have some free time to spend with me before she is tied up with the next little one. Ellie Raines is the name of the lady we've found, and she is wonderful with the twins.

"This past week, we went out to the ranch to round up cattle. She looked after them while Fran went riding with us. It was like old times, having her there. It's really the first break she's had since they were born. She wasn't too keen on getting a nanny, but I persuaded her to give it a try and now she thinks it will work out well. But we both agree that Ellie needs privacy and so do we."

"Congratulations on the new baby. You must be thrilled."

"You can't imagine how much! We both are." Colt shifted in his seat. "The other thing I need from you is the calculation of our hydro costs over the past 10 years. You can pick that up off the computer can't you?"

"It might take some time to go that far back, but I'll get it for you."

"Can you have it by Friday?"

"Certainly."

"Good. What is your schedule like for Friday right after lunch?"

Shauna Lee consulted her calendar. "Things are pretty slow right now. I don't have anything booked. Why?"

"I'd like you to come out to the farm with Brad Johnson. I think we're going to put up three or four wind-powered generators at the ranch. We'll probably have him set one up at each of the two wells on the grazing lease as well. They will provide a dependable power source for the pumps. We have those stationary engines, but they are a pain in the ass. If it's hot, someone has to go there every day and start them to pump water. If they decide not to run, you have another problem. If there is power on site, we can use a float in the tank to trigger a switch that will start and turn off the pump.

"The other thing I wanted to talk to you about is finding a manager for the farm. I need someone with a track record and good credentials. In other words, I'm looking for someone like myself. Don't you have access to people who make it their business to find people like that?"

"I'll look into it. They are out there, but whoever we find won't come cheap."

"I'd hope to negotiate for a fair wage. I can't match the big corporations, but I'm thinking about a decent monthly salary, with a percentage of the net income of the farm. I know it won't come cheap, but this is something I really want to do.

"Fran's concerned about the farm going downhill. I won't let that happen, but the ranch has always been where my heart is and Fran loves it there too. I want to raise my kids there."

"What will you do with Ollie?"

"He's there for life. As far as we are concerned he's part of the family."

"That could get to be pretty close quarters for all of you."

Colt grinned. "When I told Fran what I wanted to do, she would have moved into the old house in a heartbeat; after we are satisfied that we have found a good manager for the farm. But I plan to build a new house.

"I took her up to the site on the weekend and she loved it. She demands so little, and I want her to have a modern home with more convenience. I shouldn't say just her, I mean for us. I want a new place for our family."

"That's a lot of changes, Colt. Can you swing it all?"

"Shauna Lee, you know my business inside out. I'm not a poor man. I'm not filthy rich, but I can certainly afford to build a house without it hurting me. That's what I want to do for the woman I love."

"She's a lucky woman."

"I'm a lucky man. She has given me love, a family, and a life that I never imagined I'd have."

Shauna Lee just looked at him.

Colt looked at his watch and stood up. "I've got to get moving. Brad will phone you about Friday. I know he plans to be at the farm by one. He wants to get home in time to watch the Rough Riders play Montreal. He said something about wanting to be home by four-thirty."

He looked at his watch again. "I've got to run. Fran will be waiting for me. When Selena is tired and hungry, she's irritable and persistent! We'll talk later." He was out the door and gone.

The phone rang as he disappeared. "Line one for you, Shauna Lee."

"I've got it," she said wearily. "Shauna Lee speaking."

"Brad Johnson, here."

"Colt just left. He said you'd be calling."

"Sorry, I'm a little late, but I wanted to confirm this now because I'll be out of town until Thursday night. Did Colt tell you that we are going to be at his place at one o'clock on Friday afternoon?"

"He did."

"So I'll pick you up at your office at about eleven-forty-five? Will that give us enough time to get there? I've never been to the farm."

"That will give us plenty of time. I-I'll be waiting for you."

"OK. I'll see you on Friday." He hung up.

She sat there looking at the phone. *Just what I need; to spend time, in confined quarters, with a guy who thinks he's my shrink.*

***

Friday morning, she had the paperwork Colt wanted ready and she had put out a couple of feelers for a manager. The thought of driving out to the farm with Brad was uncomfortable and she wished she could avoid it.

Can it be Friday already? The week has gone by too quickly for comfort. I should have told Colt that I couldn't come and sent the information along with Brad. I could still plead a headache or something. It will be pretty awkward riding with Brad after our last encounter.

However, she was waiting in her office when he arrived. Brad followed Christina to her door, stepped past her, and walked into Shauna Lee's office.

Brad looked around the room, taking in all the details. It was bright, modern and tidy. "Nice digs you've got here," he said after a moment. "But there's nothing about you here. No pictures of friends, your favorite cat, or you sailing on the lake. There is nothing that gives anyone any idea about who you are."

She glared at him.

"Why?" he asked. "How do your clients get a feel for who you are?"

"This is a business, not a photo album of my life. It's professional, neat and tidy."

"And there's no personality! It's sterile. Your receptionist has pictures at her desk. I saw a horse and a picture of her having a beer with friends around a fire pit. There was a couple of others too."

"I don't have a horse or a cat, or pictures of me drinking beer with friends."

"Why?"

She snatched up the file on her desk. "I don't need you acting like my shrink. Either you get back to business and stay on topic or I'll phone Colt and tell him I'm not coming."

He chuckled as he watched her fume. "My truck is right outside." He sauntered out with a smirk on his face, winking at Christina as he passed. Shauna Lee looked like a thunder cloud when she followed him.

Brad opened the passenger door and waited for her to step up. Then he gave her gentle lift so she could make it onto the seat. He shut the door, whistling as he walked to the driver's side. He opened the door and stepped up into the cab. He started the truck, fastened his seatbelt and looked across at her. "All set?" he asked.

"Why the hell do they make trucks so high off the ground like this?" She was snarky and she knew it. "It's ridiculous."

"Actually those lift kits are special order."

"Why? What do you get out of it?"

"Well, I get to lift a shorty like you up into the cab once in a while and watch her slide her fancy little tush up onto the seat."

"Screw you!" she hissed.

"You asked. I told you. And, as I'm sure you'll recall, I passed up on that offer last time. I think I'll do the same now."

Shauna Lee flushed scarlet. "That's it! I'm out of here," she stormed, reaching for the door handle.

He put the truck in gear, ready to ease out into the traffic. "You've still got your seat belt on, and it's a long way down to the pavement if you do get it off and try to get out."

She glared at him. He gave her a long look and finally she looked away. She saw Christina watching them from her desk inside. *Oh, great!*

"Have you had lunch? I haven't, so I'm going to the drive through at the A&W and order a hamburger and coffee."

She didn't answer him. He grinned. "Cat got your tongue? Oh, that's right. You don't have a cat or a horse or—"

She threw the file at him. "SHUT UP. Why are you doing this?"

He reached out in an attempt to catch the folder and keep the contents from scattering. "Hey, I'm driving. That's not a smart move." He stopped at a red light and they both scrambled, reaching for the papers that had slid to the floor. She snatched the one he held and organized the file without looking at him.

When he stopped at the drive-thru at the A&W, she was still fuming. "That's it. I'm taking a taxi back to the office. You can take this file to Colt and explain why I'm not with you."

He grinned as she gathered up her purse and reached for the door handle while he ordered. The door wouldn't open. She tried again and then realized that he had pushed the child-lock button and she couldn't get out. "You bastard; I'll-I'll..."

He had moved the truck forward to the pickup window. He paid the cashier, took the food and eased the truck into a parking spot.

"I ordered a burger and coffee for you, too. I'm sure you haven't eaten. You need to be on top of things for the business meeting. All the angst you put out against me has to have taken a lot of energy."

He slid out the cup holder and put a to-go cup in it. "As I remember from the other night, you take your coffee black." He laid a foil wrapper with a hamburger in it on the seat and eased it toward her. "I ordered the same for both of us."

He worked his hamburger out of the package and dropped the wrapper on the seat. He took a big bite.

Shauna Lee's mouth was watering. She hadn't eaten breakfast because she had been so nervous about this whole day; the trip out to the farm and back with Brad; even being at the farm; she hadn't been there since Colt had married Frank.

"Eat the 'burger," he urged.

She picked up the packet and slid the hamburger out of it. She took a tentative bite, then another."

He turned the key and started the engine. "Can we go now?"

"Yes," she said quietly and took another bite.

Brad finished his hamburger while he drove. When he saw a sign that read, *Cantaur 12 km*, he turned. He followed the road until he came to Colt's driveway, then turned left and started down the long drive.

Shauna Lee finished the last bite of the hamburger. She crumpled the foil wrapper; picked up the one Brad had pushed against her and dropped it in the brown paper bag. "You told me you'd never been here."

"I haven't. I got clear instructions from Colt when I talked to him last night. I didn't say anything to him, but I wasn't sure you would drive out here with me. I thought you might decide to bring your own wheels."

"I thought about it. I should have."

Brad parked in front of the house. He would have spoken, but Colt stepped out on the veranda. As Shauna Lee reached for the file, he dropped his hand to cover hers and gave it a gentle squeeze of apology.

He released the child-lock so she could get out, and then

shut off the motor. As he got out of the truck, Colt came to the passenger door to help her out. His touch was impersonal but gentle; definitely different than Brad's lingering hold had been.

"One thing's for sure, Johnson, the lift job you've got on this thing would disappear fast if you ever settled down and had kids. The only thing this is good for is getting a feel of your date's bod' as you lift her up into the cab."

Shauna Lee shot a look at Brad and caught his grin as he shrugged. When he saw her look, he sobered up immediately and reached out to shake hands with Colt.

"Nice place you've got here. I think you could use three turbines right here on the farm. They would save you energy and cut your hydro costs."

Colt cuffed him on the shoulder. "I just manage the place. You need to convince the boss about that. She's inside." He turned to lead them into the house. Shauna Lee followed behind, wondering at the easy camaraderie that the two men had developed in a short time. She hesitated as she looked at the house.

She'd been here before as a guest of Colt's mom and dad. Now there was a new mistress. *Suck it up Shauna Lee.* She forced a smile as she walked up the steps onto the veranda.

Frank came to the door as they stepped inside. Colt slipped an arm around her shoulder. "Honey, this is Brad Johnson. Brad, meet the boss."

She jabbed him in the ribs with an arched look. "You all heard that," she said with a laugh. She extended her hand to Brad. "Hi. I'm Frank."

He quirked his eyebrow and she grinned. "I know — he always calls me Fran, but he's the only one who does that. My name actually is Frank."

"Glad to finally meet you." He motioned to Colt. "The way this guy talks about you, you'd think you were newlyweds. It's nice to see really happy people."

Frank gave Colt a loving smile. "Thank you, Brad."

Brad turned to Shauna Lee and looked at each of them. "Do you two know each other?"

Frank smiled warmly as she looked at Shauna Lee. "We do." She reached out and placed a hand on her arm. "Shauna Lee is one of the most generous, understanding people I have ever met," she said softly. She looked at Colt. "And she's a smart businesswoman too. That's why we wanted her here, isn't it, hon?"

Colt smiled at Frank in a way that made Brad feel a tug of loneliness.

Colt agreed and suggested that they each grab a chair at the old maple table. "I guess we had better get to this. Brad wants to be home by four-thirty so he can watch the football game, so we've got about two hours to get this finished up." He looked at Frank. "Do I smell coffee?"

She nodded and he walked to the counter and collected the tray that was already set up with four mugs and cream and sugar. Frank brought the coffee carafe and a plate of fresh cookies. Her eyes met Colt's and a knowing look flashed between them. Colt chuckled. "My favorite cookies; she made them the first time I met her at the ranch."

Frank flushed remembering. She shot Colt a look that said 'don't you *dare.*' She cleared her throat. "So where do we start, guys?" she asked, adroitly changing the direction she feared Colt's teasing would take. She sat down on a chair at the far side of the table, positioning herself and Colt across from each other and adjacent to both Brad and Shauna Lee.

Brad explained the concept of the wind turbines, affirming what Colt had discussed with her. She made sure that Shauna Lee was included in the conversation, and soon it flowed nicely with everyone's input. An hour and a half flew by.

Colt sat back and looked across the table at Frank. "So, do you think we should go with what we talked about?"

She nodded. "It makes sense. It's a new thing for us, but I agree with you; especially at the water tanks. And you want to put two others near the corrals at the ranch?"

"I was thinking in a couple of years..."

Frank's eyes glowed. "Ohhhh..." she breathed softly. "That would be perfect." *My vet clinic,* she thought. *Colt, you are such a darling!*

Colt looked at his watch. He turned to Shauna Lee. "What I'd really like, is for you to go to the ranch with Brad one day next week. You know the way out there, and you know how our business works.

"I'll call Ollie and ask him to take you guys out to both of the water tanks so Brad can get the information he needs. I've shown Ollie where I want the other two turbines put at the ranch. I want to get at this right away before the weather changes."

He looked at Brad. "I'd go with you, but I've got business to take care of here. I've got to get a mobile home set up for our nanny; a cement pad, hydro, and a sewage system. I want to get it in place as soon as possible so I beat the winter weather."

He looked at Frank with a slight smile, and Brad caught the knowing look between them. "We all need privacy." He looked around the table. "I guess that does it then. We can't make Brad late for his game."

When everyone had pushed their chairs away from the table, the patter of little feet could be heard on the top floor, headed for the stairs. The twins came bouncing down them, followed by Ellie. Selena charged into Colt, swinging on his leg as her happy brown eyes looked at each person in turn.

Sam came down and took Frank's hand. He looked at Brad and then at Shauna Lee. He hooked a finger in his mouth, considering her. "Dad, I see'd 'er."

Shauna Lee laughed. "You are such a cutie."

Brad watched her curiously, thinking how seldom she ever really smiled with a light in her eyes. And he didn't miss the wistful look that lingered, either.

Colt swept Sam up into his arms. He grinned at him and

said "Yes, you did see her yesterday when we went to her office." He looked at his watch and shook his head. "Brad, right now you will be fifteen minutes late for the game; you'd better get on the road." He turned to Shauna Lee with a smile. "Is the information that I asked for in that file on the table?"

She nodded.

"Thanks."

Frank and Colt stood in the doorway, children in their arms, watching Shauna Lee and Brad go to the truck.

Brad walked to the passenger door and opened it. Shauna Lee looked at him doubtfully. "It's okay," he said reassuringly. He bent over and clasped his hands, palms up. "Put your foot here and your hand on my shoulder, and I'll lift you up." She looked at him skeptically. "I promise, I won't harass you anymore today."

She gingerly put her foot in his hand and leaned her body into his shoulder, steadying herself with her hand as he had instructed her to do. He lifted her up effortlessly, let her lean inside the cab and move her feet onto the floor. He watched until she had turned and lowered herself onto the seat. He smiled at her and shut the door. Turning, he waved to the Thompsons as he walked around the front of the truck to the driver's door.

"I'll talk to you soon, Colt. It was nice to meet you, Frank." He slid in, started the motor and fastened his seatbelt. He looked at Shauna Lee. "Buckled up and ready to fly?"

She nodded and he put the truck into gear and eased out onto the driveway. They drove in silence until they were half way back to Swift Current.

Then, Brad sighed. "I think I envy their happiness. They're still crazy in love and they have three-year-old twins. You can't miss the looks that pass between them."

He tapped his finger on the steering wheel. "I didn't realize you and Frank knew each other that well." He looked across the cab at her.

"Actually, we haven't met very often."

"But she said...."

Shauna Lee looked out the window. "That happy family could have been Colt's and mine. I was engaged to him, when he decided he was in love with her. I didn't hold him to it. That's why she is so generous to me."

"You two were engaged?"

She nodded.

He frowned. "How can you work together now? I couldn't do it."

"We were good friends. Neither of us was looking for love and romance. We went out together off and on for a few years. There was no solid commitment, but we went to Mexico and out for dinner and—"

"I get it!" he said harshly.

"Anyway, four years ago he suggested we should get married. At first I thought he was kidding. But he was very persistent, so I agreed. I liked him, but I never had considered marriage with anyone. I didn't want children, and I didn't want to live on the farm.

"He said we would live in town. His mom and dad were living on the farm then. We were engaged for about three and a half months. After the first month, I could sense that something was wrong and as time passed, he became more unsettled. Before Christmas, he came and told me he couldn't marry me because he was in love with Frank.

"I liked him, but I wasn't in love with him, so I told him to go to her. When he found her, she was pregnant with the twins. They are his, there's no doubt of that. They got married immediately."

"Whew!"

"When I see the way he is with her and the kids, sometimes I wish I'd held on to him. If he could change so much, maybe I could have too. But it's too late now. They're married and they have the twins. He told me the other day that she is pregnant again. They're crazy about each other. I missed my chance."

They were silent until they could see Swift Current in the distance. Brad spoke softly. "Shauna Lee, do you really believe you and Colt could have been as happy as they are?"

She looked away. "Why not?"

"Well, he was engaged to you. He asked for his freedom because he was in love with her."

Shauna Lee sighed. "I've seen how happy he is; how he is with his kids. I've often thought that if I had realized that love could be like that... I'd have been willing to chance it."

He was silent until he stopped at a red light. "Seeing them together... I think they were meant to be. You two weren't meant for each other Shauna, but you could find that kind of happiness with someone else."

"I'll never have that."

"Why are you so certain?"

"Brad, please don't analyze me."

"OK, OK! I'll leave it alone."

Shauna Lee glanced at her watch. "If the game started at four-thirty, you're already half an hour late. My house is closer. You could stop and watch it there. I can order pizza in."

"Are you serious?" he asked cautiously.

"Hell no! I get a big kick out of having you turn me down."

"I didn't exactly do that... but... yeah, I do appreciate the offer."

"And know in advance that you are not invited to my bed."

Brad chuckled. "Yes, let's get that sore point out of the way; I'm not going anywhere near your bed... not yet, anyway." He looked at her intently. "I was serious the other night. You interest me, but I don't hunt where others do, and I'm not going to be another one of your boy-toys."

"Could you be any blunter?" she asked caustically.

Suddenly he changed lanes. "I have another idea. You have an oven." It was a statement, not a question. "Why don't we make our own pizza?"

She stared at him in astonishment. "Well... yeah, we could, but I have to confess, my cupboards are pretty bare. I need to go for groceries and what about the game? You're already late."

"This won't take long. We'll stop at Safeway and get what we need. It'll be fun." He grinned as he parked the truck. "Are you ready to go?"

She went into the grocery store with him and followed as he whipped through the aisles like a man who had shopped there before: an onion, garlic, red and green peppers, mushrooms, tomato sauce Shauna Lee's surprise was obvious, a bag of shredded Mozzarella cheese, a pound of hamburger, a pound of bacon and some limes. He grinned as he picked up a packaged pizza crust. "We'll cheat this time. Next time I'll make the crust from scratch."

"Do you actually do this often?"

"I sure do. Through the years, I ate in so many restaurants, I got sick of it. I decided to learn to cook. And I'm pretty good at it if I do say so myself. Tonight you're in for a treat. We'll make my Hungry Man's Pizza." He looked at her. "Have you ever made pizza?"

"No. I love pizza, but I always have it delivered."

"Lady, if you're going to hang out with me, you're going to have to learn to cook!"

When they arrived at her place, she led Brad to the couch, picked up the remote, and handed it to him as he sat down. He found the channel with the game on. It was already the second quarter.

She stood watching him. He was immediately into the game, sitting on the edge of the couch, tensing as he watched the players move, cheering when they made a good play, cursing when someone made a bad move.

"Can I get you anything to drink, Brad?"

He looked at the time. "It's only about five minutes until half time." He patted the seat beside him. "Sit here by me. Do you watch football?"

"To be honest I don't understand the game. I just kind of freak, when I see about 2000 man pounds landing on one guy at the bottom of the pile."

He hooked an arm around her shoulder as she sat down, pulling her closer. "I'll help you understand the finer points of the game."

They watched until half time. Then he took over in the kitchen. He didn't let her off the hook though. She sliced peppers and mushrooms while he chopped the onion. He chopped a clove of garlic and added it to the hamburger while she cooked it in a frying pan.

He sorted through her meager assortment of spices, selecting a handful of this and a pinch of that and tossed them into the tomato paste. By the beginning of the third quarter, the pizza was in the oven.

"Now, wasn't that fun?" he asked with a happy smile. Then he walked to the fridge and took out two of the Corona beers that they had mutually agreed upon when they had stopped at the liquor store. He hooked a lime with his little finger just before he closed the door, then went to the counter and dropped it on the cutting board. He cut a couple wedges and popped one in each bottle. "I should have asked you, would you have preferred a glass?"

"No. I drink it straight from the bottle."

He grinned as he handed her the bottle of golden ale. "You're a girl after my own heart."

At the beginning of the fourth quarter, the aroma of cooking pizza filled the room. "I'm hungry. That hamburger is long gone and that pizza smells like it's ready," he said, easing himself away from her so he could stand up.

She could see the bulge behind his zipper when he turned toward the stove. Her feminine parts were tight, singing with arousal. Sitting so close to him had sent her hormones into overdrive.

She got up and while he took the pizza out of the oven,

she went to the cupboard and took the pizza cutter from a drawer. Then she reached up and took out two plates. "Want another beer?" she asked.

"That sounds like a good plan. Is it all right if we sit over there?" He motioned to the couch.

"I eat there most of the time. I'll pull the coffee table over and you can put the pizza pan on it. I'll bring the plates and some napkins."

He cut a slice and took a bite out of it. "Mmmm, that is good! We did great a great job with this one."

"You mean you did."

"No, we did. You helped. I'll let you cut the onions next time so you'll remember that you helped," he teased.

She slid a slice of lime into each bottle of Corona and carried them to the coffee table.

He lifted a slice of pizza off the pan and held it up for her to take a bite. "Now, tell me that delivery beats this if you dare!"

She took a small bite. "Ohh... that's hot," she gasped, rolling it around in her mouth, trying to cool it.

"Sorry! I didn't think about that. Did it burn your tongue?"

"Yes."

He pushed her bottle of Corona into her hand. "Maybe this will help."

She swallowed a few glugs and then rubbed her tongue against her teeth.

He groaned, watching her do it. He reached for her, pulling her to him. "Here, let me see if I can help." He kissed her deeply, his tongue working over hers.

"The pizza isn't the only thing that's hot," he whispered hoarsely. "I've wanted to do that all afternoon." He pulled her over, laying her across his lap. As she looked up at him, she could feel the hardness of his erection against her back. She felt the wetness in her panties and she ached with arousal.

After he kissed her again, he gave his head a slight shake

as if to clear it. Then he helped her up, so she was sitting on the seat beside him again. His hand trembled when he handed her a plate with the piece of pizza on it. His eyes met hers and held. Then he cleared his throat. "Eat." His voice was husky with emotion.

What the... She was trembling when she took the plate. She sat it on the coffee table. Confused she reached for her Corona and sipped hesitantly.

He turned his attention back to the game, watching quietly. When she had finished eating, he reached over and took her hand, lifting it to rest on his thigh. She could feel the tension in his body. They sat side by side, with his hand resting on hers until the game was over. Then, Brad stood up and gathered the pizza pan and the dishes. Shauna Lee picked up the empty bottles and pushed the coffee table back.

She turned to meet his gaze.

"Shauna Lee, I have to go... *now.*" His voice was strained.

"I-- It's still early."

He closed the distance between them and slipped his arm around her waist pulling her against him. She could feel his erection push into her. "I can't tell you how much I enjoyed this... you and me making the pizza together. Having you watch the game with me. But... I have to go before I... before *we* do something we can't take back." He kissed her gently, then turned and walked to the door.

She reached out to him. "Brad, please don't go."

He shook his head. "I'm only human, Shauna Lee. If I stay, you know where we'll end up. I don't want to take you to the bedroom tonight. No, that's not true, I damned well *do* want to. But I'm not going to."

He pulled her to him. "I can't deny what you do to me," he whispered. "I've been so horny for the past three hours, my nuts are aching." He nuzzled the curve of her neck. "But, if I let that happen tonight, sex will take over our relationship. I want to get to know you first. I want to spend time exploring things together. I want to find out what you enjoy... besides

Full Circle

sex.

"I think you are going to have to discover those things out about yourself too. I may be wrong, but I think you've lost touch with who you really are. You tell me you've worked and studied, and that's about all. You say you have no family. Do you have any friends, or are your only friends the guys you bring home?"

"Brad, you don't know anything about me."

"But I want to," he whispered. He settled his mouth over hers and kissed her into silence. Then he released her and stepped away. "I *have* to go now. If I don't, I'll be no better than all those other guys." His eyes implored her. "Please... please know you are worth more than that. Stop giving yourself away, Shauna Lee."

He reached out to touch her hand. "I'll call you during the week. If you're not interested when I call, just say so. But, if you're willing to see if we can make something lasting, I'd like to explore that possibility with you."

She looked at him with the glisten of tears in her eyes.

He turned quickly and walked out of the house. She moved to the window and watched him stride down the walkway. He got into his truck and sat there for a moment, his head tilted back against the neck support, looking up at the roof. Finally, he sat up, started the motor and drove away.

It was early, but Shauna Lee turned off the lights and went into the bedroom. She took off her clothes, turned back the covers and lay naked on the bed. Her fingers slid down over her breasts to the throbbing ache between her legs. She knew she could relieve herself, but that wasn't what she wanted or needed.

She needed what he'd left her without; the warmth of human contact, arms around her, someone to laugh with, someone to share even a few hours with. He'd left her *alone* like she'd been all her life.

She cried herself to sleep.

CHAPTER SIX

The next morning she woke up early. Brad was the first person on her mind. He'd almost been cruel when he'd come to pick her up yesterday, asking questions she didn't have answers for herself. Why was he so insistent? Why did he care if her life was *sterile,* as he called it?

The phone rang. She looked at her watch. It was six-thirty in the morning. Who would call this early? She reached for the phone.

"Good morning, beautiful." The voice was soft, sexy, sleepy sounding.

"Brad?"

"I hope that's who you're thinking about. Are you still in bed?"

"Yes."

"What are you doing?"

"What are *you* doing?" she countered.

"Thinking about you; the cold shower just didn't do it last night."

"That's your own fault. I asked you to stay."

"I know that, sweetheart, but... I'm looking for something I can put my heart into. I'm serious... but for me it's got to be just you and me. I won't share you with other guys. I want to build a relationship with you. I want what I saw yesterday between Colt and Frank. I want that kind of love for you and me."

She sobbed.

"Shauna Lee? Sweetheart—"

She couldn't control her tears; she sobbed again. Then she hung up.

Fifteen minutes later the doorbell rang. She knew it was Brad. *Go to hell,* she groaned. She was not getting up to face more torment. But he kept ringing the bell. Then he went around to the back door and pounded on it.

Furious, she staggered out of bed and went to open it, not even thinking about the fact that she was naked. "Jeez, don't break the place down—" She stopped dead. He stood there in pajama bottoms, bare feet, and no shirt. "Are you absolutely crazy?"

He pushed through the door, forcing her in with him. He closed it and locked it behind him. Then he enveloped her in his arms, pressing her face to his muscular chest. He swept her up and carried her into the bedroom, laid her on the bed and slid in beside her. His hands tangled in her hair and he kissed her forehead. "Turn over and let me cuddle you," he whispered. They lay together, spooned. She felt his warmth, the strength of his arms around her. It wasn't sexual. It was peaceful, safe... like finding home after a long, exhausting search. They both fell asleep.

Shauna Lee stirred. At first she was confused, enveloped in his warmth. His arm tightened. "Good morning, beautiful," he whispered.

"Uhh..." she murmured. "What are you doing here?"

"I came by to ask you to go on a date with me. Will you come?"

She moved to turn over. He held her tight. "No. Just stay here in my arms. Let me hold you."

She was silent for a moment. "What kind of a date?" she whispered.

He whispered back to her. "Breakfast at my house, a lazy day getting to know each other, maybe watch a movie tonight or just sit around and talk. You can stay over if you want... I have a guest room. Breakfast together tomorrow morning; maybe we'll go for a drive. We'll give ourselves a chance to learn to *like* being with each other, learn to be comfortable together, learn to be friends and companions.

"And if it works this weekend, then maybe we'll do something similar again next weekend, and the next one. Until we can't imagine life without each other, until we fall in *love*. Lust is no issue. We've got that already, but like and love has to be nurtured and built upon. Are you willing to give it a try?"

She was still for a few seconds. "You are crazy." She thought for a moment. Then she nodded. "But... yes, I'm willing to give it a try."

His arms tightened around her momentarily; then he lightly slapped her naked hip. "Do you want to shower here or at my place?"

"Are you serious?"

"Well, sweetheart, I don't know if you noticed, but I'm not dressed for public places. I knew you were crying, so I bailed out of bed and tore over here. I thought I might sweep you up and take you home with me right then, but it didn't happen that way. At seven in the morning, it didn't seem to matter too much, but at eleven or eleven-thirty, it's a little different."

"Can I grab a jogging outfit now and come back later for necessities?"

"That's good thinking." He rubbed his hand along the cheek of her butt. "Out you get and be quick. I need to get back home so I don't get arrested for indecent exposure!"

Smiling, she slid out of bed and went to her dresser to

take out a pair of panties, a bra and socks. He got out of the bed and made it while she quickly got dressed. She grabbed her cosmetic bag and hair brush and stood waiting for him.

"You're good!" he said with a smile, leaning in for a quick kiss. "Let's go."

***

Shauna Lee hadn't given any thought to where Brad lived or what his home would be like. She wasn't prepared for the reality. He lived in one of the new subdivisions on the outskirts of town on a ten-acre lot. The house was big and sprawling and the yard perfectly landscaped.

"Is this your place?"

"My name is on the mortgage." He grinned at her. "If you don't like it, I'm—"

"I didn't mean that. I just thought you'd have a condo or something."

"Actually, this is what my Dad calls a *Bird House*. I bought it with the idea of settling down some time and starting a family. Now I just have to find a Bird, who will share it with me." He looked at her. "You could have first option."

She looked away from him. "Brad. You don't know me. I'm not a prime candidate."

"See, I think you are wrong there. I guess that's something we have to explore. When I first met you, I thought the same thing. I figured you were nothing but trouble; certainly not someone I wanted to have anything to do with. But even that night, at the meeting, I saw beyond the- the other stuff."

He smiled as their eyes met. "I knew you were intelligent, and people at that meeting respected you."

"What a revelation that must have been," she said bitterly.

"Shauna Lee, I'm drawn to you in spite of everything else. For whatever reason, it's different with you. You frustrate the hell out of me, but you've got me thinking about the future; love and marriage and forever; my gut tells me you are worth the effort."

"We don't want the same things and I don't want

children."

"And yet I saw you with Sam yesterday. I saw you fight tears when you looked at him, and when you reached out to him, you had such a wistful expression. I don't think that had anything to do with him being Colt's son.

"You're smart enough to know Colt's heart is taken, but you know what I think, Tweetie Bird? I think part of you wants what you see in Colt, now that he's in love, because it's safe for you to imagine that with him because it's unreachable and you know you'll never have to deal with real intimacy."

"I shouldn't have come here."

"You're wrong. You needed to come here. It's not going to be easy Shauna Lee, but I'm in for the long haul. Little by little, day by day, week by week, month by month, year by year — we are going to peel away the layers and free the woman that you really are. In my heart, I feel that you have been hurt badly. I want to be the one to show you what real love, *unconditional* love is. I want to share that with you."

He reached out and touched her. "Trust me, Shauna Lee. I don't give up easily when I really want something. And I really want to see you happy and in love with me." He opened the truck door. "Ok... session one with the analyst is over."

"Session one? More like session five, isn't it?"

"Sorry. I'll drop it for now. It's time for a shower and brunch. How do waffles and strawberries and whipped cream sound?"

He led the way to the front door, unlocked it and swung it open. "Welcome to the nest, Tweetie Bird."

Shauna Lee looked at him. "If I was smart, I'd probably fly away." She walked past him and he stepped in behind her, closing the door. She looked around the large foyer. Ceramic tile covered the floor and flowed into the kitchen and dining area. Rich dark hardwood flooring led down the hall and into other rooms. The kitchen was a modern dream. She stood and looked around in open admiration. "Brad, this is... beautiful.

You have wonderful taste."

"You remember that because I know I do." He smiled into her eyes as he brushed her chin lightly with his fingers. "OK, breakfast first or a shower first?"

"I need a shower. I must look like a nightmare."

"No, I see a beautiful dream." He winked. "I'll show you the spare room. There's an en-suite right off it." He led the way down the hall and stopped at a door at the far end. "Here you are."

She stepped into the room and looked around. It was decorated with a classic contemporary design, understated luxury. "It's beautiful, Brad."

"You'll find towels and shampoo in there. Take as long as you like. I'll grab a quick shower in my bathroom. Come to the kitchen when you're ready."

Shauna Lee luxuriated in the warmth and pressure of the shower. She washed her hair, toweled dry, and quickly put her clothes back on. She peeked in the drawers, looking for a blow dryer. *None. Well, I guess it's a curly mop for me today.*

She wandered down the hallway stopping to look at different groups of pictures on the wall as she went: family, friends, fun events, hunting pictures. This man had pictures everywhere; evidence of his life. *No wonder my place drives him crazy.*

She stepped into the kitchen and watched him beating something with a mixer. She walked quietly to his side. He removed the bowl from the stand. She could see it was filled with a deep pile of fluffy egg whites and he was shaking a dry mixture over them. Then he folded it in gently with a spatula. "From scratch?" she asked.

He grinned as he turned to the hot waffle iron, opened the lip and spooned the mixture onto it. "They're best that way."

She shook her head, knowing she'd never be able to match his cooking prowess. "Can I do anything to help you?"

"You can clean the strawberries and slice them."

"I think I can handle that."

He set out a bowl, a small knife, and a cutting board. With an economy of movement, he reached into the fridge and brought out a big carton of strawberries. "There you go," he said with a smile. He turned to check the waffles and lifted a fluffy, golden brown one off the iron. He slipped it onto a plate in a small compartment below the wall oven.

"What's that?" she asked looking at it.

"It's a warming drawer. I'd hate to be without it."

He spooned more of the mix onto the waffle iron and closed it. Then he reached for a small electrical whipping wand and started making the whipped cream.

"Can I set the table?"

He nodded. "The plates are up there," he said nodding at a cupboard, and the cutlery is over here." He pulled open a drawer to show her.

He is so organized, he scares me; everything in its place, she thought as she watched him put the waffle mix bowl directly into the dishwasher and give the counter a wipe down.

He looked at her with a happy smile. "Pull up a chair and dig in," he said as he carried the waffles, whipped cream and strawberries to the table. "I'll put coffee on for after we eat."

She sat down and waited for him to join her. "Help yourself," he said, leaning over to tousle her curls. "I like these," he said softly.

They ate with relish. "Brad this is wonderful. These waffles sure beat the toaster pop-ups I buy."

"Shauna Lee, you don't know what you're missing. And the best part of it is the fun of doing something like this with someone special... like you."

"But I didn't do anything."

He shook his head, pointing to the strawberry stains on her fingers. "Yes you did, and you set the table. You're great company. You know, it gets lonely being here, no matter how beautiful the place is."

She nodded. "I understand loneliness," she said wistfully.

He took their plates and cutlery and slid them into the

dishwasher, then poured them each a cup of coffee. "Do you ride horses? I guess I should ask if you ever have since it seems like you don't do anything much except work and—"

She put her hand up to stop him. "I rode when I was about eight. That's so long ago, I doubt if it counts now."

"Do you want to go for a walk in the pasture? I've got a couple of horses out there."

She looked skeptical but nodded. Brad got up, went to a cupboard and slipped something small into his shirt pocket. He reached out his hand and threaded his fingers through hers. "We can go out the back door."

It was a beautiful day and they wandered down a trail that ran through a large landscaped back yard, into a fenced pasture. In one corner, there was a small barn and a corral. Brad whistled sharply and in seconds they could hear the pounding of hooves coming their way.

Brad filled a small bucket with oats and stepped forward to meet the horses, then led them into the corral and shut the gate. "Do you want to come in here with me or watch from out there?"

"I'll stay out here for now."

He talked to each one of the horses, rubbing their ears softly, running his hands down the length of their backs and down over their hips. He took a curry comb and started working their coats while they stood with all their weight on three legs, resting a hind one, with bottom lip drooping, tail switching lazily, in perfect contentment.

As she watched, a familiarity from long ago rose in Shauna Lee. Her mind went back to a battered old pole corral and bare dirt. She remembered the old gray gelding that she had loved. She had ridden for hours every day; a lonely child in a dysfunctional family. Her horse had been her love, her only companion. Her eyes glistened with unshed tears. She hadn't thought of those days for years. She'd shut them away like she had the rest of the memories of that part of her life.

"Can I come in?"

"Of course you can! They're very quiet. They won't hurt you."

She entered the corral and went to stand by Brad. One of the horses singled her out, nuzzling her top. Brad expected her flinch away and was surprised when she didn't. A confidence from years ago surfaced, and she responded to the horse like an old friend. She rubbed it and petted it, crooning to it softly as she did so.

Brad watched her silently. A soft look came over her face, and she buried her face against the horse's nose. She breathed deeply several times. Brad watched with wonder, then reached into his pocket and took out a small camera. She didn't even notice that he had taken a picture and he slipped it back into his pocket. When she looked at Brad, there were tears in her eyes.

Her voice was emotional. "Can we ride?"

"Do you want to?"

She nodded, burying her face against the horse again.

"OK. I've got saddles in the barn. Let's saddle up."

"Can I ride bareback?"

"Shauna Lee, are you sure?"

"Will he be all right with that?"

Brad nodded. "The kids back home rode both of them bareback all the time."

She smiled tremulously. "Will you help me up? I'm pretty rusty at this."

Brad made a step for her with his hands and she pulled herself up and slid over the horses back. She leaned forward and wrapped her arms down around its neck. She lay on the animal's back and stayed there, her face turned away from him.

Brad watched in silence, wondering what this meant to her. Then he noticed her shoulders shaking and he heard her sob. He walked around the horse until he could see Shauna Lee's face. She just squeezed her eyes tightly, sobbing uncontrollably; tears coursing down her cheeks, dribbling down the horse's neck. He lay a hand on her thigh and let her cry.

Finally, she sat up, sniffling, hiccupping, her face streaked with the tears that had mixed with the unavoidable dust on the horse. She swiped at her eyes and glared at him. "I don't like you," she cried. "You are prodding me into places that I don't want to go."

He reached up and lifted her off the horse as he might have a child. Then he enfolded her against his chest and rocked from side to side with her. "Let's go inside," he whispered. She followed him numbly. When they got in the house, he looked at her with compassion. "Shauna Lee, I don't know what happened out there, but that was a big emotional block that you let loose. Do you want to lie down for a while? You have to be exhausted."

She nodded. He took her hand and led her down the hall, but not to the guest room. Instead, he took her to the door of his bedroom. He picked her up and carried her to the bed. He slipped her runners off, then went into the bathroom and came out with a damp face cloth. He wiped her face gently. "Lay down, sweetheart. I'll go take out some steak for supper and I'll be right back."

She was tense and curled up like a child when he came back.

He walked around to the far side of the bed and slid in against her back. He wrapped his arms around her, cradling her close. Gradually she relaxed and eased into his embrace. She fell asleep, snuffling occasionally. Brad didn't go to sleep immediately. He was lost in his thoughts, wondering what had happened to this beautiful woman.

When she woke up, she squiggled in his arms. She turned around and faced him. "I'm sorry. I- I didn't mean what I said to you out there."

He kissed her forehead. "I want to believe that."

"It's just that you won't let go. I've cried more in the past week than I have in years. Probably since I..."

"Since you what?"

"Brad, I can't talk about this now. I don't know if I'll ever be able to."

"That's all right, sweetheart. We'll take as long as you need."

"You don't know what you're asking of me. Will you just accept me as I am? Please?"

"I will, for now. But, sweetheart, you're going to have to face the past some time. You're a prisoner of it now."

She turned away and sat up. "Don't push me anymore, Brad." She stood up and walked out of the room.

When he followed, she wasn't in the kitchen. He looked in all the rooms, and then went to the back door. She was heading to the corral. He wanted to go after her but resisted, knowing he had to give her space.

It was dark when she came back in. He had made a salad, potatoes were baking in the oven and steaks were waiting to go on the grill.

She went to the cupboard, took down two plates and put them on the table. Then she went to the drawer and picked out the cutlery, adding a steak knife when she saw the steak. He put a butter dish, salt and pepper, sour cream, chives and bacon bits on the counter and she transferred them to the table. Brad reached for two wine glasses and went to the wine cooler, bringing back a bottle of red wine.

They both worked in silence, and even as they sat down to eat, it wasn't broken. He looked at her for permission to pour the wine and she nodded. They finished the meal and cleaned up.

Then, Brad silently took her hand and led her into the family room. He turned on the electric fireplace and motioned for her sit on the couch. He picked up the TV remote and selected a country music station. He sat down beside her and snuggled her against him. They sat in the quiet, the music pouring softly around them.

Brad was lost in his thoughts. Shauna Lee was drifting; suddenly the words of a song caught her attention. Brad noticed and listened to the words. "That's Aaron Pritchett singing."

She buried her face in his chest. "I didn't know who was singing. I was listening to the words. That is my song, Brad; that is me. I don't want to deal with the past. I just want to hide away. I want to find *a warm, safe place*."

"I'm here for you, Tweetie Bird. I'll be your warm, safe place."

They sat close for a couple of hours. He looked at his watch; it was ten o'clock. "You are staying the night, aren't you?"

"Is it all right?"

"Sweetheart, I want you to. This day hasn't exactly gone the way I expected. I don't want to take you home. I want you here with me."

"Be my safe, warm place?" she murmured.

He nodded. "Are you ready to go to bed? We didn't go get your things today. I'll give you one of my shirts to wear to bed."

"Will you sleep with me and hold me?"

"I have every intention of doing that. Let's go."

She waited while he shut off the lights and came to her side. He led her to his bedroom and turned on the bedside light. Then he went to his closet and pulled out a white shirt. "You'll swim in it, but it will do."

He swallowed hard when she came out wearing his shirt and looking freshly scrubbed. He groaned inwardly. *I must be a masochistic fool.*

When he came out of the bathroom, she was curled up under the covers. He turned off the light and then went to the other side of the bed. She turned and lifted the sheet for him to get in. Then she rolled to her side, her back to him, cuddling into his arms as he spooned her. She threaded her fingers through his. "Thank you," she whispered.

He squeezed her, then kissed the back of her head. They drifted off to sleep.

Hours later, Brad awoke with a start, disoriented at first. Arms were flying, fists flailing, legs kicking; a bundle of fury in his bed. *What the hell....*

Shauna Lee cried out. "No! No... not Poko!..." The words came from her private hell.

"Shauna Lee! Sweetheart, everything is alright. You're just having a bad dream." Brad tried to hold her, but she struck at him, pushing him away. Suddenly she bolted upright in the bed, sobbing, eyes wide and full of anguish.

Brad reached for her, enfolding her in his arms. "It's just a dream, sweetheart. I'm here to protect you." He let her lie against him and sob. When she finally pushed away from him to wipe her tears and her nose on the shirt that she was wearing, he let her go.

"Oh, Brad," she moaned. "You must be sorry you ever brought me here. I've been such a mess this weekend."

He shook his head and reached out to touch her wordlessly.

"I don't know what's happening. I haven't dreamed like that for years."

"Do you want to talk about it?"

She closed her eyes against the thought. "Brad... I've got so much baggage. I warned you... I don't know if I can ever be what you imagine I can be."

"You already are."

"I'm not what you *think* I am. I'm not what I appear to be. If I let you make me start feeling again... I'll have to rebuild my whole life. I don't know if I have the courage...."

"Do you want to tell me who, or what, you were fighting with before you woke up?"

She sat for a long moment, then got up and walked out of the room. Concerned, Brad followed her. He stopped at the large doorway that led into the main living area of the house. He watched her as she walked around the kitchen counter and opened the door of the cupboard where the glasses were. She took out a tall one and ran it full of water from the tap. Then she went to gaze out the window while she drank it.

Finally, she turned to look at him angrily. "I can't believe this is happening to me." Her voice was rough with emotion. "This is you... your fault. You wouldn't just leave me alone."

"Shauna Lee, I'm sorry. I had no way of knowing that bringing you here would be like this."

She shook her head. "You wanted to find out who I am. Well, now you're getting your wish."

"I care for you, Shauna Lee."

"How can you say that? You don't know who I am."

"Shauna Lee ... I don't know how to explain how I feel. It seems crazy. We've hardly known each other long enough to have any real feelings, but of all the women I've met..." His look was pleading.

"Brad, I buried an entire existence years ago. I didn't want to remember it then... I don't want to now. I built a new life and started over. You have no idea who I am; maybe I don't know who I really am."

He ran a hand through his hair. "Just believe me." His voice was rough with emotion. "No matter what the past has been, you reach a spot in me that no one else has touched. I am willing to do anything to try to make this work; anything but share you with those other guys."

"I hope you don't live to regret it." Shauna Lee came to him. "Brad, I've never known anyone like you before," she said softly. "I almost don't know how to act; how to be with you."

She took his hand and led the way back to the bedroom. She pushed her pillow up against the headboard and sat on the bed against it with her legs pulled up in front of her, arms wrapped around her knees, chin resting on them. Brad slid in on the other side and lay with his elbow propped up on the bed, his cheek resting on his closed fist.

"I didn't have a childhood like you, Brad. I sure as hell did not come from the same kind of a perfect family."

"We weren't perfect."

"Well, you were compared to where I came from. My mom and dad may have been in love once. Time changes things. But for as long as I can remember, I don't think they loved each other... I think their marriage was just a trap created by circumstances. Dad had a farm, but nothing seemed to work out for him. We were always broke, but he could afford to drink and he did... all the time." She picked at the sheet aimlessly, lost in her memories.

"When I was almost eleven, mom had another baby. Now that I'm an adult, I can't even imagine how that happened, considering the way things were between them. The baby was a boy. They called him Andre, and for once dad had something in his life that he was really proud of. Mom loved Andre because he was her child, but I also think, because for once Dad was truly happy. I loved Andre too. He was part of my heart...."

She was silent for a moment, staring at the wall. "I forgot until this afternoon... how could I have forgotten? But I did. When I stood there and watched you brush your horses, suddenly it came back to me. How I used to ride. It got me away from the house, it gave me freedom. I'd go for hours. I had a gray gelding called Poko." Her words were spoken quietly, almost as if she was talking to herself. "I loved him so much. He was an old Percheron-cross. He was probably ugly as sin, but I thought he was beautiful."

She fell into silence again. Finally, Brad reached over and touched her toe. There were tears brimming in her eyes when she looked at him. She grimaced. "Dad drank all the time, but he was happy when Andre was with him. One day, when Andre was almost four, Dad was out on the tractor...."

She bit her lip as the tears spilled over. She dashed them away with her shirt sleeve. "Suddenly Andre was there. Dad couldn't have seen him, or maybe his reactions were just too slow. He..."

She began to sob. "He was backing up. He ran over Andre with the back tire. He just laid there... his little body... Dad watched h- hi- m die." Her fingers curled tight into her palms. She looked at Brad. "Dad was so broken. He had to blame somebody."

A sick feeling flooded Brad's belly. "Not you, Shauna Lee. Tell me, not you..."

"If I hadn't been off riding, I'd have been home helping mom. I'd have kept Andre away from the tractor."

"No, Shauna Lee," he groaned. "That was so unfair."

"Dad never was the same again. None of us were. He blamed me, but he took it out on Poko too because I was riding him. He... he took his gun and sh- hot him."

Brad reached for her, but she pushed him away.

"Dad never was a strong man, but after that, he drank constantly. He'd drink until he passed out; probably to erase the memory of what happened to Andre." She pulled the edge of the sheet up over her knees and wove it through her fingers.

"And Mom..." she said sadly. "She just drew farther and farther away from everything. She just wasn't there anymore; I guess it was depression. The spring I was fourteen; actually I was fourteen and a half then; Dad caught a ride to town with a neighbor. That wasn't uncommon, but that time he didn't come home. We never saw him again."

"What happened to you and your mom?"

She smiled bitterly. "Well, it hardly mattered to Mom. But to me... it really scared me. I was afraid that if Mom went to the hospital, I would be put in a foster home."

"Christ, Shauna Lee ..."

She kept speaking, ignoring his words. It was as if Pandora's Box had sprung open and everything just came spilling out.

"I did the best I could. Mom was like... a- a zombie. She ate very little. She just sat and stared into space or slept." Shauna Lee balled the edge of the sheet in her hand.

"We had chickens for eggs, but when nobody gathers them properly, the hens set on them. In a few weeks, they hatch baby chicks. Over the summer, lots of them showed up and they grew. Dad had made me learn how to kill them and butcher them, so we had meat.

"Dad had made me plant a garden in the spring because Mom couldn't. Even though he was gone, it grew and I pulled vegetables out of the weeds. There was a milk cow and I knew how to milk.

"The neighbor helped me when I asked. He brought me firewood for winter. I didn't think about it then, but now I think that he might have paid the power bill for us because we didn't. There was no money."

She sighed. "We held on until Mom got pneumonia in January. The neighbor said she had to go to the hospital and he took her into town. She never came back. She went into a nursing home and she died six months later."

"What did you do, Shauna Lee?"

Her eyes filled with tears. Her jaw set. "I can't go there now, Brad. I just can't!"

Brad lifted back the sheet and tried to ease her down beside him.

She shook her head and resisted him. "I can't be here now. I...I'll go to the other room." She pushed herself up and stood. Then she walked away without a word.

Brad jumped out of bed and followed her down the hall, into the spare room. She shook her head as she looked at him. "No," she whispered. He watched her pull back the sheet and crawl into the bed. Then he turned around and walked back to his bed.

He was sick at heart. *This is my fault. I should have accepted her as she was or got out. No wonder she hasn't wanted to know who she was.*

Brad woke up at five o'clock, his head dull from the emotion of the night before and the lack of sleep. He became aware of warmth at his back and a slender arm around his waist. A couple of tears seeped out of his eyes, and he swallowed hard to fight back more.

Shauna Lee had come back to his bed. She was curled against him, her cheek resting against his back. She was clinging to him, sound asleep. He wanted to turn over and take her in his arms, but she was sleeping and she needed rest. He didn't want to wake her, so he stayed where he was. His mind relaxed. He held her hand, clasping it and holding it against his breast. He fell into a sound sleep.

It was noon before Shauna Lee stirred. Brad had been awake for a while. When he knew she was awake, he turned over. She was still sleepy-eyed and flushed. Her eyes were slightly red and swollen. He didn't enfold her as he wanted to. He slid an arm around her waist and gave a gentle squeeze. "You don't know how happy it makes me to wake up and find you here, snuggled up against me."

She looked at him solemnly. Then she moved into his arms. "Hold me, Brad. Please?" She lay in his arms and savored his warmth, his strength. She felt safe.

After they got up and had breakfast, Brad asked her what she would like to do.

"Can we go for a ride?" The sparkle was gone from her. The night's revelation had taken its toll.

"Are you sure you can do this today?"

"Yes."

They went to the corral and Brad whistled for the horses.

Shauna Lee smiled wanly, but she did smile as she watched them come up the trail. "I would like to ride bareback."

"Okay, we'll give it try and see how it goes. Do you want to ride very far?"

"How far can we ride from here?"

"If we go out the back of the field, we can follow a trail for a mile or so and then we can ride all afternoon through fields that a friend of mine owns if you want."

"I'm going to saddle up though. I'll be a cripple if I don't. Are you sure you want to go bareback? I have a saddle you can use."

"I've never ridden with a saddle, Brad."

"Oh." *Why didn't I realize that?* "It's been a long time since you rode, sweetheart... or am I wrong?"

"No, you're right. I never rode again."

"You're not thirteen years old anymore. You might find the saddle is easier on your body. Either that or maybe we should just ride around here in the pasture and give you a chance to get used to it again. We could go for a longer ride next weekend."

She thought for a moment. "You are probably right. Let's just make it a short ride today."

After an hour of riding, she was shifting on the horses back, trying to find a comfortable spot. "I think I need to get off him. I'm going to be sore."

A glance at Brad's watch told him it was later than he'd thought. "What do you say we go out for supper?"

"Well, I have to go home anyway. We could..."

"You don't have to go home you know. We can stop by and pick up your things and I'll take you to work when I go in the morning?"

"Brad, I can't stay here with you indefinitely. I have to go home and live *with* myself. I can't avoid my past anymore. I have to face it and- and deal with my feelings as best I can."

"I'll help you. I'm a good sounding board."

"You're a master shit-disturber," she said ruefully.

"Shauna Lee ... I'm sorry I helped to upset your world. But honestly, don't you think you would have remembered eventually? This way you were with someone who cares. I was here to offer whatever support I could. It might have been worse if you had been all alone when it happened."

"Recently, something else did happen. Suddenly I was thinking of something so... so horrific from my past... it made me physically ill. I had to deal with it that time, but it was awful." Tears shimmered in her eyes.

Brad stepped to her side. "There have been enough tears for now. No more, sweetheart. Not today." He wrapped her in his arms and kissed her gently. Then he brushed away the one or two that slipped down her cheeks.

They went to her place first so she could drop off her things and change. Then they went out for Chinese dinner. Afterward, he took her back to her house.

"Don't hesitate to call me if you need me," he said seriously after he kissed her soundly. "I'll be here as fast as possible, no matter what time it is."

She looked at him in a dazed way, slowly shaking her head. "Brad, are you for real? Can you really be this wonderful and caring? Is it possible that I can really deserve someone like you? This," she motioned with her finger between him and her. "It almost scares me... it's like-- like it's too good to be true."

He took both her hands in his and looked intently into her eyes. "I've told you how I feel and I've told you that I'll do almost anything to make things work for us. Just trust me, Shauna Lee." He turned to the door, opened it, and then hesitated. "It doesn't feel right, leaving you here."

She swallowed hard. "Just go. If I need you, I promise to call."

CHAPTER SEVEN

Shauna Lee fell into the sleep of exhaustion. The phone woke her at seven-fifteen the next morning. She smiled when she answered and heard his voice. "Good morning, beautiful. Were you thinking about me?"

"Not really. You woke me up."

"I thought I'd call and talk dirty with you for a minute or two."

She laughed and it sounded good to him. "You fool; I wouldn't know how to talk dirty with you. You've never...." She blushed and quit speaking.

"I've never...? What were you going to say?"

She took a deep breath. "You've never played "dirty" with me... other than the fact that it is dirty of you to get me all... you know... hot and bothered, and then walk out and leave me."

"Well, right now, I have a companion that's trying to break through my restraint. I'm going to need a cold shower again."

"Brad, I have no sympathy for you. Go and have your cold shower."

"Hear that, big guy? She told us to go have a cold shower. What do you think?"

Shauna Lee grinned to herself. *That man is impossible!*

"Are you there, Shauna? My friend here... he says he doesn't like cold showers."

"Tell him he missed his chance."

"Shauna? I think we just talked "dirty" and you know exactly how to do it with me."

"You're nuts. But I *do* miss you Brad; even just lying in your arms instead of...playing dirty. Actually, it's kind of nice to just be there... not *having* to... you know.... Thank you for caring about me and looking after me," she said soberly.

"I miss you too, sweetheart. I love to hold you in my arms. I'll talk to you later. Now I have to go take a cold shower and make my friend behave so I can go to work."

Brad didn't phone, and she had to admit she felt disappointed. She took a lunch break and walked downtown to do some shopping. When she got back to the office, she asked Christina if anyone had called.

Christina said 'No,' with a happy twinkle in her eye. Shauna Lee's disappointment overshadowed her impulse to ask what had made her day.

Shauna Lee went into her office and took a couple of steps toward her desk; then she stopped dead. On the corner of her desk sat a dozen red roses in a crystal vase. Her spirits lifted magically and her face lit up with a smile. She reached for the small envelope that rested on the flowers.

As she started to open it, she noticed two framed pictures sitting next to her computer monitor. She laid the envelope down and leaned over to look at them. She picked up the closest one and gazed at it. *When did he take this?*

It was an excellent picture of her with her face resting against the horse's nose. Then she picked up the other one. He had caught her riding bareback, hair flying, galloping up the trail toward him. She pressed the picture to her lips. "You wonderful man," she said softly.

"Ahh... you finally realize that!" She jumped and found herself in his arms. Then he was kissing her, hot and passionately. "It's been about sixteen hours since I did that. I'm a starving man."

"You could have had lunch with me."

"I meant touching you, kissing you, holding you, starving. I'm not hungry. I grabbed a hamburger at the A&W while I took care of some important things." He swept his hand toward the desk.

"The flowers are beautiful."

He looked puzzled. "The flowers? They aren't from me." He looked at them. "There's a card. Did you look at it?"

"Well, no. I saw the pictures and stopped to look at them. I love them, Brad. You really surprised me." She looked up at him, puzzled. "Are you serious about the flowers not being from you?"

"Totally serious. What does the card say?"

She opened the envelope hesitantly and then pulled out a card. No one ever sent her flowers. If they weren't from Brad, who were they from?

She looked at the card and began to smile. It read, "I hate cold showers." The card was signed, "Brad's friend."

She turned to Brad, and reached down and caressed the hardness behind his zipper. "Thanks, big guy, they're beautiful. Talk to Brad about why you're taking cold showers."

Brad moaned. "Woman," he whispered. "I'm waiting. I still haven't heard the words I want to hear from you."

She looked at him, puzzled.

"When you are ready, they will come. Until then, my friend and I will take cold showers." He kissed her again. "I have to go do some work now. Can I take you home with me after work and we'll make supper together?"

They had supper together every night that week. Some

nights she slept in his arms, others he took her back home. If he took her home, he always called her the next morning. He had worked his way into her life and made her want to be with him.

***

Saturday morning the ringing of Brad's phone woke them. He uncurled himself from holding her and reached for it.

"This had better be good," he growled. "I'm still in bed. In case you hadn't noticed, it's Saturday morning."

Shauna Lee heard Colt laugh. "You know people die in bed!"

"Maybe I just did. I thought I was in heaven until you called."

"Well, it's time you got your ass out of bed! It's nearly ten o'clock. What you need is a good woman and a pair of twins and a nanny in the house with you. Believe me you'd be up by now!"

"I've been giving it some thought; the good woman part, I mean. I'm not sure about the twins or a nanny. But a good woman..." He curled his arm and pulled Shauna Lee closer. "Yeah, I'm waiting for a green light and I'm in for that."

"I've got news for you, man! If you wait for a green light, you'll probably never get one. You've got to be proactive and turn on the light yourself."

He laughed and looked at Shauna Lee, knowing she could hear the entire conversation through the handset. "Women aside, what's on your mind this morning, Colt?"

"I've intended to call you all week about going out to the ranch to get the specs for the turbines. I've just been too busy getting the trailer set up. I know it is Saturday, but I wondered if you could make it today.

"I've tried to get hold of Shauna Lee a couple of evenings this week, but she never answers. I worry about that woman. I hope she doesn't get herself in a heap of trouble, doing some of the stuff that she does."

"Yeah," Brad drawled as he gave her a squeeze. "She

could get herself into a heap of trouble. I saw her last night and she looked pretty hot."

"Was she with some guy?"

"Yeah, she was."

"Damn it. You know, after that night at the restaurant, I told Frank what had gone down. She suggested maybe I should try to talk to her, but I don't want to get involved that way. I just worry that she'll find herself in a situation she can't handle one of these times."

"She easily could find herself in a situation she doesn't know how to handle. But the guy she was with last night was different than the others. I think she may be getting it right this time."

"She's a good person, Brad. As Frank said, there has to be someone out there for her. I'd like to see her as happy as I am. I'd like to see her with someone who deserves her."

"Colt, she's pretty smart. I'm sure she'll figure it out. Now, about going to the ranch today..." He looked at his watch. "It's getting kind of late. We could go tomorrow and leave early. We'll have a better chance of getting everything done if we do that."

"You're right. If we wait until tomorrow, we'll get Ellie moved into the trailer today. She's a prize, but I miss being able to run around the house in the buff if I want to or being able to grab a morning quickie with my wife."

"Okay, man, I get the picture! Do your thing and we'll go out to the ranch tomorrow. What time do you want to leave; around seven o'clock?"

"That will work for us. I'm going to bring Fran along."

"Oh great. We'll spend another day watching you lovebirds! Just seeing you two together makes me horny. You are so... Aww, forget it. I'm just envious. Bring her along. Maybe I'll take my chances and work on Shauna Lee."

Brad chuckled, as she squirmed. "We'll see you tomorrow. I'll stop in at the office today and get everything I need. I'll get Shauna Lee lined up too. We'll be at the farm by seven."

He hung up the phone and grinned at Shauna Lee. She gave him an elbow in the ribs. "You are terrible!"

"Well, I didn't think you'd want me to tell him that you were here in my bed and that I was the guy you were with last night!"

"I'd have died of embarrassment. They say women are gossips.... Jeez."

"I basically told him the truth. I just left out the juicy stuff. Speaking of juicy..." He ran his hand over her hip and pulled her back against the hardness of his erection. He groaned and pushed her searching hand away gently. "Shauna Lee, this is killing me, but I don't want to just have sex. I need to know that it means the same to you as it does to me."

"Brad... I don't know what you want. I've been ready since that night when you left me all alone. I cried myself to sleep that night."

He eased himself away. "Tweetie Bird. You've been ready for sex. I want more. I believe that eventually you will too. When I know the time is right, I'll make love to you like no one ever has. Until then," he put his hand on his swollen shaft. "More cold showers and lovers nuts, buddy." He stood up and headed into the ensuite.

Shauna Lee glared at him. "Fuck you!"

He stopped and looked at her. "I'm counting on you doing that! But not before we make love, sweetheart."

"Bull! I'm beginning to wonder if you aren't gay."

He stopped short and stared at her. Then he laughed harshly and with one swift move pushed his pajama bottoms over his hips and let them drop to the floor. He walked back to the bed. A flash of fire burned in his eyes as he pulled her up onto her feet.

He jerked her against him, then grabbed her hand and pushed it against his erection. "If I'm gay, why does this happen every time I think of you? And that seems to be damned near all the time lately."

She pulled away and ran to the spare room. She ached for release. "What the hell does he want from me?" She fought tears of frustration, as she showered, dried off and blew her hair dry. Then she pulled on a pair of jeans, and a red long-sleeved top. She was still angry when she went to the kitchen. He was whistling to himself as he made breakfast and she had an urge to hit him. *Jeez! How can he be so happy?*

She walked around him and went to the cupboard. It was a familiar ritual now. Two plates, two coffee cups, two sets of knives and forks. *Like a couple,* she thought. *Who don't have sex. Cripes!*

Bacon was sizzling on the grill, and she saw him look in the oven and check on the hash browns. She set the table and got the ketchup from the fridge for his hash browns. Then she moved to the toaster and popped in three slices of toast; two for him, one for her. She took the butter down from the shelf and got a knife to spread it. The moves were automatic now. It was part of their routine.

He came up behind her and slid his arms around her. She stiffened. He turned her into his arms, even though she resisted him. "Not talking to me?" he asked softly. He ran a hand up her back, along the length of her neck and through her hair. She felt herself melting.

"This looks great, but I still prefer your curls when we're here by ourselves on the weekends." Then he kissed her gently and held her close against him. "My Tweetie Bird," he whispered on a sigh.

Then, he stepped away, going back to the grill to turn the bacon. She watched him crack three eggs onto the grill. He cooked his sunny side up and hers over easy and firmer the way she liked them. *He so maddening about some things, but then he is so wonderful too.*

"Breakfast is ready," Brad announced cheerfully as he put everything on a plate and took the hash browns out of the oven. Shauna Lee picked up the coffee carafe and carried it to the table. They ate in silence that wasn't broken until she looked at him and said, "That was yummy. Thank you."

"I enjoy doing it for you, sweetheart. I love having you here with me."

Her expression turned to frustration. "I'm so mad at you."

"I sense that."

"You're tormenting me; you are a tease."

"I'm not teasing, Shauna Lee. I'm betting the rest of our lives on this."

She stood up. "Damn you," she cried. She turned and flounced to the back door. Her runners were there. *As if I live here*, she thought as she put them on.

She went outside and followed the trail to the pasture. She got a bucket of grain from the barn and called the horses. She smiled when she heard them running through the trees.

When they reached her, she let them take turns eating out of the bucket. When the grain was almost gone, she poured the remaining kernels on the ground and then petted them both. Finally, she put a bridle on *her* horse (that was how she thought of it now) and swung up onto its back.

Brad watched her from the backdoor as she rode bareback down the trail and out of sight. He sat down on one of the chairs and gazed into the field where she had disappeared. *Am I expecting too much?* He rested his elbows on his knees and buried his face in his hands. *She's been hurt so much. Who knows what she hasn't been able to tell me? But I don't want to settle for less than love.*

He sighed deeply, then stood up and went inside to his office. He turned on the computer and pulled up a file, considering what he needed to take with him the next day.

He was still at the computer when Shauna Lee came back into the house two hours later. He heard her come in but decided that he would let her seek him out when she was ready. He listened to her footsteps as she looked for him, stopping in each room as she went.

He didn't look up when he heard his half-closed office door push open. She hesitated uncertainly before she stepped into the room.

He looked up at her. "Enjoy your ride?"

She nodded and moved to his side. He swiveled the chair so he could reach out and slip his arm around her waist, then pushed back from the desk and pulled her down onto his lap. She sat there and let her eyes hold his in a long look. Then she broke the connection and laid her cheek against his shoulder. He nuzzled her hair, noticing the smell of the crisp freshness lingering in it.

"Brad?" she said softly.

"Uh-hum?"

She sat up and threaded her arms around his neck. "I'm sorry I acted the way I did this morning. Sometimes I act more like a petulant teenager, than a grown woman. You are so wonderful to me." She looked past his shoulder, avoiding eye contact. Her voice grew hoarse with emotion. "You...you confuse me. I've never met a man who wouldn't have sex with me. And with you...it...it *hurts* so much to know that you won't. I don't know how to do what you want me to do; I don't understand what you want from me."

He sighed. "Sweetheart, I..."

She cradled his face with her hands. "Brad, you know I've had meaningless sex with lots of guys."

He grimaced. "Don't—"

"No! I need you to understand. I didn't realize it then, but now I know that I was lonely. I wanted companionship, but you've changed all that." She looked deep into his eyes. "Brad, with you it wouldn't be meaningless. You've given me so much."

She bit her lip. "I- I *want* to be with you that way. I want to give myself to you. I need to feel you inside me. Don't you see? Being together with you that way... it's the closest that I can get to you. It hurts that what I have to give isn't enough. That you are looking for something more."

Now he was fighting emotion. "Tweetie Bird, it's not that what you have to give me isn't enough." He closed his eyes and swallowed hard. "I- I'm not rejecting you. I never, ever wanted to *hurt* you. You mean too much to me to do that."

He sighed. "This hasn't been easy for me. I love to hold you close, but I'm a man. A night hasn't gone by that I haven't ached with wanting you."

He shook his head, his eyes reflecting his anguish. "I- I don't want to fight this anymore. Maybe I've been unrealistic." He helped her stand up, and then took her hand as he stood. "Come with me."

He led her to his bed.

He wrapped his arms around her and held her close. As he kissed her, he slid his hand up the back of her shirt to caress her. It moved around to cup her breast. He played with the nipple through her bra. He shifted his mouth to trail down her neck, nipping her, kissing her, licking her lightly as he went.

She whimpered.

Desire flooded through him like a tsunami. He was so hard he ached. *Maybe I've been a fool,* he thought. *She wants this. God knows, I want this.*

He pulled her against him as his fingers fumbled to undo her jeans. He pulled down the zipper and eased them over her hips, letting them slide to the floor. Feverishly, he slid his hands into her panties and inched his fingers slowly downward. He slipped them into the small patch of fluff at the entrance he sought and he gently invaded her.

He groaned. She was hot and moist.

She gasped and bucked against him. He reached for the hem of her shirt with both hands and pulled it up over her head. He unhooked her bra, slid it down her arms and let it fall.

Fire raced through him, burning away all his former reasoning. *The rest doesn't matter right now; I just have to trust her feelings,* he thought as he undid his jeans. He let them slide to the floor and he jerked off his shirt. He ripped his socks off and threw them to the side, then picked her up in his arms and laid her on the bed.

He tugged off each of her socks, leaning over to lick the toes of each foot as he exposed them. She jerked her foot away. She squirmed as he kissed his way up her legs, moving along the inside of her thighs until he found her juicy moistness. His tongue danced and probed, as she twisted and sobbed.

He continued his way up, worshipping her body with his mouth; tracing his tongue along her belly, thrusting and twirling it deeply into her navel. Every inch of her was sacred to him and he kissed her everywhere. When he reached her breasts, he suckled them and slathered his tongue around each hardened nipple.

Her fingers threaded through his hair and she tried to reach his mouth with hers. Finally, he laid his body over hers, giving her what she sought. He took her mouth in a hot, probing kiss. She was twisting, grasping him.

Their eyes met. "Brad, are you sure?"

He groaned. "There's no going back now, Tweetie Bird." His voice rasped. He cried out as he pushed into her. He tried to go slow, but he was beyond control. This moment had been put off for far too long. He was taking her hard and deep. She made a muffled sound against his neck and he felt her convulse inside, squeezing around him. Their cries mingled.

"God, oh God, oh my God," he whispered as he collapsed and rolled off of her.

She was crying softly, running her fingers through his hair as she kissed his mouth: his eyes: his neck. She buried her face into his chest and he felt the wetness of her tears. He gathered her close and held her.

They lay there, bathed in perspiration, satiated until their breathing steadied.

"Brad... this is okay, isn't it? I know you didn't want to... you're not disappointed are you?"

He groaned. "Sweetheart, how could I be disappointed? We- I- you left me breathless." He kissed her forehead. "I love you, Tweetie Bird. I just wanted to know that you loved me before we went this far. I don't want to get my heart broken."

She looked at him sadly. "I hope I never... I *won't* ever break your heart, Brad. I want to be with you; *only you.* Even when I was so mad at you this morning, I realized how much a part of my life you've become in such a short time; how much like a couple we've become. It's been so many years since I've let anyone into my heart; given anything from deep inside me to anyone. *You* have that."

Brad reached for her hand, his love shining in his eyes.

She let him take it, but her eyes filled with tears again. "But I can't let myself love you. I can't even think about that." She dashed the tears away impatiently. "Everyone I've ever loved has either hurt me or left me or died. I can't ever do that again and I can't lose you."

"Sweetheart, I'm not like the others. I'm here for the long haul."

"Brad, when someone dies they don't have a choice. That is the long haul for them."

They lay entwined together, silent for a long time. When Brad stirred, he realized that he'd dozed off. He was hungry. He looked at his watch. It was after six in the evening and they had things to do.

"Tweetie Bird," he whispered. "I'm hungry! That took a lot of energy, and we still have to go into town and get what we need for tomorrow."

Shauna Lee stretched. She reached up and traced his lips with her fingertip. "I don't want to move, in case this is a dream that will fade away when I wake up."

"This is a dream, sweetheart. It's a dream come true. It's not going to fade away. But we have to get going. I have to go to the office and pick up supplies and you probably have to do the same. Then I think we should go out and celebrate in the best restaurant in town."

"That's right here in your kitchen, isn't it?"

"It's the cook's night off. Do you like seafood?"

"Brad, anything is all right; even a hamburger at A&W."

She moved tight against him and buried her face into his chest. "I want you to know, being with you wasn't... I couldn't be a virgin for you, but it's never been that way for me before," she whispered. She shivered involuntarily. "It wasn't just sex... it was so far beyond that ...."

She leaned her head back and looked at him. "I just want to wrap my arms around you and pull you inside me and *feel* like that forever."

He chuckled. "I don't think we can stay like that forever. We'll need to eat, and go to work occasionally. But, Tweetie Bird, I told you that first day when I brought you here; you have the first option on my heart, everything I am."

"How can you be so sure? We haven't really known each other very long. There's still a lot that you don't know about me, Brad."

"It's a knowing, like recognition in my heart. All that other stuff has nothing to do with you and me. It's what happens from this day forward that counts."

He rolled onto his back and eased away from her. "Right now, we have to get moving. We'll come back here later, I promise."

He gently slapped her naked hip. "Up and at it girl. We've got things to do, and breakfast was one hell of a long time ago."

She groaned in protest as she rolled to the edge of the king-sized bed and sat up. "Party-pooper."

"I'm just going out for re-enforcement! You can have the bathroom," he said as he pulled on his shirt and jeans. "I'll go down the hall to the spare room."

Even though Brad was hungry, they went to their respective offices first and collected what they needed for the next day. After asking if she needed to stop at her house, he drove to one of the nicer restaurants in town. They ate their meal as they drank wine and looked into each other's eyes, savoring their happiness.

When they were leaving, they met Josh Kendall in the lobby. He sneered when he saw Shauna Lee. "Got another sucker on the line, eh, bitch?"

Before Shauna Lee could even flinch, Brad leaned forward, catching Josh by surprise as he shoved him against the wall. "You're the only sucker here, Kendall. And now, I'm telling you what you told me the first time I met you, you weasily little prick; *You're out of luck this time, buddy. She's mine for tonight!*"

Brad pushed him against the wall a little harder. "In case you didn't get the message, I'm telling you again. She is mine tonight and every night now. Got it?"

He glared into Josh's shocked face. He released him from against the wall and gave him a firm shove. "You're the loser. Take my advice and stay away from her or you'll answer to me. One more thing; don't *ever* call the woman that I love a bitch again."

Then he slid his arm around her protectively and guided her out to the truck. Josh stared after them, sputtering idle threats and straightening his shirt.

CHAPTER EIGHT

Colt Thompson glanced at his watch as he stepped out on the veranda. It was almost seven o'clock and darkness still hung over the land. He stretched and inhaled the crisp, fresh air. The sky was cloudless, the partial moon riding high in the sky. The smell of coffee brewing in the kitchen wafted on the air, and he could hear Frank and Ellie in muffled conversation behind the half-closed door behind him.

Brad should be here soon, he thought. *Hopefully, he tracked down Shauna Lee. We need to get on this today. I want to get those turbines in place before it gets too cold to pour the cement for the bases.*

He watched as lights came into view on the main road and grinned when the signal light flashed and the vehicle made the turn into the laneway. *Right on time. The more I have to do with Brad, the better I like him.*

The truck pulled up in front of the house and Colt walked down to greet its passengers. As Brad partially opened his door, the interior light came on, revealing that Shauna Lee was with him. They were laughing about something and he saw Shauna Lee reach across the seat and slap Brad playfully with the file folder that she held in her hand.

Colt opened the passenger door as Brad got out on the driver's side. Shauna Lee was relaxed and happy when she smiled at him. "Good morning, Colt. You owe me big time for this! He rousted me out of bed at a quarter to six this morning; on a Sunday no less!"

Brad laughed. "And she's been nattering at me all the way out here. Even the fact that I stopped at the drive-thru at Allan & Wright's and bought her a coffee and a breakfast sandwich didn't stop her."

Colt reached up to help Shauna Lee slide out of Brad's 'monster truck' as he laughingly called it. "Johnson, you need to put a pull-down step on this thing so short people can get in and out."

"You are missing the point, Colt. It gives me a chance to get up close and personal when I help a shorty get in. Besides, I don't travel with many short people; just her." He nodded at Shauna Lee with a grin.

"Come in. Fran's got coffee on. We'll grab a quick cup and head out."

Frank greeted them with a happy smile and motioned to the coffee pot and the cups set out beside it. "You've been here before, guys, so you don't qualify as 'guests' anymore. You have to pour your own this morning. I'm going to run up and say goodbye to the twins. Ellie is upstairs with them."

Colt looked at them. "Help yourself, guys. I'll run up and get a hug too. We'll be right back."

Shauna Lee poured two cups of coffee and handed one to Brad. They shared a quick kiss, followed by a look of conspiracy. "We'll keep it our secret for a while?" she asked in a whisper. He nodded in agreement and they sat down at the table. Moments later Colt and Frank came downstairs hand in hand, laughing happily.

Frank poured a cup for each of them and carried it to the

table. She looked at Shauna Lee and reached out to touch her hand. "I like the curls, Shauna Lee. You look so relaxed and happy."

Shauna Lee smiled warmly. "I didn't have time to use a curling iron. This getting up with the birds...."

Brad grinned. "Tweetie..."

Shauna Lee blushed softly. Frank caught the rise in color and the quick little look that passed between the two of them. *Hmm. Am I imaging things, or is there something going on there?*

Colt missed it all. He guzzled his coffee and stood up. "Shall we hit the trail guys?"

"Colt," Frank protested. "Give us a chance to finish our coffee."

"Oh... sorry. I'm just anxious to get going."

Brad stood up. "We need to hit the road. We have a lot to do today and it's a two and a half to three-hour drive to the ranch."

He looked at Shauna Lee, a smile dancing in his eyes. "Hustle it up, girls."

Frank smiled as she collected the cups and put them by the sink. *Something is going on between those two!*

"We can my truck," Brad offered. "Everything we need for today is in it."

Colt nodded as he put on his coat. When they got out to the truck, Shauna Lee turned to Colt. "You can sit up front with Brad. I'll get in the back."

"Are you kidding? Have you any idea how seldom I get to sit in the backseat and make out with my wife? We never got to do those things before we got married," he said, giving Frank a hug. "Now I'm grabbing every chance I can get. Before too long, the baby will be taking up cuddle room." He rubbed his hand over her slight baby bulge and grinned. "But I'll happily move over."

He looked at Brad. "You'd better get with it. You have no idea how wonderful this baby thing is."

"Give me time, man." He lifted Shauna Lee so she could

get up onto her seat. He made an exaggerated show of running his hand down her leg. She slapped at him, flushing scarlet.

"I'm going to work on Shauna today and see if I can make any headway."

"Johnson, I've got witnesses. That's harassment. It can get you into trouble. Maybe more than you want to deal with."

He laughed as he shut her door. When he got in, he looked across at her. "I might be willing to take my chances."

"Brad!" she protested.

He chuckled and looked over his shoulder. Colt had his arm around Frank and held her tucked close. "Alright you two, no indecent behavior back there. I don't want any distractions while I'm driving."

"Keep your eyes on the road. You'll be fine. This seat is too small for any more than a little necking."

"You guys," Frank protested. "Get down to business."

"I'm trying to, but I keep getting interrupted," Colt responded.

Frank jabbed him in the ribs with her elbow.

Shauna Lee looked out the window, a soft flush in her cheeks and a faint smile on her lips.

***

They arrived at the ranch at eleven-thirty. Ollie met them at the door. He looked at the four of them, then past them to the truck. "Didn't you bring the twins?"

Colt answered. "Not this time. It would have been too crowded."

Frank smiled as she watched some of Ollie's excitement deflate. "You know, Ollie, you can stop by anytime for a visit."

"Yeah, I know. I just—"

"Now that you have Patch here to spell you off, you don't have a reason not to. Speaking of Patch, where is he?"

"He went out to check the cows. He's really conscientious. This morning, one of them was kicking at her belly. She might have eaten something that gave her a bellyache. Anyway, he went out to check on her again."

Frank looked up. "Should I go out too?"

"That might be a good idea; take the quad. It'll be at the shop. Patch walks everywhere."

Frank turned and headed out the door. Colt went to the cupboard to get cups and Ollie brought the coffee pot to the table. "Does anyone use cream and sugar? Never mind, Patch uses both so I'll put it on."

"Who is Patch?" Shauna Lee asked.

"He's a new ranch hand. Ollie met him through the Kowalski boys. He was looking for work so Ollie talked to me and I gave him the go ahead to hire him. He's been here for about 6 weeks; I just haven't gotten the paperwork from Ollie. You'll meet him when they come in."

He glanced toward the door as if expecting them. "Ollie is really impressed with him. He's kind of quiet and reserved, but a good cowhand."

Ollie poured the coffee and they each took a cup. Colt took a few sips and then turned back to Shauna Lee. "Have you found anything new in your search for a manager for the farm?"

"I've got a couple of possibilities. Just names on my desk right now, but I've got feelers around, checking them out."

Brad joined the conversation. "Are you looking for a manager for the farm, Colt?"

"Yes, I've told Shauna Lee to start looking for one."

"What exactly are you looking for?"

"I want someone to take over the operation and the management of the farm. He has to have the right credentials and experience. I've been thinking about offering a percentage of the net income of the farm, as well as a competitive wage. By competitive I mean comparative to this situation, not to a big corporation."

"What are you going to do? Move out here?"

"This is where I had always intended to be until dad had his heart attack. Then, I had to take over on the farm. But I love it out here and Fran does too."

He smiled and shook his head. "She was working here when we got together. I refused to accept that I was in love with her and I almost lost her because of my stupidity. I did my best to push her away and she left."

He moved a finger between Ollie and Shauna Lee. "I have to thank these two for urging me to go find her."

Ollie snorted. "Well, he was moping around like a sick calf. He just needed a good kick in the ass. Those two were a perfect fit right from the beginning, but they were both too stubborn to admit it.

"I knew she was head-over-heels in love with him when she left. When I confronted her and asked her if she was pregnant with Colt's baby, she admitted it. But she was just as stubborn as he was and she made me promise not to tell him."

Colt was sober. "He didn't tell me either. He just tore a strip off me and told me to suck it up and act like a man. He did begrudgingly give me a hint as to where I could find her though."

Ollie chuckled. "The best phone call I've ever gotten was that New Years Eve when they woke me up at two o'clock in the morning to tell me they were getting married right away and they were having twins! I danced a jig and then I couldn't go back to sleep."

Colt looked at Brad. "Yeah... well now you know all our dirty laundry!

Brad shrugged his shoulders. "A lot of people have dirty laundry, Colt. Thankfully our past doesn't have to control our future."

"You're right, Brad, and now we are moving on. I plan to build a house up on the bench and move my family out here. It will be a wonderful place to let the kids grow up."

Brad looked thoughtful. "I'm thinking; I have a friend who might be what you are looking for as a farm manager.

He's from the Peace River country. He has degrees in agriculture. I'm not sure what all, but he's a smart businessman and he ran the family business for twenty years and made it pay.

"They had thousands of acres of grain farm and all the modern machinery; you know, the GPS stuff and 'white shirt cabs' with stereos and air conditioning, 70 foot plus wide air seeders, fancy sprayers. You name it, they had it.

"Then his dad died. His mom had died a few years earlier, and there was no one to curb the inheritance free-for-all. There are six kids in that family and the fight was on. Everyone wanted their share of the pie in cash and they all thought they were going to be multimillionaires. In the end, between everyone's greed and the lawyers, the family business had to be sold. A major corporation bought it."

"Did they offer him the management position?"

Brad sighed. "They did. But while the inheritance fight was on, his wife divorced him. Last I heard, he was just looking for a new start, anywhere away from there. If you want to check him out, I'll give you his phone number and address when we get home. His reputation has been solid. He might be your answer."

Colt nodded. "I have confidence in your judgment, Brad." He nodded to Shauna Lee. "You can give her the information. I'm going to be flat out with everything else going on. She knows what I'm looking for and she has good instincts about that sort of thing."

Shauna Lee smiled. "Thanks, Colt."

"Well, it's true—" He stopped as he heard the door open. "They're back." He stood up and walked down the hall.

"Hi there, Patch." Patch nodded to Colt as he hung up his coat. Colt looked at Frank. "So how is the cow?"

"I think she's alright. She's eating. Her eyes are clear and her nose is moist. I couldn't get close enough to examine her so Patch will keep an eye on her."

She smiled happily. "It felt good to be out there again. We

have to find a manager and get started on the house so we can move out here next year!"

"We were just talking about that, and Brad knows someone who might be what we are looking for as a manager. He's going to give Shauna Lee the guy's phone number and address. She'll check him out."

He slipped his arm around her shoulders. "We'll take time for you to grab a coffee and then we'd better get moving."

They walked into the kitchen and Shauna Lee handed Frank a cup of coffee. She was pouring another for the new hand when Ollie introduced him to Brad.

When Patch spoke in acknowledgment, a shiver went up her spine. She trembled as she sat down the coffee pot and slowly turned to look at the newcomer.

Colt motioned to her. "Patch, this is Shauna Lee Holt. She's been our accountant..."

The color drained out of Shauna Lee's face. She reached for the countertop to steady herself. Brad was instantly on his feet and at her side. He slid his arm around her waist. "Shauna ... are you alright?" Her hand grabbed his shirt and clenched it. "Sweetheart...?"

She didn't seem to hear him.

Everybody's eyes flashed to Patch. Shock whitened his face. "Leanne?" he whispered.

Colt shook his head. "No. You're confusing her with someone else."

Patch stared at her. "No," he said hoarsely as he reached out to her. "Leanne?"

She leaned into Brad. He could feel her trembling. "No," she whispered.

"I know my own daughter. Those eyes! No one could miss them and that golden curly hair. No matter who you call yourself, you are Leanne Bergeron."

The floor seemed to slide away and Shauna Lee collapsed against Brad. He held her against him and then lifted her in his arms. "Shauna... sweetheart... talk to me."

He looked at Patch in confusion. "What the hell is going on here?"

Shauna Lee was alert in a moment. She looked into Brad's eyes as tears filled hers. "Take me home," she whispered. "Get me away from here, away from him... please, just take me home."

He glared at Patch. "If you really are her dad, you are a heartless bastard. Do you have any idea how much damage you've done to her?"

He looked at Colt. "We're headed home. I'll come back during the week and do the job."

Shauna Lee put her arms around his neck and pulled herself up so she could look into his eyes. She shook her head. "I'm sorry. This was just a terrible shock. Please put me down, Brad."

"Are you sure, sweetheart?"

She closed her eyes and nodded. He let her feet slide to the floor, so she stood beside him.

She stepped toward Patch and looked him straight in the eyes. Her voice trembled, but she held strong. "Leanne Bergeron does not exist any more, so you are not my father. You never were a father to me. You didn't care about me. You walked out and left without a backward glance. Mom was so sick—"

"Leanne...what I did was cowardly; inexcusable. But there are things you don't know about your mother and I. I read about Marie's death. I read about you and what happe—"

She flew at him, beating him backward. "Shut up! SHUT UP! Don't you dare! Don't you *dare* go there!" She slapped him. "I buried Leanne Bergeron along with everything else that I left back there. I'm Shauna Lee Holt. I have made a new life. I have become a new person."

She started to cry. "And guess what; nobody noticed. Nobody cared. Nobody even gave Leanne Bergeron another thought." She pushed past him and ran outside.

Brad was right behind her. He caught her before she got

to the end of the cement sidewalk. He grabbed her from behind and pulled her against him. "Everything is alright... I'm here with you." He turned her into his chest, enfolding her in his arms, pushing his hands gently through her hair.

Frank followed them, carrying the shoes they had left inside. She came up beside them and stretched her arms around them to hold them both. Then Brad picked Shauna Lee and carried her to the truck.

He motioned for Frank to open the back door and he slid her in. He reached for the shoes that Frank handed him and put them on her feet. Then he pushed himself up onto the seat beside her and slid his arms around her shoulders.

She leaned into him and rested her face against his chest. "I'm sorry I'm such a screw-up."

Frank watched as he kissed Shauna Lee's forehead. *Thank goodness she has Brad.* She went around to the passenger side and pulled herself up onto the front seat, staring out the window as she waited for Colt.

Colt didn't come outside for several minutes. When he did, he slid behind the steering wheel and turned to look at Brad, who gave him a nod. He started the truck, fastened his seatbelt and headed for home. The entire drive was made in silence.

When they arrived at the farm, Brad lifted Shauna Lee out of the back seat and stood her on the ground. He led her around to where Frank waited by the passenger door. As he bent to lift her up, Frank rested her hand on his sleeve, her eyes imploring. He nodded and she stepped in front of him and wrapped her arms around Shauna Lee.

She felt Shauna Lee stiffen momentarily, then relax into her embrace. "I'm glad you've got Brad," she whispered. "I want you to know that Colt and I are here for you."

Shauna Lee hesitated, then lifted her arms and hugged her in return. "Thank you," she whispered. Frank stepped away and let Brad put Shauna Lee into the truck. He closed the door and walked around to the front to meet Colt.

"Don't leave her alone tonight, Brad," Frank said softly. "She needs somebody. If it can't be you, I'll come. This obviously was a dreadful shock to her."

"You don't know the half of it. Anyway, I'm not leaving her alone. She's coming back to my place tonight. We'll see how things are tomorrow. I may phone her office and just tell them she's not coming in. If that happens, I won't go to work either."

Colt looked at him with concern. "Are you guys..."

"Together? Yes. It hasn't been easy, but we are. I know it must seem sudden, but it's like I've been waiting for her, like I've always loved her."

Colt sighed and reached to shake Brad's hand. "Hang in there, buddy. She's worth the effort if you love her."

"I know that. I'll talk to you in a couple of days. Then, we'll work something out to get this job done."

CHAPTER NINE

Brad looked at Shauna Lee as they entered the Swift Current city limits. "How are you doing, sweetheart?"

"I'm alright," she answered dully.

"I'm going to swing into the drive-thru at A&W and pick up a coffee. Do you want to grab something quick to eat, too? I'll make pizza when we get home."

She shook her head. "Just drop me off at my place."

He was silent while he ordered coffee and a hamburger for both of them. He pulled forward and picked up the order, then drove into a parking space and shut off the motor.

She looked at him questioningly. "What are you doing?"

"We're going to eat. I'm hungry. That bacon and egg sandwich we had for breakfast is long gone." He opened a hamburger wrapper and handed it to her. "Eat," he said softly as he handed it to her.

She shook her head. "Just take me to my place."

"Shauna Lee, please. It's been hours since you ate. You need something now. Then, we'll talk about going to your place. You've had a tough day."

When she took the hamburger and looked at him, tears were shimmering in her eyes. "I'm such a screw-up, why don't you just give up on me? Take me to my place and just forget about me."

He opened her coffee, pulled out her cup holder and sat the to-go-cup into it. Then he looked at her. "Is that why you want to go to your place? Because if it is, you should know that if I take you to your place, I'm staying there with you. I'm not leaving you there alone. I'm not giving up on you. I'm not forgetting about you." He took her hand. "And in my opinion, *you* are not a screw-up. Now your old man... he's another thing."

She started to sob.

"Sweetheart, this was a mistake. We'll just go home." He started the truck and she didn't protest when he headed for his place.

He parked, then got out and walked around to the passenger door. He opened it and reached for her. She leaned into his arms and let him lift her down to stand on the ground; then she slipped her arms around his waist and clung to him. He wrapped his arms around her and held her. They stood like that for what seemed to be countless moments. Then she pulled back and looked up at him. "Thank you," she whispered.

"Let's go inside," he said gently.

Once inside, Brad looked at her closely. "What do you want to do, sweetheart? Do you just want to lie down?"

"I must sound like such a baby, but I honestly don't know what I want to do. I'm exhausted. I'm numb. I-I don't know."

"Why don't you have a rest while I grab something quick to eat and start making pizza for supper?"

She nodded and turned toward the hall. He slid his arm around her shoulder and led her to his bedroom. He pulled back the cover and stepped aside as she lay down. Then he pulled the cover back over her and leaned down to drop a kiss on her cheek.

"Have a nap, sweetheart. I'm sure you'll feel better then. And remember this; I'm here for the long haul, so don't ever think that I'll abandon you."

She reached up and touched his face gently, then closed her eyes.

He went to the fridge and took out a beer, then made the pizza crust and set it aside to rise. He went to the bedroom to check on Shauna Lee; she was lost in the oblivion of sleep. As he looked at her, he replayed her confrontation with Patch in his mind.

What happened to you, Tweetie Bird? he wondered. *What was so terrible that you wanted to completely forget your life? Even go so far as to change your identity? Surely more than having your deadbeat father leave you and your mom.*

Troubled, he went back to the kitchen. He leaned against the counter and finished his beer as he gazed unseeingly out the window. *There are things you don't know about your mother and me.* Patch's words rang in his mind.

"Secrets and lies destroy lives time after time." He shook his head. "People never realize how much they can hurt others without physically touching them. Bruises and broken bones heal. Scars in the mind stay there forever."

Brad went to the fridge and got another beer. Then he started preparing the topping. When he finished browning the hamburger and chopping onions, peppers, celery, and mushrooms, he kneaded the dough and rolled it out to fit the pizza pan. He arranged the toppings, then put the pizza in the oven and set the timer. He checked his watch. It was almost five o'clock.

He slipped into the bedroom and checked on Shauna Lee again. She was still sleeping peacefully. He touched her hair gently and went back to sit in front of the TV and flipped through the channels until he found a football game. The Rough Riders were playing in Edmonton. He turned the volume down low and sat there, not really watching, lost in his concern for Shauna Lee.

He didn't realize she was there until she touched his arm. He looked up startled. "I just checked on you and you were sleeping."

She smiled wanly. "I woke up as you were leaving. I felt you touch me."

He took her hand and tugged her over to sit by him on the couch. He slid his arm around her. "Feeling any better?"

She nodded. "I needed that." She took his hand and lifted it to her lips, pushing against it with a soft kiss. "Are you watching the game?"

"Not really. It's just on. I couldn't concentrate. I was just sitting here, thinking about today."

She sighed. "I was totally blindsided. I haven't seen him since I was fourteen and a half. After all these years, I couldn't have imagined seeing him there. When I heard his voice..."

"That bastard."

She shook her head. "I think he was as shocked as I was. He's hidden himself so well for all these years... I'm sure he never imagined he'd run into me there."

"It's interesting that you'd mention that. He didn't try to distance himself from you. He claimed you. He could have just slipped away and left the place. It'll be interesting to see if he quits his job, that's if Colt doesn't put the run on him."

She shook her head. "Colt shouldn't fire him if he is working out well at the ranch. It doesn't matter to me if he works there. As far as I'm concerned he's not my father. The girl who was his daughter has been buried for twenty years.

"There's no reason for me to see him again. I do the accounting for Thompson Holdings. Aaron Bergeron is just a name... but then he doesn't call himself Aaron anymore, does he. Who is he now? Patch? Whatever... it means nothing to me."

"Shauna Lee, you know it's not that simple. You and I need to talk about all of this eventually; your dad, you; all that stuff. But let's just sit and relax for now. The pizza will be ready in a few minutes. I think we should eat first. We can talk as much as you are comfortable with later this evening."

She nodded, biting her lip.

"We can't brush all this away and pretend it never happened." He kissed her cheek as he squeezed her gently. "I love you, Tweetie Bird. I've told you before, I'm not cutting out. But you can't keep living a lie. I know you had to have been hurt beyond comprehension to take such drastic actions. That kind of thing doesn't heal in a hundred years if you bottle it up and try to lose it inside yourself. It's still there. It's still hurting you."

She sighed and laid her head against his shoulder, closing her eyes. They sat like that until the timer went off. She shifted and sat up so he could move. He stood up and took her hand, helping her to her feet.

They walked to the kitchen hand in hand. He turned off the timer and took the pizza out of the oven. She went to the cupboard; *2 plates, 2 knives, 2 forks, napkins. He loves me. He must. I have to tell him. Can I open up to all that pain again?*

He put the pizza pan on the table. He went back to grab two bottles of Corona and a lime from the fridge and snagged the pizza cutter on his way back to the table. They sat down together and she waited as he made the first cuts.

"Mmmm. That smells yummy, Brad. I just realized that I am hungry." She looked at him. "Did you eat something earlier?"

He nodded at the beer. "I got a head start on you. I had a couple while I made the pizza. I checked out the hamburgers, but they were cold and unappetizing, so I ditched them in the garbage."

"I'm sorry. I just couldn't eat then."

"And I should have realized that. You see, I don't always know what the best thing to do is, even when I think I do. It's a man thing, I guess." He reached out and brushed her cheek. "You proved that when you forced my hand yesterday."

She blushed.

"And I can tell you, it felt so damned good to give in and admit you were right. I felt like I'd gone to heaven, and it made such a change in you. You relaxed..."

"It wasn't just the sex, Brad. That was incredible, but it was having you accept me..."

He smiled. "I've accepted you for quite a while, sweetheart. One day soon, I hope you will be able to accept that I love you unconditionally and that you are worthy of my love."

Her eyes misted.

"No more tears now. Eat!" He cut the lime and stuffed it into her bottle, then slid it over to her. They ate in silence, then gathered up the dishes and loaded the dishwasher. Then they stood looking at each other in an awkward silence.

Shauna Lee reached her hand out and took his. "I guess... we have to talk," she said haltingly.

"We do, Tweetie Bird." He pulled her close and kissed her gently.

"Where shall we sit? Where are you most comfortable?"

"On the bed?"

"Are you trying to distract me? It might work for tonight, but we still need to talk about this; if not tonight, then tomorrow."

"Kiss me again?"

He cupped her face in his hands. "I think I could." He dropped his lips to hers. The kiss lit the fires that always sprang to life when their lips met, only now he wouldn't deny them. He picked her up and carried her to the bedroom.

They made love slowly, sensually. It was a deeply satisfying, healing experience for both of them. Afterward, they lay on the bed quietly.

Shauna Lee snuggled against Brad, as soft and pliant as melting chocolate. Brad's heart was full. He watched her lashes drift down to rest on her cheeks. *I love you so much, girl. We'll talk tomorrow. I can't bear to make you face all that ugliness tonight.* He kissed her cheek softly and drifted off to sleep.

A few hours later, Brad stirred from his slumber; something wasn't right. He stretched his arm out, feeling for Shauna Lee. She wasn't there. He got up and wandered through the house, but didn't find her. His heart was pounding. *Where can she be?*

He turned on the light in the kitchen and looked at his watch. It was midnight. "Shauna Lee, where are you?" he wondered out loud. His truck was in the driveway, so she hadn't taken it and gone home.

He ran a hand through his hair. "Okay, settle down, Johnson," he said to himself. "Where would she go? It's dark. Would she have gone out to the horses? She's happy with them."

He stepped out the back door. The sky was full of stars, the moon shining brightly. Suddenly he saw movement, a dark image running up the path toward him.

"Brad," he heard her call. "I'm here." She flew into him with arms outstretched. "I woke up and couldn't go back to sleep. Suddenly I felt I had to come out here." She hugged him close. "I didn't think you'd wake up. When I saw the light go on in the kitchen, I knew you were looking for me. I'm sorry."

"You gave me a scare. I searched through the house and you weren't there. I saw that the truck was still there, so the next thing to do was look out here."

"I wouldn't take your truck without asking," she said, stepping back to look at him. She reached down and took his hand. "Let's go in. It's chilly out here and I'm wide awake now."

Brad shivered. He had just pulled on a pair of pajama bottoms. He looked her over. She had put her clothes on and grabbed one of his jackets from a coat hook by the back door. "At least you got dressed! Did you find what you were looking for out there?"

"I think so. I know I have to talk to you about what happened today. Can we do that now? Before I chicken out?"

"Anytime you want. Do you want me to make coffee and

sit in here, or on the couch? Or do you want to go back to bed? What will work best for you?"

"Coffee would be good. Can we sit here? This isn't easy for me. I don't want to take any more bad memories into the bedroom. I want to have happy memories in there; like earlier tonight."

Brad hugged her. "Coffee is coming up."

She drummed her fingers on the table while she waited. When Brad sat two cups on it, she sighed as she reached for hers. She played with the handle and then looked at him. "Where do I start?"

"Well, is there anything more that you need to tell me about your dad? Did he abuse you?"

Her eyes widened. "You mean sexually? Heavens no! He wouldn't even give me a hug. He sure as hell didn't do that."

"I'm glad, Shauna Lee. I would kill him if you told me he had."

"Brad, please! He has caused enough pain in my life; please don't let him take you from me too. If you went after him, that's what would happen."

"I just would like to even the score for what he did to you!"

"It's the past."

"But it isn't in the past, Shauna Lee. It is still part of you. It has colored your whole life."

She shook her head. "I told you everything about dad. He walked out and left us flat broke. Mom died and I was alone."

"Yes, and you were afraid Social Services would take you. When I asked you what happened to you after that, you said you couldn't talk about it then. Sweetheart, none of this justifies you taking an assumed name, starting life over. That's big."

"I- it's so hard, Brad. I—"

"Sweetheart, I love you. The choices that you made back then won't change how I feel about you. But I need you to be honest with me. I need to be able to understand you."

Full Circle

"Brad... I was 15 years old. I had no home, no money, nobody to care. I moved in with Dave Trutcher. He was in his twenties and he lived in the neighborhood. He was a rough and tumble farmer. I- I got pregnant immediately."

She looked down at her hands as she twisted them together. "The baby was a boy. I called him Ben." She swallowed hard. "He was born with a bi-lateral cleft lip. To me, he was beautiful and, even though, his mouth was badly deformed. He was part of me and I just loved him even more because of the problems he had. He needed me. I knew that he'd need special care and eventually he would need a lot of surgeries to repair his lip. But he was mine and I loved him with all my heart.

"Dave was revolted by the way he looked. He always referred to Ben as 'the freak,' and he wouldn't touch him. He insisted that my genes were responsible for the defect because no child with his genes would have been born looking like that."

Brad exploded. "What an asshole! Where does the pain end for you, Shauna Lee ?" He held her in his arms and rocked her.

"It- t- 's not the end yet. There's more."

"Ben would have started to have corrective surgery when he was about eighteen months old." She began to cry. "But he- he didn't l-i- v- e.. l- ong- g en- ough for that."

Tears filled Brad's eyes and trickled down his cheeks. Shauna Lee wiped them away.

"I changed my name after that. I- I decided to bury Leanne Bergeron with her baby and start life over with a clean slate. I became Shauna Lee Holt. That was my grandma's name — my mother's mom." She mused for a moment. "She was the only person who ever truly showed me that she loved me."

Brad grabbed her hands and held them to his lips. "You've got me now."

She sighed wearily. "I know that... I'm so tired, Brad."

"I know. I'm sorry I prodded you to talk about all this. I wanted to help you, to understand you, not to hurt you more."

"Brad this isn't your fault. Seeing Dad today was a shock... but he obviously knows about my baby. He started to bring it up this afternoon at the house. I couldn't listen to him; I couldn't let him do that to me."

She sobbed. "I guess I blame him for what happened. If he had been a father to me; if he hadn't been such a drunken coward, if he'd have stayed and made a place for us to live, I wouldn't have been in such a mess. I had nowhere to go."

Brad's heart ached for her. "He is the poorest excuse for a father that I've ever heard of." He leaned forward and brushed her lips with his. "And for tonight, you've told me enough; I've heard more than enough. Let's go to bed. We need to get some sleep and I want to hold you and make you feel safe."

She nodded and stood up, reaching for his hand. They walked together to the bedroom. He helped her slip out of her clothes and slide her naked body onto the sheets. Then he gently covered her, dropping a kiss on her forehead as he tucked the blanket around her.

He undressed quickly, turned off the light on his side of the bed and eased himself in behind her. The feel of their bodies touching, skin to skin, was warm and comforting. She relaxed against him, settling into his arms. Sleep soon claimed her.

Brad lay for a long time, listening to her even breathing. He couldn't forget her words; *he didn't l- i- v- e l- ong enough for that.* He cursed her father and Dave Trutcher. No wonder she had closed herself off. Everyone who had been a part of her life had hurt her, had let her down.

He finally slept fitfully for a couple of hours. When he woke up, he checked the clock on the bedside table. It was six-thirty in the morning. Shauna Lee was still asleep and he was emotionally and physically exhausted. He considered for a moment and then shifted so he could reach his cell phone on the night table.

He dialed his office and left a message saying he would be in on Tuesday. Then he dialed Shauna Lee's office and left a message for Christine, telling her that Shauna Lee wouldn't be in until the next day. He shut off the phone and put it back. Shauna Lee stirred lightly, reaching for his hand in her sleep. Brad smiled and kissed her shoulder, then fell asleep.

It was noon when he woke up. Shauna Lee was gone from the bed. He listened for sounds of movement in the house and then smiled as the aroma of coffee wafted on the air. He was just starting to get up when she tiptoed to the door. She smiled when she saw that he was awake and walked to his side of the bed, bending down to slip her arms around his shoulders. She sat down beside him, held him close and kissed him.

She leaned back and looked at him. "I just talked to Christina. She said you phoned in earlier and said that I wouldn't be in. Thank you. When did you do that?"

"I didn't sleep very well. I woke up early and knew that I wasn't in any shape to go to work today. I thought you needed some time to recoup too, so I made an arbitrary decision, without checking with you first. I hope that's alright."

"It's fine. I appreciate you thinking about my needs and taking care of things. I'm not used to that."

"Get used to it, Tweetie Bird," he said with a soft smile as he reached to tangle his fingers in her curls. *She's slipped right back into happy mode,* he thought. *How does she do that after everything that happened yesterday? It must be a defense mechanism. I guess that's how she has survived all these years.*

"I made coffee." She smiled shyly. "And, I made breakfast... or at least, I tried to."

Brad grinned. "What? Did you buy a package of frozen waffles?"

She punched him lightly on the shoulder. "No. I made

pancakes from scratch." She wrinkled her nose. "I think they are alright."

He pulled her close and rubbed his face in her hair. "I'm impressed! I'm hungry, so let's go eat."

When they went into the kitchen, he was surprised to see that the table was set and everything ready. "Sit down," she said with a proud smile. She went to the warmer and took out a plate of golden brown pancakes, as well as a plate with crisply cooked bacon. Then, she brought the coffee carafe and poured two cups full.

Brad took two pancakes and commented on how light and fluffy they were. He slathered them with butter and drowned them in pancake syrup. Then he took a couple of bites. "Tweetie Bird, these are really good! You've been holding out on me."

"No. I just paid attention to what you did and tried to do the same thing. So, are they really good or are you just being nice to me?"

"No kidding. Try them yourself!"

She smiled after she took the first couple of bites. "They are good. Hey, I did alright."

Later in the afternoon, Brad went into his office and Shauna Lee sat watching TV.

"Shauna," she heard him call. "Will you come here for a moment?"

When she came into his office, he swiveled his chair so he could slide his arm around her waist and pull her close. "I'm looking at my schedule for the next few weeks. I have to go up north for a maintenance check at a couple of places where I've installed turbines. I could do it on the November eleventh long weekend. Would you come with me?"

She smiled as she ran her fingers through his hair. "How far north?"

"Well, I've got one set up by a dugout near Glaslyn, and we put two up at a house on Chiteck Lake a couple of months ago. They aren't big jobs, just maintenance checks before winter sets in. It'll be quite a bit of driving, but the roads are good. It will be an easy weekend away from home, and we'll get to spend it together."

She looked into his eyes and smiled brightly. "I think it could be fun. Besides, what would I do for three days without you? I'd miss you like crazy."

He squeezed her gently. "I'm happy to hear that." His look turned sober. "I've got another trip to make, too. I'll be gone for a week. I've been trying to ignore it, but it's something I have to do. At the end of November, I have to fly to China. Several months ago I had an inquiry from a company over there. They are interested in finding out more about the turbines.

"This trip will basically be a fact-finding mission, testing the water. If this contact materializes, it could be a real boost for Windspeer, but nothing is certain and it's not going to happen overnight."

"Brad! That is so exciting."

"Yeah, but I won't be able to take you with me this time."

"I'll be all right. It's just a week."

"I know, but I may not even be able to call you. I'm not sure what the situation will be over there."

"But you'll be safe?"

"I wouldn't go if I wasn't certain of that. I plan to spend many, many years with you!"

"Then I'll sleep in your shirt every night and be waiting here when you get back."

CHAPTER TEN

"Want another coffee?" Frank asked, holding up the coffee pot.

Colt nodded. They were catching precious minutes alone before Ellie came over to the house and the twins woke up.

"I wonder how Brad and Shauna Lee made out last night. She seemed pretty shell shocked."

Colt was thoughtful. "It's hard to realize that I've known her so many years and have no idea what her life has been all about. What could have happened to her that she would have totally denied it: she changed her name and lived as a different person?"

"Well, she certainly was stunned to see Patch at the ranch." Frank thought for a moment. "He was shocked too. But did you notice that he acknowledged her, even claimed her. But she would have made him vanish if she could have."

"Well, it's clear that there's some painful history there and Brad knows about some of it. He was really defensive of Shauna Lee, and he certainly expressed his anger toward

Patch."

"I'm glad he's there for her."

Colt grinned. "Yeah. The sly dog; she was probably with him when I talked to him Saturday morning. It's pretty sudden, especially to say he's in love already."

Frank gave him a little nudge with her toe. "Not everyone is such a hard sell as you were!"

Colt grabbed her hand and kissed it. "I was pretty thick headed. But when I got it right, I fell hook, line, and sinker."

She smiled. "And you don't even fish! When we're at the ranch, we're going to have to teach you how to relax a bit and fish. Every kid should learn how to drop a hook. I did that with my dad."

Colt grinned. "Riding horses is just as relaxing."

Frank smiled. "I agree, but it's good to learn something new, too. Anyway, back to Patch... he seems like such a nice guy. I guess people can change."

"He offered to quit yesterday, after what happened between Shauna Lee and him."

"What did you say?"

"I told him I didn't want him to. What happened between them years ago has nothing to do with his work on the ranch now. He may have been a lousy father, but he and Ollie work well together. His references are second to none. He stayed at the Gang Ranch for over fifteen years, through different changes in ownership. I didn't vet Ollie when he came. Who knows what his history is, but he's a good man and we'd be lost without him."

"I'm glad. At this point, he seems like a good fit. You can make sure that he and Shauna Lee don't have to be in contact."

Colt nodded. "Which reminds me; I should call Brad's office and see if he's working. I want to get moving on the turbines."

Frank handed him the phone. Colt dialed and waited for an answer, then shut off the phone. "I just got the answering machine. He's not going to be in until tomorrow. Things must have been tough for Shauna Lee last night. I'll check in with him this evening and see if we can go out to the ranch tomorrow."

"So, what are we doing today?"

"Do you want to go into the office and look at house plans? We should get started on that too."

"Let's do it. The kids aren't up yet and Ellie will be here any minute."

Frank collected their cups and put them in the dishwasher. Colt took the coffee pot back and slid it onto the coffee maker. They reached for each other's hand and walked to the office.

"Where do we start?" Frank asked.

"I picked up a few books of house plans. That will give us a place to start."

"Have you looked at them?"

"Yeah. I found a few that might work, but I want you to go through these on your own. Then we'll see if there are any that we both like."

"Ah, no outside influence, eh?"

He smiled and nodded. He handed her the books and motioned to the chair behind the desk. "Take your time. I'll go check in on the twins and then I'll make a few phone calls from the kitchen. We'll compare notes later."

The twins came into the office to say good morning and then Colt took them back into the kitchen where he and Ellie supervised their breakfast routine. Frank could hear squeals of laughter and general banter between the four of them. Afterward, the house fell silent when Colt took the twins out for a walk.

She heard Ellie go upstairs to tidy their room and then come down and go to the laundry room. *We are so lucky to have found her. She is so much more than a nanny! I hope she stays until all the kids are grown up. And then we could keep her on as a member of the family.*

By lunch time, Frank had carefully looked through all the plans and picked out three designs that she liked best. Colt was back with the twins and she could hear them all in the kitchen.

When she joined them, Colt was at the stove. Ellie had Sam settled in his chair at the table and was putting an obstinate Selena into hers. *Her patience amazes me*, she thought

"What's for lunch?" she asked.

Colt motioned to two empty boxes of Kraft Dinner lying on the counter. "Ellie got out voted this time, but we had to agree to eat some carrot sticks, cucumber slices, and red pepper strips along with the Mac 'n Cheese. It's ready now."

Frank picked up the plate of vegetables and Colt took the pot of Mac 'n Cheese to the table. He dished a portion onto each of the twin's plates and Frank held out the vegetable plate and let them help themselves.

While everyone ate, Selena and Sam told Frank what they had seen on their walk. After lunch, Ellie took them upstairs to their room and Colt and Frank cleaned up the lunch dishes.

"Did you find anything that you liked?" Colt asked.

"Actually, I found three. They all have good points. It's hard to pick out one, but we can make adjustments, can't we?"

"For sure. These plans just give us a place to start. Mona Blake is an architect that I know in Swift Current. She's good and she's flexible. She'll have ideas of her own to suggest, but she'll make sure we both get what we want. Let's go compare notes."

They went into the office and Frank showed Colt the plans she had chosen. He looked at her with a twinkle in his eye. "We've picked two of the same ones."

"Show me the other ones that you liked," Frank said. He showed her three others and she could see good ideas in each of them. "So, now what?" she asked.

"I'll phone Mona and see if she has time to work with us now. I want to get on this right away. The sooner we get our design finished and blueprints ordered, the sooner we can talk to a contractor."

"This is exciting, Colt. I love this old house, but I can hardly wait to be out at the ranch! But we've got to find a manager first."

"We can do both. Brad and Shauna Lee will collaborate on finding a manager. We'll work out the plans for the house and we'll have everything on the go as soon as they can start building in the spring."

Frank gave him a warm hug, excitement lending a flush to her cheeks and a sparkle in her eyes. Then she handed him the phone.

Colt's call was answered on the second ring. He talked extensively with Mona. When the conversation was finished, he looked at Frank with a smile. "She's just finished up a big job. She says she'll let her assistant tie up a couple of other loose ends and she wants to see us any day this week."

"I'm going to phone Brad in an hour. I don't want to press him too hard, but if it's possible, I'd like to go out to the ranch with him tomorrow and get the turbine setup underway."

"In the meantime, we could pick apart these plans and decide what we want to incorporate into our house. If we have an idea of what we want before we go to Mona, we'll have a head start."

Colt reached into the bottom drawer of the desk and pulled out a pad of graph paper. Then he took a yellow notepad out of the top drawer. Frank pulled up a chair and sat beside him and they started dissecting the various plans, making notes about what they liked, what they would tweak and what they each wanted to add.

Time slipped by quickly. When the phone rang, Colt glanced at his watch as he answered it. It was four o'clock already. He pointed to the time as he answered. Frank looked surprised. She slipped out of the room to put on the roast that she'd taken out the night before and put five potatoes in the oven with it for supper.

When she came back to the office, Colt wore a satisfied

smile. Frank gave him a questioning look.

He stood up. "That was Brad. We're a go for tomorrow. But the even better news is that he tracked down his buddy from the Peace River country and talked to him. Shauna Lee talked to him too. She thinks he's a good candidate for a manager. He's interested, so he's going to fax his résumé to her tomorrow, and I'll get it from her on Wednesday."

He hugged her. "Things are going our way, hon."

"Speaking of Shauna Lee, did Brad say how she was?"

"No, and I didn't ask. He may not want to say anything. It may be something that stays between the two of them. I talked to her though and she sounded fine."

"That's pretty amazing. After what happened yesterday... how could she just put on a happy face and be okay today?"

"It could be because she has always done that. If you think about the things that were said between her and Patch yesterday, I'd say there's probably more to the situation than we have any idea about. She's obviously lived with something painful for a long time. He said that he heard about when her mom died and then he started to say something else and she flew at him."

Frank was thoughtful, remembering. "She did. And she was yelling at him to shut up, and warned him not to go wherever she knew that conversation was going." She sighed. "What happened to her, Colt? She said she'd buried the person she'd been and nobody had even noticed. No one had cared." Tears shimmered in her eyes. "What a terrible thought to live with."

***

Brad arrived at the farm at seven the next morning. Colt asked him in for coffee and Frank joined them.

"Brad, is Shauna Lee okay?" Frank asked.

Brad sighed. "It's amazing how she bounces back. I can't talk about this with you guys. She's trusted me enough to confide in me. But her life has been..." He rubbed his hand across his face. "Sometimes you have to wonder how much one person can take."

"Brad. Please let her know that we support her."

"She could use your friendship if she'll let you in. She has closed herself off for years..."

Frank frowned. "Shauna Lee has really invested herself in her work. When I was working at the clinic, everything centered on my work too. Any relationships I had were pretty impersonal. Everyone I knew was just an acquaintance.

"Some of us are not social butterflies, Brad. Truthfully, I- I haven't made many close friends either. I have one girlfriend that I've been close to forever, but she lives in Calgary. But other than that, I lived in a 'man's' world until I got married. Now I have Colt and the twins. They are the center of my world. Well, throw Ollie and Ellie in there too, but I'm busy; I don't have time to make friends. I never feel like I need friends."

"But you have a family... you have *someone* in your life...." He shook his head. "It's hard to love someone and see so much pain."

"At least she has you now, Brad."

He smiled. "Yes, she has me." He turned to Colt. "I guess we'd better hit the road."

"I'm ready. Let's get rolling." Colt leaned over and gave Frank a kiss. "If you have time, you could look at those house plans some more. Anything you think of, just write it down. We have an appointment with Mona at three-thirty tomorrow afternoon."

Frank nodded. "I'll spend some time looking at the plans again. I'm so excited I can hardly think about anything else!"

She walked to the door with Colt and Brad, waiting as they shrugged into their jackets. She kissed Colt again. "Travel safely, love. See you later."

Brad and Colt talked about everything, except Patch and Shauna Lee, as they drove to the ranch. When they got close, Colt said, "We probably should go right out to the water wells on the grazing lease."

"That makes sense. Just tell me where to go."

"Take the road through to Loch Levan. There will be a sign coming up pretty soon. When we get there, we'll go through the park, across the Gap road and then I'll give you directions to the first one at the corrals."

"This really is different country, compared to the Swift Current area," Brad commented as he drove.

"It is. It's totally unexpected in this part of the world. I love it out here; the hills and the different trees, the different animal species. It's like a small piece of the foothills set in the middle of the flat prairies. My heart is here, and so is Frank's. That's why I'm going to move heaven and earth to get us out to the ranch by next autumn."

Brad nodded. "That's where you should be if you feel that way."

"Speaking of that, thanks for getting in touch with your friend in the Peace River country. Shauna Lee seemed to think he is a really promising prospect for the manager's position."

"I think he could be, but you'll have to decide that for yourself, Colt."

The time went quickly as they traveled to the two water tanks. Brad took measurements and explained how the bases would be made so the turbine towers could be anchored and set up solidly. They both realized that they were working against time, as the probability of winter cold loomed on the horizon.

"These are the critical ones for now. Those at the ranch can be installed next year. Right now, they'll just be a fill-in on the power grid, but their end purpose will be to power a vet clinic for Fran to work out of. That'll be a couple of years down the road after this next baby arrives and we get settled in at the ranch."

"Frank's a vet?" Brad asked.

"A good one and I want to give her a chance to use her training. She spent years in vet school. She should get to make use of it. I think the locals will use her services once word gets out."

"I never even thought of her being a vet. People are full of surprises."

"Aren't they?" Colt said. "Anyway, I think we can head back to the ranch now. I'll show you where I plan to set up the other two turbines. We might as well cover them all while we're out here."

Brad pulled into the driveway that led to the ranch's home site. Colt noticed that Ollie and Patch were across the field, working on the fence. He pointed them out to Brad.

Brad's countenance visibly shifted. "I'd rather not have to see that asshole right now."

"Patch?" Colt looked across the field. "You probably won't have to. If Ollie comes in, he'll leave Patch to work on the fence."

"If I ran into him today, I'd want to strangle the bastard."

"I understand Brad. I know it's got to be awkward for you, but he's a good worker and his resume is sound. Ollie likes him..."

"Colt, when it comes to that man, my give-a-shitter is broken. He was an inexcusably rotten father to Shauna Lee. The way he treated her, the way he walked out and left her and her mom; those things have scarred her for life."

"I get it, Brad. But I'm not going to fire him for what happened years ago between him and Shauna Lee. He works well with Ollie. Shauna Lee is my accountant. She doesn't usually come out here. She never has to see him again."

"That's the amazing part. Shauna said exactly the same thing, but I'm telling you, man, I'd kick his ass all the way to Timbuktu. He'd never get a chance to screw with her mind again."

Colt looked across the field at Ollie and Patch. He didn't answer, but instead directed Brad to take a turn onto a trail that led toward the corrals, where he wanted to put the remaining turbines. They discussed the site and agreed it would be a better plan to install them in the spring.

When they were finished, they got back into the truck and Brad made some notes on his iPad. When he had finished and started the truck, he noticed Ollie coming across the field on the quad. He noted with relief that Patch had stayed at the fence line. He looked across at Colt. "I guess we'll wait for Ollie to get here."

Colt nodded.

Ollie pulled up next to Colt's window on the passenger side. "Howdy do, boss." He nodded to Brad too. "Guess you're checking out the turbine sites, eh?"

Colt nodded, then said "I see you're fixing fence."

"Yeah, it needs to be done. And Patch has been pretty bummed out since Sunday, so I've been trying to keep him busy and work with him so he doesn't have so much time to think."

Brad clenched his jaw but kept quiet. Colt nodded at Ollie. "It's smart to tie up loose ends like the fences; one more thing to cross off the to-do list. I'm going to take Brad up to the bench and show him where we're going to build the house, so I guess we'd better get moving. I'll give you a call this evening."

While Ollie drove away, Brad put the truck in reverse. His anger was simmering, barely below the surface and Colt knew it. He sought to divert Brad's explosive response to the mention of Patch's feelings, by changing the focus of his thoughts.

"Drive back to the driveway, and turn right. You won't go far and you'll see a trail to the left. That will take us up on the bench where we plan to build. I haven't gotten too far into thinking about this, but I've been toying with the idea of putting two or three turbines on the ridge behind the house. I like the idea of the house being energy independent of the power grid, and I'm sure we'll get enough wind up there to make it work."

Brad drove up to the bench in silence, but when they arrived, he looked at the panoramic view and smiled. "You've got it all here, Colt. This is great. What house design are you looking at?"

"We're looking at plans now. We're both pretty much set on a rancher style. It'll fit in well up here."

Brad nodded. "I can see it." He looked up at the ridge above the house. "Are you thinking of putting turbines up there?"

"Yes. What do you think? Will two do the job? Or should I put up three to be safe?"

"That depends on how much you plan to have going on. Three would make a total of seven turbines. I'd have to sharpen my pencil a bit, but I'm sure we could work a package deal, and save you quite a bit.

"Not only that, but you probably would be eligible for federal and provincial grants for green energy. On top of that, you could feed the extra energy into the power grid and it would bring in a substantial income."

"Well, let's put our heads together over the next couple of weeks and see what we can come up with," Colt agreed. "I'll have Shauna Lee look into what's available for grants, too."

Brad nodded in agreement. "We need to get started putting up the forms and pouring cement out at the water tanks. This weather isn't going to hold forever. It'll be too late to get everything lined up by the time we get back today, but could you go out there with me on Thursday? We could probably do both sites."

Colt thought for a moment. "I'll make that work. Fran and I have an appointment with the architect tomorrow and I need to get on that, too."

They talked amiably as Brad drove toward home. Once they reached the main highway, he reached for his cell phone and hit a speed dial. Colt could hear it ringing. Brad smiled as he spoke into the phone.

"Hi there, Tweetie Bird," he said softly. "How are things going today?"

Colt could faintly hear Shauna Lee's laughter, but her

words were indistinguishable to him. Brad chuckled. "I'll see you in about two hours. Love you."

Silently, Colt marveled at how invested Brad had become in his relationship with Shauna Lee in such a short time. *Love,* he thought. *There is no accounting for it sometimes.* He smiled as he recalled how hard he and Frank had resisted it. Brad was the exact opposite. He had plunged right in, heart first.

***

Frank and Colt went over the house plans again that evening, comparing notes and looking for anything they might have missed. "Mona will make suggestions. She'll look at this with a fresh eye."

Frank smiled. "And she has so much more experience, she may think of things that never crossed our minds." She hugged him. "I am so excited, Colt. Everything is falling into place so neatly." She touched her small baby bulge and Colt rested his hand over hers. "A new baby, a new house, us moving to the ranch.... Sometimes I want to pinch myself to see if I am dreaming!"

CHAPTER ELEVEN

Shauna Lee looked at her watch. It was eleven o'clock. It was Wednesday morning and the office was slow. She picked up the picture of her and 'her horse' that Brad had put on her desk the first time he'd introduced a personal touch into her office.

She ran her thumb softly over the glass as she looked at it. *Brad*, she thought, remembering how defensive and supportive he had been of her when she had met her dad at the ranch. *There's never been anyone like him in my life before.*

She put down the picture and reached for the one he had brought in most recently. She smiled softly as she examined it. She had known when he had taken this one. He had put his camera on a tripod and set the timer. He had stepped behind her and aligned his face with hers. He had pulled her slightly into him and the camera had caught them in a joyful, laughing moment.

He makes me smile, she thought as she stood looking at it. She looked at the other pictures sitting in different places around the room. "He's determined to build a life for me," she said with a sigh. "He cares so much, it scares me. I'm afraid something will go wrong; that I'll lose him."

The ring of the phone startled her. She reached for the handset. "Hello."

"Morning, Tweetie Bird. What have you been doing since I saw you two and a half hours ago?"

"You goof," she said softly. "It's been pretty slow so far. But I did some checking on Timothy Bates. Everything he put on his resume checks out; but then of course you knew that. I'm going to suggest that Colt have him come for a personal interview."

"That sounds great! I called to tell you that I made plans for the evening, without consulting you first. I hope you don't mind. Colt and Frank have an appointment with an architect this afternoon, so we decided to meet at The Steakhouse at around five o'clock. They want to get home before eight so they can tuck the kids in."

She smiled. "That's fine. I can leave here anytime after four-thirty."

"I still have to go to the lumber yard. It'll save time tomorrow if I have all the pieces cut to length."

"I'll be ready when you get here." She hesitated. "Brad, I hope you know how much I appreciate your thoughtfulness."

"I think I do, sweetheart." There was a smile in his voice. "I'll see you as soon as I get things finished up here. And, Shauna Lee, you know that I love you." Then the phone went dead.

She swallowed hard. She couldn't tell him she loved him; it was just too frightening.

That evening, Colt and Frank were bubbling with excitement about their plans for the new house. Colt and Brad talked about what they needed to do when they went out to the ranch the next day. Shauna Lee filled Colt in on the information she had about Timothy Bates and he told her to set up an interview as soon as possible. He wanted them to meet at the farm. These were all impersonal things that she felt totally comfortable with.

She was less at ease with Frank; she could feel her reaching out to her. *She goes out of her way to be friendly, even suggesting that we get together for a girl's day. A girl's day? I wouldn't know how to act. And...with Frank?*

She found herself watching Colt and Frank interact. *They are so happy,* she thought. *Brad was right. They are meant for each other.* She looked at Brad. His eyes met hers and warmth flooded through her. *Could we be like them? Could I be that happy? What if something goes wrong?* She reached out and touched his arm. He took her hand in his and pulled it under the table, resting it on his thigh. Her fingers entwined with his. He squeezed her hand gently.

As they were saying goodbye, Frank hugged her. Shauna Lee stiffened momentarily. She couldn't remember when a woman, other than her grandmother when she was a child, had shown her affection, had hugged her. *Except for when Frank hugged me that Saturday.* Her thoughts were conflicting. *It feels good,* she finally admitted, fighting tears. She hugged Frank back tentatively.

Frank's lips brushed her cheek as she released her. She smiled as her eyes met Shauna Lee's and she trailed her hand down her arm to her hand. She squeezed it gently and said softly, "Take care."

Then she nodded at Brad and turned to take Colt's arm. "We'd better get going, daddy," she said with a smile. "We don't want to take advantage of Ellie. Heaven help us if she went on strike."

Brad was smiling as he put his hand against the small of Shauna Lee's back and guided her to the truck. She was silent and thoughtful as he helped her up into it.

"They are so pumped about life right now. Everything is coming together for them; the new baby, moving to the ranch, planning the new house."

Shauna Lee nodded. "When I think of where Colt was five

Full Circle

years ago; bitter and angry, defensive and determined to never fall in love again...it's good to see him like he is now. It makes me wonder if..."

"If...?" Brad prompted.

"You know... could *we* ever..." She stopped, color suffusing her face.

"Could we ever be like them?" he prompted, with a smile. "I know we can."

***

The next morning they were up early so Brad could meet Colt at the farm by seven o'clock. Shauna Lee's car was still at her place, so Brad had to drop her there on his way out of town. He had walked her to the door and went in with her. She chuckled as he made a tour through the place, making sure everything was all right before he would leave.

When he was satisfied, he kissed her goodbye and made her promise she'd be at his place when he got back that evening. He and Colt would work until dark before they started home. He left after telling her that he would call her at the house when he was on his way into town.

Shauna Lee put on a pot of coffee and looked around. It felt strange to be there. She had spent the last month at Brad's place, only stopping in to make quick checks periodically or to grab a few clothes from her closet. She realized that *home* was there with him now.

As she drove to work later, she caught herself missing Brad's company, wondering where he was. She checked her watch and calculated where he'd be. *Somewhere near Maple Creek if they got away from the farm right away.* She smiled. Brad had planned to slip into the drive-thru at A&W for a coffee and breakfast sandwich on his way out of town. *He's been doing that a lot lately,* she thought. *He should own shares in the place.*

The office was busy that day and time went by quickly. She contacted Timothy Bates and set up a date for him to meet with Colt at the farm. They consulted their calendars and decided to set a date in mid-November, after the long weekend. She told him she would double check with Colt and confirm the time.

Her phone rang at about two o'clock. To her surprise, it was Frank.

"Hello, Shauna Lee. I have to run into town to take the architect some more information. I know the guys will be ravenous when they get in, so I'm putting on a pot roast before I leave. Could I pick you up and bring you out here? The four of us can have dinner together. We'll hear about their day and you can ride home with Brad. I'm pretty certain he'd like that."

Shauna Lee's first instinct was to say *no* and close the door on the invitation. She quickly said, "Oh, I have my car here today."

"Couldn't you drop it off at your place? I'd follow you there and pick you up."

Shauna Lee grimaced. *Jeez!* But a little voice whispered in the back of her mind. *This would make Brad happy. It won't hurt you. Open up just a little bit, Shauna Lee.* She swallowed hard and heard herself say, "That would work and Brad would be thrilled."

"Good! I'm looking forward to having you come. What time can I pick you up?"

"I've got things pretty much under control here now. I have an appointment with a client at three-fifteen. He's just bringing me some paperwork so it won't be a long meeting. Any time around four o'clock should be all right. Christina will close up the office at five if I ask her to."

"That'll be perfect. I'll see you then."

Shauna Lee hung up the phone, misgivings stirring in her mind. She tried to squash them, but old habits die hard. *What am I doing?* The tentacles of old fears tugged at her. She wanted to phone back with some excuse and cancel. She reached for the phone, but the thought of Brad made her stop. *If I'm going to make things work with him, I have to get past this,* she thought. "And I want to make this work," she whispered.

Slowly Brad's persistence, his unflagging understanding, his declarations of love, had worked a fine crack into the bastion of the lifetime of defenses she'd built. The fortress hadn't crumbled yet, but she knew he had given her a glimpse of something that she didn't want to lose. She closed her eyes.

Her heart twisted with fear. *He wants love, and he is worthy of love. But am I? Can I truly let all this pain go and freely give him what he needs? It should be easy; he offers me so much. But this fear of losing again...it just keeps coming back. It haunts me.*

She turned back to her desk. "I can do this," she said with determination. "Going to Colt and Frank's tonight is a start. I won't let myself be held captive anymore."

When Frank came to the office, Shauna Lee was ready to leave. She greeted her with a smile, then went to her car and started it. As Frank followed her to her place, a lump burned in her chest, but she resolved to push it out.

When she got into Frank's van, she felt like a frightened child; she wasn't in control now, she couldn't just walk away if she wanted to. She'd given up that thread of comfort and security when she'd left her car at her place. But she vowed to take control of her emotions, of her heart, of her mind. This was another step toward a new, happier life. She would make it work.

Frank saw the uncertainty behind Shauna Lee's smile. *She's uncomfortable.* Frank smiled warmly, hoping to ease her mind. She concentrated on driving, giving Shauna Lee time to relax. She commented on what a nice day it was and maintained a neutral conversation. Gradually she felt Shauna Lee relax. By the time she turned on to the long, tree-lined lane that led to the farm, the conversation was much easier. Shauna Lee had even laughed a couple of times.

When they went into the house, the twins ran to greet Frank. They hung on her legs, talking excitedly over each other, each one vying to get her attention first. She bent down and encircled them both in her arms, holding them against her breasts in a warm, loving embrace. "Okay, kids, we have company. Remember Shauna Lee? Be nice now and say hi."

Selena went to Shauna Lee and reached out her hand. Shauna Lee took it as she looked down into her smiling, beautiful face. Her dark eyes were dancing with mischief.

Selena tugged on her hand. Her little body twisted with exuberance as she braced herself to pull. "Come on," she commanded with a giggle. Frank had picked up her son and nodded when their eyes met. Shauna Lee gave herself up to the child's persistence and followed her into the kitchen.

Selena guided her to a chair at the table and patted the seat, indicating that Shauna Lee should sit down. "Would you like some coffee?" she asked in a matter-of-fact way.

Shauna Lee chuckled and gave Frank a quick look. Frank nodded. Shauna Lee looked into those sparkling eyes again. "That would be very nice, Selena."

Selena whirled to her mother. "Coffee, Mom." She pointed to Shauna Lee. "She wants coffee."

Frank bent down to put Sam on the floor. "It's coming right up, Selena. I'm proud of you for being such a good hostess. Do you want to help me make it?"

Selena ran to pull a chair away from the table and slide it up to the cabinet, next to the coffee maker. "Can I put the coffee in, Mommy? I know how. Four scoops. Isn't that right?"

Shauna Lee watched with interest. *This is how it should be*, she thought remembering her 'children should be seen and not heard' childhood. Suddenly she felt fingers tug on her pant leg. She looked down to see Sam looking up at her, his big blue eyes calm but interested. "Oou 'no me?"

Her mind flashed to her last visit and her heart did a somersault. *He remembers!* She reached down and picked him up, setting him on her lap. He twisted so that he could look into her eyes. He touched her face thoughtfully and smiled. "I 'ike oou."

For Shauna Lee, time seemed to stand still. She took his hand in hers and lifted it to her lips. She held him close and whispered. "I like you too."

Selena was still bubbling over and talking to her, but Frank had turned in time to see the interaction between Shauna Lee and her son. For that fleeting moment, Shauna Lee had let her guard down. Frank saw the pain and longing in Shauna Lee's face as she hugged the child and whispered to him.

There's so much more to her than we know, Frank mused thoughtfully, as she took two coffee cups down from the cupboard. She poured the coffee when it was ready and carried the cups to the table. "You take it black, don't you?"

Shauna Lee nodded and let Sam go. He looked into her eyes and smiled, then slid off her lap. He walked over to his mom and looked at her solemnly. "She 'ikes me, Mommy."

Frank smiled at her son. "You are a very special little boy, so I can see why she likes you, Sam." He leaned on his mother's knees and stuck his thumb in his mouth. He looked at Shauna Lee for a long moment. Then he smiled and it was like sunshine in Shauna Lee's heart. He pointed at her. "I 'no oou. I 'ike oou."

Shauna Lee smiled as she lifted the cup Frank had put in front of her. The eyes she lifted to meet Frank's had the shimmer of unshed tears. "You have such sweet kids, and you're such a good mother. Not all children are so fortunate."

"Thank you, Shauna Lee. These children," she touched her tummy, including the new one, "are such a gift. Colt and I are so lucky."

The twins ate early, and Ellie ate with them. Then Frank took them upstairs and bathed them. After they had been dressed in their pajamas, they came back downstairs to play until Colt arrived home to say goodnight and tuck them in.

Sam came over and took Shauna Lee by the hand. "Come," he said tugging on her hand. Shauna Lee smiled at him and stood up. He pulled on her hand, leading her to a box of toys in the family room. He sat down on the floor and patted the spot beside him as he looked up at her. "Oou sit."

She smiled and sank down on the floor beside him. He took a toy tractor out of the box and showed it to her. Shauna Lee smiled. Then he took the toy and pushed it around on the floor. "Vrrrrm," he said looking at her as he moved it. "Daddy goes 'ike this."

Frank watched Shauna Lee play with her son. *Colt said she swore she never wanted to have children, but look at her; she's good with them.* She watched as Selena introduced Shauna Lee to her stable of toy horses. Shauna Lee picked up a gray horse and looked it over. "What is this horse's name, Selena?"

"His name is Starlight."

"Do you ride your daddy's horses?"

"No, not yet. Mommy says they are too big for us to ride. Isn't that right, Mommy?"

Frank looked up at her and smiled. "Yes, they are Selena. This summer we will check out the ones at the ranch. There may be one there for you guys to ride."

Frank turned to Shauna Lee. "Do you ride?"

"When I was a child, I rode all the time. Brad has a couple of horses and I've gone for a short ride a couple of times on one of them."

Sam sidled up to her, tapping her on the arm. "Whatss oou 'orses name?"

"My horse was called Poko. He was my best friend and I loved him very much."

Selena took some plastic panels for toy corrals out of the toy box. "Will you help us build a corral?"

Shauna Lee slid down and rolled over on her stomach. She began to fit the pieces together, helping Selena make them into a corral. Sam brought a toy barn to her and set it in front of her. She smiled at him as he plunked down beside her.

When Colt and Brad came in the door, the first thing they saw was the three of them playing on the floor. Brad's eyes flew to meet Frank's. She read his surprise and nodded as she smiled at him.

As soon as the twins heard Colt's voice, they jumped up

and ran to greet him. Sam was carrying the gray horse by its back leg. "Dad, dad." He held the horse up to show him. "Is Poko." He pointed to Shauna Lee. "Poko iss 'er 'orse."

Shauna Lee had stood up. Her eyes met Brads. She smiled softly as he winked at her. *She told them her horse's name was Poko,* he marveled. *Oh, Tweetie Bird. You are making progress.*

He walked over and put his arms around her, dropping a light kiss on her lips. "This is nice... finding you here. Now I don't have to drive home alone. Frank told Colt you'd come out with her."

She nodded. "It's been... fun."

He squeezed her shoulders. His gray eyes were bright. "I'm proud of you," he whispered.

Frank had the table set in no time. Ellie had gone to her trailer earlier, so Colt took the twins upstairs and tucked them into bed. The four of them lingered over dinner, discussing the events of the day.

Finally, Colt yawned and looked at his watch. "Well I don't know about the rest of you, but this has been a long day and I'm ready to hit the sack. It's nine-thirty already, and it'll be another early morning tomorrow. We have to go back to the ranch and finish the job."

He looked at Brad. "Are you sure you don't want to spend the night here?"

Brad shook his head. "It's not that far. Shauna Lee has to go back to town anyway."

Colt nodded. "It's your call. We're ready to pour the cement now. We shouldn't need all day to do those two forms. Maybe we can make it a little later."

"Let's see how morning feels. I'll give you a call when I'm leaving Swift Current. I'd sooner get to work earlier and make sure we get the job done. We can always come home early, but I'd rather not have to go back on the weekend."

When they got to Swift Current, Brad and Shauna Lee stopped at her place to get her car. She looked at him and smiled softly. "You're tired. We could spend the night here you know. There are no groceries so you'd have to stop at A&W in the morning again, but we are right here and we could be in bed in 10 minutes."

Brad yawned. "You're right. It'll simplify everything in the morning, and you won't have to drive your car home alone now." He parked the truck on the street and they went inside.

"Brad, do you want me to throw your clothes in the wash? I'll put them in the dryer first thing in the morning before I make the coffee. They'll be dry in half an hour or a bit more."

He looked at his jeans and his shirt. "That might be a good idea. They are a little worse for wear."

When Shauna Lee came back from the laundry room, Brad had turned back the sheets and was already in bed. He had fallen asleep while he waited for her. She smiled as she turned off the light and slid in beside him. He stirred in his sleep and mumbled something as his arm slid around her.

The next morning Shauna Lee was awake by five o'clock. *I can't believe I am awake this early!* She swung herself out of bed and darted into the laundry room to put Brad's clothes into the dryer. Then she wandered out to the kitchen and made coffee.

Humming she looked through her cupboards. "Pretty bare," she murmured to herself. "And there isn't any milk or eggs. Ahhh, what's this?" She pulled a plastic package off the top shelf. "Buttermilk pancake mix. All it needs is water." She smiled. "I know it's almost sacrilege, but we could have breakfast together."

She opened the sealed package and measured out the ingredients. She added an extra teaspoon of baking powder and water and stirred it with a whip. As the electric griddle heated, she rifled through the freezer and found some bacon. She popped it into the microwave to thaw while she poured four portions of pancake mix on the hot griddle.

She was intent on her cooking and did not hear Brad slip up behind her. She jumped with a squeal as he slid his arms around her waist, pulling her back against his chest. "Are you sick?" he asked, reaching up to feel her forehead. "You're singing in the kitchen while you're cooking... at five-thirty in the morning?" He stuck his finger in the pancake mix. "And you told me you didn't have any groceries.... what is this?"

"Oh, just some of my magic."

"Hmmm... I never thought of your magic showing up at the stove at five thirty in the morning." He turned her toward him. "This is where I've always found your magic." He pulled her close and settled his mouth on hers. The kiss was deep and passionate. His response was immediate. So was hers.

"Breakfast or dessert?" she whispered.

"Both?" he whispered, sweeping her into his arms.

"Turn off the grill," she said with a giggle.

He unplugged the electrical cord and carried her to the bed. He slipped off her housecoat and let it fall to the floor. He laid her on the bed and they made love, fast and furious and passionately. In ten minutes, it was over except for the deep breathing, the little shivers of ecstasy and the marvelous afterglow.

"You are going to be late."

"Colt won't mind if I'm late; he even suggested it. And since you went to all that effort to make breakfast, I'm going to eat it."

"It's just a mix," she confessed.

"No; not just any mix. It's a mix that the woman I love made, with a song on her lips, after she dried my clothes... I hope."

She smiled. "I didn't forget! I'll do almost anything for the most important man in my life. Even get up at five o'clock in the morning to dry his clothes and find a way to make breakfast so that I can share it with him."

He pulled her close and kissed her again. "If I don't get out of here, I might have to stay at the ranch to finish the job up tomorrow. That wouldn't be good for anyone... because I plan to do this properly tonight; slow and simmering, not like this morning's firestorm." He sat up and swung his legs off the bed. "And if I have to stay at the ranch... they'll have to tie me up to keep me from pounding your old man to a pulp."

"Brad, he's not worth it."

She went into the kitchen and plugged in the grill. Then she opened the package of bacon and put some on to cook. Brad was dressed when he came out and found her going through the fridge looking for pancake syrup. She found a bottle with half an inch in the bottom. She waved it triumphantly, grinning as she opened it and put it on the table.

Brad went to the cupboard and took out two plates and two mugs. She smiled at him as she went to the cutlery drawer. She smiled even broader as she picked out two knives, two forks, and two spoons.

"What are you thinking?"

She looked sheepish and shrugged her shoulder.

"Fess up!" he said, wrapping his arms around her.

"Just silliness."

He looked into her smiling eyes. "You are going to make me very late, Tweetie Bird."

"Two plates, two mugs, two knives, two forks, two spoons, the two of us, here or there. Just silliness."

"That's not silliness; it makes perfect sense to me!"

She took the pancakes out of the oven and put the bacon on a plate, then took it to the table. She bent down and whispered in his ear, "Eat. You've got five minutes until you have to hit the road. I want you home tonight."

They ate breakfast and finished their coffee and then Shauna Lee stood up and led him to the door. He kissed her deeply before he put his shoes on.

As she followed him out the door, his hand snaked out and grabbed her wrist, pulling her close. "I love it when you're happy like this," he said before dropping his lips on hers for one more kiss. Then he walked down the steps.

Shauna Lee was chuckling when she went back inside.

She looked around the room. "Yesterday this place seemed so empty, so uninviting. This morning it feels like home. He makes any place feel like that when I'm with him."

Shauna Lee left work early that afternoon, with Christina's promise to close up the office for the weekend. She stopped at Safeway and bought a pork tenderloin roast, as well as some broccoli and a head of Romaine lettuce. She selected two smooth, new potatoes for roasting and made her way through the till. Then she headed home to Brad's place.

When Brad got home, the house was filled with the savory smells. The table was set and candles flickered in the dim room. He sniffed appreciatively. "I can see we need to create a morning firestorm more often." He pulled her into his arms and nuzzled her hair. "What a welcome home, he whispered. "I've been thinking about this all the way home." He rubbed himself against her so she could feel his arousal.

"Dessert first?" she asked.

"I want to so badly, but you've gone to all this trouble." He shook his head. "And I am hungry too... for food, that is. I don't want to rush anything tonight. Not this," he said rubbing against her again. "And I don't want to rush supper either. Let's relax and enjoy it while we eat here in the candlelight."

Shauna Lee laid her head against his chest. "We have the whole evening." She stepped back, running her finger along his bottom lip. "I still have to steam the broccoli. Can I get you a beer or a glass of wine to help you relax while it cooks?"

"I'll have a beer."

Shauna Lee went to the fridge and took out a bottle of Corona. She grabbed a lime and cut it, then slipped a piece into the bottle and handed it to him. She poured herself a glass of wine, turned on the steamer, and took his hand.

"Let's sit on the couch. We can nurse our drinks while you tell me how your day went."

He sat down and pulled her beside him, tugging her to his side. He bent to kiss her, but she shook her head. "Enjoy your drink, and tell me about your day. Consider it a bit of foreplay before we eat, okay?"

He groaned. "I've been in foreplay mode ever since I left this morning."

She giggled. "You're the one who was worried that I would let sex take over our relationship."

He shook his head. "No... I said it would take over our relationship; I didn't say that you would be the only one to let that happen. I knew how much I wanted you."

"I want to hear about your day."

He put a hand on her thigh and held her next to him. "What do you want to know? We went to the water tanks and poured cement at both sites for the turbine bases." He tugged at the crotch of his jeans as he looked at her. "And I had lover's nuts all day. I also had trouble concentrating, just like I am right now."

He put his Corona on the end table at his elbow; then he took her glass of wine away from her and sat it down. "Damn it, woman," he groaned. "You're torturing me." He pulled her on top of him as he slid down on the couch and drew her into a passionate kiss. She reciprocated. Then she let her hand slip down to his bulging crotch, moving further down to massage his scrotum through his jeans. He broke the kiss with a gasp.

A beep from the steamer signaled that the broccoli was cooked.

"To hell with the broccoli," he rasped.

Fifteen minutes later Brad kissed her forehead. "We'd better get up; the broccoli will be mush."

She giggled, rubbing her head against his chest. "To hell with the broccoli," she said softly.

"I'm hungry now."

They slowly got up and dressed. Brad shook his head as he looked at her. "What have I gotten myself into? I think I'm way in over my head."

She slapped his butt. "Which one? The big one or the little one?" she teased. He made a grab for her, but she eluded him and went into the kitchen.

She took the meat out of the warmer and set it on the counter. She reached for the carving knife and laid it next to the meat, smiling as she looked at him and motioned to them. He sauntered around the counter and took out a plate, gently slapping her hip as he passed her. Grinning, he picked up the knife and started to carve the meat.

Shauna Lee took baked potatoes from the warmer and put them on a plate. She noted that the broccoli was cooked to mush, when she put it in a bowl. She took the salad out of the fridge. She retrieved Brad's beer and her glass of wine from the end table. "Do you want a glass of wine?" she asked.

He looked at the table and smiled. "Anything that sumptuous deserves wine. I'll finish the beer later." He walked to the cupboard and got another wine glass, then carried the meat to the table and sat down across from her. "You've outdone yourself, Tweetie Bird. This looks great."

They relaxed and took their time, enjoying the meal; settling into normal couple talk. The sexual tension had been relieved. Brad was able to think clearly now and willingly elaborated on the work that he and Colt had finished out at the ranch. They were sitting back, enjoying a cup of coffee when Brad looked at her and chuckled. "The twins were outside with Frank when I dropped Colt off. They have put it together that you are with me now. Sam asked about you."

Shauna Lee looked surprised. "What did he say?"

"Where's Poko?"

She laughed. "He is so cute. You just have to love him."

"He's no dummy. At first I wondered if he was a little slow," Brad commented. "But Selena is so advanced for her age that I think she makes him seem that way."

"She is so hyper. He is so calm and laid back. They are two totally different personalities."

"Well, he sure likes you." Brad smiled softly. "And from what I saw last night, the feeling is mutual."

She looked at her cup for a moment. "I like both of them,

but all I have to do is look into his calm blue eyes and... he touches me here." She placed her hand over her heart. Her look was wistful, but there were no tears.

"That's good, sweetheart," he said softly, reaching out to touch her hand. "I could tell you were enjoying them last night when we came home. It made my heart stop for a moment; seeing you down there on the floor with them. Sam was sitting so close to you, leaning on you, watching you and Selena playing with the horses. He was holding the gray one. When he called it Poko I knew you had told him about your horse."

She turned her hand over and entwined her fingers with his. "It's odd, but it was easy to tell Selena and Sam about him and how much I had loved him."

CHAPTER TWELVE

Saturday morning, Brad and Shauna Lee woke up to the warm glow of the sun streaming in through the bedroom window. They shifted onto their backs and looked at each other. Shauna Lee reached for his hand and threaded her fingers through his. "Good morning," she said softly. He smiled and raised her hand to his lips. He kissed the back of it gently, then turned it over and slowly licked the palm, with a glint in his eyes as he measured her reaction.

"Brad." It was a plea.

"What?" he teased.

"You know what."

"Tell me."

"You're driving me crazy."

"Tweetie Bird, who would have imagined we would be so well matched."

"Yeah, especially since you refused to have sex with me for so long that I was beginning to wonder if you were gay."

"That was a low blow, but I think we've cleared up that

misconception now," he said lazily.

They drifted languidly in the morning sun that shone on the bed. Finally, Shauna Lee stirred. She lifted her head and looked at him. "People die in bed, you know."

"I am certain I've died once or twice already. I've seen a golden-haired angel. I'm sure I have."

She tickled him. "You're mistaken. This angel has just turned into a devil... a hungry devil." She hit him with a pillow and then jumped out of bed. "I'm going to take a shower. Haul your ass out of there or I'll go to A&W by myself."

Brad laughed as he got up and headed for the shower. He was sitting in the kitchen when Shauna Lee came down the hall. He smiled at her as he stood up and held out his hand to her. "Come on, you little devil."

He drove downtown and passed the A&W. He grinned when she threw him a questioning look. "I need a real breakfast."

Brad stopped in front of Smitty's Pancake House. "It's time to eat." He glanced at his watch. "It's ten minutes after twelve. I guess this is lunch!"

They shared lighthearted banter as they ate. When they were finished, Brad reached across the table and touched her hand. He was smiling. "I love it when you're like this."

She wrinkled her nose at him, but her heart was light and happiness bubbled out of her. "Like this?"

"All bubbly and happy."

She squeezed his hand. "I have you to thank for that, Brad."

"I'm just playing a supporting role, Sweetheart. You're doing the hard work." He stroked her fingers with his thumb. "I'm proud of you, Shauna Lee."

She looked down at their joined hands. "Thank you. I am trying. I want to..." She looked up at him. "I want to make this work. I want to trust. I want to be able to give you what you want; what you give me so freely. I want to be able to love you, Brad."

He leaned forward and kissed her hand. "You already do Sweetheart. You already give me what I want, what I need. Shall we go?"

He helped her into the truck, shut the door and got in on his side. He looked at her as he reached to turn the key. Her eyes were swimming in tears. He slid over and pulled her close. "What's wrong, Shauna Lee?" he asked softly.

She smiled tremulously. "Nothing, Brad. These are happy tears."

"Oh..." He kissed her gently. "So, uh..." *Happy tears...Tweetie Bird, you just threw me off track,* he thought as he looked into her tear-washed eyes. "Well... It's a beautiful day. We aren't likely to get many more like this before winter sets in. What would you like to do? "

"Can we go home and go for a ride on the horses?"

He tousled her hair. "I like that idea."

They took the horses out through the gate at the back of the horse pasture and followed the trail to the gently rolling fields. They rode in companionable silence, enjoying the crisp, fresh air and the serenity of being away from everything else.

Shauna Lee sat astride her horse and threw her arms wide open, embracing the world. "I love this: total solitude, no sounds of traffic, no telephones, and no computers!" She turned to smile at him, happiness overflowing.

"I know what you mean. I get that same feeling when I go hunting in the mountains. Dad and I ride way off the beaten track. You feel like no else has ever been there. The mountains are so majestic, the air so clean and the scenery so spectacular. It's like being transported into a totally different world. For two weeks, we become different people. I always think we become the people we really are meant to be. Life is simple, with no outside pressures. It recharges my batteries. One day I'd like to take you with me."

Shauna Lee shook her head. "I couldn't go hunting."

Brad looked out over the fields. "Shauna, man has been a

hunter for centuries. Dad and I always use the meat we take. How can I explain it to you? For us, it's almost a spiritual thing; being so close to nature, to the creator."

"So why can't you just go out into the mountains?"

"I could. But I'd miss pitting myself against the animals. They are cunning and they have instincts that man can never equal. Spotting a goat or a herd of caribou on a mountain ridge across a valley is only the beginning of an arduous journey. You can ride your horse so far, but after that you are on your own. You are the one on foreign terrain. They are right at home and they know the trails. They are sure footed and travel a lot faster than you ever can.

"It's hard work, often outright dangerous, when you're climbing high up in the mountains. But it's such a thrill when you stalk them and beat them at their own game. In truth there have been many times when I've dragged my ass back to camp, so exhausted that I've wondered if I'd collapse on the trail before I got there and I've never even gotten close to them. I'm driven by the challenge and I'll go out again the next day."

She looked at him thoughtfully. "I could be interested in going for the trip, without a gun."

He shook his head. "That would be foolish, sweetheart. Certain animals see everything as prey, including humans. You need a gun for your own protection." He looked thoughtful. "But we could take a camera along if you wanted to go into the mountains with me and make picture-taking the main reason for being out there. I'd love to share that experience with you."

"Did you go this year?"

Brad shook his head. "No, I was too busy, but who knows, maybe *we'll* go to the mountains next year and hunt with a camera. We'll take a gun along for a backup in case we need it." He glanced at his watch. "We'd better start for home. It's four o'clock already. It'll be getting dark soon."

"I hate to see this day to end." Her face was relaxed and

beaming. "I've enjoyed this ride so much. I have always ridden alone before; it was wonderful to be able to share it with you."

They took their time on the way home and it was dusk when they got back to the corral. Brad unsaddled his horse and took the saddle to the tack room in the barn. Shauna Lee slid off her horse and petted it, telling it how much she loved it.

Brad handed her a curry comb, then poured a measure of grain in the trough for each animal. While the horses ate, Brad and Shauna Lee curried them, lifting their coats to allow fresh air to move through the hair and release the moisture and salt from their sweat, cooling the animal naturally. The horses' postures changed, reflecting their appreciation.

Darkness had settled in by the time Brad and Shauna Lee put away the grain pail and the curry combs. They joined hands as they walked the along the path to the house. When they reached the back door, Brad slid his arm around her shoulder. "This has been a great day all the way around, hasn't it?"

Shauna Lee tilted her head against his shoulder. "It has been incredible. Thank you, Brad."

He squeezed her shoulder gently, then opened the door and let them inside.

That night they ate leftovers from the night before. Afterward, they each took a bottle of beer and settled on the couch to watch TV. Brad surfed through the channels without finding anything that caught his eye. He handed the remote to Shauna Lee. She clicked on CSI and snuggled against him to watch.

In minutes, she noticed a change in his breathing. He had fallen asleep.

Hours later Brad stirred and looked at his watch. It was one o'clock in the morning. Shauna Lee was snuggled against him, sound asleep. His shirt was damp where she had drooled on it as she slept. He eased himself away from her letting her slide to the seat. He stood up and worked the kinks out of his limbs before he lifted her in his arms and carried her into the bedroom.

He hesitated deciding what he should do. He laid her on top of the bed, unbuttoned the waist of her jeans and eased the zipper down to make her more comfortable. He reached for a blanket that lay on the chair in the corner and placed it over her. He took off his jeans and socks, then eased himself under the soft cover and moved over to lie against her. She automatically rolled onto her side and eased her back against his chest.

He slipped his arm around her waist, a soft smile curving his lips. *It's a habit already...like coming home.* Sleep claimed him in moments.

Sunday morning they awakened to another clear, beautiful day. Shauna Lee stretched and then realized that she must have fallen asleep watching CSI. She turned in Brad's arms and traced her finger along his lips. His eyes remained closed, but he smiled. "Are you awake?"

"I am now," he said lazily.

"What time did you bring us to bed?"

"One o'clock."

"Are you serious?"

"Would I lie?" he asked sleepily, his eyes still closed.

"Yeah, you might, but this time I believe you. I must have just died!"

"Well, you were out like a light, but you were still breathing so I took that as a good sign."

She pinched his nose gently. His eyes opened slightly when he grabbed her hand. "You are asking for trouble, Tweetie Bird."

She tickled his ribs. "What kind of trouble?"

He moved to grab her. "Damn," he groaned.

"What?"

"I'm sore in places I forgot existed. I haven't been on a horse that long for a while."

She chuckled. "Poor baby!"

She heard him chuckle as she left the room. She went to the kitchen and made a pot of coffee. She poured a cup for herself and considered what she could make for breakfast. "I don't feel like doing this right now, but I guess I'd better suck it up."

When Brad came into the kitchen, she was browning hamburger in a pan. She had tossed in chopped onion, diced red and green peppers, a minced clove of garlic and added a generous helping of Taco spice and salt and pepper. She had another pan on the grill heating.

"What have we got here?" he asked, looking over her shoulder.

"An omelet surprise."

He got a spoon and dipped it into the hamburger mixture. "Umm. Taco... Mexican flavor. That's good."

He watched her whip two eggs with a fork, add salt and then pour it into the second pan. She pulled the mixture into the middle until it was starting to set.

"What kind is it? I assume the hamburger mix is the filling?"

"It's a Mexican omelet. You put salsa and sour cream on it. I ordered it in a restaurant once and I liked it. I've kind of guessed at the recipe. I hope it turns out all right."

He reached out and took her hand. "It'll be wonderful. The hamburger tasted good, so let's try it. I'm hungry."

They took their first few bites. Brad lay down his fork and looked at her. "This is good, Shauna Lee. I really like it."

"Are you serious?"

He nodded. "You never fail to amaze me. My mother would like this recipe."

Shauna Lee smiled as the warmth from his praise flooded through her.

He picked up his fork and started to eat again. When he finished, he pushed back his plate and picked up his coffee. He smiled at her as he spoke. "Speaking of my mom, I've been thinking about Christmas. How would you feel about going to my folks for Christmas this year? I want you to meet my family."

Shauna Lee tensed.

Brad shook his head. "Don't stress about it now, sweetheart," he said softly. "We've got a while to think about it before we have to decide. If it makes you too uncomfortable to go for Christmas, we'll go another time. We can stay here or go somewhere warm."

"That isn't fair to you," she protested. "You should see your family at Christmas."

"No. I'm going to be with you; wherever that is. You're my priority now. What do you usually do for Christmas?"

"Not much. Christmas has never meant much to me. Sometimes I've just stayed at home. A few times I've caught a last minute trip to Mexico or somewhere warm."

"Well, Tweetie Bird, Christmas is a big deal to me. I'm going to have a lot of fun sharing it with you!"

She smiled. "I haven't had anyone to share the holidays with for years, but you have a way of opening new doors for me. I'm sure it'll be fun!"

"Count on it!" He looked out the window. "You know... it looks like today is going to be another great day. What shall we do?"

She gave him a wicked grin. "We could go riding again."

He grimaced. "I was thinking of something less painful." He frowned. "You rode bareback all afternoon. I don't understand why you're not in major pain."

She stood up and reached over to tweak his ear. "You've done some pretty serious riding out of the saddle the past couple of days. Maybe that's what has caught up with you."

Brad slapped her butt lightly and grinned. "Careful...," he said softly.

She looked deep into his eyes. "You're too sore to back that up," she teased. "So what were you about to suggest we do today... since you don't want to ride?"

Brad thought for a moment. "I've never been out to the Big Muddy Badlands. Have you?"

She shook her head. "Where are they?"

"About two hours southeast of town. It would be a nice drive and we'd get to see some new country. There's lots of history in the area. There's a natural formation called Castle Butte. It apparently stands out there all by its self; sort of a mini-mountain in the middle of a desert like area.

"There are some caves out there, too. American outlaws used to come across the U.S. border into Canada and hide out in them. I checked the area out on the internet a while ago. There was mention of Butch Cassidy and the Sundance Kid and some other guy."

He snapped his fingers, trying to remember. "What's his name... Sam Kelly! It is said that he enlarged a wolf den for his living quarters and the cave is supposed to still be there, pretty much as he left it. He was into a lot of shit in the U.S., but he and his gang specialized in stealing horses and cattle. They would hide them in caves close by for a while and then they would take them back into the U.S. and sell them."

Shauna Lee's eyes sparkled. "Good grief, it was the original wild west!"

"Part of it anyway. So, are you up to it?"

"Absolutely! Should we pack a lunch and some coffee?"

"No, we'll go to a little place called Coronach for lunch. There are a couple of restaurants there. We'll find out where to go from there."

"Let's go. I'll grab my purse and a jacket and put my runners on."

When they went to the truck, Brad took her hand and led her to the driver's side. "I want you in here, right beside me, nice and close."

It was shortly after noon when they stopped for lunch. The locals were friendly and happy to tell them how to get to Castle Butte. When Brad inquired about the caves, the owner of the restaurant said that they were only accessible through private property and the people who owned the ranch were away.

Brad paid for the meal and they went outside. As they got into the truck, one of the locals followed them. Brad lowered his window and talked to him. The man told him that it was the end of the season for the guided tours.

Nobody lived in the old house on the Giles Ranch anymore, but he knew the owner. He told Brad he would have to park the truck on the road, but if they crawled through the barbed wire fence and followed the trail, they would find the caves. He gave him directions to the old ranch and Brad thanked him.

He was grinning when he started the truck. He put his hand on the inside of her thigh. "Are you game for an adventure?"

"It sounds like fun."

Brad pulled up to the ranch gate and stopped. He read the sign; "Giles Ranch: Trespassers will be given a fair trial, then hung." He smiled crookedly as he turned to her. "Hangman's noose and all! Do you think we should risk it?"

"Well, it sort of makes us outlaws. I guess that's fitting with the history of the area."

He chuckled as he hooked his arm around her shoulders and pulled her against him. "Are you ready?"

Shauna Lee nodded and they got out. He grabbed the camera, then pressed the automatic lock and shut the door. They walked to the fence and he put a boot on the bottom wire and took the middle one in his hand, pulling them apart so she could crouch and go between them. When she had slipped through the fence, she did the same for him.

He whistled a soft tune as they walked hand in hand down the trail. They had gone a fair distance before they saw what appeared to be a cave at the bottom in the coulees.

"That could be what we are looking for!" she said, excitement sparkling in her eyes.

They stopped and looked out over the terrain. "Can you

Full Circle

image what this country was like just over hundred years, with outlaws and Indians roaming these hills? If I remember correctly, Sitting Bull even hid out here a time or two," Brad mused.

Shauna Lee's face glowed as she turned to him. "I never knew about any of this, and I've lived in Swift Current for thirteen years!" She threaded her arms around his waist. "Brad, you are the best thing that has ever happened to me. You just keep showing me more about life."

He pulled her tight against him and lifted her face to meet his. "That is a two-way street, you know. I love having you to share things with." He looked deep into her eyes. "For the first time in my life, I've finally found what I've been waiting for. You are the missing piece of the puzzle." His arms tightened around her. "You make my life complete." He kissed her. "Let's go." His voice was rough with emotion.

He took her hand and led her down the trail to the caves. They saw a sign that read 'Sam Kelly's Outlaw Caves.' He smiled as he pointed to the sign. "We've hit pay dirt! Will you stand over there by the sign and let me take your picture?"

She took his picture, too, and then he found a dead branch with a crotch in it. He pushed it into the light soil and put his camera in the join. After he had assured himself that he had everything lined up, he set the timer and ran to her. They stood one on each side of the sign when the camera flashed. He grinned. "That's another picture for your office!"

They looked in the cave that was largest. "This is probably the one they used for the animals," Brad said looking around. "It's huge."

He hooked his arm around her shoulder and walked with her to the other one. It had been reinforced. "I think he actually lived in this one for a while after he gave up rustling and came back here to settle down." They stepped through the opening and looked around. The ceiling was low and Brad had to stoop to avoid bumping his head on it. "He must have been short."

Shauna Lee smiled as she looked at him. "Not tall, dark and handsome like you." Shauna Lee looked around, taking in the dirt walls and floor. "Can you imagine living in a wolf den? He had to have enlarged it a lot."

"I guess he did what he had to do."

It was four o'clock when they got back to the truck. Brad looked at her as he unlocked the door. "Should we go any farther today or should we come back another day?"

"I'm content to go back. It's going to be late by the time we get home anyway."

They sat shoulder to shoulder and thigh to thigh on the drive home, chatting easily. The November long weekend was coming up and they discussed the trip they were going to make to the northern region of the province. They decided to leave on Thursday so they could be home by Sunday night.

CHAPTER THIRTEEN

Thursday morning, Brad and Shauna Lee were on the road to Glaslyn by eight o'clock.

"How far is it?" she asked. "Will we get there early enough for you to do the maintenance check at that site this afternoon?

"It's roughly a six-hour drive; maybe six and a half with stops for fuel and food." He gave her a teasing look. "Mind you, if we park somewhere on a back road for a quickie, it will take longer."

"Brad! We're making this trip so that you can do a maintenance check on the turbines. Let's just focus on that for now. No side trips."

"I love it when I get you all tied up in a knot!"

They drove to North Battleford where they stopped for lunch and fuelled the truck. Brad had stopped teasing her and the trip had relaxed into a pleasant drive. When they got in the truck after lunch, Shauna Lee asked how much farther they had to go.

"It's roughly an hour's drive from here to Glaslyn. The turbine is set up in a pasture about fifteen kilometers out of town. I should phone Bob Matzlan now and let him know where we are. He's going to meet us at the site."

Shauna Lee listened as he made the call. She realized that she hadn't seen him interact with clients. She'd seen him with Colt, but they had a friendly relationship as well as a professional one. It bordered more on casual, but now as she listened to him talk to Bob Matzlan, she glimpsed the truly professional aspect of the man.

He shut off the phone and put it back into its holder. "He'll meet us there and he'll be on time, which is good." He looked at his watch. "It's almost two o'clock now. If everything goes like I expect, it'll take about an hour to check out the turbine; an hour and a half max. I should be done by four-thirty.

"Spiritwood is about thirty-five kilometers from Glaslyn. That may be the best place to go for a motel. When I went online and checked out the town, I saw a fairly new one on a service road adjacent to the highway. The rooms looked decent and there are a few restaurants downtown where we can catch something to eat."

"That sounds good. What is Bob Matzlan like?"

"He's a nice guy. I'd guess that he's in his late fifties or early sixties. I think his father-in-law lives there with him. The boys call him Grandpa, but as I remember, Bill didn't introduce him as his dad. Come to think of it, I've never met his wife, but there are 3 boys. The oldest is about thirty-two, and I'd guess the youngest is about twenty-five."

"Are the boys interested in farming?"

"Bill is the oldest one. He has taken over the family farm, but Bob is still working with him."

Shauna Lee shook her head. "I can't imagine anyone wanting to farm."

Brad looked at her curiously. "Why? It's a time-honored way of life that has been the backbone of this country."

"And a lot of the time it's been a damned skinny old cow, with every vertebra of that backbone almost poking through the hide."

Brad frowned. "Shauna, you must have quite a few accounts for farmers and ranchers. A lot of them are very successful. Colt seems to have done well."

Shauna Lee looked out the window. "Yes, Colt and his dad have done well. But, Brad, I lived on a farm when I was a kid. Believe me; our life was nothing like theirs."

He squeezed her hand. "Probably not; but that was thirty-five years ago or more. Times have changed a lot since then. Farmers like your dad scarcely exist now. A quarter-section is not enough to survive on unless the owner really specializes in something unique. I know a couple who raise fancy little dogs and they do really well, but they cater to their buyers and they understand marketing."

"I know you're right about that. But, I can't shake the memory of the smell of cowshit, dirt and dust and poverty."

"Well, there still is an odd one like that. They've gotten stuck doing what their father did, what their grandfather did. The majority of those people have never gotten an education beyond the basic reading and writing and arithmetic. And honestly, most of them have no vision; they can't even begin to imagine creating a better life. I think a lot of those guys have other social problems. Alcohol is a big one, but some of them get into drugs too. How the hell they can afford it is beyond me."

Shauna Lee snorted. "But they always do. Dad could always squeeze out enough money to buy his whiskey. It didn't matter what else didn't get taken care of."

Brad slowed down and signaled, turning right at the intersection. "We don't go right into Glaslyn. We turn here and go east for about five kilometers. Then we turn off on a gravel road and go in about ten kilometers, to the turbine.

"Bob Matzlan is a pretty sharp guy. He is one of the thoroughly modern farmers. He and his son farm several thousand acres. I don't know how much education Bill has, but he is no dummy. He was the one who got interested in wind turbines and researched them on the internet. He and Bob came to Swift Current to meet me."

Brad slowed down and signaled to turn left onto a gravel road. He smiled when he saw a white crew cab parked on the side. As he pulled up behind it, all four doors opened and four men got out and walked back toward them. He got out and shook hands with all of them.

When he came back to the truck, they followed the other vehicle down the road. They turned into a field and a few hundred yards further, as they rounded a curve in the road that passed a clump of poplar trees, Shauna Lee caught her first glimpse of a wind-generated turbine mounted on a tower.

Brad's smile was one of pride. "There it is! And they are happy with the setup." He opened the truck door and slid out. "Are you going to get out? The air is a bit nippy, but it's refreshing. I'd appreciate it if you'd take a few pictures for me; some of the four of them and me looking at the tower and working around it. I have to check the storage batteries and I want to climb up and look at the turbine too."

"Where is the camera?"

He opened the back door, reached inside and took a small leather pouch out of a storage box he had set on the seat. "Just click away. I'll keep the ones I can use and discard the rest."

She took it from him. He gave her a quick hug and joined the others. Shauna Lee played with the camera, adjusting the focus from close-up to wide angle. When she was satisfied, she followed the men and took pictures.

To her surprise, Bob Matzlan came over and stood beside her. "I don't think we've been introduced. I'm Bob Matzlan."

She looked at him and smiled. "I'm Shauna Lee Holt." She looked at him closely, attracted by his startling blue eyes.

"I'm pleased to meet you, Shauna Lee. It's strange, but there's something very familiar about you like I've known you from somewhere before."

Shauna Lee's heart skipped. She tried to sound casual, but all the red flags were up. "I don't think so."

"Funny. It's just a feeling. I'm trying to think. You said your name is Holt. Are you married?"

Surprise registered on her face.

"Pardon me. That was rude of me. I was just wondering if that was your family name."

She swallowed. "It is a family name." She looked at him. "There is nothing familiar about you to me."

"I guess it's just my imagination. You are a very striking young woman; one that would stick in a person's mind."

She smiled at him. "I guess I should take that as a compliment. Thank you."

She moved away from him and kept taking pictures. She could feel his eyes on her and it unnerved her. *I have never known anyone from Glaslyn.*

Bob approached her again as she was taking a picture of Brad climbing up the tower. "Do you live in Swift Current?"

She nodded and then took another picture.

"Do you know if any of your family ever lived in this area?"

Jeez! He's like a dog with a bone. "No. In fact, I'm sure they didn't."

"Life is funny. When I was a young man, my first love was a pretty, young woman named Marie Holt. You remind me of her. I don't know why because you don't really look alike..."

Shauna Lee almost choked, but he didn't notice. He was lost in his remembering.

"We lived at Medstead at the time, then my family moved to Glaslyn and we lost touch. I never forgot her. In fact, I happened to run across her a few years later at a house party in Junor. She hadn't forgotten me either, but she had married a Frenchman. That night he got so drunk he passed out and she was really mad at him. We'd been drinking and dancing and one thing led to another. We went outside and ended up in the barn. It wasn't the right thing to do, but I've often wondered...."

Shit, shit, SHIT! This is way too much information. She felt sick. *How can this be happening? All these freaking years later!*

She was relieved to see Brad walking toward her. She smiled as she stepped forward to meet him and handed him the camera. "Do you want to check the pictures and make sure some of them are what you want?" He studied her face as he took it. *Something has upset you, Tweetie Bird.* He glanced through the pictures quickly and assured her that she had done well.

Then he glanced at his watch and turned to Bob. "Everything is working fine. Like I mentioned when we installed the turbine, they are very simple in design and require no regular maintenance. But if it's reasonably close, I make it a policy to check out every installation before the first winter, as a precaution. It helps me keep on top of any possible problems too."

He shook Bob's hand again and said he had to be getting on the road. Shauna Lee smiled and said goodbye, then led the way to the truck.

Brad didn't say anything until they reached the highway and headed east again.

"What happened back there?" he asked.

"Wh- aa- t do you mean?"

He took her hand. "This is me, sweetheart. My radar picked up on something back there. What was it?"

"You're like a damned lie detector machine."

"So what was it?"

She sighed and rested her head back against the seat, looking up at the roof of the truck. "Jeez! I can change my name and run, but it seems that I can't hide."

"What are you talking about?"

"Bob Matzlan. He kept asking me questions and telling me that I reminded him of someone." Tears shimmered in her eyes as they met his. "It turns out he... he had a thing for my mom when they were young. After she was married to Dad, they met again at a house party. Dad was so drunk he passed out, and mom was mad at him. Bob said one thing led to another, and he and Mom had sex that night." She wiped away the tear that spilled over on her cheek. "He told me all that. He just started talking and blurted it out. Jeez! As if I needed or wanted to know all of that."

Brad was thoughtful. "Did you tell him who you were?"

"Are you kidding? I just kicked myself over and over for using Grandma's married name. I should have chosen VanWinkle or something like that, instead of Holt. Mom was gone, Grandma was gone and Grandpa was dead before I was even born. I never imagined anyone would connect the dots."

"Well, Bob's curiosity probably won't go any further. You gave him a happy glance into the past. I'm pretty sure he won't give it another serious thought."

"I hope not. I don't want any more ghosts from my past to raise their heads. I thought I had put all of that behind me years ago, when I changed my name."

"Where did your parents live, Shauna? You said you lived on a farm, but where was it at?"

"A few miles from a little place called Junor. In the early homestead days, it was a thriving little community. The railway line ran by there, but when we lived in that area, there wasn't anything much left of the town."

"Is that near here?"

"I couldn't honestly say. I never went very far from the farm when I was growing up and I left there when I was fourteen and a half. I've never been back."

Brad took her hand. "Would you like me to help you find it?"

"NO, No, no! I don't want to go anywhere near the place."

"Okay, sweetheart, we won't do it. I just thought... well sometimes it helps to face our demons. It can take away the power that they have to hurt us and lay them to rest."

She shook her head. "I don't want to. I can't!"

Brad pulled her against him and held her there as he drove the last few kilometers to Spiritwood. He turned off the highway and drove along the service road until he came to the motel that he was looking for. "Here we are," he said as he pulled up in front of the office.

Shauna Lee waited in the truck while he went in to make arrangements for the room.

He came back to the truck and got in. "Are you all right?"

She nodded. "Where is our room?"

"Down at the far end. I'll park in front of the door." He started the truck and moved it, and then they both got out and went inside.

Brad looked around the room. It was large and comfortable with a table and two comfortable chairs and good lighting.

"I rented it for two nights. It's about a forty-five minute drive to Chitek Lake from here. I'll finish up early there and then we'll come back here. We're in no hurry. We can sleep in. We'll still get home in plenty of time Sunday afternoon."

"I like the sound of that."

Brad grinned. "I'm hungry. The receptionist said there's a restaurant on Main Street that she'd recommend. She said the food is great. Shall we go check it out?"

They drove around downtown and then parked in front of an older, rundown-looking building. When they went inside, the decor was just as dismal, but the waitress was neat, her clothes clean and her shoes shiny. They looked at the menu and both decided to order Salisbury steak."

Brad picked up his coffee cup, took a sip and smiled. "Ahh...that is a great cup of coffee."

The waitress brought them both a cup of beef vegetable soup and a fresh dinner roll. Brad dipped a spoon in and tasted it. "Hey, this is good!"

When their Salisbury steaks arrived, they looked across the table and gave each other a thumbs up. The food was excellent. When they were finished the meal, the waitress brought two pieces of carrot cake for dessert.

Shauna Lee groaned. "I can't eat this now." The waitress amiably suggested that she could put it in a takeout box, so they both decided to take dessert back to the motel.

Once they were inside, Brad swept her up in his arms and sat her in the middle of the bed. He picked up the remote and turned on the TV, then sank down beside her. They both scooted up to sit against the headboard. He pulled her against him while they listened to the last few moments of the evening news. After the news, Brad flipped through the channels and finally selected a channel that played soft music.

"I didn't get my job done today," he said softly, as he turned to pull Shauna Lee into his arms and kissed her.

"You did."

"Not this one. I didn't get into the fo—"

"Foreplay." She finished the word as she touched her lips to his again. "I think you made a really good start," she whispered against his mouth

He tossed the extra pillows on the floor, then pulled back the sheet and let her slide into the bed. He rolled into it beside her and they hungrily reached for each other. They made love slowly, savoring the pleasure. When they were satiated, they lay hand in hand, side by side.

Shauna Lee became very silent.

"What are you thinking?" Brad asked softly.

"Nothing."

"Sweetheart, you can't lie to me. What's going on in that pretty head of yours?"

"I was thinking about what Bob said today."

"And?"

"Brad... you'll hate this..."

He pushed himself up on his elbow. "Spill it, Tweetie Bird. What are you thinking?"

"Brad, you know my past... about all those guys."

"Sweetheart, don't do this. You were lonely. You were needy. You were looking for affection."

"But what if that isn't the reason. Bob said mom had sex with him at a party where dad was passed out. Brad, that's acting like a slut. What if I'm like her?"

"You're not a slut!"

"I've acted like one, so did she."

"Sweetheart, you can't assume that about your mother. Maybe she was empty and lonely, just like you were."

"But, she was married."

"The marriage may have been empty and lonely. It could have felt like a trap if she hadn't married the man she loved."

"But why would she do that? Why would she marry Dad if she didn't love him?"

"Bob told you his family had moved and he'd lost touch with her. Maybe she loved him. Maybe she thought she'd never see him again, so she just got married. In those days, women didn't have the choices that they do today."

He reached for her and pulled her against him. "You are a wonderful person, who has never known love before. Even your mom couldn't give that to you. Maybe she just didn't have it left to give."

"I hope I deserve you," she whispered.

"I have no doubt about that." He turned off the music and the light. She rolled onto her side and he pulled her against his chest. He held her close and waited for sleep to come.

The next morning they went back to the same restaurant for breakfast. They were on the road to Chitek Lake by nine-thirty. Brad had phoned to let his client know that they were on their way.

Brad parked in front of a modern, two-story house situated at the edge of Chitek Lake. The lawn was beautifully maintained and she could see the two turbines spinning in the breeze.

Brad opened the door and helped her out of the truck. "You'll like these folks. They are down-to-earth people." When they got to the door, Brad knocked. They could hear footsteps scurrying through the house.

Full Circle

The door opened and a petite gray-haired woman smiled as she looked at Brad. "Come in. I just put the coffee on and I made fresh cinnamon rolls this morning." Her eyes slid to Shauna Lee. She hesitated, shock whitening her face. "Oh, my! LeeAnn, is it really you? She reached out and pulled her close. She kept repeating her words. "Oh my. Oh my! LeeAnn." She looked over her shoulder and yelled. "John, John... hurry up. You'll never believe who's here."

Brad watched in stunned disbelief. *Oh, Tweetie Bird. The past is determined to find you on this trip.*

John Potter came bounding to the door. "Who is here?" He slid to a stop. "LeeAnn? LeeAnn Bergeron? Oh my God, it's really you. It's been so long since we've seen you."

Shauna Lee faltered. Brad reached out and steadied her. "I'm sorry, sweetheart. I had no idea that you knew the Potters."

"Come in, come in," John Potter insisted. He reached to pull Shauna Lee into his embrace. "How have you been, LeeAnn? We tried to find you several times throughout the years, but we always hit a dead end. It was as if you'd just vanished. I guess I couldn't have blamed you if you had, after everything that happened."

Brad put his arm around her protectively. "John, she didn't know we were coming to your place, and I had no way of knowing that you knew each other. Can she sit down and have a chance to collect herself?"

"Yes, of course. Come in and sit at the table. Bring her a cup of coffee, Marion."

Shauna Lee sank onto the chair. Her face was pale and she looked devastated.

Brad looked at their hosts. "John and Marion; we're together now. Once she is settled and comfortable, I'll go out and check the turbines. I- I think it might be good if the three of you had a chance to catch up. Obviously, there has been a connection between you. I- I'm going to be honest about this. There are still things I don't know about her past. I just know that it was painful." He hesitated. "Please be kind to her."

He turned to go outside, aware of the puzzled looks on the face of the Porters. He was almost at the door when Shauna Lee called to him.

"Brad... please stay." There were tears in her eyes. "You have to hear about this sometime. I tried to tell you that night, but you said..."

He nodded. "I know. I said we both had dealt with enough that day. Are you sure you want me to stay?"

"Yes," she said softly. "I want to get this all out in the open now. You know most of it, but this part is the most painful, the ugliest." The sadness in her eyes hit him like a kick in the gut.

Brads heart faltered. *How much more could there be?* John was looking at her with compassion. Marion's eyes swam with tears. He pulled over a chair and sat next to Shauna Lee, reaching for her hand. She smiled at him wanly.

"I don't remember much about the months after Ben's death. They are a blur; a nightmare of pain that just steam-rolled over me. My arms ached with emptiness. My heart was broken. I would have gladly died. I wished I could, but I didn't. John and Marion saved me; saved my sanity."

She looked at John and Marion. "I need to tell you something right away. I changed my name after you took me to Saskatoon. That's why you couldn't find me. I'm Shauna Lee Holt now. I buried LeeAnn Bergeron along with Ben when I left here."

Surprise flickered over John and Marion's faces.

Shauna Lee's look was apologetic. "Please forgive me. I knew I should have told you. You had been so kind to me." She looked down at the hand that Brad held in his. "So much had happened. You know the huge coverage that the trial received in the news

Brad stiffened. *Trial? What the hell?*

Shauna Lee continued. "LeeAnn Bergeron was a household word. Everyone knew that name, even if they

Full Circle

didn't know me. I couldn't face all the questions, people's pity, never knowing when the media would be in my face, asking me stupid questions or just keeping tabs on what I was doing.

"I wanted anonymity; to simply disappear and start a completely new life. I didn't want *anyone* to be able to find me." She looked at them, imploring them to understand. "If one person knew, it could slip out and others would find out. The next thing I knew, people I didn't want to know could find out. So I didn't tell anyone.

"My Dad had walked out. Mom had died. Grandma was the only person who had ever made me truly feel loved. She died when I was six. I decided to take her name. Why I kept the Lee part, I'm not sure now. Maybe deep down I did want to keep a little piece of myself. Whatever; I became Shauna Lee Holt and that is who I have been for the past twenty years."

She looked at John and Marion. "I told Brad about Ben being born with a cleft lip, and how his... father... felt about him. I told him that Ben didn't live long enough to have the surgery he needed. I haven't told him what happened though. This is so painful..." Tears slipped down her cheeks as she looked at Brad.

"Ben was a fussy baby. He had trouble swallowing and he'd get infections. I was so tired that night. I fell asleep with him cradled in my arms. He had one of the ear infections that he often suffered from and he'd cried and cried for hours. He started to cry again and it took me a few moments to wake up fully.

"Before I realized what was happening, Dave jerked Ben out of my arms. He was shaking him furiously and Ben was screaming. I jumped out of bed and tried to take Ben away from him. He... he swung Ben into me like he was a baseball bat. I fell down. He dropped Ben onto me." She was sobbing. "Ben wasn't crying anymore. He was just dangling silently over my arm."

Brad closed his eyes. Pain knifed through him. *Oh, Shauna Lee, no.* Tears were running down everyone's cheeks now, including his.

"I was terrified. I screamed at Dave, telling him that he had to take us to the hospital, but he just turned away and grabbed a bottle of rum off the table. He- he just kept saying that the little freak had finally shut up and went out the door."

"The fucking son of a bitch," Brad looked up, shocked at what he'd said out loud. "I'm sorry, guys, but..."

John waved his hand, dismissing Brad's apology. "We've all said and thought that about him, and much worse! I could have strangled him with my bare hands. I often wished that he'd have gotten shot while resisting arrest, rather than put LeeAnn through the ordeal of the trial."

Even though Brad was holding her, Shauna Lee hugged herself, pushing away the coldness that ran through her, struggling to swallow the bile that rose in her throat. Her stomach rolled as she remembered holding her son's precious little body close to her breast. "I ran across the field to John and Marion's."

John read her pain. He reached across the table and touched her hand. His voice was full of compassion. "Let me tell the rest, Lee... Shauna Lee."

She nodded, sobbing. Brad held her close, smoothing her hair. *I feel so helpless.*

"The baby was dead when she came to the door. She was clutching his body against her chest, but he was blue and still. She was crazy with fear, babbling incoherently and crying hysterically, begging us to take them to the hospital right away.

"Of course, we took her. While it was clear that there was nothing to be done for the baby, LeeAnn was falling apart. She needed help. Dave had never hidden how he felt about the baby. He had nothing but contempt for Ben and LeeAnn.

"Today we would have reported his behavior to social services and had her taken out of the situation, but twenty years ago you minded your own business. I did go into the back room and phone the police before we left. I reported what had happened and they came out and took Dave into custody."

Marion's expression was full of compassion. "You were so young, just a girl yourself. I don't know how you dealt with his cruelty."

Shauna Lee sobbed. "I- I had nowhere else to go. I had a roof over my head and food to put on the table and a place to sleep. I didn't grow up in a very loving home and until the baby was born, life with Dave wasn't that bad. But after Ben was born..." She buried her face in her hands. "He despised me and poor little Ben. Dave would have h-h-it him over the head like he did the ru-n-t pigs and thro-w-n him on the manure pile with them. H-ee told me he wou-ld. But Ben was m-my ba-by. I lov-ed him."

John Potter spoke, breaking the sickening mental image. "LeeAnn came here after she got out of the hospital and she lived with us until after the trial. It took several months for the case to get to court. Lee, sorry... it's going to take a while to think of you as Shauna Lee; Shauna Lee testified against Dave. He should have gotten life without parole, but they gave him twenty-five years.

Brad sat upright. "Twenty-five years!" he exploded. "It won't be long before he's released. He could be out on parole now if he behaved himself in jail."

"That was one reason I changed my name, leaving no trail. He hates me. I was afraid he would come after me."

John nodded. "He hated a lot of people. We'll all be looking over our shoulders when he is released." He looked at Shauna Lee. "Do you live in Swift Current now?"

She nodded. "I've been there for thirteen years."

Brad's voice reflected his pride in her. "She's worked hard and she's done very well for herself."

"What did you do after you left here?" John asked.

She sighed. "I rented a single room in a private home. I

did housework and cooked meals for board and room. The couple both worked. They liked me and eventually they recommended me for babysitting and house-sitting jobs on the weekends. I stayed with them until I finished high school.

"I... I was determined to leave fear and poverty behind me. I vowed to make a good life for myself and never be dependent on anyone else for my survival again. I vowed I'd never be vulnerable to my emotions again. I would be the master of my own ship. Nothing was going to stand in my way. And on the surface I've done that."

"What do you do?" Marion asked.

"I became a chartered accountant. I worked for an old accountant in Swift Current and when he retired, I bought the business. It was a good investment for me."

John and Marion both nodded with approval. "Good for you," Marion said.

John drummed his fingers on the table. "Did you change your name legally?"

Shauna Lee shook her head.

"How did you get into school?"

"Well, when I enrolled in high school, I simply registered as Shauna Lee Holt, but I realized that I had to get a birth certificate that I could use." She grimaced. "I did what I had to do. It took me a while, but once I had that, I got my social insurance number too. Then I could get a real job."

John's eyes were sad as he looked at Shauna Lee. "I wish you had come to me."

"You'd already done so much for me, John. My top priority was to disappear and leave my old existence behind. If I turned to anyone for help, I would lose my anonymity. I was totally focused on building a new life. I did what I had to do."

Her expression was pained as she looked at Brad. "I even resorted to... to prostitute a few times. It paid a lot more and I needed money." She hid her face with her hands. "I'm sorry, Brad, but it's true. I hope you can forgive me."

Brad closed his eyes and squeezed her hand. *Oh, Shauna Lee.* . "The past is the past, sweetheart. I've told you that before and I still mean it. What happens from here on is what matters." He dropped a kiss on her hand.

John looked at Brad with admiration. "You are a fine man, Brad. I am so glad to see that Shauna Lee has someone like you in her life."

"Thank you, John. From what I've heard here today, you were probably more like a father to her than her own dad was."

"She needed someone."

John looked at Marion. "Can we have some hot coffee and some of those cinnamon buns, Mom?"

She nodded and went to make a fresh pot of coffee.

Shauna Lee looked at John. "I didn't think that anyone would recognize me. I've changed a lot since those days... or at least I thought I had."

John looked at her thoughtfully. "You have changed a bit. You're older and you've filled out, but those eyes are unmistakable. On first glance, I may have missed the resemblance because I wasn't expecting to see you, but on a second look, it would be hard not to see it."

Marion had brought small plates and the cinnamon buns to the table. "I knew you right away."

Shauna Lee sighed. "Obviously I'm not as invisible as I'd thought I was."

Brad held her close. "You've spent too many years hiding, Shauna. You can't do that anymore. We'll face this together."

After they drank coffee and enjoyed Marion's fresh cinnamon buns, Brad and John went out to inspect the towers. Shauna Lee and Marion chatted, catching up on the past twenty years. When Brad and Shauna Lee left for Spiritwood, the Porters assured them that Shauna Lee's secret was safe with them.

Brad was sick at heart as he watched Shauna Lee huddle against the passenger door. She had refused to sit next to him when he'd ask her to. She'd become strangely calm; as if she had removed herself from the situation. *That has to be how she has survived all these years.*

At eighteen, Shauna Lee had been stripped of everything she cared about in her life. Emotionally she had been numb. She'd had no possessions, no education, no family, no life. But she had drawn on strength deep inside her, one that had always been there and that was how she'd survived. Now she was doing that again. Would she lock herself in that world, or would she reach out to him?

When he drove up to the motel door, Shauna Lee sat up and opened her door. Brad was relieved when he saw that she sat on the edge of the seat, waiting for him to help her down to the ground.

Before he opened the motel door, he glanced at his watch. It was four-fifteen. He swung the door open and let Shauna Lee step inside. He followed her and locked the door behind him. He watched her as she stood at the end of the bed, looking at him uncertainly.

He stepped in front of her and unzipped her jacket. She let him take it off her and then she turned and sat down in one of the chairs. *She's keeping her distance,* he thought sadly. He took off his jacket and laid it on the bed beside hers. He hesitated and then sat down in the other chair. He was silent for a moment. Then he cleared his throat. "Do you feel like talking?" His voice was soft.

"What is there to talk about?"

"You could tell me how you feel. I'm here for you and I'm a good listener." He smiled gently. "I'm even better at it if I can hold you in my arms.

She smiled wearily. "I'm numb. I don't know what to say."

"Can I hold you?"

She shook her head. "I need some time, Brad."

"Do you want me to leave you alone for now?"

"Please."

"Maybe you should lie down and relax. I can sit here and watch TV."

She hesitated and then nodded. He stood up and extended his hand. She placed hers in it and let him help her to her feet. He led her to the bed and let her sit on the side of it. He bent down and removed her shoes, then swung her legs up. He squeezed her hand, then walked back to the chair and pulled it over so he could watch TV.

He flipped through the programs but found nothing that interested him. Finally, he selected a soft music channel and sat slouched down in the chair, letting the music wash over him. He let his head fall against the back of the chair and stared at the ceiling. He was deep in thought, going over the horrific story he had heard that morning. *Someone should have killed that bastard,* he thought. *A man that would kill his own child; Jesus! Poor Shauna Lee, no wonder she just shut down and locked up.*

"Brad." He jerked up in his seat. She was sitting up, looking at him.

"What, sweetheart?"

"You don't look very comfortable there. Why don't you come and lay down?" She patted the far side of the bed.

"I don't want to crowd you."

"If you lay there, you'll be more comfortable and you won't be crowding me."

"Are you sure? I'm okay, you know."

She smiled wanly. "I'd like to know that you are close enough that I can reach out and touch you if I want to."

His heart lightened. He kicked off his boots and lay down. He fought his desire to hold her close, to protect her. Instead, he forced himself to breathe deeply and relax. He vowed to give her the room she needed.

Slowly he drifted off to sleep. Sometime later, she rolled over beside him and placed her hand on his arm. He surfaced briefly, smiling as he turned toward her. She mumbled in her sleep as she rolled over and snuggled her back against his chest. He slipped his arm around her waist and they fell sound asleep.

When Brad woke up, the TV was still playing music. He looked at his watch. It was two o'clock in the morning. They had slept for at least eight hours. He was wide awake... and hungry. The coffee and cinnamon buns were long gone. He shifted carefully, trying not to awaken Shauna Lee, but with his slightest movement she stirred. She stretched, then turned over and looked at him.

"What time is it?" she whispered.

"Two in the morning," he whispered. Then he grinned. "Why are we whispering?" he asked softly.

"Because it's two in the morning," she replied just as softly. "Jeez, we've already had a full night's sleep, and I'm hungry!"

"So am I. We didn't eat that carrot cake the other night. There's a coffee maker in here. We can make coffee and eat the cake."

"Right now that's better than nothing." She rolled off the bed and went to set the coffee maker up to brew. Then she opened the small fridge and took out the two pieces of cake. She came back, sat down beside him and handed him a piece.

They gulped it down, then looked at each other and laughed. "I'm wide awake," she said.

"So am I." He got up to pour them each a cup of coffee and brought her one. He looked at her as he sipped. "Well, what are we going to do now?"

She looked at him. "We could head for home and sleep the rest of the day after we get there."

He looked at his watch again. "It's twenty to three. If we leave right away, we'll be home around nine o'clock. That'll leave us time to stop for breakfast too."

She leaned forward and kissed him softly. "Let's go."

They quickly packed up their bags and were on their way. When they reached North Battleford, it was still dark, but they decided to have breakfast at a twenty-four-hour truck stop.

An hour later, they were back on the highway.

Brad looked at his watch when he parked in front of the house. "We're home," he said with a smile. "It's nine-thirty."

CHAPTER FOURTEEN

Frank and Colt sat at the kitchen table, enjoying their morning coffee. Colt looked out the window and shook his head. "I can't get over the way this great weather is holding. November tenth and it is plus six degrees. I can't remember when I've seen this before."

"It must be global warming," Frank said with a smile.

Colt chuckled. "Whatever it is, it's just what we need. If these temperatures hold for another week, Brad and I should get the towers and turbines up at the water tanks before winter sets in for real. That will be a big load off my mind. It'll make things so much easier next summer."

"Modern innovation is amazing isn't it?"

Colt nodded. He glanced at the clock on the wall. It was seven-thirty. "We have half an hour before the twins get up. Could I talk you into joining me on the wicker lounge out on the veranda? We could snuggle and have another coffee."

"It's warm for this time of the year, but it's still chilly."

"That's the reason for cuddling. It'll be refreshing and the morning sky will be beautiful."

Frank laughed. "Well, it's either a very romantic idea or an insane one. I'll get a warm jacket."

"You're a real trooper. I'll refill our cups and put my coat on."

They settled on the wicker lounge, cups in hand. Colt hooked his arm around Frank and pulled her into the curve of his shoulder. "Look at that sunrise," he said softly. The sky was flushed fuchsia and pink with touches of yellow.

"It's beautiful."

Colt looked toward Ellie's trailer. "It looks like Ollie stayed overnight; at least both vehicles are there."

"Don't be nosey," she chided.

"I'm not nosey. I'm proactive. She's our nanny. He's our ranch foreman. I don't want anyone screwing up the system."

"Colt! That sounds awful!"

"Well, what did you think when Ollie showed up here yesterday?" He laughed. "He was as nervous as a teenager going out on his first date! He shocked the hell out of me when he asked if Ellie could have the afternoon off."

Frank shook her head. "Not me! I saw that coming when we were out at the ranch for the roundup. Ollie got a light in his eye and a spring his step the moment he set eyes on her." Frank chuckled. "I remember thinking that there might be snow on the roof, but Ollie still had a fire in the stove! I'm surprised he took this long to make a move."

"You're kidding! I missed all that. I guess I didn't expect it of him."

"Why? Because he's older? Even old guys get lonely... and horny!"

"Horny?" Colt laughed. "The old dog spent the night there. Do you think..?"

"Colt! Now you really are being nosey. If they did, that's up to them. They are old enough to make their own choices, with no observations from you."

He looked at her with a twinkle in his eye. "So, are you

willing to make a bet?"

"Do you think he's going to come out here and tell you everything, you pervert?"

"If he's wearing a shit-eating grin and walking bowlegged, we'll know."

She gave him dig in the ribs. "He already walks bowlegged and he could be grinning from ear to ear because he's happy."

"Because he got to grease his pole!"

"That is crude! You're disgusting." They heard the trailer door close. "Shhh... here they come."

They watched Ellie and Ollie walk toward them. When they saw Colt and Frank sitting on the lounge, they spoke quietly to each other. Then they both laughed.

"See that shit-eating grin?" Colt murmured.

Ollie let Ellie precede him up the steps onto the veranda. Frank stood up and smiled. "Good morning, you two. We came out to drink our coffee and admire that fabulous sunrise." Her eyes met Ellie's. "Did you have breakfast or are you going to join us?"

She led the way indoors and Ellie followed her.

Ollie looked at Colt with a twinkle in his eye.

Colt couldn't control his grin. "So, you old dog, did you have a good visit?"

"Sure did. She's one hell of a woman. We were awake half the night." He stepped toward the door and then looked back at Colt. "Get your mind out of the gutter, you young pup. We weren't having sex. We were talking. Not that it's any of your business, but I can hear the wheels turning and I don't want you to disrespect such a wonderful lady."

Colt had the grace to look embarrassed.

Ollie laughed. "Gotcha! We took a bet on it when we saw the two of you sitting there. She didn't believe you'd think that, but us guys... well, we all think pretty much alike. I could read your mind as soon as I saw you sitting there."

"For God's sake, don't tell her. She's our nanny! I couldn't face her..."

Ollie was still chuckling when he went through the door. Colt followed him a few moments later, hoping his discomfort didn't show.

Ellie and Frank had gone upstairs to get the twins dressed. Colt offered Ollie a cup of coffee and asked him how everything was at the ranch. Ollie's eyes still twinkled, but he took up the conversation and Colt's embarrassment eased. When Ellie and Frank came down with the twins, pandemonium broke out. They ran to meet Colt and then they crawled all over Ollie.

Ollie's affection for them was undeniable. He beamed with pride like the grandfather he never would be, might have done.

Colt offered to help make breakfast, but Ellie and Frank shooed him out of their way. He suggested Ollie join him and they went into his office.

"I'm going to give Brad a call and see if we can finish putting up the turbines this week. I'm anxious to get that out of the way before we get cold and blowing snow."

The phone rang several times and finally went to the answering machine. Colt leaned back in his chair. "He isn't answering. He was going north to check out some of his turbine installations. He was taking Shauna Lee with him, but he said they'd be back today."

Ollie checked the time. "Well, it's only nine-thirty. They probably aren't back yet."

Colt nodded, tapping his pen against the desk. "You're right. And who knows what they'll end up doing." He grinned. "He and Shauna Lee seem to have a good thing going."

"Shauna Lee." Ollie looked thoughtful. "I wish she would sit down and talk with Patch. There are things that she needs to be told. He has talked to me some. I'm not excusing his actions, but there seems to be more to the story than she knows."

"It's hard to imagine that happening. Brad is extremely defensive of her. He has no respect for Patch whatever. He sees red whenever his name is mentioned."

Ollie shook his head. "Everyone has a story, Colt, but sometimes they aren't interpreted correctly."

Colt opened his mouth to speak just as the telephone rang. He looked at the call display and smiled. "Good morning, Brad."

They exchanged ordinary conversation and then Colt got to the point. "Could we finish installing those turbines this week while this weather is still holding?"

"That's at the top of my list. I have a few things to finish up before I head off to China on the twenty-third of this month. I can work with you tomorrow and the next day if that fits your schedule. We should be able to finish up by Tuesday night."

"We could stay at the ranch tomorrow night. It would speed things up."

"You can. I'm coming home. I want to spend as much time with Shauna Lee as I can before I leave. I'm going to be gone for a whole week."

Colt laughed. "You've got it bad, man!"

"Keep your opinions to yourself. How often do you go away for a week without Frank? Besides, Patch is still at the ranch isn't he? The more I learn about Shauna Lee's past, the more I want to strangle that bastard."

"Brad, there may be another side to ..."

"Screw that noise! I'm not interested."

After breakfast, Ollie and Ellie took the children for a walk. When they came back, Frank volunteered to give them a snack and put them down for their nap, giving Ellie the afternoon off.

Ollie and Ellie walked back to the trailer.

Frank and Colt went out and sat on the wicker lounge again. She looked at Colt and grinned. "So, you pervert. Are you mind peeking into Ellie's bedroom again?"

He grinned sheepishly and shook his head. "That sneaky old dog, I asked him if he'd had a good visit. He gushed about what a wonderful woman she was and about how they'd been awake half the night. I didn't say a word, but then he told me to get my mind out of the gutter. He informed me that they hadn't had sex, they had just talked."

"That is priceless!"

"That's not the best part. Or is it the worst part?" He grinned. "That old bugger guessed what I'd been thinking and he'd made a bet about it with her."

"Colt! That is awful!" She covered her face with her hands and groaned. "What did Ellie think?"

"Let's hope we never find out."

Ollie left at five o'clock that afternoon. Colt grinned and shook his head as he watched him drive down the road. "He's going to get home late. I guess age is irrelevant when you've got the hots."

"Do you realize that teenagers and twenty-year-olds probably think we are too old for sex? What do you think your parents' love life is like?"

"I've never actually given it much thought. After Dad had his heart attack..." He grinned. "But he is my dad. I guess he's probably still interested. I'm sure I will be at ninety-five. And I'll probably have to run to keep up with you."

CHAPTER FIFTEEN

Brad and Shauna Lee sipped beer as they watched the evening news. When it was over Brad looked at her. "I'm curious. How did you get your new birth certificate?"

"Brad... do we have to go through this?"

"I'm just curious."

She shook her head. "I'm not."

"You were a kid. How the hell did you do it?"

"You just have to get in touch with the right people."

"But how did you do that?"

"Jeez, Brad..."

"I'm not judging you. I'm just ... it boggles my mind."

She sighed heavily, knowing he wouldn't give up until she told him, "I... well, I told you that I- I slept with guys for money."

"You said that before."

"Well... one of the guys I got to know was a salesman. He traveled all over the country and he knew lots of people."

"How did you meet him?"

"I met him at the bar." She brushed away Brad's angry expression. "I know, I know... I was too young to be in bars, but when I dressed sexy, and put my hair up and wore makeup, I seldom got checked for ID. It only happened a couple of times."

She sighed. "Jeez, Brad, I don't want to tell you all this stuff. I really didn't... sleep with many guys, and after I met him, I didn't go with anyone else. He only came to town once in a while. He was older, probably thirty-five or so. Actually, he was a really nice guy. He realized how young I was after the first time, and we never had sex again.

"He wanted to know why I was doing what I was doing. He didn't like it. I explained what had happened. I told him that I just wanted to be anonymous and start over again and I was trying to save money so I could find a way to get a new birth certificate. I needed to have one so I could get a social insurance number and get a real job.

"After that, when he came into town, he would take me out for dinner and we would just talk about all kinds of things. He always paid me a lot and he was nice to me.

"When he came through town one time, he told me he had talked to someone who knew someone, who could take care of everything for me. I was thrilled. I told him I wanted to keep the name I was using and my birth date because I was already using that information.

"Three months later when he came back, he had everything I needed.

"I had a complete identity as Shauna Lee Holt and a complete history to back it up. I was born in Nunavut. My parents were Gregor and Helena Holt. They worked independently as geologists, doing mineral exploration around Ennadai Lake. I was born in a small cabin by the lake, out in the wilderness. My father delivered me and the place of birth was recorded in latitude and longitude.

"My parents were friendly with the Ihalmiut Inuits. Sometimes I stayed with them while my mom and dad flew out to camps further away. When I was five years old, my parents were killed in a plane crash. An Inuit family took me in and I lived with them until I was seventeen. Then I came to Saskatoon and started going to high school. They even included some background information about what it would have been like to live with my imaginary Inuit family."

She shook her head. "Brad, my new life was complete to the last detail. I could have been that girl; I became that girl."

"How much did it cost you?"

"He refused to take any money and he never told me how he got the paperwork. I've built my whole life around that information. For the first few years, I was scared to death, always looking over my shoulder, afraid that someone would show up and expose me as the fraud that I was. But once I got through university, I relaxed and accepted my life."

"So, what did this guy want in return?"

"Nothing; he made two stipulations. First, I had to use my new identity to get a real job, which was what I wanted it for anyway. The other was that I would never make money... selling my body... selling sex... again, but when he came to town, he wanted to see me. Honestly Brad, he never slept with me again. He only came back a couple more times and then I never saw him again. I often wondered what happened to him."

"This is kind of freaky, Shauna Lee. Think about it; if he could get you a new identity that quickly, you weren't the first one they'd done that for. Whoever did it was pretty sophisticated, and methodical. They would have needed access to government records, or I don't know how it could have worked."

Shauna Lee sighed and buried her face in her hands. Then she looked at him. "I know. It used to drive me crazy. For a while, I would go online and search to see if Gregor and Helena Holt really existed or if they were just made up. It took me awhile, but I did find them for real, Brad. They did live in Nunavut and they were geologists and they did die in a plane crash up there."

"That's identity theft. Well, not exactly, but it's certainly manipulating a dead person's identity to create another."

She sat staring at the TV. "I didn't mean any harm. I was just trying to protect myself." She wrapped her arms around herself. "But, I really am just a fraud, Brad. My whole life is a lie." Tears shimmered in her eyes. "I'm sorry I got you involved. I know you love me, but you need to walk away. Sometimes, no matter how much you care, the price is too high."

A look of shock crossed Brad's face. "Shauna that is *not* what I was getting at. No one could blame you for wanting to escape your past. After what I learned this weekend, I don't know how you held yourself together. I am proud of you.

"I'm even... I'm grateful that guy helped you. No matter what other shit he may have been involved in, he was sort of a... a guardian angel for you. It's the old double-edged sword; good and evil. Life is seldom black and white; there are always shades of gray. It depends on the point of view you look at it from. From your ... from *our* point of view, he did a good thing for you. He gave you a chance to escape a horrific past that was the result of a seriously dysfunctional family. He gave you a chance to build a new life."

He pulled her hands into his and held them tight. "But think about it, there are actually people out there doing that kind of thing. You read about it in books and you see it in movies. I've heard that people use false ID's, but I never dreamed that they did such a thorough job. It's unnerving. Can you trust anybody or anything?"

"I've been me, like this, for over twenty years. I trust in me."

He groaned. "I just keep pushing my foot farther down my own throat; when will I ever learn to leave good enough alone?" He pulled her into his arms. "Sweetheart, none of this really matters now. I wasn't judging you and please don't keep thinking that I'm going to leave you. It isn't going to happen. I'm stuck to you like crazy glue."

Shauna Lee was strangely calm; withdrawn and solemn. When he pulled her to her feet, she didn't respond with her usual smile. He put his arm around her waist and guided her to the bedroom, but her movements were automatic. *I've hurt her.* He reached to help her unbutton her shirt, but she shook her head and brushed his hand away.

"Shauna?"

"Not now, Brad."

He turned away and went into the bathroom. His heart was heavy. When he came back to the bed, she was lying on her back, staring at the ceiling. He slid into the bed from the other side and reached for her, but she didn't turn into his arms, and she didn't turn so he could hold her and spoon her from the back. She just lay there. The message was clear. She didn't want to be close tonight.

He reached for the hand that lay at her side next to him. He enveloped it in his, needing to touch her, to reconnect. She didn't pull it away, but let it lie limp in his clasp. Eventually, Shauna Lee fell asleep. Brad lay beside her, cursing himself for pushing her once again. Tears of anguish squeezed out of the corners of his eyes; spilling his grief for the pain she had suffered.

The next morning Shauna Lee responded to his touch. She kissed him, and she gave him a hug, but he still felt the emotional barrier she had erected. The sparkle wasn't there, the spontaneity. He felt like they'd lost their special connection and his heart ached.

Colt noticed his preoccupation when he picked him up. They had driven for several miles when he looked across at Brad. "Okay, man, something is going on here. Do you want to talk about it?"

Brad shook his head. "I'm sorry. I didn't realize I was such an open book. I can't really talk about this."

"Is it Shauna Lee?"

Brad nodded. "Her past just keeps coming back to hurt

her. I want to help somehow, but sometimes I think I do more harm than good."

"Well, you're right. This probably isn't something we should talk about. All I can suggest is that you have patience, man. I'm sure that you have gotten closer to her than anyone else. If you love her, don't give up."

"I'm not giving up. I just don't want her to shut down on me."

Shauna Lee was making dinner when Brad got home that night. She turned to smile at him. "I wasn't sure what time you'd get home. You're a little earlier than I expected."

"We have one tower and turbine up and ready to go. We'll do the other one tomorrow. I didn't want to be late tonight." He walked over to stand in front of her and put a hand on each of her shoulders. "It bothered me all day; you know, the way things went between us last night. I know you were trying this morning, but you weren't there yet. I just wanted to get back here so I could hold you like this." He wrapped his arms around her. "And I wanted to kiss you like this." He bent his head and claimed her lips. He felt the resistance in her yield and soften against him. "I love you, Tweetie Bird."

"I know that, Brad." She cradled his face between her hands. "It's just that sometimes I feel like I'm such a liability."

Brad worked his hands over her back, across her shoulders and up her neck where he threaded his fingers in her hair. "Tweetie Bird, you have never been a liability. You are not a liability. You never will be a liability." He looked into her eyes. "Quit questioning my judgment and good taste. You'll give me an inferiority complex."

She pressed her cheek against his chest. "I hope you'll always feel that way."

"There you go, questioning my judgment again." He kissed her forehead and then looked toward the stove. "I'm hungry, and something smells wonderful. What are you making?"

She lifted the skillet lid. "I cheated tonight. I picked up a package of Hamburger Helper and some fresh hamburger. I sautéed some chopped onions, peppers, celery and garlic and added it to the hamburger and left the meat to brown. After I added the hamburger and pasta mix, I threw in a fancy mix of frozen vegetables and left everything to simmer."

"It smells yummy. How soon can we eat?"

"After the table is set and I finish making the dressing for the salad." She opened the fridge, took out a salad bowl and set it on the counter. "Do you want a beer?" she asked as she reached for a dressing mix container.

Brad nodded as he went to the cupboard and took down two plates. Shauna Lee grabbed a lime and two bottles of Corona out of the fridge and put them on the counter. She grinned as Brad took out the cutlery.

He bumped her hip as he walked past her, murmuring softly in a sing-song voice. "Two plates, two cups, two knives, two forks, two spoons, always the same..."

She giggled. The sparkle was back in her eyes and her face was soft again.

They relaxed as they ate and shared the events of the day. Shauna Lee leaned forward and touched Brad's hand. "I got a call from Timothy Bates today. He'll be in Swift Current on Wednesday. He's going to meet Colt on Friday."

"That's great news." He looked thoughtful. "Would you...?"

"Would I be comfortable if you invited him to stay here for a few days?"

He nodded.

"I thought about that earlier. You know that it is instinct for me to close up, but I know you would enjoy having him stay for a few days. So the answer is yes. Go ahead and invite him."

"But, will you enjoy having him here?"

"He's your friend, so I probably will. It's not like he's going to be here forever and it'll give me a chance to get to know him a bit. I may have to take him out to the farm on Thursday. Colt wants him to go out there so he can show him around. At least he isn't anyone that can spring any more shocking news from my past on us!" She smiled apologetically. "I hope not anyway."

"Can you take Friday off?"

"Why?"

"Well, I leave for China on Sunday night."

"Already? I forgot it was so soon."

"Well, it is and I want to spend as much time as possible with you before I go. If you can play hooky, I will too."

She gathered the dishes off the table and put them in the dishwasher. "I'll have to give Christina a week off for filling in for me so often, but I think I can persuade her to let me off the hook for Friday."

"Tell her I'll bring her something special from China."

***

Timothy Bates arrived at eleven-thirty, Wednesday morning. He had called Brad when he came into town and got directions to the Windspeer office. He chuckled when his old friend came pushing through the door as his pickup rolled to a stop. Brad was opening his truck door before Timothy undid his seat belt.

"Hey there, guy. Is it ever good to see you. How was your trip?"

"It was pretty good, except for your crappy roads. Don't you guys pay your taxes? I came across from Edmonton to Lloydminster; the roads were perfect. I spent the night in Lloyd' and then headed down here this morning. Man, talk about narrow and rough roads; even the pavement is falling apart."

"They're working on them and things are getting better. Now that you've had your bitch session, how is everything else?"

"Well, your folks say hello. I really appreciate you putting in a word for me here. I hope this works out. I want to get away from the Peace River country. There is still a lot of stuff going on with the family. Marsha is still twisting the knife, wanting to bleed some more out of me. You were smart to never get married. I'm counting on you to hit me on the head if I ever get stupid enough to consider it again. Put me out of my misery before it gets started!"

"Ouch! You are a tad bitter. They're not all like Marsha, Tim."

"Show me one who isn't. In a hundred years, I might be interested." He closed the truck door and turned to Brad. "So what is Colt Thompson like?"

"I've done business with him and we've become friends. As far as I'm concerned he's an all-around, straight-up guy. He's got a good operation at the farm and I think you'll find him fair to work with. He's looking for a manager because he wants to move back to the ranch that he owns in the Cypress Hills. He's got a great wife, twins, and another one on the way. They are a happy family."

"And Shauna Lee Holt? I talked to her first. Is she his accountant?"

"She is. We're meeting her for lunch in about ten minutes. I think she's going to take you out to the farm tomorrow."

"Does everybody know everyone else in this town?

"It just turns out that way, in this case. I certainly don't know everyone in town. Anyway, we should get over to Shauna Lee's office."

Brad considered their recent conversation. He hadn't seen Tim for two or three years and he was surprised by his attitude. *He's so bitter. I hope I didn't stick my neck out to get it chopped off by giving him a good reference to Colt.*

He pulled up in front of *Swift Current Accounting and Bookkeeping Services*. "This is it. Shauna Lee owns the place and she handles Thompson Holdings accounting. So if you and Colt work out an agreement, you'll get to know this place well. Let's go in."

Christina's smile lit up her face when Brad walked in. "So

what will you bring back for me from China?"

"Give me some ideas! I'll do my best to find something worthwhile; maybe a statue of Buddha."

She laughed. "Yeah, I'll put it in my shrine to you!" She nodded toward Shauna Lee's office door, "Just go on in. I think you know the way," she said with a wink. "She's expecting you anytime, now."

Tim found himself wondering what was going on between Brad and the receptionist as he followed him to a half-closed office door. Brad pushed the door open and stepped inside. A petite, blue eyed, blonde turned from an open filing cabinet to greet them.

Her smile was radiant when she saw Brad. "You're here!" Her gaze shifted to Tim. "And you have to be Timothy Bates," she said extending her hand.

He took her hand and smiled. "Call me Tim."

"Ok, Tim. Did you have a good trip?"

Brad laughed. "He's really impressed with our roads!"

Shauna Lee chuckled as she grabbed her coat and purse. "Shall we go?" Her eyes met Brad's and held. As she walked up to him, he slid his arm around her waist and dropped a quick kiss on her hair. "I take it you're playing hooky on Friday."

"Did Christina tell you that?"

"Not exactly. She just asked me what I was going to bring her from China."

She gave him a quick smile. "I gave her next week off too. She's filled in a lot for me lately and if I keep really busy while you are gone, time will go faster for me." She reached up and touched his cheek.

Brad looked at Tim. "Sorry, I should have introduced you. This is Shauna Lee Holt. She is Colt Thompson's accountant, but she's my Tweetie Bird. You'll get to know her better when you stay over at our place tonight."

Tim's surprise was obvious. *Tweetie Bird,* he thought. *Whoa, fellow! I'm way behind the times here. Brad tied up with a woman, and she's living at his place! I hope he knows what the hell he's getting into.*

Tim nodded his acknowledgment to Shauna Lee, then followed Colt and her out of the room. Shauna Lee stopped at her receptionist's desk.

"Tim, this is Christina Holmes. She's my receptionist and right hand around here."

"Christina, this is Timothy Bates. He is a friend of Brad's from B.C., and he is here for an interview with Colt. You remember when he had us looking for someone suitable to manage the farm? Well, Tim is the man Colt decided to go with."

Christina stood up and reached out to shake hands with Tim. As they shook, she could sense his closed attitude. The energy he gave off was flat, the look in his eye was guarded and cool. Christina's bubbly nature immediately sensed his remoteness and she drew back. *Yuk! What a bloody cold fish*, she thought.

Shauna Lee's smile included both of them. "If things work out the way we hope they will, you two will get to know each other well."

Don't hold your breath, Christina thought.

The next morning Shauna Lee decided to drive her car out to the farm and have Tim follow her. Then she could come back to Swift Current to meet with Brad, and Tim could decide if he was coming back to Brad's place for the night, or if he would stay overnight at the farm. Brad had shown him where the spare key was so he could get in.

He had made it clear that he was taking the day off to spend time with Shauna Lee because he was going to be away.

They spent a lazy day at home, enjoying each other's company. Then Brad insisted on taking her out for supper. They enjoyed the meal, drank wine and relaxed. When they came home, Tim hadn't returned, so they spent the evening cuddling, kissing and stoking the sexual fire that shouldered between them. When it had fanned into a hot flame, they retired to the bedroom and exhausted it. They fell asleep in each other's arms.

Sunday morning came too quickly for both of them. Brad held her against him as they lay in bed. "I don't want to go, Tweetie Bird," he whispered. "I'm going to miss you."

Her fingers traced his lips. "I'm going to miss you too. Just be sure you come home to me."

He laid his head against her hair. "I promise you, I will come back."

"I'll be here waiting for you. We'll make up for the lost time when you get back." She kissed him, darting her tongue between his lips. "Remember this." She flicked her tongue again. "Take the memory with you and bring it back to me."

Brad smiled and pushed back the sheets. "Let's go make breakfast. I want to remember you sitting across the table from me, with those big blue eyes sparkling and that mass of soft blonde curls bouncing." He pulled on his pajama bottoms and went out to the kitchen.

She put on a cotton wrap and followed him. By the time she wandered into the kitchen, he had the coffee brewing.

He nodded to a brown paper bag on the counter. "You can empty that bag. I'll make scrambled eggs and bacon."

She looked at the bag. It was a large heavy brown paper one. As she reached for it, Brad glanced over his shoulder. "It's delicate. Be careful how you open it."

"What are you up to now?"

He just smiled as he turned back to making breakfast.

Shauna Lee opened the bag carefully and peered inside. She looked in quickly, pulled back, then looked again and frowned. "What on earth?" she said softly. She reached in again and touched a mound of black hair. Suddenly it moved, squirming, wiggling. Two dark eyes looked up at her. She gasped and jerked her hand back.

Brad laughed out loud. "It's not going to hurt you. Take it out and hold it. You'll love it."

"What is it?" She reached her hand into the bag again and a tiny tongue licked her fingers. She let her fingers close around the squirming, twisting little ball and she pulled it out. Brad watched her, savoring her incredulous expression.

"Oh, you little darling." Her eyes filled with happy tears as she buried her face in the tiny ball of fluff. "Brad, this is so... so special. What a tiny little puppy!"

She walked around the counter and leaned in to kiss him. "How old is he? Or is it she?"

"She is fourteen weeks old."

"She's so little. What is she?"

"She is a toy Havanese. She will always be a tiny little bundle of energy. She doesn't shed and apparently she is anti-allergenic. I wanted you to have something to keep you company; something for you to love and cuddle with while I am gone. When I get home, we'll both love and cuddle her, but she is yours. Her name is Karma."

"Karma." She nuzzled the puppy. "I like that."

"There is just one thing I want to make clear. She does not sleep in our bed with us. I refuse to share you there."

She snuggled the puppy in the crook of her arm and slipped the other one around Brad's neck. She pulled his ear down to her lips. She hesitated, then grinned as she shot the tip of her tongue into his ear and twirled it around. "She wouldn't be any competition for you, no one would."

Brad chuckled. "I hope not! I think we'd better eat now. We have to leave for Regina by ten o'clock."

Shauna Lee looked at him. "What am I going to do with her?"

"There is a small carrier in the back entry for her. I thought you'd want to take her with you; at least until she gets used to us and the place."

She gently placed the squiggly little package in his arms and ran to get the carrier. It was full of goodies: tiny doggy bones, some little toys, a dainty little collar and leash, water and food bowls, a soft pad on the bottom for her to lie on.

Shauna Lee's eyes sparkled. "Brad! You've thought of everything! You'll be a perfect daddy. To Karma I mean!" She blushed.

Brad's eyes met hers and held them. "I intend to be a perfect father when the time comes. And you'll be a perfect mother." Shauna Lee looked away. She picked up the puppy and deposited her in the carrier. She petted and talked baby talk to the dog as she reluctantly closed the door and secured it.

"Brad Johnson. You are the most wonderful, thoughtful man I have ever met." She wrapped her arms around his neck and rested her cheek against his. "I don't know how I'd live if I ever lost you."

He grabbed her by the arms and looked into her eyes. "I don't want you to think that way anymore. You are not going to lose me."

"I'm sorry. I've been afraid for so long, the thought just comes without me thinking about it." She buried her face into the curve of his neck.

As she watched his flight taxi down the tarmac, lift into the air and disappear in the distance, tears trickled down Shauna Lee's cheeks. A tight knot twisted in her stomach as she walked outside and went to her car in the parking lot. She unlocked the door, reached in the back seat, took out Karma's carrier and put it in front of the seat beside her.

She opened the door, took the little black ball of fluff out and tucked it into the curve of her neck. She sat, stroking it absently, her mind winging through the sky with Brad. Loneliness overwhelmed her. She broke down and cried.

Ten minutes later she placed Karma back in the carrier and started the car. She glanced at her watch. Brad was one-third of the way to Calgary already. At four-thirty, Alberta time, he would board his connecting flight and he would be in Vancouver at four-fifty nine, B.C. time. It would be six-fifty-nine in Swift Current, when he landed in Vancouver. She sighed. "The provincial time changes really mess up your head when you look at your watch."

She grabbed her purse, took out her cell phone and turned it on. He would probably call her when he landed in Calgary and she didn't want to miss him. She wanted to hear his voice.

Brad called before she was halfway home. His voice was full of love and concern. They talked briefly, because he had to hurry to make his connection to Vancouver.

Shauna Lee arrived at the house at six-thirty. She brought Karma's carrier into the house and took her out of it. The puppy stretched, enjoying her freedom. Shauna Lee put out a small dish of soft food and some water and watched her eat daintily.

Her cell phone was on the floor beside her and she answered it on the first ring. "Brad?"

"Hi, Tweetie Bird. Are you home yet?"

"We got home about half an hour ago. I'm sitting on the floor with Karma. She's eating out of the new bowl you bought her...Daddy. Where are you?"

"I'm waiting for my luggage to arrive on the carousel, Mommy. One day we'll discuss this mommy and daddy stuff, but now isn't the time for that."

"Brad..."

"We'll take everything in little steps, just like we have up 'til now. I miss you, sweetheart. I can almost feel you right here beside me. I can't tell you how many times I've already reached for your hand. It's almost a shock when I realize that you're not there."

"I miss you too. I'm going to sleep in your shirt and take Karma to bed with me."

"Just don't let her get the idea that she belongs there. Remember... I won't share you; even with her."

"Where did you get Karma?"

He chuckled. "I owe Christina big time for that. She helped me."

"Have I told you how much you mean to me?" she asked

softly.

"I'm listening. Tell me more."

"I miss you."

"I miss you too. My luggage just went around for the fourth time. I guess I'll have to go, love; I'll talk to you in the morning before I leave. I have to get to bed soon because I have to be at the airport at three in the morning. I fly out at six o'clock, B.C. time.

"Okay." She kissed into the phone and said goodnight.

Loneliness washed over her as the line went dead. She scooped up Karma and went to sit on the couch. She cuddled her and caressed her. Karma luxuriated in her affection. Shauna Lee bent down and dropped a kiss on her head. Memories flooded through her. For a moment, she was holding Ben again. Her heart filled with love as she looked into his beautiful little face.

Karma jumped up and tried to lick her face. Shauna Lee startled, coming back to reality with a jolt. Her eyes brimmed with tears as she lifted the puppy to her face and kissed it. *My baby.*

She turned the TV on in an effort to dispel her loneliness. She surfed through the channels, finding nothing that held her attention. Finally, she went to bed, taking Karma with her. She slept fitfully, missing Brad's warmth, his arms around her. Karma was a comfort, but she couldn't compete with Brad.

When the phone rang at six o'clock, she snatched it from the night table. Before she could say hello she heard Brad's voice saying, "Good morning, beautiful. I hope you slept better than I did." His voice spilled over her, rich and sexy.

"Didn't you sleep?"

"Not much. I missed you."

"I missed you, too. As sweet as Karma is, she is no competition for you."

"That's a big relief. I was worried."

"You adorable goof. Where are you?"

"I'm waiting in line at the airport. I'm calling a little early, but I wanted to hear your voice."

"Brad, do you have to be gone for a whole week? Couldn't you do all this over the internet and come back home?"

"I've already done as much of that as I can. I'll be home earlier if I possible, but my schedule is pretty tight, as it is. I'll call you when I get to Beijing. I have to go now, Tweetie Bird, I'm next in line. I love you."

"I hope you know how much you mean to me, Brad."

"I do sweetheart. Maybe you even love me a little bit."

Tears filled her eyes. "Maybe," she whispered. "Hurry home to me!"

"I will. Bye, love. I'll talk to you soon." The line went dead.

She held the phone to her lips and kissed it. *Maybe you even love me a little bit.* "Why can't I say it to him?" she whispered. "I love you. Three little words, but they just won't come. I know he loves me and I know he won't leave me. Cripes, he knows everything about me now and he's still here. What's wrong with me?"

Shauna Lee had a busy week. She had made sure of that when she had given Christina the week off. She took Karma to work with her every day. The junior associates made a fuss over her, but for the most part she stayed in the carrier under the reception desk, by Shauna Lee's feet.

Colt and Tim stopped in on Tuesday. From all appearances, everything was working out and Tim would probably take over management of the farm. Colt was taking him around town and introducing him to the merchants that he dealt with regularly.

They were still negotiating some of the finer points of the agreement, but everything sounded positive. Shauna Lee smiled when they left her office. It felt good to know that her intuition had not let her down.

Brad called three times that week. Each call was a hurried message, filled with loneliness and love. The stress of doing business in an unfamiliar environment, as well as being away from her, was wearing on him. He knew he couldn't hurry the trip, but he was chafing to be on his way home.

When Shauna Lee opened the office Friday morning, loneliness was heavy in her heart. She was early and she sat behind the reception desk with Karma on her lap. Shauna Lee stroked her and talked to her softly, thankful that Brad had anticipated her loneliness and given her something cuddly and living to focus on. "One more sleep and Daddy will be home," she whispered.

Christina stopped in for coffee at three o'clock. She brought each of them coffee from Tim Horton's and half a dozen donuts. Christina took over her chair at the desk and picked up Karma. She looked at Shauna Lee with a smile. "Isn't she a sweetie?" She ran her fingers over the puppy's head with a smile. "Shauna Lee, I hope you realize how lucky you are. Brad is so crazy about you. I might even consider marriage if I met a guy who loved me the way he loves you."

"I do know how lucky I am. He is wonderful and I've missed him like crazy. I'm counting down; one more sleep until he's home. Karma is a sweetie, but she is definitely not him."

Christina laughed. "He's good for you. You probably have no idea how much you have changed since he's come on the scene."

"I know one thing. I never imagined anyone could work their way into my heart like he has. I don't know what I would do without him now."

"I'd say you don't have to worry about that." She held out the box of donuts. "Eat! You look like you have lost five pounds this past week. You'll blow away if you keep it up."

Shauna Lee drained her cup of coffee and tossed it in the garbage. "Will you stay at the desk while I go to the washroom?"

"Go!"

When Shauna Lee came back down the hall, she heard Christina talking. She stepped into the reception area and stopped dead. Her face went white and momentarily, she couldn't find her voice.

Christina looked at her with surprise. "Shauna Lee? What is wrong?" She turned to look at the man in front of her, puzzled.

"I'm her dad. She doesn't want to see me, but I have to talk to her."

When Shauna Lee spoke, her voice was filled with anger. "How dare you come here? You know I don't want anything to do with you."

Patch Bergeron stood his ground. "I'm not leaving until we talk."

"Screw you!" Shauna Lee yelled. "You didn't want anything to do with me thirty-five years ago. I haven't seen you for over twenty years. Why the sudden urge to see me now?"

Shock registered on Christina's face. *What is going on here,* she wondered.

Patch nodded, his hazel eyes holding Shauna Lee's blue ones. "I was wrong. In twenty years, I've come to realize that. I am ashamed of what I did, but I need to explain; to tell you the truth."

Shauna Lee stormed into her office and slammed the door. Christina stared after her and then looked at Patch.

"I'm not leaving until I talk to her."

"I- I'll go in and see what I can do." Christina slowly opened the door. "Shauna Lee," she said softly. Shauna Lee was standing at the window, staring outside. Her cheeks were wet with tears when she turned to face her.

"He says he's not going to leave until he talks to you."

"Jeez, I wish Brad was here. He'd throw him out into the street. What does he think he has to say that's so important now, after all these years?"

"Shauna Lee, I don't know your history with him, but he's determined to talk to you. I'll come in and sit with you if you want."

Shauna Lee shook her head and dashed the tears from her cheeks. "Send the useless bastard in here. There's nothing he can do or say that will make any difference now."

Christina went out and brought Patch to the door. Shauna Lee glared at him as he closed it behind him. She crossed her arms over her chest, symbolically closing him out. "Alright. Have your say and then get out."

"LeeAnn, will you sit down... can we sit down?"

"LeeAnn does not exist anymore."

"No matter what you call yourself, you're still LeeAnn Bergeron."

She sneered. "I guess you'd know, wouldn't you. How did you decide on Patch?"

He looked at her steadily. "My first name is Patrick. It always has been. Aaron is my middle name. My family called me that because my dad's name was Patrick, too. Patch is the nickname the ranch hands gave me. After all these years, it's become my name.

"And after all these years, I am Shauna Lee Holt." She walked to her chair behind the desk and sat down. She motioned to him. "Sit down and let's get this over with. Tell me your story and get out."

"It's not a story, it's the truth."

"As if I would believe anything you said."

Patch ignored the jibe. "Lee... Shauna Lee. Your mom and I..."

Shauna Lee bristled. He didn't miss that fact.

"Just listen, please. When I married your mom, I was crazy in love with her. She was beautiful. You remind me of her... except for your coloring and those... those big blue eyes.

"She was sexy and full of fun. But after three years of marriage, I discovered that I- I... that she didn't really love me. I was just a fill-in."

"How can you say that?"

"One time when she was mad at me, she told me so and I knew that she meant it." He twisted his hands together. "I was devastated. I should have set her free, but part of me still loved her and another part of me wanted to hurt her the way she'd hurt me.

"Besides that, where would she have gone? What would she have done?" He looked at her. "In those days, it wasn't like today. We didn't have any money. We would have both been struggling on our own. And I had my pride. What would people think?"

He shrugged. "I started drinking. It helped me forget; it helped me make her angry; it helped me get even with her for what she'd done to me. The bottle became my lover."

He looked out the window and swallowed hard. "Then she got pregnant. I felt ashamed. I'd never touched her with love since she had told me there was someone else." He shook his head. "We had sex, but I never made love to her. She submitted to me, but I made sure she knew that I... that I hadn't forgiven her."

He stood up and walked to the window. "When you were born, I was so proud, and I loved you completely. You were beautiful, but as you got older... you didn't look like either one of us. You had blonde curls and those beautiful big blue eyes. No one in my family had blue eyes. And your mom's eyes were so dark, they were almost black. Your Grandma Holt's eyes were as dark as your mom's."

He turned to look at her. "Your eyes were so striking. I kept thinking about them. Then one day I remembered where I had seen them before."

Shauna Lee sucked her breath in. *Oh, no, no, no!*

"It was like a kick in the gut when it came back to me. One night we were at a house party. A guy I didn't know was there and I suspected that Marie had known him before. She danced with him all night. She flirted with him; they were all over each other. I was jealous and I drank until I passed out.

"When I put it all together in my mind, I confronted her with my suspicions. She denied everything, but I wouldn't let it go. I constantly kept after her about it. One day I pushed her far enough; she defiantly admitted that she had gone to the barn with him.

"I couldn't stand looking at you after that; seeing your curly blonde hair and those blue eyes was like a knife in my heart. I couldn't deny what stared me in the face every day. You were not my child. I knew you were his."

Shauna Lee covered her face and sobbed.

Patch walked over to her. He put his arms around her for the first time in thirty-five years. She stiffened and then collapsed. "I am so sorry, LeeAnn. I couldn't think clearly for years; not until I left and got away." He shook his head, sadly. "Your mom and I were both selfish and filled with anger and misery. Without thinking about what we were doing, we hurt you the most, and you were the only innocent one." He kissed her forehead.

"I've had twenty years to think about what we did to each other, and to you. I was so stubborn and proud that I wouldn't forgive her. She knew she'd hurt me. Eventually, I just wore her down and she became lost in the defeat of my endless rejection. We continued to live in that same vicious cycle year after year, destroying each other and everything around us."

Shauna Lee sobbed and he held her until she pulled away.

"When I got older, I realized that you didn't love each other," she said. "I have wondered how Andre was ever conceived."

"I forced her one night when I was drunk. I'm ashamed to admit that I did that quite often in those days, but she never got pregnant. I thought I was sterile. When she got pregnant, I thought she must have been with someone else. But she was so despondent, that I couldn't imagine her having sex with anyone else.

"When Andre was born, he looked like me right from day one. I couldn't deny it. And I loved him like I loved no one else; except your mom when I first married her."

"Things were better between you and Mom for a while

weren't they?"

"Yes. It's amazing what our guilt and our love for Andre did for a time. And then..." Patch walked back to the window. His shoulders were shaking and she heard him smother a sob.

Shauna Lee did the unimaginable. She walked over to him and put her arms around him. "And then Andre died," she whispered sadly.

He shook his head. "No! Then I *killed* him. I was drunk and I ran over my own son with the tractor."

"It was an accident."

Patch was crying, his body wracked with sobs. "I'll never forget that... seeing him lying there. I wished I could trade places with him. You can't know much how I wanted to.

"I couldn't face what I'd done. I needed to blame someone else, so I blamed you. And I shot your horse. I was so... I was so cruel to you... and to your mom."

He tried to collect himself and control his emotions. "After that, I totally lost myself in the bottle, and your mom lost herself in the black hole I'd forced her into. Then, like a coward, I ran away and left you to fend for yourself."

He pulled away from her. "I've been a coward all my life, Lee... Shauna Lee. I didn't have the guts to try to make things work with your mom. I made her life hell. I was a shameful bastard to you.

"I don't expect forgiveness. I don't deserve it. I can't forgive myself. I've thought about ending it all, but in some way, I believe that living with the understanding of what I've done is my punishment. I live in my own hell every day."

They clung to each other; two strangers crying together; a father and a daughter as they had never been.

Patch cradled Shauna Lee's head. "It's too late to change the past, but I had to tell you the truth. I couldn't live with you believing that your own flesh and blood could have treated you the way that I did. Real fathers don't do that. I realize that I was the only dad you ever knew, but I never truly was a dad to you."

There was a gentle tap at the door. Shauna Lee looked at her watch, knowing it was Christina. "Just lock up and go home, Christina."

"Are... are you sure? Are you alright?"

"We'll be done here pretty soon. And Christina, thanks for filling in for me."

Shauna Lee walked back to her chair and sat down. Patch looked at her uneasily. She motioned for him to sit down as she reached for the box of tissues. She pulled out a couple and handed them to him, then took some for herself. After they had both wiped away the tears and blew their noses, they sat and looked at each other.

"I'll leave now if you want me to."

She shook her head. "I'm not sure what we do now." She sighed. "I wish Brad was here. He'd know what to do."

Patch smiled ruefully. "If he was here, we'd never have had this conversation. Ollie mentioned he was out of the country, and I knew this would be a chance to talk to you. That's why I came today."

Shauna Lee was shocked. "You came here today because he was away?"

"Well, he's so protective of you that he's like a bloody guard dog. He has no use for me; he's made that clear." His smile was drawn. "I'm glad that you have someone like him in your life. It's obvious that he loves you and he makes it his business to take care of you. He's a good man Shauna Lee." He looked at his watch. "I don't know how you feel, but this has been really tiring for me. I'm hungry. Would you let me take you out for supper?"

She pleated the sleeve of her shirt with her fingers. "We can't go back and change the past. I closed the door on my life as LeeAnn Bergeron over twenty years ago. I tried to bury everything and forget it ever happened. But Brad says it has colored my whole life and it still is part of who I am. He has helped me deal with a lot of memories. Meeting you at the ranch that day was such a shock."

She looked at him. "Good, bad or indifferent, you are the only dad I've ever known. To be honest, until Andre was born I didn't realize that you didn't love me. I guess even then, I didn't get it. Sometimes I wished you would play with me the way you did with him. I knew you and Mom fought. I was devastated when Andre died, but when you shot Poko... then I despised you. And I have ever since."

Patch shifted in his seat uncomfortably. He swallowed hard and looked away.

She sighed. "Instinctively, I want to slam this door closed right now." She shuddered. "But I guess that would just continue the cycle of pain and the lack of forgiveness that made such a mess of all our lives from the very start. Neither of us can start to heal until we face this."

He looked at her then, his eyes brimming with tears.

"I'm glad you insisted on this meeting," Shauna Lee continued. "What you've told me has made sense of some of the things I couldn't understand. I understand how hard it had to be for you to look at me every day and know what had happened." She shuddered as she covered her eyes with her hands.

Patch swallowed hard. "It doesn't excuse how I acted; you were innocent, the product of our selfishness."

Shauna Lee shrugged and reached for her purse. "I can't tell you that I'll ever be able to love you, but after what you have told me, forgiveness is not an issue. I guess we have twenty years to work through. I'll go for supper with you."

She stood up and reached for her jacket. Patch stood and went to the door. He opened it and waited while she shut off the lights and stepped past him. His hand reached out to touch her arm.

"Thank you," he said softly.

She nodded and went to the reception desk. Christina had closed Karma's carrier and left it on top of it. Shauna Lee looked at Patch. "I need to let her out to run around for a bit. She is trained to use a box in the back and I should give her something to eat. Is it all right if we wait about fifteen minutes?"

He nodded. "She's a cute little thing."

"Brad gave her to me the day he left for China. He wanted me to have her so she would keep me company."

Patch smiled. "He's a thoughtful man."

Shauna Lee smiled. "He is wonderful." She thought for a moment and then reached for her cell phone. "I'm surprised I haven't heard from him." She checked her messages.

"Jeez," she said softly. "He called four times. How did I miss him?" She checked her phone. "Oh, the ringer's shut off. He's probably left Beijing already. With the time difference... he'll be in the air by now. And he'll be worried about me."

The evening went quickly and Patch and Shauna Lee made a tenuous start toward healing their relationship. He filled her in on his years at the Gang Ranch. She shared with him how she had gone to university, got her CA, and ended up buying *Swift Current Accounting and Bookkeeping Services*. He didn't bring up anything about the baby and if he had, she would have refused to discuss the subject.

They parted easily. She knew she could have offered to have him spend the night at the house, but she didn't. She needed time to absorb everything and time to think. It had been a day full of unexpected revelations and she wished Brad were there.

CHAPTER SIXTEEN

Brad arrived in Vancouver at nine-thirty Saturday morning. It was ten-fifteen by the time he reached the luggage carousel. He hadn't been able to connect with Shauna Lee before he'd left Beijing. Worry and anxiety gnawed at his gut. He flipped open his phone and dialed her cell again. It rang three times before she answered.

"Brad?" she cried. "Is that you?"

Relief flooded through him. "Tweetie Bird. You had me worried. I couldn't get you before I flew out yesterday. Where were you?"

"When I realized that I'd missed you, it was too late. I accidentally shut the ring tone off. Yesterday was a crazy day. Normally I would have been checking it constantly, but yesterday I was fighting to keep my equilibrium."

"What happened?"

"I'll fill you in when you get here. Just hurry home. I've missed you like crazy. I needed to feel your arms around me so badly last night."

"Where are you now?"

"Karma and I have just left home. We're on our way to Regina." She smiled. "Do you want me to book the honeymoon suite at the Coast Inn or do you want to drive home and sleep in our own bed?"

"Do you mind if we drive home? I want the comfort of our own bed tonight."

"That sounds good to me. We can sleep in tomorrow."

"I can hardly wait to feel your body against mine. I love you, Tweetie Bird."

"Uh huh, maybe, too. I've missed you like crazy!"

"Did I hear you say you loved me?"

She smiled. "Maybe."

"Be careful, sweetheart. One of these times, you are going to slip up and say it. I'll see you at about four-thirty."

She smiled as the line went dead.

Shauna Lee was at the airport two hours early. It was a cool afternoon. She walked Karma through the parking lot, letting both of them stretch and get some exercise. Excitement bubbled in her mind, anxiety knotted in her gut and sexual anticipation tightened in her groin.

She alternated between checking the time and peering longingly into the sky. Her logic told her that Brad's plane was barely halfway to Calgary, but her emotions told her that time was passing at an agonizingly slow pace.

She stooped to pick up Karma and snuggled her in the curve of her neck. "I love you," she whispered. *Both of you,* she thought. She closed her eyes and swallowed hard. *I don't know if I should dare to think that, but I do love you, Brad.* A flicker of uncertainty rippled through her, followed by a shimmer of fear. "No," she whispered, pushing it away. "Brad would never hurt me."

At four o'clock, she put Karma back in her carrier and put it on the back seat, out of the sun. Even though it was getting chilly, she lowered all the windows a fraction and locked the doors to keep her safe. While she approached the airport terminal, she looked into the sky, searching for Brad's plane.

When she stepped through the door, she realized that her heart was pounding and she felt nervous. She stood looking out the airside viewing area, watching for it to land. She heard the arrival announcement and then it was taxiing up the runway.

She moved to stand near the escalator. She was shocked to realize that she was trembling. She wrapped her arms around herself, attempting to control the involuntary reaction. Her eyes were glued to the landing at the top.

She was so intent that she almost missed seeing Brad come bounding down the stairs next to it. His eyes were focused on her and the smile on his face was dazzling. When their eyes met, she gasped and moved toward him. Tears of joy filled her eyes, as he enfolded her in his arms.

They were kissing hungrily, their hands pulling each other close.

"Shauna Lee," he whispered. "I never knew a week could be so long." He pulled back and looked into her eyes, smiling as he brushed her tears away. "Tweetie Bird, I missed you so much." He hugged her against him again. "I can't tell you how much I love you."

"I love you, too, Brad."

She felt him tense and then he looked into her eyes. "What did you say? Did I hear you right?"

She smiled through her tears. "Maybe."

"We'd better get out of here before I embarrass us." He grabbed her hand and led her outside. "Where are you parked?"

"What about your luggage?"

He looked surprised, then grinned sheepishly. "I got so excited I forgot about that." He turned her toward him. "You did say you loved me, didn't you?"

She smiled. "Maybe."

"I guess I'm going to have to make love to you slowly until you are begging me for mercy and then you'll say it again. After this past week, I'm definitely up for the challenge." He grasped her hand and pushed it against the hardness in his jeans. "Wouldn't you agree?"

She kissed him quickly. "Quit talking and get your luggage. I'll bring the car around to meet you."

He watched her dart across the parking lot, then turned and went inside. When he came back out, she was waiting at the curb for him.

He was grinning from ear to ear. "It is so good to be home and have you close. I can't wait to get even closer."

"Hang on, big guy. This car is pretty small. We'd better get on the road. We've got a two and a half hour drive ahead of us."

He groaned as he reached across the console and slid his hand along the inside of her thigh. She shivered and grabbed it in hers, holding it still.

"I've changed my mind. I can't wait that long. I've dreamed of the feel of your skin against mine all week; and my poor friend here..." He stroked the hardness behind his zipper. "He's so tired of cold showers, it's a wonder he doesn't have hypothermia."

He leaned over and slid his tongue into her ear. "Find a motel or a hotel room... whatever, just make sure it's soundproof and has a king-sized bed. I don't want everyone else to hear you begging... just me."

She pulled away as his tongue twirled around in her ear. She shivered. "Behave yourself and help me decide where to go."

"It can't be that hard to find. There's a Days Inn near the airport. I remember looking at it online and it had king-sized beds."

"Karma is here too."

"I'll put her in my garment bag."

"You're bad."

"But I'm good at what counts!"

When they walked into the King Suite at the Days Inn,

Shauna Lee whistled softly. "Brad, how much did this cost?"

"Insane, but I intend to get my money's worth." He grabbed the *Do Not Disturb* sign and put it on the door. Then he reached for her. His kiss left her weak in the knees, clinging to him. He groaned as he rubbed himself against her. He reached for the hem of her shirt and started to lift it.

She pushed him away. "We have to take Karma out of your garment bag." She smiled softly as she traced his lips with her finger. "And I think we are going to be busy for a while, so we'd better give her something to eat and some water before we get too involved."

He groaned. "You're right." They laid bath towels in the tub and put Karma onto them. Shauna Lee gave her some soft food on a saucer that she took off the counter by the coffee pot. She put water in the ice bucket and set it by the drain. "I feel mean, putting her in the tub."

"It gives her more freedom than she'd have in her carrier, and she's fed. And I'm hungry," he said as he reached for the hem of her shirt again, "for you."

She sighed as he guided her out of the bathroom and back to the bed. Everything happened quickly. Blatant lust fuelled their urgency. There would be time later to savor their lovemaking but for now, the overwhelming need won out.

"So much for making you beg," he whispered. "I've missed you. I've missed us... I kept reaching for your hand; on the train, in a car, in the bed. It felt like part of me was missing."

"I missed you too."

His arms tightened around her briefly. "I love you so much, Tweetie Bird."

She buried her face against his chest. "I..." She shut her eyes. "I love you too, Brad." She raised her face and looked into his eyes. "There. I- I said it." Tears filled her eyes. "I love you," she whispered.

He expelled a deep breath. "I wasn't sure that I'd ever hear you say those words." He cupped her face. "I've waited so long for you to tell me that. Sweetheart, you can't imagine what it means to me."

"I'm afraid, Brad. I can't lose you. Anything I've ever loved...."

He touched his finger to her lips. "Shhhh... remember, you aren't supposed to think that way anymore. That is not going to happen."

"What if I am a jinx?"

He held her close. "You're not a jinx! Shauna Lee, everything and everybody that you have lost; that all happened before you were eighteen years old, and none of it was your fault." He nuzzled his face into her hair.

"And look at what you have done since then. You are strong and resilient and what you have achieved is beyond most people's imagination. You started over with nothing and you fought tooth and nail to build a life for yourself, and you've done it."

She rolled onto her back and stared at the ceiling. "When it comes down to it, I am the reason that everything went wrong in the first place."

"Shauna Lee ..."

"I had a visit from my dad... I mean Patch, yesterday."

Brad shot up on the bed. "That bastard!"

"He came to the office and he wouldn't leave until he had talked to me."

"You mean he came to shift more blame onto you. What an asshole!"

"He didn't do that. He apologized for being such a bad father."

"I guess he should have," Brad responded heatedly.

"Nothing is simple, Brad. He explained things that made more sense about what I remember happening between him and Mom."

"Why would you believe anything he said?"

"I probably wouldn't have if I hadn't gone to Glaslyn with you."

"What has that got to do with him?"

"Do you remember what Bob Matzlan told me about him and Mom meeting at a party?"

Brad thought for a moment and then he nodded.

"Well, Dad pretty much confirmed what he said."

"No...."

"Dad didn't know who Bob was, but he knew Mom had been with him."

"Shauna Lee ..."

"He told me he was crazy about Mom when they got married. A couple years later, they had a fight and she told him she had always loved someone else. He was hurt and angry and he couldn't get past it. He started drinking.

"One night they were at a house party and some guy showed up. He said Mom and the guy danced and flirted all night. He said they were all over each other. Dad was angry and jealous and he drank until he passed out.

"Later when Mom was pregnant, he was excited because he thought it was his child. Even when I was born, he still thought so. But I was blonde and I had these blue eyes. It bothered him because there were no blue eyes in his family. Mom's eyes were so dark they were almost black and so were Grandma's. Eventually, he remembered the guy at that party; his blonde hair and blue eyes, and he knew. I guess eventually Mom admitted that she'd gone to the barn with him."

She turned and looked at him. "I was a constant reminder of her betrayal, and he... he couldn't stand to be around me."

"That would be hard," Brad admitted. "But why didn't he divorce her instead of making your life hell."

"He said he should have, but part of him still loved her and part of him wanted to punish her for what she'd done. He never forgave her. They just lived year after year in their own hell, and I was the reason."

"That is not true. I could pound that man into the ground. How dare he dump that on you?"

"No, Brad. That's not what he did. He wanted me to know

that my own flesh and blood had not treated me the way he had."

"Damn! I leave you for a week and this happens."

"I really wished you were here last night, but I can't count on you to rescue me all the time." She looked at him seriously. "Brad... he couldn't have told me this if you'd been here. You would have run him off."

"Damned right, I would have! The nerve of him; coming to your office."

"But, I'm glad he did. Finally, I understand what happened. When I was young, it was hard to accept that he wouldn't play with me, especially when I saw him with Andre. I couldn't understand why he wasn't the same with me. He wouldn't even touch me."

He pulled her close. "Sweetheart, that doesn't make you a jinx. That was their problem. You were a victim."

"It seems like my whole life has been like that."

Brad shook his head. "No, sweetheart... that first part of your life was, but everything that happened then, including you ending up with that Dave jerk: all of that happened because you didn't have a real family."

"Brad, do I know how to be different?"

"Shauna Lee ..." His voice was filled with anguish. He shook his head. "I wish my love could heal you, but you have been through so much." He looked into eyes. "Sweetheart, maybe we need to get professional help."

She stiffened. "What are you saying?"

"Maybe we need to go for counseling."

She pulled away. "No! I'm not going there!"

"Shauna Lee, you've been hurt so badly and you have never really dealt with any of it. You just pushed your pain down and buried it." He reached for her chin and tried to turn her face toward him.

"Brad, you say you love me. Why can't you ever just accept me the way I am?" She pushed his hand away and rolled over, turning her back to him.

"Sweetheart, it's not that I don't accept you. I don't want you to live in fear or always feel that you are not worthy of happiness."

"Well, it feels like you're telling me I'm not good enough the way I am!"

Brad's heart fell. "Shauna Lee... that is not what I meant. I would be with you every step of the way. I need to understand all this, too."

He slid his arm around her waist and tried to snuggle against her, but she pushed his arm away.

"Well, you can forget it. I am not subjecting myself to that. I've bared my soul to you and now that isn't enough."

"Sweetheart?"

She lay tense and didn't answer.

Damn, I stuck my foot in my mouth again. He groaned.

They both tossed and turned, but sleep wouldn't come. At nine o'clock Brad got up and walked to the window. Shauna Lee got up and went into the bathroom. She came out with Karma in her arms.

Brad turned to face her. He could see the hurt in her eyes. He crossed the room and pulled her into his arms. Karma wiggled between them. Shauna Lee did not relax against him.

He sighed. "Shall we go home? This hasn't turned out the way I planned." He walked away to pick up his garment bag. "I think it's got to be these King-sized beds. The last time we rented one, we didn't sleep either." There was no humor in his voice, only anxiety.

Shauna Lee picked up the dog carrier and put Karma into it. She collected Karma's things from the bathtub. She gathered up the towels and threw them on the bathroom floor. Wordlessly, she put Karma's toys in her overnight bag and picked up her jacket.

Brad tucked Karma into the garment bag and looked around. "I guess that's everything. Are you ready to go?"

Shauna Lee nodded and opened the door. She stepped into the hall and Brad followed. They took the elevator down

Full Circle

to the lobby. The clerk looked puzzled when Brad dropped off the key and told him that they were checking out.

Shauna Lee handed him the car keys and the two and a half hour drive home was made in uncomfortable silence. When they drove into Swift Current, Brad pulled into the A&W drive-thru. "I'm starved. I haven't eaten since breakfast. How about you?"

Shauna Lee swallowed hard. She started to shake her head and then changed her mind. "Yes. I'm hungry."

"Do you want a hamburger?"

"Yes, please."

Brad ordered two cups of coffee and three hamburgers.

"I guess you are hungry," Shauna Lee said with a faint chuckle.

"I am. I was so excited about coming home that I didn't think to grab lunch. And then I couldn't wait to make love to you..."

"And I spoiled that," she said sadly.

He reached for her hand and she let him take it. "You didn't spoil it, Tweetie Bird. I should have thought before I spoke. I didn't intend to upset you. You have to know I would never hurt you; that I was only thinking of what would help you.

"I know, but I don't want to talk to a stranger about my life."

"We'll drop the subject. It was just a suggestion."

They stopped in the parking lot and ate. When Brad was finished, he sighed with satisfaction. "I was hungry. And, that was my first hamburger since I touched down on Canadian soil again."

"I needed to eat, too. It's going to feel good to go home and fall into our bed now," she said with a faint smile.

Brad reached out and squeezed her hand. "I've missed cuddling with you."

Tears glistened in her eyes. "I have missed it too. Karma is adorable, and she did sleep with me, but she is no substitute for you."

They went straight to bed. Their sexual desire had been subdued. They both needed the healing comfort of feeling skin against skin; Brad's chest against Shauna Lee's back with his arm around her waist holding her against him, their legs tucked together.

Shauna Lee lifted his hand to her lips and kissed it softly. "I do love you, Brad Johnson," she whispered.

"And I love you, Tweetie Bird

The skies were gray when they woke up the next morning. Shauna Lee turned in Brad's arms to face him. She ran her hands along his jaw, up over his cheeks and into his hair.

Brad shifted onto his back and eased her into the curve of his shoulder. "Hmm. This feels good, holding you like this."

He was silent for a few moments, then pushed up on his elbow and looked into her sleep-flushed face. "Tweetie Bird, this may not be good timing and it isn't the way I planned to do this, but I want you to think about what I'm going to say. I thought about it all the time while I was away, and I want to marry you. I want to spend the rest of my life with you."

Her blue eyes widened. She looked frightened as she shook her head.

He kissed her. "I did say I wanted you to think about it for a while." He lightly brushed the tip of her nose. "You always say 'no' at first. I haven't asked you yet, but I'm going to do it now. Will you marry me, Shauna Lee Holt?"

Tears filled her eyes.

He smiled. "I know what your answer would be right now. Just think about it for a few days or hours and then give it to me."

She shook her head. He placed a finger across her lips. "Not now," he said with a teasing smile. "Get used to the idea. And remember, when I really want something..."

"...you don't take no for an answer." She finished his sentence. "Brad you know this scares me to death."

He nodded. "That's why I told you to think about it. The question is open-ended, with no pressure! Well, not much anyway. I'll wait an hour or two for your answer." His hand slipped down to tickle her ribs.

She writhed and he laughed. "I thought about that when I was in China, too. I didn't know if you were ticklish. I had to find out before I married you."

She smacked him playfully. "No pressure eh?"

"Of course not. Just say 'Yes' and I'll go shopping for a ring tomorrow like I'd planned to do before I lost my head just now and jumped the gun.

CHAPTER SEVENTEEN

Sunday morning, Colt sat behind the desk in his office. He smiled across it at Tim Bates. "So are you satisfied with everything?"

Tim reached across the desk and Colt clasped his hand. "I think the arrangement works for both of us. I'm happy if you are."

"So now we just need to find a place for you to live."

"I'll check around town. Brad should be back this weekend. He may have some ideas."

Colt stood up and stretched. "We'll come up with something between the two of us. Let's go have a coffee."

They went into the kitchen. Frank was sitting at the table poring over house decorating magazines. She rubbed her lower back as she looked up them. "Ideas, ideas, ideas! This is so exciting, but how do you decide which way to go?"

"Talk to Mona. It's her job to help you decide." He walked over to the coffee pot and set it up to brew. "Tim and I have come to an agreement. We just have to do the paperwork and he will officially be the new manager of the farm. Next, we have to find a place for him to live until we move out to the ranch."

Frank grimaced when she stood up. "That's great news, Tim." She leaned forward and rested her hands on the table.

Colt moved to stand beside her and placed his hand on her lower back. "Is your back still aching?"

"Yes, it is. In fact, it seems to be getting worse. I think I'll lie down for a while."

"Can I do anything to help?"

"Would you heat the gel pack for me? Not too warm, though."

"Is it still in the hall closet?"

She nodded. Colt frowned as he watched her go up the stairs. "She never complains about anything. She has to be really bothered, for her to let it show." He went to the closet, got the gel pack and put it in the microwave.

Concern showed on Tim's face. "How far along is the pregnancy?"

"About nineteen weeks. She's due in April."

When the beep signaled, Colt took it out of the microwave and bounded up the stairs. He offered to massage her back, but Frank insisted that he go back downstairs and have coffee with Tim. He helped Frank position it under her lower back and looked at her with concern. "Should I take you to the doctor, hon?"

She shook her head. "I'm sure everything will be alright. My body is probably just stretching, making room for the baby."

"Did this happen when you were carrying the twins?"

"No, but every pregnancy is different. Just let me rest for a while." Frank lay closed her eyes. The warmth didn't seem to help. Her discomfort drove her from the bed into the bathroom. She pulled down her jeans and sat on the toilet. "This never happened with the twins. It must be gas." She found no relief, so she stood up and began to pull up her panties. She stared in shock when she noticed a red stain on the crotch. Fear struck at her heart. *Blood! There shouldn't be blood.*

She pulled up her jeans and went back to the bedroom, and sat on the edge of the bed. "Alright... I just have to get hold of myself. I remember reading somewhere that spotting is not unusual. It's not heavy. I'll just rest here and see if it gets any worse."

She lay down and tried to relax. In half an hour, she was up again. She went into the bathroom to check her panties. There was more blood, but it was still light in color and not heavy. When she stood up, she noticed that the ache in her lower back seemed to reach around into her stomach and pelvic region. *Maybe I should call the doctor. There shouldn't be a problem, but this didn't happen with the twins. Still, I don't want to be an alarmist. I'll just lie down again.*

Colt came into their room and sat on the side of the bed. "How are you doing? Any better?"

"Not really. There's a bit of blood on my panties, but not very much. But the ache has moved around into my tummy and the pelvic area. I'm not sure what to do. This didn't happen when I was carrying the twins."

"Fran, why don't I take you to the hospital? We don't want to take any chances with your health or this precious little bundle." He rested his hand on her tummy, looking concerned.

"I guess you're right. I just didn't want to overreact. I've read that sometimes spotting can be normal."

Colt took her hand and helped her sit up. He put his arm around her and guided her down the stairs. Worry was etched on his face as he looked at Tim.

"I'm going to take Fran to Emergency. We want to make sure that everything is all right. The twins are sleeping. Would you go over to the trailer and tell Ellie what's happening? I know Sunday is normally her day off, but she'll have to fill in here while we're gone. I'll call home when I know more."

"Don't worry. Between the two of us, everything will be looked after." He gave Frank a serious look. "It's good that you're going in now."

She smiled uneasily and followed Colt out to the truck. After he had helped her get settled, he got in and started the truck. He reached for her hand while he let the motor warm up. "I've been pretty preoccupied with Tim and getting this farm manager thing set up. I guess I haven't asked how you've been. Have you had any problems before now?"

"Not really. I've been more tired than usual; not sleepy, just no energy. And my stomach has been a bit queasy the past few days, but I think that's just part of being pregnant. I remember feeling that way early on with the twins."

"You didn't say anything."

"Colt, I can't run to you with every little hiccup. You were busy. Getting things settled with Tim is huge in the big picture."

"Honey, you and my family are the big picture for me."

"I'm sure everything is all right. But you are right, it is best to check this out and know for sure."

They checked into Emergency. The doctor who attended her was a woman. She asked Frank who her OB/GYN was, along with a few general questions. She placed the stethoscope at various locations on her tummy and gnawed on her bottom lip while she listened.

Concern filled Colt. "Is everything all right?"

She smiled. "I'm sure it is, but this little one isn't co-operating. I'm not finding its heartbeat, but that is probably because of how the baby is positioned."

She consulted Frank's chart. "You are nineteen weeks now. Are you feeling movement yet?"

Frank frowned. "Not yet. But that's not unusual is it?"

"It's your second pregnancy, so it is possible that you could, but it's not unusual that you haven't. I'm going to send you for an ultrasound though. We want to cover all our bases."

Colt's stomach tightened, even as he smiled reassuringly at Frank. *Everything has to be all right,* he thought. Frank got dressed and sat on the bed. Colt was holding her hand when Dr. Wilfred pulled back the curtain and stepped in by the bed.

"Hello there, Frank." He looked at Colt and reached to shake his hand. He looked down at the chart he was holding, and then touched Frank's shoulder kindly. "So, tell me exactly what has been happening."

Frank explained what had happened that morning and mentioned her tiredness and the couple of days of nausea. He smiled reassuringly and reaffirmed that they would do an ultrasound as soon as the technician was available.

The technician appeared with a wheelchair almost immediately. Frank protested that she could walk, but the doctor assured her that this free ride was one of the few that people got in the medical system and she should enjoy it.

Colt went into the ultrasound room with Frank and stood out of the way, as the technician prepped her; then he moved up and stood on the far side of the bed, where he could watch the sonogram screen, too.

Dr. Wilfred watched intently as the technician dabbed jelly on Frank's tummy and started to move the transducer probe around on it. Tension grew heavy in the small room as she searched for the pulsing of the heart. There was no telltale rhythm. Frank's face crinkled, as tears filled her eyes. "Where is the heartbeat?" she pleaded anxiously.

Doctor Wilfred and the technician looked at each other, and then quickly broke contact. The technician cleaned up and pushed the machine back. Doctor Wilfred looked at Colt sadly, and then reached for Frank's hand.

"There is no heartbeat, Frank. I'm afraid the baby has died. What you are experiencing now is the body releasing the uterine lining and expelling it because it senses that the embryo is no longer viable."

Frank began to tremble. "But why? Why would my baby die in-si-de me? What did I do wrong?" Tears spilled and she

Full Circle

looked at Colt, her eyes imploring him. "I'm sorry. I'm so sorry I didn't take better care."

She collapsed into inconsolable tears as Colt bent over her. He pulled her close. "Fran don't. Honey, this is not your fault. You didn't do anything wrong."

"But I didn't keep it safe. I... I let it die."

Doctor Wilfred stepped up and laid a hand on each of them. "Ten to twenty percent of known pregnancies end in early miscarriage. It is the body's way of saying that the fetus is abnormal and not growing correctly, so the uterus expels the embryo. We don't know why this happens, but it does.

"As a rule, the baby has already died before the miscarriage starts. That is what has happened here. Even if you had come in before the heart had actually quit beating, once the process starts it is almost impossible to halt. Something didn't fit together genetically with this embryo. Nature takes over in these cases and neither one of you could have done anything about it."

Colt brushed away his tears. "So, what happens now?"

"We'll go back to Emergency. I need to examine Frank and see how far she has dilated. She's not bleeding heavily yet, which indicates to me that this process is just starting. We will do a D&C in the next day or so, and scrape the womb to remove all the embryonic tissue and make sure that there is no chance of infection.

"I know this isn't comforting right now, but this does not mean that you will not have another child. You have successfully carried twins already."

Frank started to sob again. Colt helped her sit up and supported her as she moved to the wheelchair.

When they arrived back at Emergency, Doctor Wilfred looked at Colt. "Frank will stay in the hospital until after we've done the D&C. It's standard protocol to give her sedation so she gets a good rest."

Colt nodded. "I agree, but I'm going to stay here with her."

Dr. Wilfred secured a private room and had Frank moved into it. While he examined Frank, Colt went to the parking lot and phoned the farm.

Ellie answered. She shed emotional tears when Colt told her what had happened and encouraged him to take as much time as needed to get Frank back on her feet. She assured him that she would look after the twins and everything at home would be fine.

He thanked her and then wandered over to the truck. He opened the door and slid inside. He leaned his head back against the headrest. His chest was tight, aching with unreleased emotion. *All our hopes and dreams for this baby; poof and they are gone.*

He squeezed his eyes tight, fighting disappointment and loss. Tears trickled down his cheeks, and finally, he gave in to the pain. His sobs were deep and ragged. He gave them free rein and let the intensity of his emotion exhaust itself. Then he wiped away the tears and collected himself. *I have to stay strong for Fran. This is going to devastate her.*

He locked the truck and went to join her in her hospital room. In the few minutes he had been out, the doctor had examined Frank and the nurses had gotten her settled and administered a sedative. She hovered in the hazy twilight zone between the medically-induced fog and the blessed nothingness of sleep. When he came into the room, she reached out and pulled him close. She had been waiting for him. "I'm so sorry," she whispered as she succumbed to the drug.

Colts eyes swam with tears. *She can't keep blaming herself. She didn't do anything wrong.* Colt was exhausted, too. He drifted off to sleep, his forehead resting on the bed, her hand clasped in his. He woke up an hour later when the nurse checked in to see how the patient was doing. After she had left the room, he went outside and phoned Frank's parents.

Cameron and Rayelle Lamonte were shocked by the news. Their immediate concern was how Frank would deal with the loss. They said they would leave early the next morning and be in Swift Current before nightfall. They would stay with Frank and Colt as long as was necessary.

Then Colt phoned his parents. Selena and Bob were out, so Colt left a message for them telling them he would call in the morning.

When Colt went back to Frank's room, she was sleeping soundly. *I don't want to be gone when she wakes up, but I'm going nuts just sitting here thinking.* He walked down the hall, looking for the nurse who had stopped by Frank's room.

"Mr. Thompson, you should leave the hospital for a while. Your wife will sleep for at least eight hours and when she wakes up the doctor has left orders to sedate her again. She needs the rest and so do you. You have a lot to deal with, too."

She put an arm around him. "Go kick a tire, shake your fist at the sun, swear at the moon, cry a few tears or talk to a friend, whatever it takes to help ease your pain. Your wife is going to need your support and you'll need hers too. Doctor Wilfred has requested a cot in the room. Come back later and we'll have it there for you."

Colt walked out into the dreary, cloud-filled day. Somehow, he was glad the sun was not shining. The clouds were more appropriate. He unlocked the truck and got in. *What am I going to do now?*

He linked his hands together and rested them at the top of the steering wheels. He gazed off into space. "I'll call Brad and Shauna Lee." He took out his cell phone and dialed Brad's number. He sighed with relief when Brad answered.

"Hello, Colt. How are you?"

"I need someone to talk to. Can I come over?"

"Sure, but what's up, man? You sound serious."

"I... it is serious. I'll fill you in when I get there. See you in fifteen minutes or so."

Brad's mind went around and around, as he tried to figure out what was going on with Colt. When he told Shauna Lee what Colt had said, they both were puzzled.

When Colt came to the door, one look told them that something was very wrong. His face was drawn; his eyes were strained and red.

Shauna Lee gasped. "Colt!" She pulled him into her embrace. "What has... where is Frank? What has happened?"

"She... the baby." His eyes filled with tears. "We lost it today. Fran's in the hospital."

Brad stepped forward. "Is Frank all right?"

"Physically, she will be. But she is blaming herself for what happened and it's nobody's fault."

"What happened?"

"The doctor says it happens fairly often. Today Fran woke up with a backache and then she started spotting. We came to the hospital and they did an ultrasound." He shook his head. "There was no heartbeat."

Shauna Lee paled. "Oh no!"

"We've been able to share everything about this pregnancy. I've regretted that I missed so much with the twins. Fran carried the full load that time. This time it was going to be so different and we were looking forward to the baby's birth, but now..."

Brad put his arm around Colt's shoulder and gave him a gentle hug. "Words are pretty hollow right now, Colt. I don't know what to say, except that we're here for you. If there's anything that we can help with, just let us know."

Colt looked at Brad and Shauna Lee. "It helps to be able to let some of this go, to talk about it. I can't fall apart in front of Fran. We haven't had a chance to talk very much because they sedated her right away, but the little that she has said makes it clear that she's blaming herself and feeling that she let me down." He shook his head. "Of course that isn't true. But how do I make her see that?"

Full Circle

Brad looked at Shauna Lee. Her eyes shimmered with tears when she spoke.

"Colt it's hard to lose a child. She has carried the baby for all this time. No matter how much you love it, it's different for her. That child is literally part of her." A tear spilled over. "Just be there for her and have lots of patience. I don't think Frank is the kind who will be able to just let this go and move on right away."

Brad looked uncomfortable, not quite knowing what to say or what to do. "Colt, can I make coffee or get you a beer or something?"

"Make it coffee, please. I can't drink. I have to drive back to the hospital. They're putting a cot in Fran's room so I can stay with her." He sighed. "Could I have a sandwich or something? I haven't eaten since breakfast."

Brad went to the cupboard and took out a mug. "We just ate and there's chili left over. Would you like some?"

Colt nodded wearily. "I just need something to eat."

Brad set a steaming cup of coffee in front of him while Shauna Lee filled a bowl with chili. She grabbed a spoon on her way to the table and placed both of them in front of Colt, and then brought him two dinner buns and a small plate of butter.

Brad sat down on a chair and pulled Shauna Lee down onto his lap. He held her hand, his thumb rhythmically caressing hers. *I feel so helpless,* he thought. *What do I say to make things better? Is there anything I can do?*

He held Shauna Lee closer and her eyes met his. *Life can be so uncertain... we take so much for granted.*

Colt ate in silence. Shauna Lee and Brad sat with him, not knowing what to say; feeling that they should be able to do more, but not knowing what they could do. When Colt was finished, he pushed the bowl aside and sipped at his coffee. He sat staring out the window. Then he shifted and looked at his friends.

"Thanks, you guys. You have helped more than you can

imagine. I needed to get all this off my chest; you know, just to breathe, just to talk about losing the baby and my concerns about Fran. I'd better go to back to the hospital now. I want to be there if she wakes up."

Shauna Lee stood up. "Colt, have you called Frank's mom and dad?"

Colt nodded. "Yes, they'll be here tomorrow. I called my parents too, but I had to leave a message. They'll get back to me."

Brad cleared his throat. "And your nanny is with the twins?"

Colt nodded. "Tim is out there too. We came to an agreement this morning. Now we need to find a place for him to live until we get the house built at the ranch." He looked at Shauna Lee. "Could you work on that for me?"

She nodded. "I'll do that." She swallowed hard. "And Colt, say hello to Frank. Tell her we are thinking of her...of both of you."

***

Frank was still sleeping when Colt slipped into her room. He tossed his jacket on the cot, and then sat down beside her. He took her hand in his and lifted it to his lips. "I love you, hon," he whispered. "We'll have another baby in time, but right now we have to come to terms with this."

An hour later, Frank began to stir. Colt was still holding her hand when her eyes fluttered open.

"Hi there, love," Colt whispered. She smiled softly, and then her eyes flew open.

"Colt? Where am I? Oh... the baby..."

Colt kissed her hand. "We lost the baby, honey. It was one of those things that no one could have prevented. We... we loved it while we could. Now we... we have to let it go."

Tears filled her eyes. "I... we... wanted it so much. How could this happen?"

"Dr. Wilfred says it happens quite often and they don't know why." He laid his head on the bed beside her. "I'm sorry this happened to us. You have nourished this little one and looked after it so carefully. You are such a wonderful mother." He kissed her cheek. "I called your mom and dad. They'll be here tomorrow night."

"Thanks. I'm glad you did. When can I go home?"

"They have to do a D&C first. Maybe they'll do that tomorrow. I'm not sure if they'll keep you in for a day or two after that. Dr. Wilfred will tell us later."

Frank's tears spilled over. "I want to go as soon as possible. I want to see the twins."

"Yes. We are so lucky to have them to go home to."

She turned her face away and her tears ran freely. "I know that, but I wanted to share this pregnancy with you right through to the birth. Now that will never happen."

"Not this time, love, but maybe in the future."

"I'm so tired," she whimpered.

"Go back to sleep. Dr. Wilfred wants you to get plenty of rest. He gave you a sedative." Colt squeezed her hand gently. "I'm staying here with you. They've put a cot in here for me."

She nodded and closed her eyes. "Is this real? Or is it just a bad dream?" she whispered.

He swallowed hard. "No, sweetheart, this isn't a bad dream. It's real life." Tears swam in his eyes, but he blinked them back. *I have to be strong for you, my love.*

Dr. Wilfred made his rounds by eight the next morning. He came in and told Frank that she was scheduled for a D&C at eleven o'clock. He explained what the procedure would entail and told her that she would certainly go home the next day, possibly even that evening if he felt it was prudent.

Colt followed him out of the room. "If she could get a good sleep here in the hospital tonight, it might be best. Her mom and dad are coming late this afternoon. No matter how much she wants to go home, there is going to be so much activity and emotional stress. If everyone sort of gets settled in first, I'd feel better about taking her home."

"Let's weigh everything when I see her later on. Some of it will depend on how pressed we are for beds."

At four-fifteen, Frank stirred and slowly woke up. She smiled wanly when she opened her eyes to see Colt beside her. "Have you been here all day?"

"I slipped down to the cafeteria for coffee and an egg salad sandwich. But other than that I've been right here where I want to be, next to you." He leaned over and kissed her softly on the lips. "I had a call from your mom and dad. They left at four o'clock this morning. They'll be arriving at the farm anytime now."

She smiled wanly. "They can help Ellie with the twins."

"I talked to Ellie just after lunch. I asked her to change the sheets in the spare room. Tim is going to stay at Brad's place until he finds a place to live. I asked Shauna Lee to help with that."

"Did you see her?"

He nodded. "I- I went out to Brad's yesterday after they sedated you. I- I needed to talk to someone. I'm comfortable with Brad and I've known Shauna Lee for so long. They listened to me and they gave me coffee and some chili. It helped."

He lifted her hand to his lips and kissed it. "They were both concerned and Shauna Lee said to be sure that you knew they were thinking about you. She was really upset."

"She likes children, Colt. You can see it when she is with the twins, especially Sam."

"And yet she always swore she didn't want any."

"Well, we don't know what has happened in the past. There may be a reason why she feels that way."

"I hope you don't mind, Fran, but I asked your mom and dad to wait until we come home to see you."

"Why...?" she started to protest.

Full Circle

"If you really want me to, I'll call them. But they've had a long drive and I thought it would give them a chance to settle in. They can visit with the twins. You've had a full day. I'm hoping they will give you a sedative tonight so you get a good rest. How are you feeling now?"

"I'm cramping a bit."

"Dr. Wilfred said he'd stop by later."

"That's good. I'd like to talk to him."

Seconds later, a nurse came into the room. "How are you feeling, Mrs. Thompson?" She took her temperature, blood pressure, pulse and listened to her chest. She looked at Colt. "I'm going to ask you to leave while I check your wife."

Colt chuckled. "I think I'm old enough. Besides that, I've seen it all before."

"Don't be cheeky! It's the rules. Out you go."

Colt dropped a kiss on Frank's lips and went out into the hallway. While he was waiting there, his cell phone rang. He glanced at the call display and smiled. *Mom* and *Dad!* "Hello, you guys. Where are you?"

Colt was shaking his head when the nurse stepped outside and told him he could go back inside to see his wife.

"I just got a call from Mom and Dad. They made a last minute decision to take a bus tour to Florida with some friends. They offered to come home, but I told them there wasn't any need to do that. Everything is covered at this end and they never travel like that, so they'll see us when they get home."

"I'm glad you did that. Things will be better by the time they get back."

Colt took her hand and rubbed his finger over the back of it in an unconscious gesture. "What did the nurse have to say?"

"Not a lot. The cramping is pretty normal and I am bleeding, but not abnormally. It will just take time. She said Dr. Wilfred had a busy afternoon and he will be in early tomorrow morning." She smiled. "I'll be able to go home then. I want to see the twins."

"And your mom and dad are there."

Frank nodded. "I'm happy to see them, too." Her eyes filled with tears. "But honestly, as much as I love them, I just want to be home with you and the twins. I have to come to terms with the fact that we won't have this little one."

She touched her tummy automatically. Tears spilled down her cheeks. "It's still hard to get my head around this, to accept that its little heart just stopped beating." She sobbed. "I don't even know if it was a girl or a boy."

Colt sat on the bed and drew her into his embrace. "We'll get through this together, hon." He swallowed hard, fighting his own emotions. "I'm sure Dr. Wilfred will tell us what our baby was, a boy or a girl." He felt her collapse against him. "And then we'll help each other heal emotionally, and we'll enjoy the two children that we have. In time, we'll have another one."

"But not this one," she replied sadly.

"No, not this one," he agreed.

The next morning everyone came out onto the veranda to meet them when they arrived at the farm. Cameron and Rayelle Lamonte couldn't hide their sadness for their daughter's loss and Ellie's face was full of concern. But Selena and Sam were bubbling with excitement when they bounded down the steps to meet them. Frank's face broke into a radiant smile, for the moment, her grief shoved aside by her love for her children.

Colt knelt down, so his eyes were level with theirs. He took their hands in his. "Mommy is really happy to see you, but you guys have to be really careful. She has a sore tummy and she can't pick you up for a while because she can't lift anything heavy... and you are both getting to be big kids. So when we go inside, you have to wait until she sits down and then you can sit by her and hug her and kiss her, but you have to be careful not to jump on her tummy. Do you understand?"

They both looked at him with big eyes, and then turned to Frank. "Can we hold her hand?" Sam asked.

Frank nodded and smiled as she reached out to them. "Please take my hands. I can hardly wait to hold you close."

She leaned over to give her mother a kiss as she passed her, but her hands held her children's tightly. She smiled at her dad and brushed his cheek. Ellie smiled as their eyes met and she ran her hand down Frank's back as she walked past her.

The twins propelled her to the couch and waited for her to sit down. They crawled up beside her and wiggled over to sit close to her. She put her arms around them and cuddled them close. Her eyes filled with tears. She bent to rub her head against each of them. "Mommy is so happy that she has you two," she whispered.

They lay their heads against her breasts, each being careful not to touch her tummy. Sam looked up at her. "We missted oou, Mommy."

Selena flew off the couch and ran to Colt. "We missed you too, Daddy. And Grandpa and Grandma came to visit while you were gone." She danced with excitement.

Frank hugged Sam again. "I want to say hello to Grandma and Grandpa now," she said softly as she helped him get down off the couch. He slipped his thumb into his mouth and stood beside her, hugging her leg.

Ellie made coffee and everyone sat around the table and talked. Frank tried to minimize her parent's concern for her, insisting that while the loss was a disappointment, she would be all right.

Rayelle Lamonte frowned. *My dear daughter, all of this is much more difficult than you are pretending it is. I know, I have been where you are now. No matter how brave a face you are putting on, this is going to hurt for a while.* Her heart ached for Frank.

Frank's parents stayed for a week, and she felt relief as she watched them drive down the lane as they left. Colt slid his arm around her waist as they waved. Ellie took the twins inside when the car was out of site. Frank laid her head against his chest and heaved a big sigh.

"Are you all right, hon?"

"I am such an ungrateful daughter. I know Mom and Dad are concerned and they wanted to do everything to help here, but honestly, I couldn't wait for them to leave. I just want to be here alone with you and the twins."

"And Ellie; you need Ellie's help."

"Of course. She's part of our family now." She turned to him. "Colt, can we go for a walk? Just you and me?"

"Are you sure it won't be too much for you?"

"We don't have to go very far. I just need some quiet and fresh air, and some time to look into the morning sky and say goodbye to our little girl with you." Her eyes glistened with unshed tears.

Colt held her tight. "Shall we walk down the lane?"

She nodded. They held hands as they started to walk. "What shall we name her?"

Colt was startled. *I should have thought of this myself.* Guilt flooded through him. "We hadn't discussed a name before. What have you thought of?"

"I've been thinking about Cherish. I will always cherish our dreams for this little girl. She will always be a part of me, even though she never got to be here with us."

Colt swallowed hard as he turned Frank toward him. He tried to push away the tears, to be strong for her, but he lost the fight as he looked into her eyes. A tear slipped down his cheeks. "Cherish is a perfect name for her."

Frank reached up and brushed the tear away. He grabbed her hand and kissed the palm. "We'll plant a tree in memory of her; maybe a weeping willow or a flowering plum? What do you think?"

"I'd like something happy. The flowering plum would be a beautiful reminder of her every spring. The blossoms are pink, for a little girl."

"We'll plant a flowering plum. Should we plant it here or at the ranch? Or maybe we should plant one at each place?"

"Can we do that? She would have been born while we are here, and we would have taken her to the ranch with us."

***

Life at the farm fell into a steady rhythm. Frank spent most of her time with the children, reaffirming how lucky she was to have them. She pushed away the sadness that constantly threatened to creep in. When she couldn't control the emptiness, she went to the bedroom to take a nap and let the tears flow. Other times, she made an excuse to go to the bathroom, and after she'd cried, she'd wash her face and try to hide the evidence.

Colt heard her sobs when she thought he was asleep. Anxiety knotted in his breast. He tried to talk to her about her feelings, but she brushed his concerns away.

Ellie saw the stress in her eyes. *I've never had a miscarriage,* she thought. *But she is not the happy person she is trying to appear to be.*

Ten days after she came home, Colt took her into town for her checkup with Dr. Wilfred. Doctor Wilfred confirmed that she was healing nicely, but he advised them to put off having intercourse for another two weeks. He suggested they make an appointment before the new year for another checkup.

CHAPTER EIGHTEEN

Brad and Shauna Lee had gone to their respective offices on Tuesday morning. When Tim arrived at *Windspeer*, Brad had phoned Shauna Lee and asked her if she could leave early and go home with them. They were anxious to hear news about Colt and Frank, but Tim could tell them little, except that Frank's mom and dad had arrived. Shauna Lee felt relief, knowing that.

She picked up Karma and cuddled her in the curve of her neck. She was surprised how much it had hurt her when she had learned about Frank's miscarriage. Feelings of her own loss had flooded through her.

True, the circumstances were different, but it was still the loss of a mother's hopes and dreams and her heart ached for Frank. She thought about how devastated Colt had been and realized that in normal circumstances it was a crushing loss for both parents.

She looked at Brad. *He will be a loving father*, she thought. She stopped petting Karma and swallowed hard. *Will be?*

What am I thinking?

She walked out of the room and went and to sit on the bed where he had asked her to marry him. He hadn't pressured her for an answer. He was giving her time. She got up from the bed, walked into the bathroom and stood in front of the mirror. She looked into her own wide blue eyes.

"Why am I waiting?" she whispered. Suddenly she knew. "I'm a fool. I shouldn't wait. I won't! He loves me and I... I love him. I don't need to be afraid."

Brad came to the bedroom door as she turned. "Here you are! You just disappeared. Are you alright?"

She nodded, her eyes shining with unshed tears. She leaned down to put Karma on the floor. Then, she reached up and threaded her arms around his neck. "I know this isn't the right time to tell you this, but the answer is YES!"

"Yes?" She saw understanding flare in his eyes. "Tweetie Bird, there is never a wrong time to tell me that!" He laughed, then spanned her waist with his hands and lifted her off the floor, twirling her around. "Shall I send Tim away?"

"No." she whispered. "But is it all right if we keep it our secret for now? I just admitted it to myself. I want to be your wife and when you came in here now, I had to tell you, so I didn't get cold feet and change my mind."

"Tweetie Bird, you have made me the happiest man in the world!" He took her hand and led her back to the kitchen.

Tim looked at them with amusement. *Fools in love; they've got it bad,* he thought. *I only hope it lasts longer than mine did.* He looked at Shauna Lee. "Brad says you may have a place for me to rent until the Thompsons move out to the ranch."

Shauna Lee gave Brad a puzzled look, and then understanding crept into her eyes. "Yes...yes I could have." She gave Brad a happy smile. "I do. I have a house in town and I never stay there. In fact, I won't be living there, now that we are getting married." Her hand flew to cover her mouth and she blushed scarlet.

Brad hugged her with a happy grin. He looked at Tim. "I

asked her to marry me when I got home from China. Shauna doesn't make hasty decisions about things like that and she kept me waiting until just a few minutes ago. She wanted to keep it a secret for a while, but now you heard it from her. We're getting married!"

"Congratulations, you guys. It must be something in this Saskatchewan air. You two are like the Thompsons." Tim's expression darkened as he looked out the window. "I hope you are always this happy." Brad caught the bitterness in his voice.

"We're going to make sure we stay this way. We're not young kids and we know relationships need to be worked at." He smiled at Shauna Lee. "In fact, we've had to work hard to get this far."

Shauna Lee laid her head against Brad's chest. "This man never takes *no* for an answer. He simply wouldn't give up on me. And now," she reached up and caressed his cheek. "I can't imagine life without him."

Brad winked at Tim. "I offered to kick you out for a while this morning after she told me the answer was 'yes', but she said not to."

"Brad! You are so bad." She struggled to hide her embarrassment. "Just ignore him, Tim. Getting back to my house; it's fully furnished, and it's comfortable enough. You can take a look at it and see what you think."

"I'm not fussy. It's just a roof over my head and a place to sleep."

Brad chuckled. "Until you get caught up in this Saskatchewan air. Look at what happened to me."

"Been there and done that once already and believe me, I have no intention of getting burned again." He stood up. "Tell me how to find your place and I'll get out of your hair right now."

"No, Tim," Shauna Lee protested. "We'll go with you. If the place works for you, I need to take my personal things out of there. There isn't much left, but I'd like to tidy up a bit."

Brad released her and stepped away. "Are you ready to go now?"

Shauna Lee nodded. "I'll get a jacket and my purse." She went into the bedroom and picked up her purse. She scooped Karma up off the floor and carried her into the kitchen. "Can we take her, or would it be better to leave her here?"

"We're going to be busy at the house. Maybe we should put her in the carrier and leave her here. We shouldn't be more than a couple of hours."

Tim liked the house. He walked through it, looking into each room. "This works for me. In fact, it's more than I expected to find, and the furnishings work for me too. Does the TV stay?"

Shauna Lee laughed. "I don't need it, so I guess it stays."

"All right, let's draw up an agreement, and I'll move in tonight." He grinned. "I've never liked being the odd man out. I'll leave you two alone to celebrate your engagement."

"You don't have to run away!" Shauna Lee protested.

Brad grinned. "You can move in tonight if you want. We can do the paperwork tomorrow."

Shauna Lee blushed. "Brad. That's rude!"

Tim laughed. It was the first genuine laughter Brad had heard from him since he had arrived in Swift Current. "Think nothing of it. As you said, this guy doesn't take *no* for an answer. I doubt if a quick kiss when you told him 'yes' is what he has in mind to celebrate your acceptance of his marriage proposal."

Brad grabbed Shauna Lee and pulled her close. "Spoken like a man who understands a man!" He gave her a squeeze. "Go gather up all your lacy bras and panties, and whatever other sexy stuff you have left around here."

"Brad," she protested, blushing again.

"I'll help you. I saw a laundry hamper by the washer." He went to get it.

Shauna Lee looked at Tim. "I'm sorry..."

"Don't be sorry. It's good to see him so happy. In all the

years I've known him, he's never been like this. He's like a teenager again. I could envy him, but I've been there already and I hope this works out better for you guys than it did for me."

"Don't let bitterness rob you, Tim. I... I was like you. Brad should have run like hell from the person I was back then, but he wouldn't let me hide behind my pain. Like I said, he is a persistent man when he decides what he wants. I believe in love now. He has shown it to me in so many ways. You may find it too."

"I'm cured of that illusion."

"Colt Thompson thought that once too. Look at him now."

"Good for him, but it's not in the cards for me."

"Don't be too sure, pal." Brad leaned against the bedroom door, a smile on his face. "Maybe we should toss a sexy nightie into his bed. You don't wear them anymore!"

Shauna Lee gasped. "Brad! Will you stop that?" She took the hamper from him and started going through the drawers, gathering up the few remaining personal items.

Brad went into the bathroom and collected the remnants of makeup and medication, including an empty birth control package. "Are you still on these?"

"Are you kidding? I'd have been pregnant within the first week after we had sex if I wasn't."

"Hmmm... well a guy can hope." He dropped the things he'd collected in the laundry hamper. "Is that it now?"

"I'm pretty sure." They walked into the kitchen to find Tim looking through the cupboards.

Brad chuckled. "You won't find much in there. I'm sure this woman never cooked when she lived here, but she's pretty good at it now."

Tim grinned. "I was checking to see what I could pack up for you, but you're right, there isn't much in here."

Shauna Lee shook her head. "Tim, I'm not taking anything. The pots and pans are yours. Brad is a great cook

Full Circle

and he already has everything. If there's anything you can salvage in the cupboards, feel free to use it. Otherwise, throw it out."

"I'm getting a sweet deal here. And it already feels good to know that I'll have a place of my own; a fresh start, without painful memories around every corner. Thanks, guys."

Brad looked at Shauna Lee. "It's seven o'clock and I'm hungry. I think we should take your new tenant out for supper. What do you think?"

Tim protested, but Shauna Lee agreed. Brad opened the door. "Hurry up, man. The invitation was only for supper. Then, you can come back here and I'll take this woman home and thank her properly for agreeing to be my wife."

The next morning Shauna Lee was sitting in her office, doodling on a yellow notepad when her cell phone rang. She smiled as she reached for it. "Hi, Brad," she answered softly.

"Hi, Tweetie Bird. What are you doing?"

"Not much. I've been acting like a lovesick teenager, daydreaming and practicing my new signature. I'm trying to decide whether it should be Shauna Lee Johnson or maybe just Shauna Johnson since you call me Shauna. Or... I could make it Tweetie Bird Johnson." She giggled. "Or, I could be Lady Bird Johnson. What do you think?"

"I like Tweetie Bird Johnson. It has a great *ring*... no pun on words."

"The ring! Ohhh... did you find one?"

"Sweetheart, I want you to go with me."

"Brad... I'd like you to pick out the ring. I'll love it just because you chose it."

"You know me, I never take *no* for an answer. Anyway, can we go for lunch together?"

"Hmmm, let me check my calendar. I've almost filled this page, practicing my new name. I think I can manage it. What time do you want to go?"

"What is your schedule for today? Do you have any

appointments?"

"No, today is a paperwork day."

"Could you take the afternoon off? It's a beautiful sunny day. We could go to Regina."

"I left early yesterday and now again today? You're a bad influence on me." She laid down her pen and pushed the yellow pad away.

"I'm sure Christina will take care of the office and everyone else is working hard. I'm the only one off in la-la land, so I might as well get out of here. When are you coming?"

"Give me forty-five minutes, and I'll be there."

Shauna Lee stood up and stretched. Then she walked out to Christina's desk. "If I cut out again this afternoon, will you cover for me?"

Christina grinned. "Well, if Brad brings me something as gorgeous as that silk kimono that he brought me from China, I'll cover for you anytime. Where are you off to today?"

"Brad just called me on my cell. It's a nice day so he would like to go to Regina. I feel guilty about taking off but—"

Christina brushed her words away with the sweep of her hand. "Don't! It's one of the perks of owning the business." She grinned as she looked at Shauna Lee's happy face. "That man has made such a difference in you. You are so alive now and we all notice it. It is good to see you happy.

"Thanks, Christina. You know, I always vowed I'd never let myself fall in love with anyone." Shauna Lee's eyes sparkled. "But Brad wore down all my defenses and now I love him so much it scares me."

"Anyone can see how much he loves you. You have nothing to be afraid of except your own fear, Shauna Lee."

"I actually do know that, but I... I have a ton of emotional baggage from... from before, and sometimes the past creeps up and bites me."

Christina smiled at her. "Do you know something? We've

worked together for ten years and I have learned more about you in the last few months than I ever even got a glimpse of in all those years."

"Have I really been that unapproachable?"

"You have been all business and nothing else. I guess that worked for you, but the rest of us have become kind of a family. We don't know everything about each other, but we know each other's spouses, their children, and their interests. On occasion, we get together socially.

"But we really know nothing about you as a person. You are a fair and consistent boss, but until Brad came along, your personal life didn't seem to exist. I felt sorry for you. I couldn't imagine living such a lonely life."

"I didn't have a personal life. I was lonely, but I was afraid to let anyone get close to me." Shauna Lee smiled sadly. "That really bothered Brad. Remember that day when he followed you into my office?"

Christina smiled and nodded.

"He did that on purpose, so he could see if my office was a 'sterile' as my house. It drove him crazy that I didn't have any pictures. He was unrelenting about it, wanting to know how anybody who dealt with me got an idea of who I was." She sighed. "I honestly didn't think it mattered. I wanted to keep my life private."

"I know that. He gave me a big wink when he walked out, and you followed him looking like a thundercloud." Christina chuckled. "And when he helped you get into the truck, I had to laugh. You looked like you were ready to kill him, and he was enjoying the whole thing!"

Shauna Lee found herself laughing. "He's got that lift kit on that truck and those big tires. I'm too short; I just can't get into it without help."

Christina was laughing too. She glanced up as the door opened. "Speak of the devil! Here he is."

Brad grinned. "Was she telling you our secret?" He looked at Shauna Lee. "You couldn't wait?"

Shauna Lee shook her head frantically. "No, Brad..."

Christina looked from one to the other. She reached out and grabbed Shauna Lee's hand to check her ring finger. "Are you getting engaged?" She let out a squeal of happiness. "Is that why you're going to Regina; to look for a ring?"

Shauna Lee flushed and Brad reached over to hug her. He placed her hand against his coat pocket and she felt the tiny box in it. Her eyes widened. "You got it?" She reached into his jacket and pulled it out of his pocket. "Show me!"

"Hey, I wanted to do this right."

"To hell with doing it right," Christina blurted. "Hurry up and show her. I want to see it, too."

Shauna Lee was fumbling with the box. Brad took it from her. "Are you sure?"

"Yes! I don't want to wait."

Brad opened the box and watched her expression. The beautiful blue eyes filled with moisture. "Oh, Brad... I love it. The setting is gorgeous. It's so unique."

He took the ring out of the box and slipped it onto her extended finger. Then, he shoved the box back into his pocket and took her in his arms, oblivious to the fact that Christina had rushed through the office and collected all of the other employees. All six of them applauded as he kissed her.

"Alright, you two," Christina said with a laugh. "Go get a room! But let's see that ring first."

Brad turned Shauna Lee in his arms, so her back was against his chest and she was facing her staff. She held out her hand and let them admire the ring. They all oohed and aahed over the diamond set in the unique combination of white and yellow gold.

Christina winked at him. "I knew you were a keeper the first time you came in here with Shauna Lee."

"Thank you. It didn't take me long to know that she was a keeper too. And believe me, she hasn't come easily!"

"I'm glad you hung in there Brad. She has become a different person since you came into her life." She shifted back and rested a hip against her desk. "So when is the wedding?"

Shauna Lee blushed again. "Jeez—we just got engaged! Give me time to catch my breath."

Brad laughed. "I like the idea of a winter wedding. Or better yet, we could elope this weekend."

"Don't you dare!" Christina exploded. "We want to celebrate your wedding." She turned to the others. "Eh, guys? We want to put on a bridal shower and all that stuff, right?" There was a course of cheers. Christina shook a finger at Brad and Shauna Lee. "No cheating! You cannot elope!"

Brad leaned around and looked into Shauna Lee's face. She shrugged and they both laughed. "I guess she just laid down the law."

"I just had to make sure you've got that straight. Now you two get out of here and do whatever newly engaged people do." Christina threw her arms around Shauna Lee. "I am so happy for you!"

She grabbed Brad's hand. "Congratulations!"

When they got into the truck, Brad pulled Shauna Lee close against him. "Well, once again, I'm going to have to take you home and thank you properly. How is it that nothing goes quite the way I plan for it to?"

Shauna Lee touched his cheek. "It turned out perfectly." She stretched out her hand to look at her ring. "I love, love, *love* my ring. You have beautiful taste."

He kissed her. Shauna Lee shot a quick look at the office window. Christina was standing there, pretending to be watching them through binoculars. She laughed. "Let's get out of here. They're probably all watching us!"

Brad started the truck and pulled out onto the street.

"Where are we going?"

"I had planned to take you to the park and give you the ring there. That's where we first spent time together at the car show. It's sunny and nice out. Do you feel like going there?"

"You are so romantic. Let's do it. And then let's go home and have a beer and make pizza like we did the second time."

He chuckled. "But I'm warning you right now, I *am* going to bed with you tonight."

They walked through the park and sat on a bench for a while. Shauna Lee told him about her conversation with Christina, explaining to him how her staff viewed her. "Now I realize that you were trying to tell me that, but I couldn't see it."

"Sweetheart, that's because you have hidden away all your life. You struggled to be anonymous. And you did the same thing with your staff." He hugged her. "You tried to do it with me."

"Why didn't you just move on?"

He chuckled. "I must have been drawn to your pheromones! I *wanted* to know you. I guess it's meant to be because I would have run a mile from anyone else like you. But with you, I never considered giving up."

When they got back to the house, they discovered Tim had left a message on Brad's cell, wondering about the rental agreement. He had gone to Shauna Lee's office and Christina and he had obviously clashed. In his message, he had referred to her as *that officious bitch*.

Shauna Lee laughed. "Christina thinks he's a cold fish."

Brad chuckled. "Wouldn't it be funny if they got together?"

Shauna Lee was thoughtful. "I'm ashamed to admit that I really don't know anything about Christina, except that she's not married. She's worked for me for ten years and as far as I know she hasn't even dated."

"I'll phone Tim and tell him not to worry about the agreement today. We'll get at it tomorrow."

Shauna Lee sighed. "I'll phone Christina and ask her to pull the forms and fill in all the information that she can. I'll see her in the morning and get everything finished up. Then, I'll give him a call and he can come down so we can both sign them."

They worked together and made pizza just as they had

that first evening. As they worked, they discussed Christmas.

"We can go to your family's place for Christmas," she offered.

"I wanted to at first, but after you told me how you've always celebrated Christmas, I made up my mind to celebrate it with you, right here in our home. We'll buy decorations and lights for the house and the tree.

"And we're going to have company. We'll have Tim and Colt and Frank and the twins for dinner: a day with coffee and donuts at the shop for my clients; one for your clients at your office; a Christmas party for your staff right here at the house so they get to know us. December is going to be full and overflowing."

Shauna Lee groaned. "Brad! Why don't we just have a Christmas wedding? We could do everything at once."

"You just want to take the easy way out." He grinned and shook his head. "There isn't enough time. You have to meet my family. I want us to have a real wedding. It's the first one for both of us and I want to look back on the memories and the pictures and admire my wife in her beautiful dress."

"Who will we invite?"

"My family, the Potters, Colt, and Frank, Tim and your staff; it will be big enough for a celebration, but not over the top enough to unnerve you."

She sighed. "You know me! I hate being the center of attention."

"Yes, I know you, but everything will be alright. Trust me. And you know, if we didn't have a wedding, Christina would never forgive us."

"I know... it's just uncomfortable for me. Who will I have for a bridesmaid? I don't have any friends."

"Tweetie Bird. That's not true. Frank is a friend, and I'll bet Christina would love it if you asked her to be your bridesmaid. And Selena could be your flower girl and Sam could be the ring bearer."

"Who would be your best man?"

"I'd like to ask Colt."

"Not Tim?"

Brad thought for a moment. "Well, Tim will be living here and he is an old friend, but right now he is so bitter about love and marriage."

"So I've noticed." She looked at her ring again.

"When do you think we should get married?" he asked.

"We're into tax time at the office after the New Year, but I don't want to wait until June! I want to be your wife sooner than later."

"I love hearing you say that." He kissed her gently. "December is going to be busy and if it's all right with you, I'd like us to fly to Dawson Creek for the New Year. We'd only be away from home for four days if we left Regina on the twenty-ninth and came back on January first.

"We can sleep on the flight back because we'll be tired. My family will protest because I haven't been home for a while, but I'm thinking of work... and you. Families can be overwhelming if you aren't used to them."

"I appreciate that you realize that," she said softly. "And... I am fine being with your family for the New Year." She chewed her lip. "I have no idea how long it takes to put a wedding together. I could ask Frank. I know they were married within a couple of weeks. But her mom helped her with the details. I'm not sure how Frank is feeling now. She's probably struggling emotionally."

"Maybe it would be a good diversion for her." He took her hand. "Let's go into the office and check out a calendar." They looked at different dates, and then decided that she could ask for Frank's help in a couple of weeks. In the meantime, Shauna Lee would phone Christina and ask her if she'd ever helped plan a wedding.

Christina was delighted when Shauna Lee called her. She said she had helped her sister four years earlier and she would call her and pick her brain. She was dancing with excitement when she hung up, telling Shauna Lee she would talk to her at the office in the morning.

"You were right, Brad. Christina is wild with excitement."

"Tweetie Bird, once you open up to people, you'll be amazed at how helpful and friendly they are."

"I feel like I don't deserve it. I didn't intend to be distant and unapproachable, but I guess I have been. They must think I am a terrible snob."

"Just be the person I've come to know, sweetheart. If they ever thought that way, they'll soon forget it."

She threaded her arms around his neck. "I'm glad you are so persistent. I love you, Brad Johnson."

Brad phoned his parents and told them about the engagement and that he was planning to bring his bride-to-be home for New Years. He also shocked them when he told his mom that they were planning to have the wedding in late January or early February. He could hear the unspoken questions. He chuckled while he assured her that he wasn't going to make her a grandmother for a year or so.

Shauna Lee blushed as she listened to him. He was grinning when he ended the call. "Everyone will be buzzing now!"

Next he phoned and made reservations for their flight to Dawson Creek. Shauna Lee cringed when she heard him affirm the cost, but Brad just smiled. "Sweetheart, I have waited forty-two years for you. I'm not a bottomless pit, but I've never been a playboy, and I've invested wisely. The cost means nothing to me."

He slid his hands around her waist and lifted her up, twirling her around. "I am as happy as a kid! It feels like I have known you forever."

"I know. Sometimes it scares me when I realize how short a time it's really been. Are we rushing things?"

"Do you have any doubts?"

"No... I don't. But I could see why people might think we are crazy."

"I know in my heart that this is right. If you don't have

any doubts, I don't care what anyone else thinks." He sniffed the air. "And I smell pizza. Let's go eat!"

They ate pizza, drank beer and jotted down ideas for the Christmas holidays. By the time they went to bed, Shauna Lee felt good about what they had come up with. With Brads input, planning for the holidays would not be so daunting. It had been a wonderful day.

CHAPTER NINETEEN

The next morning, Christina was dancing with excitement when she arrived at the office. She looked at Shauna Lee. "Did you sleep last night?"

Shauna Lee smiled. "Yes. Why would you ask me that?"

"Because I didn't; I'm so excited that you asked me to help with your wedding. I talked to my sister Julie last night! She gave me a few suggestions and ideas. Have you set a date?"

"As soon as possible! Well, not in December. It's too busy already. Brad wants a real wedding... fancy dress, cake, invitations, etc."

"Shauna Lee! You want it too."

"Yes, once I got past the intimidation of the whole idea, I admit I do too." Her smile sparkled. "I am excited. So, how quickly can we put a wedding together? The office really gets busy by the end of January with tax time and I have to be on the ball then; I can't be distracted by planning a wedding, but I don't want to wait until spring. Soooo...."

"So, we'd better get the ball rolling! I know December is

busy, but we can order invitations, book a caterer, book a church, book a photographer, and make the guest list. You need to get your invitations out as soon as possible since the wedding is going to be coming up fast."

"I'll call Brad and see if we can meet for lunch. If he's free, could you have lunch with us today, so we could discuss some of these things?"

"I'd love to."

"I'll get a hold of him right away. If I call his cell, I'll be sure to get him."

Brad chuckled when he answered the phone. "Let me guess; you're up to your neck in wedding plans!"

"Are you psychic, too?"

"No, but I can imagine you and Christina at it."

"You're right. What are you doing for lunch?"

I have an appointment at one, but I'm pretty flexible until then. What's on your mind?"

"We need to make some decisions. Could you come over before lunch?"

"I could come right now if you want."

"Umm... all right, we can get together in my office. We need to set a date and we need to think about where we are going to get married so we can order invitations. Things like that."

"I'll be right over. Shall I stop at Tim Horton's and pick up some donuts?"

"That's a great idea. Bring enough for the whole staff. And Brad, please bring a large coffee each for the three of us."

Shauna Lee phoned Christina. "Brad has an appointment at one, but he's free right now so he's on his way over. And he's bringing Tim Horton's coffee for the three of us and donuts for everyone; I mean the staff as well."

Christina chuckled. "I wish I had met him first! I like that man."

Brad arrived twenty minutes later, bringing coffee and a varied selection of donuts. Christina brought a paper plate into Shauna Lee's office and let everyone pick two goodies each, and then she took the box into the coffee room. She turned on the intercom at her desk so they could hear if anyone came in, and they sat around Shauna Lee's desk with a calendar.

They decided on the first weekend in February. Shauna Lee was surprised to learn that Brad's family was devout Baptists. *I wonder what other little things we don't know about each other,* she mused.

He grinned as if he had read her mind. "When we go there at New Year's, we won't be allowed to sleep together."

Christina howled with laughter.

Shauna Lee looked shocked. "Are you serious? We live together!"

He chuckled. "Not as far as my parents are concerned! Sleeping together in their house is a definite 'no-no' until we are married. That's another reason why I only plan to spend two nights there!"

She shook her head. "I guess Tim will have to sleep at the house on the weekend of the wedding, so I can move back into my place."

"Or you can live at my place for a few days," Christina volunteered.

"Would you do that for me?" Shauna Lee asked, her eyes glinting with a sudden flood of unshed tears.

"Of course I would. It's one way to make sure I get invited to the wedding," she said with a laugh. "Besides that, it's bad luck for the groom to see the bride before the wedding, so you couldn't stay at the house the night before the wedding anyway. I want you two to be 'Happy Ever After' so I'm going to be the watchdog." Christina shook a warning finger at Brad.

He reached over and grabbed her finger. "We will be 'happy-ever-after' regardless."

They all laughed and then Shauna Lee reached over and touched Christina's arm. "Brad and I talked about this last night. Would you be one of my bridesmaids?"

Christina looked stunned. She jumped up and hugged Shauna Lee. Her eyes brimmed. "As long as the bridesmaid dress isn't a chartreuse color and it doesn't make me look fat!"

"I'm going to ask Frank Thompson to be my maid of honor. I hope she is up to it by then."

"Why wouldn't she be?"

"Oh... Christina, I thought you knew. She had a miscarriage last Sunday."

"Oh no! I am so sorry to hear that." She blinked hard. "That would be such a painful thing to go through. One day you'd be so happy and full of anticipation. The next, all your dreams would be gone."

Brad changed the subject. "I guess we need to count up the guests. For my family, there could be nine adults and if the kids all come that would add another seven. So that is a total of sixteen, and Tim makes seventeen. And you will want to invite the Potters, won't you?"

She nodded. "Frank and Colt and the twins make twenty-three, and I want to invite all the staff from here."

Christina counted on her fingers. That's another fifteen if the children are included. That makes thirty-eight... and *me*. That makes thirty-nine, plus you two, that totals forty-one."

"Is there anyone else you would like to invite, Shauna Lee?"

"No..."

"What about your dad sweetheart? As far as I'm concerned he's an asshole, but he was, or I should say *is* the only dad you've ever had. It's up to you."

Shauna Lee chewed her bottom lip as she stared at the floor. Brad and Christina waited for her answer. She sighed. "He is the only remnant of family that I have. Would you hate it if I asked him?"

"Tweetie Bird, I hate what he did to you. He hurt you in so many ways. But if you want to invite him to the wedding, I'm fine with that."

Full Circle

"It's still hard for me to accept him, but after what he told me." She shrugged. "We were all hurting, Brad. Am I any better than him... or Mom... if I shut him out? We need to heal." She shook her head. "I know it would mean a lot to him. He's a troubled man, too."

Brad took her hand and gave it a gentle squeeze. "Maybe we should invite Ollie, too, so he'll feel more comfortable."

"And we can't forget Frank & Colt's nanny, Ellie."

How many is that now? Forty-four?"

"We were going to have a small wedding!"

"Don't worry; you'll love it."

Christina and Shauna Lee accomplished a great deal by the end of the first week in December. They had reserved the church; the reception and catering arrangements were in place, a photographer was booked and the invitations were at the printers. Brad met them after work on Friday and the three of them went for supper The Steak House.

Brad looked around the room after they sat down. He took a second look and then grinned at Christina. "Tim is sitting over there by himself. Maybe we should invite him to join us."

"Don't go out of your way to do it on my behalf," Christina grumbled.

Brad chuckled. "The poor guy doesn't know anybody else in town. It's got to be kind of tough."

"I'm not running an escort service. If he'd get off his high horse he might meet other people, but he is so bitter and defensive, he doesn't exactly attract anyone to him."

"Get used to him, girl," Shauna Lee said with a grin. "He'll probably be your escort at the wedding. Brad's going to ask him to be his best man. He's going to ask Colt too, but I'm sure he'll be with Frank."

"Crap... when I said no chartreuse dress, did I forget to say no Tim? I'm sure that man hates women."

Shauna Lee took a sip of water, then said, "He just went

through a very nasty divorce and he doesn't have much use for the fairer sex right now. You're right though, you can almost feel his scorn." She gave Christina a wicked smile. "You could take him on as a challenge."

"Not likely. Brrr... he'd freeze me to death."

Brad looked thoughtful. "We've been friends for a long time, but I have to admit he is pretty jaded right now."

Shauna Lee and Christina were toasting their success with the wedding plans when Tim walked up to their table.

"Tim! Grab a chair and join us." Brad motioned to the empty spot beside Christina.

Christina glared at Brad while she moved her purse. She barely acknowledged Tim when he sat down.

Shauna Lee sent him a warm smile. "Are you getting settled, Tim?"

"Yes. I'm very comfortable. It's a perfect place for one person."

"I always liked it, until I met Brad." She looked at Brad and smiled. "But the last time I stayed there by myself it felt empty. It just wasn't home for me anymore."

"I'd buy it from you if I wasn't going to be moving out to the farm next fall. It's perfect for my situation."

"How are things at the farm?" Brad asked.

"I go out there every day. I'm getting familiar with the books and the equipment. I'm impressed with Colt's management style. He's flexible and open to new ideas, which is something I appreciate. I think we'll work well together. I'm excited about taking the place over."

"How is Frank doing?" Shauna Lee asked.

"She's putting on a good front, but losing the baby has been hard on her. It's been hard on both of them. Colt struggles with it, but he tries to be strong for Frank. And Frank tries, but the sparkle that was there when I first met her is missing now."

"Well, it hasn't been very long. It was a huge loss for them," Shauna Lee said soberly.

Full Circle

When Brad and Shauna Lee arrived home, they talked about Colt and Frank. "Brad, could we invite them for supper on Sunday night? We need to talk to them about the wedding. I don't feel comfortable that we haven't told them yet."

"I did mention that we were engaged when I phoned Colt the other day."

"I am glad you did. I wanted to phone Frank. She reached out to me before, but it almost feels wrong for us to be so happy when they are hurting so much right now."

Brad pulled his cell phone out of his pocket. "I'll give them a call now and invite them over Sunday afternoon. We could get a tree tomorrow and some decorations. We could put it up on Sunday. The twins might have fun helping us decorate. I'll run the idea past Colt."

Brad was smiling when he clicked off his phone. "Colt asked Frank how she felt about coming over on Sunday and she was open to it. And not only that, they always get their tree from a farm where they pick their own and cut it. They went there last summer and tagged one. We may not find one we like, but it could be fun to go with them. What do you think?"

Shauna Lee hesitated.

Brad chuckled. "I know what you are thinking. Look, just think about it overnight. I'll let him know in the morning."

Am I so predictable? That is silly. I have to change and the time to start is now. "No, phone him now, Brad. We should give them as much time to plan as possible."

Brad pulled her to her feet and kissed her. "That's my girl! I'll call right now."

Saturday morning, Brad and Shauna Lee met the Thompsons at the highway junction. The weather had changed and the morning was cold and frosty. Everyone was dressed in warm jackets, gloves, and winter boots. It was a two-hour drive to the Christmas tree farm, but everyone was caught up in the spirit of the season and no one seemed to mind.

The tree farm offered rides on a wagon pulled by two gray horses. The wagon was stacked with hay bales and the driver took them down the trails through the rows of trees, stopping periodically so they could look at them. Colt and Frank cut down the Scotch pine that they had marked earlier in the year. Brad and Shauna Lee selected a Spruce to take home.

It was snowing by the time they got back to the old barn, where the tree farm office was located. Everyone had hot chocolate and warmed up around the wood stove. Snow was falling heavily when they left for home. Winter had come and they would have a white Christmas.

Brad stopped at the A&W when they got to the city. "I'm hungry. That cup of chocolate was just a teaser. Can we make this supper? It's quick and easy."

Shauna Lee nodded. "I'm starved, too."

Brad peered out at the snow as they waited for their order. "I want to put lights up on the outside of the house, too. How do you feel about stopping at Costco after we finish eating? We can get decorations for the tree and lights for the house. They have all kinds of stuff there."

"That sounds like fun. We need to shop for groceries, too. We have to get food for supper tomorrow night."

Two hours later, they were laughing like kids when they came out of Costco with two shopping carts filled and spilling over. Their excitement carried into the evening while they ate popcorn and examined their purchases.

Brad leaned back, watching Shauna Lee when she sat on the floor in the living room, boxes scattered around her while she examined the brightly colored ornaments they had bought. Her eyes were sparkling, excitement bubbled from her. *She's like a child,* he mused lovingly.

He pushed boxes away so he could crouch down beside her. "What are you thinking, Tweetie Bird?"

She was caressing an old-fashioned looking angel tree topper that she had insisted on buying. "This reminds me of my grandma. That's why I wanted it." She laid her head against his shoulder. "She always made Christmas special. She made all of the decorations for the tree: strings of paper links, snowflakes that she cut out, and I can remember stringing popcorn on thread and putting it on the branches. But she had an angel tree topper." She pressed the angel to her cheek. "This one reminds me of it."

"So your family celebrated Christmas when you were young?"

She nodded. "Yes; especially when grandma was alive." She was thoughtful. "We never had a lot of gifts, and they were always things that we needed. Mom and Dad would give me winter boots or a coat. Grandma knitted socks, gloves and scarves. Grandma used to bake and she gave it away as gifts.

"But Christmas was about getting together with neighbors and having fun. She was Roman Catholic and we always went to mass on Christmas Eve. She was a happy person and she embraced everyone around her. She made me feel so loved and special."

"After your grandma died, did your mom and dad still celebrate Christmas?"

Shauna Lee sighed. "They went through the motions until Andre died. After that, they didn't bother with anything."

Brad stood up. He reached down to take her hand and helped her to her feet. He pulled her against him, brushing away a curl that fell over her eye. He smiled as he looked into her eyes. "There is plenty of love in this house, Tweetie Bird, and we are going to enjoy Christmas the way your grandmother did. We can even go to Mass on Christmas Eve if you want to."

She laughed. "What would your Baptist family think of that?"

"About as much, as they'd think of you and me living together in sin. I live my own life, I have since I left home."

Sunday morning they were up early. It was still snowing,

but Brad had shaken the snow off the tree when he'd taken it out of the truck box the night before and he had stood it up in the garage so it would dry off. They worked together, deciding where to put it and then setting up it in the tree stand.

They were putting the outdoor lights up when Frank and Colt arrived. Colt offered to give Brad a hand while Frank and Shauna Lee watched them. The twins burned off their energy in the snow. When the lights were up across the front of the house, Brad declared the job done for the season. He gathered up the unopened boxes and took them to the garage.

When they went inside, Shauna Lee made hot chocolate for the children. Brad put the potatoes in the oven to bake and put the cooked pork tenderloin in the warmer. Then he made rum and eggnog for the adults and they all sat around the kitchen table.

Frank asked Shauna Lee to show her the engagement ring. She admired it and asked if they had set a wedding date.

Shauna Lee smiled. "Yes and the planning is well under way. We are getting married at two o'clock on Saturday, February fourth." She reached out and rested her hand on Frank's. "I want to ask you if you'd be my maid of honor."

Frank looked surprised and then smiled tremulously. "I would be honored, Shauna Lee. I'm so touched that you would ask me."

"I wanted to ask you earlier, but it was after..."

"After the baby..."

Shauna Lee slipped her hand around Frank's. "It's hard for me to feel right about being so happy, when I know how painful things are for you."

Frank shook her head. "No... life has to go on."

"How are you doing, Frank?"

Frank tried to give her a bright smile. Shauna Lee shook her head. She took her hand and led her into the bedroom. "Frank, I've never gone through what you have; you and Colt were so excited about the baby. He was so broken and worried about you the day... the day you found out."

Tears filled Frank's eyes. "I feel so guilty. I blame myself. I don't understand how it could have happened. Maybe I shouldn't have gone riding..."

Shauna Lee hugged her. "Frank, what happened isn't your fault. It was nobody's fault." She led her over to the bed. She pulled Frank down beside her.

Frank covered her face. "That's what Colt tells me. He's been so wonderful." Tears slid down her cheeks. "But... I feel so alone, so empty. I'm angry. I'm angry at myself. I'm angry at God. I'm angry at everything. Sometimes I'm even mad at Colt, and that is so unfair."

Shauna Lee brushed the tears away. "I think that's pretty normal. Frank, nobody around here, knows this except Brad, but I know how devastating it is to lose a child. I lost my little boy when he was fourteen months old. I... I totally lost myself. It took me years to get over it. In some ways, I never have. Brad has helped me to move on in many ways, but I'm certain no one ever forgets *that* child. It is always a part of you."

Frank looked shocked. "I had no idea, Shauna Lee."

"I found my own way to cope, Frank. I wanted to die with him, but I didn't, so I shut myself off from that part of my life and built a new one. You don't want to go there. You have the twins, and Colt loves you so much. He would do anything for you. Hold on to what you have..."

"I know all that Shauna Lee, but I have to make my way through this... in my own time. I am feeling better physically. Now, I just try to keep busy and not think about it. But at night... sometimes I just can't escape...."

"If it ever helps to talk, I'm here for you, Frank."

"Thank you. Sometimes it's easier to talk to another woman. I've just never cultivated any friendships with women. You are the closest thing to a girlfriend that I have around here."

"It's the same for me, but you will get to know my secretary, Christina Holmes. She's going to be my bridesmaid.

She's worked for me for ten years. I'm ashamed to say I've never taken time to get to know her until now, but she's nice. I think you'll like her." Shauna Lee grinned. "Maybe we'll form a girl's club, just the three of us."

Frank smiled wanly. "Maybe we should go check on the others and see if the twins have terrorized your puppy."

Colt and Brad were in the kitchen. Brad had put the carrots and vegetables on to cook, and he was making a salad. Colt was carving the pork.

"Brad, you should have called me," Shauna Lee protested.

"We can handle this. We figured you girls must be talking girl stuff. Did you ask Frank to be your matron of honor?"

"Yes, did you talk to Colt?"

Colt was grinning. He reached for Frank and pulled her close. "So, I guess we are going to walk down the aisle together, again."

She nodded and laid her head on his shoulder. "What are the twins doing?"

Brad laughed. "They're sitting in the living room. I plugged in the Christmas tree lights and they are sitting there, fascinated."

CHAPTER TWENTY

December passed quickly. Shauna Lee and Brad made dinner for her staff and their families. She was amazed at how warm and friendly they were, and how appreciative they were for the invitation to her home.

For the first time since they had worked for her, Shauna Lee had seen her staff as people with families, rather than simply as employees. She had seen individual members of their families before, but she realized that she had never seen each family together as a unit. And it proved true, that Christina didn't have anyone in her life.

Shauna Lee sent out invitations to her clients, asking them to join the staff for coffee and goodies and most of them stopped by. Everyone expressed appreciation for getting to meet all the staff, and the staff members felt appreciated and happy too. Each client received a box of chocolates to take home.

On December twenty-first, Shauna Lee spent the afternoon at Brad's office, helping him host an afternoon of appreciation for his clients and people who had expressed interest in the wind turbines. Shauna Lee was chatting with James Turner from Eastend, when a hand touched her shoulder.

She turned her head and looked into Bob Matzlan's blue eyes. Hers widened with shock.

Bob smiled. "I wondered if you would be here. I haven't been able to get you out of my mind since you were in Glaslyn with Brad."

"Oh..."

James Turner looked at them closely. "Are you two related?"

Shauna Lee swallowed a gasp. "No."

Bob Matzlan looked at him with a cautious smile. "Why would you think that?"

"Your eyes are almost identical. It's very noticeable."

Shauna Lee swallowed hard when she turned to look for Brad. He happened to glance her way and caught the stress in her expression. His eye slid to the person she was talking to. *Jim Turner; he shouldn't be a problem. Who is the other guy? Oh shit...*

Brad excused himself and strode to her side. "Bob! What a nice surprise. I wasn't sure you would make it." He turned to Shauna Lee. "Sweetheart, would you bring coffee for Bob?"

She nodded. "Do you take cream or sugar or both?"

He smiled, his eyes drinking in her face. "Neither. I drink it black." She turned away, anxious to escape his scrutiny. *Those eyes; they are like mine.* A knot tightened in her belly. *But why is he here? I know Brad invited him, but he must have looked me up first because Brad hadn't seen him.*

When she returned with Bob's coffee, Brad and he were deep in conversation. Bob reached to take the cup from her trembling fingers. He looked directly at her. "I have invited Brad and you to have supper with me after you are finished here."

Her eyes flew to Brad's. He reached out and touched her

arm. "I told Bob we'd be happy to join him, Shauna Lee."

Bob sensed her anxiety. "Shauna Lee, I don't want to disrupt your life. I just need some answers. This thing won't let me go."

Brad slid his arm around her shoulder. "It's all right, Tweetie Bird. I'll be there with you." He looked around the room. The crowd had thinned to just two people, and they had put their cups down.

"I'll go say goodbye to them." He glanced at his watch. "It's after five. We can close up as soon as they leave. We'll go for supper right away. I'll come back tomorrow and clean up."

Shauna Lee bit her lip as she looked at Bob. "How does your wife feel about this?"

He eyes saddened. "My wife died five years ago. She had cancer."

Shauna Lee reached out to him, her hand touching his arm. "I'm so sorry."

"She was a wonderful woman and I loved her. We raised a good family and I've lived a happy life. This..." he motioned between Shauna Lee and himself. "This has nothing to do with how I felt about her."

"Then maybe you should leave it in the past."

He smiled sadly. "I wish I could, but I can't ignore what I believe to be true."

She turned away and moved to join Brad. Bob followed her. Brad scanned her face with concern. Her discomfort reached out to him. He took her hand and turned to Bob. "We can go now. What do you like; Chinese, steak, seafood?"

Bob chuckled. "I like to support the beef industry, so let's make it steak, but more than anything, I'd like a quiet spot so we can talk."

Brad looked at Shauna Lee, but she wasn't looking at either of them. He sighed. "Let's go to The Steakhouse. We can pick one of the back booths. It's still early. The crowd won't be coming in yet."

Brad helped her up into the truck. He rested his hand on

her thigh and nudged her close to him. "I know you don't want to do this, but he's determined. We may as well talk to him now so we can move on. I'll be right there with you. You already know what your dad told you. Bob can't hurt you."

She gritted her teeth. "I've done everything I can to leave my past in the past, where it should be, but it just keeps coming back to haunt me."

"This isn't going to haunt you. You already know where he's coming from."

When they arrived at the restaurant, Brad took her hand and led them inside. He looked around the room and walked to a booth at the back. He asked the waitress to wait until he signaled for her to come to the table, explaining that it would probably be half an hour or more before they would order.

When they sat down, Bob Matzlan placed a brown envelope on the table and slid it over in front of Shauna Lee.

She recoiled from it.

"Don't be afraid. I don't want to hurt you. Please open it."

Shauna Lee stared at the envelope but didn't reach for it.

Finally, Brad picked it up. "Do you want me to open it?"

"I don't want to see it."

"Do you mind if I look?"

She shook her head and glanced away. Brad opened the envelope and took out the contents. There were three pictures. Brad picked up one and looked at it. A corner was torn and the picture was faded. It was a close-up of two people; a blond haired teenage boy with distinctive blue eyes and a dark-haired girl with eyes so dark they were almost black. He was hugging her and they were both laughing.

Brad looked at Bob, knowing he was the young man. He picked up the second one and looked at it. It portrayed the same couple sitting on the hood of a car, looking happy and in love. The third one showed the young woman looking back over her shoulder, as she stood in front of the boy with her arms wrapped around his waist. They both were smiling and vibrantly happy.

Brad's breath caught in his throat. *That has to be Shauna Lee's mother,* he thought. *That woman looks like her, except for the eyes and there is no doubt that is a young Bob.*

He looked at Bob. He nodded, turned to Shauna Lee, put his arm around her and pulled her head into the curve of his shoulder. "Sweetheart, you need to look at these." He held one up in front of her. Shauna Lee squeezed her eyes shut. Brad nudged her. "They're happy pictures, sweetheart. Look at them."

She sighed and opened her eyes. Her eyes widened as she looked at the picture. Then she reached for it. Tears filled her eyes as she studied it. She looked at Bob. "This is you?"

He nodded. "And Marie Holt. I believe she was your mother."

She nodded, as she caressed the picture with her thumb. "I never saw her look so happy. She was beautiful here." She looked at Bob. "Were you really in love with her?"

"I always loved her."

"But you told me you loved your wife."

He smiled. "I did. She was wonderful and we raised three terrific boys."

"What do your sons think about this?"

"I haven't said anything to them, yet, but I will, if what I believe is true. I think that you are my biological daughter."

"That could only hurt them. Why would you do that?"

Bob leaned his elbows on the table and looked at her. "Did you take a good look at my sons?"

"I only saw them briefly when we were there that day. What are you getting at?"

"When we got married my wife was a widow. Her husband had died in an accident. He had been my best friend. The three of us had been extremely close. The three boys are their children. After Randy was born, Suzanne had her tubes tied, so she and I never had any children.

"I adopted the boys and raised them as my own. I love them like they are my own and the boys know that. They would be happy for me if I found out that I had a biological child, a daughter of my own. I'm sure they would welcome you as their sister."

"You raised another man's children and you loved them?"

His look was puzzled. "Their dad was my best friend. They had been part of my life from the time they were born. I was part of the household. I loved those kids long before I married their mother. Being a father goes beyond depositing sperm, Shauna Lee."

Her tears threatened to spill over, but she managed to push them away. She looked at Brad.

"It's your call Shauna Lee, but I think you need to get it all out in the open."

Her tear-filled eyes met Bob's. "I'm sure you are my biological father. It's hard to ignore our eyes, but..." She pleated the paper napkin on the table in front of her. "A few weeks ago, I saw my dad for the first time in twenty years. I didn't want to talk to him, but eventually he insisted, just like you have tonight." Pain filled her eyes as she looked at Bob.

"There were so many things about my childhood that I couldn't understand. My dad and mom..." She shrugged. Brad took her hand again and gave it a gentle squeeze of encouragement. "For as long as I could remember, they didn't seem to like each other, and Dad wouldn't have anything to do with me. I didn't know any better. I just thought that was how parents were. When I was eleven, my mother had another baby. It was a boy. Dad was so happy. But, that baby died when he was four. In the end, Dad left Mom and me.

Bob sat up straight, his face tight, his hand flexing open and then closing.

"When Dad came to see me, he told me that he had loved Mom with all his heart when he married her. He was thrilled when Mom got pregnant, and he loved me when I was born. Sometime later, when they were fighting, she told him that she didn't love him, that she had always loved someone else. As I grew older, because of my hair and my eyes, he began to suspect that he wasn't my father."

"Oh, no," Bob said softly.

"Eventually he remembered the man at the party at Junor and he put it all together. He confronted Mom about it. Of course, she didn't want to admit what had happened, but I guess he wouldn't let it go. She finally told him the truth. He said that every time he looked at me, it reminded him of her betrayal."

"Why didn't he divorce her?"

"He should have, but he said part of him still loved her and another part wanted to hurt her like she had hurt him." She sighed. "So they destroyed each other. Dad was bitter and drank all the time. Mom lost herself in depression."

Bob eyes shone with unshed tears. "And you? What happened to you?"

"It made me a survivor."

Bob bowed his head. "I'm sorry Shauna Lee."

"You know, Bob, I hated my dad for years but after he told me what had happened, as much as he hurt me when I was a child, I can't hold it against him now. And Mom and you... I can't hold it against you, either." She picked up a picture and looked at it. "You were so happy, then. I'm glad to know Mom had some happiness in her life."

She laid her head on Brad's shoulder. "Life is hard sometimes, but once in a while, we get lucky. Brad has changed my life. He has changed me. He loves me for who I am."

Brad signaled to get the waitress's attention. Bob reached across the table and touched Shauna Lee's hand. "I want you to keep the pictures and I hope you'll let me be a part of your life."

"Can you imagine? For thirty-five years, I didn't have a father who would acknowledge me. Now, I have two.

***

It was Christmas Eve! Shauna Lee cradled Karma in her arms while she stood on the front porch and watched the huge snowflakes float down with the softness of goose down. Halos formed where the street lights shone through. The colored lights that Brad had threaded around the big spruce tree at the edge of the parking area shimmered like twinkling ghosts. The snow edged down the roof and slid off to dollop on the bottom step.

Brad opened the door and stepped out behind her in his sock feet. He threaded his arms around her waist and pulled her back against his chest. "It's beautiful, isn't it?"

She nodded. "It is. I'm so excited. I feel like I'm ten years old! I can't believe that I never noticed all this beauty for all those years. How could I have been so blind?"

"Most things are better when shared, especially times like this. You know there are a lot of people that feel the same way about Christmas that you did."

She was thoughtful. "I wonder how my dad feels about it; probably the same. I think he regrets the way he reacted when I was a kid. He has to feel lonely."

"Shauna, do you want to phone and see what he's doing? You could invite him to dinner tomorrow if you want."

"I don't know. You don't like him. How would you feel about it if we did that?"

"Sweetheart, I hate how what he did has affected your entire life. But in a way, he was a victim, too." He turned her around and led her inside. "And if you want to go back further, then we could blame Bob and your mom."

"And then we could blame Bob's family for moving away," she continued. "But really, it's just circumstances and life. Maybe it's time to let go of all the blame and anger and move on."

Brad wrapped his arms around her. "It would be a healing thing for all of us. Are you ready to do that?"

"You'll have to help me. Can you stop calling him an asshole?"

"Tweetie Bird, I'll do anything to help you move on with your life."

Full Circle

"It's kind of late to call now, isn't it? Tomorrow is Christmas."

"Who knows, sweetheart? Some people would hitchhike through a blizzard to get here if they got that call."

"I don't have a gift for him."

"What would you give him; a sweater or a tie that he probably wouldn't use? I'll bet he would be happier if you gave him a second chance. You could wrap up an invitation to the wedding and give it to him. Have you thought about asking him to walk you down the aisle?"

She smiled at him. "You are so wise. Do you have the phone number for the ranch?"

"Come with me. It's in my office."

She dialed the ranch but didn't reach anyone. She was deep in thought when she came back to the kitchen. "There was no answer there. They must be out feeding or something."

"Let's eat and then you can try to call again."

Brad took the small beef roast from the oven while Shauna Lee took a salad out of the fridge and mixed the dressing. Brad was setting the table when the doorbell rang.

They looked at each other. Brad shrugged. "It could be Tim. I don't think he was going home for Christmas. I told him to stop by if he wanted to."

Shauna Lee nodded. "I'll get it."

A man stood staring out at the snow, in much the same way as she had done earlier. He turned to face her when she opened the door. Her jaw sagged.

"I didn't come to stay. I just wanted to give you this and I'll go." He held out a thin package.

Shauna Lee was momentarily stunned. He leaned down and laid the package on a lighted reindeer ornament on the porch. Then mumbling that he was sorry, he turned to walk down the step.

She reached out and grabbed his coat. "Dad, please don't go." He turned to face her. "I tried to call you. There was no answer at the ranch."

He hesitated. "Ollie and I fed late. We fed enough so I don't have to feed until tomorrow afternoon. I knew I would be late getting home tonight. Ollie went to the Thompsons for Christmas. Ellie invited him over for supper tonight."

"Come in." She stood aside for him to enter.

Patch stepped up beside her. He looked into her eyes solemnly. "Thank you," he said softly. "I didn't expect you to ask me in. I... I just wanted to do something now that I didn't do when you were a child."

Shauna Lee hugged him. He hesitated then hugged her back. Brad stood back and watched as a tear seeped down the older man's cheek. She released her hold and gently nudged Patch inside, closing the door behind them.

Brad's eyes met Patch's. They measured each other for a moment. *He was a victim too,* he thought. *No matter how hard it is to understand the way he treated her. If she can try, so can I.*

Brad stepped toward the man who had been Shauna Lee's unwilling parent and extended his hand. "Welcome, Patch and Merry Christmas." He looked at Shauna Lee. "I'll put another plate on the table."

Shauna Lee's look was grateful. She nodded when she took Patch's coat and hung it up.

Supper was quiet and awkward. No one knew exactly what to say. When they finished eating, Brad poured coffee for the three of them. Brad sat down and looked at Shauna Lee. "Did you show your dad your ring?"

She looked at her hand and then held it out for Patch to see. "Brad and I are engaged. We are getting married on the fourth of February."

Patch studied the ring and then turned to Brad. "I'm glad she met you. I think you're a good man. It's time someone loved her and looked after her, and I'm sure you will do that."

"Thank you, sir. I love your daughter with all my heart."

Patch looked from one to the other. "Always be honest with each other and don't keep secrets. They destroy love."

Shauna Lee swallowed hard as she looked at Brad. She gathered up the dishes and put them in the dishwasher. Brad wished he could have a drink, but decided against it because he knew Patch was an alcoholic. He invited him to join him in the living room. The conversation relaxed as Brad turned it to the ranch and Patch happily talked about what was happening there.

Shauna Lee slipped into the spare room. She opened the box on the bed and took out an invitation and a reply card and envelope. She went to the cupboard and took out a small, thin gift box that she had purchased earlier.

She got a sheet of paper from Brad's desk and quickly wrote a note, then folded the paper and placed it under the invitation, which she nestled in a froth of tissue in the box. She took a tag and inscribed it: "To Dad."

She slipped the tiny package under the tree with the other gifts. She and Brad had agreed not to go overboard; even so, a few packages were nestled under the branches. One of the gifts was for Christina, who would be coming for Christmas dinner and another had Tim's name on it. Shauna Lee felt guilty when she looked at the small package she had placed there for the only man she had known as her Dad.

Brad and Patch found they had experiences to share and other things to talk about. Patch had become a hunter after he went to the Gang Ranch. He was a fly fisherman, too. Brad and he were soon swapping stories.

Shauna Lee sat back and listened, observing them both. In Brad, she saw a passion for things that she and he didn't share. In Patch, she got a glimpse of a side of the man that she had never known. They had things in common.

She loved Brad. She didn't know if she would ever be able to say she loved Patch. She hadn't forgotten how he had treated her. She knew he regretted their past. Could she give him another chance in her heart?

The evening went quickly. Finally, Brad looked at his watch and then looked at Shauna Lee. The look held a question. She nodded and stood up. "Will you stay overnight and have Christmas dinner with us tomorrow?" she asked.

"Thank you, but I hadn't planned to do that."

Brad leaned forward. "We'd like to have you stay."

"I don't want to impose on you two. I just wanted to give something to Shauna Lee." He looked around. Panic registered in his voice. "Where did I put it? Did I leave it outside? I don't want it to get wet." He got up and went to the door. Relief showed on his face when he saw it resting on the reindeer, cold but sheltered from the snow.

When he handed the package to Shauna Lee, Brad intercepted it and carried it to the tree.

"We'd like to have you stay, Patch. We talked about this earlier and Shauna Lee phoned the ranch to ask you to come for Christmas dinner. But, of course, you weren't there."

Patch hesitated. "I should run it by Ollie, first. The cattle have plenty of hay, but it is snowing. He thought I was going back tonight."

"I'll call Colt. You can talk to Ollie. You should stay the night. You'd have a long drive to the ranch and it's still snowing hard." Brad dialed Colt's number.

When he answered, Colt told him that Ollie wasn't there. "He's over at Ellie's place." Colt chuckled. "He's probably getting his Christmas present if you get my drift. Why did you want to talk to him?"

"Patch stopped in earlier and we'd like him to stay overnight. It's a long drive home and it's snowing like crazy."

"Ollie and I talked about that earlier. Ollie said they put out extra feed. He said Patch shouldn't even have to feed tomorrow, so tell him to stay as long as he likes, as long as he gets home so he can feed the next day."

"Thanks, Colt. Did all the parents arrive? It sounds like you have a house full."

"Everyone is here. The place is overflowing. The kids are going crazy with excitement. We had to let them open a few gifts this evening."

"How is Frank doing?"

"She seems to be doing alright. She's busy and that helps. We just take one day at a time. She has good days and tough days."

"Well, Merry Christmas, Colt."

"Same to you Brad. I'm glad you guys invited Patch for Christmas dinner. He is a tormented man, and everyone should be with family for the holiday."

Shauna Lee showed Patch to the spare room. She took the box of invitations into the office and then showed him where the towels were in the bathroom.

Patch looked at his clothes. "I didn't come prepared to stay for Christmas. I don't have a change of clothes."

"If you give me your clothes, I'll put them in the washer and I can have them ready for you in the morning."

"Would you do that for me?"

"Of course I would. There's a house coat that'll fit you in the closet." She slid the door open and took out a forest-green, velour garment that Brad had left there.

Patch looked at it. He smiled at her. "It's nice. I've never owned one."

Shauna Lee told him to leave his clothes on the floor by his door. She went out to the kitchen where Brad had taken the turkey out of the refrigerator to finish thawing. "I'm going to wash his clothes, so they are clean for tomorrow. I told him to use the housecoat that was in the closet. He said he's never owned one."

She picked up Patch's clothes and put them in the washer. She and Brad worked in the kitchen doing the preparation for the turkey dressing and the vegetables for the next day. By the time they were finished, everything was ready to put into saucepans to cook and minimal time would be needed to put the dressing together and have the turkey in the oven the next day.

The next morning Brad finished the turkey and put it in the oven. Shauna Lee pressed Patch's clothes and hung them on his doorknob. Then, she made coffee and heated cinnamon buns in the warmer.

She and Brad were as giddy as kids. When Patch appeared, they each grabbed a coffee and a cinnamon bun and went into the living room. Brad selected the gift he wanted to give her and handed it to her. She picked out the one she wanted to give him. Then she gave Patch her gift.

Patched looked at her in surprise. "I didn't expect a gift."

"Dad, this isn't much."

He opened the box and pushed back the tissue paper. He lifted out the invitation and his eyes filled with tears. "Are you inviting me to your wedding?"

"Yes." She said softly. "There is folded sheet of paper in there too. You should read it."

He moved the invitation and the reply card. He picked up the folded sheet and opened it. The words blurred through his tears as he read them; *Dad, will you please walk me down the aisle at my wedding?*

He put the box down on the end table beside him and stood up. Tears streamed down his cheeks when he stepped toward Shauna Lee. "This is the most incredible gift you could have given me. I'll be honored to walk you down the aisle. You cannot know what this means to me."

He turned to the tree and picked up his gift for her. "This is all I had to give you."

Shauna Lee's finger trembled as she opened the package. "Oh," she cried softly. In her hands, she held a picture taken on her mom and dad's wedding day. They were both smiling and looked very much in love. "Where did you find these?"

"I took them with me when I left. Your mother had hidden them away years before. I knew she would never miss them. She was too deep in her sadness and depression. But, even though I was running away, I wanted to remember that once there was some meaning to our tortured lives."

Shauna Lee studied the picture. She looked at Patch. "She looks happy. She looks like she is in love with you here."

"I think she was. I've thought it about it since I talked to you. That's when I got those pictures out and looked at them again. Your mom had a sharp tongue. She was mad at me when she said that she'd always loved someone else. Now I wonder if she was just lashing out at me. She was so scornful when she said it and it hit me where it hurt the most. She was beautiful and I was always insecure; always amazed that she had married me. I loved her so much and I was devastated when she threw that at me. I couldn't let it go."

Shauna Lee looked at him sadly.

"There's another picture there, Shauna Lee."

She stared with surprise. "I didn't notice. I was so amazed to see this one." Her fingers slipped under it and pulled out another one. Tears flooded her eyes.

"That's your mom and me, when you were born."

Patch was holding her in his arms. Her mother was standing behind him with her hand on his shoulder. Patch was a proud father.

"I wanted you to know that I did love you when you were born. It just became too painful when I realized that you weren't mine." He looked away. "I let my foolish pride destroy our lives, our family. I'd do it differently now, but it's too late."

Shauna Lee hugged the pictures to her breast. "Thank you, Dad. These are so special! I'm grateful that you gave them to me. We can't change what happened in the past. You and I can only move on from here."

After they had opened their gifts, Brad went to the kitchen to check on the turkey and Patch and Shauna Lee chatted about the past. She hesitated and took a deep breath. "Dad, I recently met my biological father."

Patches eyes widened in surprise. "How—"

"I'm starting to believe everything unfolds the way it is supposed to in spite of us. When I met Brad, I wasn't a very nice person. He should have run like crazy, but he looked beyond the surface and fell in love with me. I tried to push him away, but he wouldn't go.

"And then, everything started to happen. I started to recall things I had buried deep in my consciousness. Then, I saw you again.

"After that, Brad and I went to check on some of his installations. The first place we went, the man challenged me, asking about my background. He... he sensed something about me. It was bizarre, but he ended up telling me about himself and Mom. But, he didn't know who I was and I didn't tell him.

"We went to the second place and it turned out to be people who had supported me when..." She shook her head.

"When that no-good man—"

"Yes." She bit her lip and fought back tears. "I blamed you for that. I thought that if you'd stayed, if you'd loved me, none of that would have happened. I realize now that that wasn't fair, but it took Brad to make me see that."

"But, it was my fault."

"No, Dad. We were all victims. After we got back, Brad went to China and you came to see me. You told me what happened with you, Mom and him. I realized then that he had to be my biological father because your stories were the same."

She looked at him imploring. "I'm not trying to hurt you, but I want you to know everything. Last week he came to Brad's open house at Windspeer. He wasn't really looking for Brad. He wanted to talk to me.

"Actually he did what you did. He insisted on talking to me. He took Brad and me out for supper and he gave me some pictures. They were of him and Mom when they were teenagers; a couple of kids and their first love. He was blonde and his eyes are blue, just like mine."

Patch stood up and paced across the room.

"He and Mom did... I was conceived the night of that party. He said she was mad at you because you were drinking and you passed out and one thing led to another and they..."

"Your mom admitted that."

"Later, he married the widow of his best friend. She had three boys. He adopted them, but he never had any children with her. He told me that he loved her and he loves those boys like they were his own, but I doubt if he was ever with anyone else other than Mom before he married. When he saw me... the blonde hair and the eyes; our eyes are the same. He began to wonder if...he wanted to know if he had a biological child. He said once he saw me he had to know."

"I guess he wants to be your father now."

"He is my father, and yes he did ask if he could be part of my life, and I will be honest, I want to get to know him and his children."

Patch looked out the window. "So, why did you give me that note, asking me to walk you down the aisle?" She could hear the dejection in his voice.

Shauna Lee stood up and walked over to him. "He fathered me, but you are my dad. I'd like you to walk me down the aisle."

"You want that, even though I was such a poor one?"

"Dad, we all need to heal and move forward. It's time for honesty and forgiveness, not anger and blame."

"Is that why you asked me to be in your wedding?"

"Partly; but mostly I asked you because I *want* you there."

Tears glinted in his eyes. "I'm amazed that you can be so forgiving."

"Dad, to be honest, this hasn't been an easy decision for me. Six months ago I wouldn't have asked you; I couldn't have. But, thanks to Brad, I have learned that love can change our lives and I want to move forward and heal. I believe that you have changed. My biological father is part of who I am, but he can never replace the fact that you were in my life from birth."

"Will he be at the wedding?" Patch asked.

"I haven't asked him. I'm sure he would like to be, but I wouldn't ask him without giving you a chance to think about it. I won't ask him to come if you say you don't want me to. I can see where it might make you uncomfortable, but all of that happened a long time ago. We are all different people now."

Patch looked out the window.

"Dad, I don't want your answer now. You have a week or so to think about it. Brad and I are flying to Dawson Creek to meet his family, at New Years. When we come home, it will be only five weeks until the wedding, so I'll have to make some decisions then.

CHAPTER TWENTY ONE

It was almost Christmas and the Thompson household bubbled with excitement.

Bob and Serena Thompson had arrived on the twenty-second. They were loaded down with gifts. The twins were wild with excitement and constantly on the go.

Frank was drowning in the confusion. *I love Colt's mom and dad*, she thought. *But right now I could do without all this madness. It is driving me crazy.* She put on her coat and slipped out to sit on the veranda and soak up the tranquility, oblivious to the cold. *Tomorrow Mom and Dad will come, and everything will ramp up another notch.*

Five minutes later, Colt came out to check on her. "It's pretty crazy in there isn't it?" He sat down beside her and reached to slip his arm around her. He felt her stiffen and withdraw. "Are you all right?"

"Of course I am," she snapped. "I just came out here to be alone for a few minutes. Is that too much to ask?"

Colt's heart sank. Frank hadn't been the same since the

miscarriage. *She just needs more time,* he thought. He sat beside her for a few minutes. The uncomfortable feeling grew between them. She did not respond when he put his hand on her thigh. She would not look at him and her face remained tight. Finally, he stood up and went inside, leaving her there alone.

When he went inside his mother was quick to ask about her. Colt smiled, hiding his pain. "She just needs some quiet time. It's pretty chaotic in here."

Cameron and Rayelle Lamonte arrived early on the twenty-fourth. They brought even more gifts and Rayelle had baked a lot of goodies. She and Serena took over the kitchen and Ellie looked after the twins.

Frank distanced herself from everything. She wandered through the house, tidying here and there. She put in an appearance but kept herself emotionally shuttered. She went upstairs to lie on the bed. *Just three more days; then everyone will go home. I just have to hang on that long.* She sighed and closed her eyes. *Just three more days.*

Colt came upstairs an hour later. She heard his steps and feigned sleep. *He hovers over me all the time. Sometimes, I just want to scream. Can't he see that I just need time alone?*

Colt sat on the bed and took her hand in his. She couldn't jerk it away and still pretend she was asleep. She felt him caress it gently. She looked up at him and saw the pain in his eyes. Her heart warmed and she inched over and tugged him to her.

He smiled softly and lay beside her. He wrapped her in his arms and held her close. She relaxed against him, her cheek against his chest. He kissed her forehead and she heard him sigh. Frank let herself slip into the comfort of his warmth and strength.

She lingered there until Colt stirred. "I worry about you, Fran. I want to help you, but I don't know how."

"I'll be all right. I'm just tired and there is so much going on all the time. I need to get away once in a while." She leaned

Full Circle

back so she could look into his eyes. "I'm sorry I'm so miserable. I don't mean to hurt you. I just... I feel so empty. I know I should be happy. It is Christmas time. I should be down there with the twins, but the truth is, I just wish it would all go away. I could care less about Christmas this year."

"I understand that. Everything is being looked after, so do what you need to and don't beat yourself up." He eased her close to him. "It feels good to hold you like this. I know it's early, but I miss having my friend and companion here with me."

She reached up and touched his face. Her eyes swam with tears. "It feels good to me too. I'm sorry. I don't know what to do. I wish I could just flip the happy switch and be there, but I can't."

"It's all right, hon; but please don't shut me out. I want to be there for you, but I can't if you won't let me." He dropped a kiss on her forehead. "I guess I should go back down and see what everyone is doing."

Frank sat up. "I'll come with you."

It was Christmas Eve and the kids were hyper, and looking forward to opening their gifts. Finally, Colt relented and said they could each open two. Eager hands ripped the wrapping and tossed it aside. Then they lost themselves in the excitement of their new toys.

Christmas day was a melee of gift opening and excitement and noise. Frank slipped away to the bedroom and shut the door. Her emotions overwhelmed her: sadness for the little girl she had lost, the huge ball of loneliness in her heart and the desperate emptiness she felt in her arms.

Heart-wrenching sobs wracked her body and tears drenched her pillow. Colt slipped into the room. He lay on the bed and pulled her against him. He didn't speak. Instead, he let her exhaust her tears and fall asleep.

His own tears dried on his cheeks. *I am totally useless here.*

Nothing I do helps her.

Bob and Serena left for home the next day.

Rayelle Lamonte wanted to talk to her daughter and comfort her. She had experienced four miscarriages herself. She understood what Frank was going through, but she didn't get a chance to talk to her. Frank had erected an emotional wall around herself and she gave nobody opportunity to intrude into the space behind it. Rayelle and Cameron left the next day. Rayelle was frustrated, her heart troubled.

Colt was just as troubled when he took Frank for her checkup just before New Years. She had developed a sharp tongue, lashing out at everyone; himself, even Ellie and on occasion even the twins.

She spent little time with the children now and Ellie had taken over in the house when his mom and Rayelle had gone home. She seemed to be tired all the time and all through Christmas, she had sought to escape everyone's company.

Dr. Wilfred said that Frank was physically healed and they could resume having sex, but he warned them to take precautions so she wouldn't get pregnant immediately. He asked her how she was healing emotionally.

Colt looked at the doctor intently, hoping that he would sense the anguish he knew that she was trying to suppress. When Frank gave him a bright smile assuring him that she was doing well, Dr. Wilfred sat back in his chair and looked at her with compassion.

"Frank, I know that isn't true. No one, who wanted their child as much as you two, gets over it in one month. I hope you discuss your feelings honestly with each other."

"We do. Colt is doing fine, and so am I."

Colt shook his head. "No, honey, I'm not doing fine and neither are you. I'm hurting like hell for what we've lost and so are you. When I try to talk to you about it, you shut down and refuse to talk.

"But when I hear you crying at night and when you go for a nap during the day, I peek in and see tears on your cheeks.

And I notice when you come down from the bathroom, your eyes red from the tears you have tried to hide, and it tears me up inside."

She stared at him. "But you are moving on. I'll get there in time."

"No, I'm stuck in this spot, just like you are. I am trying to be strong for you Fran. Neither one of us can move on until we deal with this."

Dr. Wilfred cleared his throat. "Frank and Colt, we have counselors who help people deal with what you've been through. If you try to ignore your pain, it will eat at you and it will probably eat at your relationship too. Colt, you don't have to be so strong for Frank that you deny you own feelings. With proper guidance, you can help each other heal and face the future together."

Colt looked at Frank. She looked away from both of them as her eyes filled with tears. Anger surged through her. "Can't I grieve for my baby? What is wrong with that! She was real to me."

Dr. Wilfred reached across his desk to her. "Frank," he said gently. "Of course, you have to grieve, and so does Colt, but there is more involved here for you. You are still flushed with pregnancy hormones. On top of that, your file shows that you have suffered from depression before and we don't want you to slip into it again. I would like you to see a psychiatrist."

Frank jumped up. "No! I'm not crazy."

"Frank, no one thinks you are. He is not going to have you lie on the couch like in the movies. Colt can go with you."

"We don't need a marriage counselor, either."

"Believe me; he doesn't have time to be a marriage counselor. He will assess you and offer advice to help you cope. He may prescribe a medication, but that is his expertise. He has more knowledge about the treatments available for the best results than I do."

"Give me a break. I just lost a baby. I cry. I didn't feel like celebrating Christmas. I need some time and space, but you have got me headed for the loony bin already." She glared at Colt when she turned to the door. "I'm leaving here. Are you coming or are you going to plot with him to put me away?" She slammed the door as she went out.

Colt jumped up to follow her. As he opened the door, Dr.Wilfred said, "Keep an eye on her, Colt. Call me anytime."

She was at the truck door, waiting for him to unlock it when he came out. She was fuming mad. They both got inside. Colt turned to her. "What would you like to do now?"

She glared at him. "Get away from you."

"Fran..." He reached out to touch her.

"Leave me alone. You went in there and made it sound like there's something wrong with me."

"Honey, you're not yourself."

"You have got to be kidding! What do you expect from me?"

They drove home in silence. Colt felt sick. Frank's anger burned stronger with every kilometer. When they arrived, she ran into the house and slammed the entry door in his face and rushed passed the twins when they ran to meet her. She strode upstairs into their bedroom and locked the door. Then, she lay down on the bed and cried.

Colt hugged the twins, explaining that Mommy wasn't feeling good. He looked at Ellie helplessly and then went up the stairs to their bedroom. She had locked the door, and he could hear her sobbing. He stood there, not knowing what to do. Reluctantly he turned and went back down the stairs.

Ellie looked at him with concern in her eyes. He shook his head. "I don't know what to do."

"Give her time, Colt."

"She's shutting me out. I'd like to hold her and comfort her. I wish we could talk about losing the baby, but she won't."

"Can I get you a cup of coffee, Colt?"

Frank stayed in the bedroom for the rest of the day. That night Colt slept in the spare room because the door was still locked. The next morning, Colt ate breakfast with Ellie and the twins. Frank was still barricaded in the bedroom. When he had repeatedly knocked on the door, she had finally told him to go away.

Colt felt as if his world was falling apart. His wonderful, loving wife, had morphed into a cold stranger in such a short period of time.

He wandered through the house aimlessly, trying to get himself grounded. He went into the office and sat down. *She will come around. We lost Cherish, but we still have the twins. And she loves them. She loves me. I just have to give her space and more time.*

He pushed a pen around on his desk. "I don't expect her to be done grieving yet; I want her to be able to cry and talk about how she feels," he murmured to himself. *But, I didn't expect her to shut everyone out. It's not like her. She didn't talk to her mom about what happened; she was barely here emotionally the whole time everyone was here at Christmas. She doesn't spend time with the twins.* "She doesn't want anything to do with me. It's scary."

The phone rang. It was Mona with questions about the house plans. Colt hesitated and then told her he would come into her office. He went to the bedroom door and called to Frank. "Hon, Mona called. She wants us to check out what she has done on the blueprints."

He heard her moving around. Finally, she opened the door. She had changed into pajamas, but her skin was pale and her hair disheveled. She leaned against the door frame. "You can go see her. I'm not into it now."

He reached out to touch her shoulder. "Fran, it might make you feel better if you got out."

She glared at him and pulled away. "As if you would know how I feel." She closed the door against him and locked it.

Colt felt like she had gut-punched him. He went down to the kitchen. Ellie was bustling around. The twins were playing in the family room. "I have to go see the architect. I'll take the twins with me and give you some time off, Ellie."

"They haven't had their afternoon nap. They could get tired and whiny."

"I'll manage. You have a rest and take some time for yourself."

"What about Frank?"

"I talked to her, but she said to go without her. It'll be good for me to get out and do something else. Don't worry about supper. The kids and I will go out for chicken nuggets. They will love it."

Colt took the twins with him to Mona's office. The changes Mona had made were small and he approved them and told her to go ahead as planned. As Ellie had predicted, the twins were getting tired and cranky. When they got back into the truck, Colt buckled them into their car seats, and he slid behind the steering wheel. *I don't want to go home yet*, he thought. *Besides, I told Ellie I would take the twins out for supper.*

He sat for a few minutes, and then decided to drive over to Tim's place. If Tim was at home, he could let the twins nap and the two of them could talk. Tim was just hanging out, watching TV when he arrived. He was surprised to see Colt, but readily agreed to let the twins have a nap on his bed.

They were both asleep in their car seats. Colt brought them in one at a time and laid them on Tim's bed. He took off their boots and unzipped their jackets, then covered them with a light blanket that Tim handed him.

Tim offered him a beer, but he declined, knowing he would have to drive home. Tim was watching boxing and Colt settled on the couch beside him. It wasn't his favorite sport, but it was a diversion.

Tim made coffee, brought a box of donuts from the counter and sat it on the coffee table. Colt picked up a new farm publication that lay there and leafed through it. He and Tim talked about a couple of articles in it and passed two hours in comfortable companionship.

Sam woke up first and quietly wandered out to join them. Colt took off his coat and sat him on his knee. He looked at Tim and smiled shyly. Then he pointed to the donuts, indicating that he wanted one. Tim chuckled, and gave him one and then went to get him a glass of milk.

Half an hour later Selena woke up with a wail. Colt looked at Tim and grinned. "The princess calls." He sat Sam down beside Tim and went to get her. She was crying when he carried her into the sitting room. They sat down by Tim. "I want Mommy."

"Mommy's at home."

Tim handed her a donut, which she took and her cries became a whimper. Tim looked at Colt. "How is Frank doing?"

Colt looked down at Selena before he answered. When he looked at Tim, the strain he felt showed in his eyes. "She's having a tough time."

Tim nodded. "My sister miscarried and she was a mess. But her husband was a jerk. His attitude was to just move on, and they'd have another kid."

"But I don't feel that way, Tim. I understand that she needs to mourn. I do, too." He shook his head. "She has just closed down on everyone. It's hard to know."

"I can't help you, bud. My ex was too busy to have kids, so I have no experience with births or miscarriages."

"I told Ellie to take the evening off. I couldn't have managed without her. She's taken over and looked after everything. I'm going to take the kids for chicken nuggets at Smitty's. Do you want to join us?"

Tim looked at his watch. "It beats eating alone."

Colt and the twins arrived home a few minutes before seven o'clock. The outside light was on and Colt thought Ellie must have come over. He guided the twins up the steps onto the veranda and opened the door for them. He helped them take off their coats and he hung them up. He helped them take their boots off and reminded them to put them on the boot mat. "Okay, kids. It's time to go upstairs and get ready for bed."

"I want to see Mommy," Selena complained.

"Mommy's not feeling very good. She's probably sleeping."

He heard footsteps in the family room, and Frank came around the corner. "Mommy's here, Selena."

Selena ran to her and Sam followed on her heels. Frank pulled them close and hugged them to her.

She looked at Colt, tears shimmering in her eyes. "It was terribly quiet here, with everyone gone."

Colt smiled at her, his love reaching out to her. "I told Ellie to take the afternoon off. The twins and I went to Smitty's for chicken nuggets."

"AnnnTim went too," Sam said.

"Yes, son, Tim went with us, too." He looked at Frank. "They needed a nap, so we went over to Tim's after I went to Mona's office. They slept for a couple of hours. I asked Tim if he wanted to go to Smitty's with us. Did you have something to eat?"

"I had a cup of coffee and some toast."

"It's good to see you up."

She nodded, her eyes brimming with tears. She stood up and took the children's hands. "Let's get you ready for bed." She led them upstairs.

Colt hesitated, not certain if he should follow. She looked back at him from the top step and smiled wanly. He bounded up the steps to join them.

After the children had settled in bed, she motioned for Colt to go ahead and she closed the door to their room. He wanted to take her into his arms and hold her, but he wasn't sure how she would react. She looked at him and then stepped toward him, hesitantly.

He reached for her and enfolded her in his arms. "I've missed you," he whispered.

"I'm sorry, Colt. I can't explain how I feel. Sometimes, I'm just overwhelmed."

He bent his head tentatively. She lifted her lips to meet his and he kissed her gently. "I love you, Fran."

She nodded. "I love you, too, Colt. I honestly do."

"Do you want something more to eat? Toast wasn't very much."

"I'm not hungry. Will you come to bed with me and just hold me? I...I need to know that you are here with me."

"Honey, I've always been here for you."

"Just come and hold me, please?"

He led her to the bed and helped her get in. He stripped to his t-shirt and shorts and lay beside her. He pulled her close and held her against his chest. She was tense. He ran his hand up and down her back and she gradually relaxed, letting her cheek rest against his chest.

"I'm sorry," she whispered."

"Honey, you have nothing to be sorry about."

"I mean, I'm sorry for locking the door last night. I was so mad at you. I felt like you had betrayed me."

"Honey, that's not what I did. We both have to work our way through this, but we have not been communicating."

"I understand that." She pushed away from him. "But a psychiatrist? That was insulting."

"Hon, please, let's not do this. I don't want to argue."

"You said we haven't been communicating. I'm trying to communicate."

"Not now. Not this way. Please."

Frank pushed him away. "You only want to communicate if we do it your way."

Colt stared at her in dismay. "Fran, you are looking for a fight. I don't want to do that. I'm going to the spare room." He rolled out of the bed and walked out of the room.

Frank stared after him, tears running down her cheeks. She jumped up and slammed the bedroom door, locking it.

Colt strode to the spare room. His heart was pounding, his mind in a whirl. "What the hell happened?" he groaned.

"One minute she wanted me to hold her, the next she wanted to pick a fight. I can't seem to win." He lay on the bed, trying to think. His mind wouldn't settle and he knew he would never fall asleep.

He got up and went downstairs. He turned on the corner light and sat on the couch. Anxiety filled him, chased by fear. His eyes settled on their wedding album. He reached down and picked it up. He turned the pages looking at the pictures one by one.

"We love each other," he whispered. "How could losing the baby tear us apart like this?"

His eyes rested on the picture of Frank and her friend Becky Freemont. Becky... He remembered Frank saying that Becky was her closest confidant. "I wonder if she's talked to Becky about the miscarriage. Probably not." He looked at the picture for several seconds. *What is her husband's name? Ron? No... Russ. That's it. Russ is his name.*

He stood up and went to the office. He called information and got their phone number. Then he placed a call without taking time to think it over. When a man answered, he asked for Becky, without explaining who was calling.

"Who is this?"

"Colt Thompson: I'm married to Fran Lamonte. Becky was her bridesmaid."

"Colt! How are you guys doing?"

"Fran had a miscarriage in November and things have been pretty rough around here. I need Becky's help."

"Just a minute. Becky's the one you want to talk to, here she is."

"What's up, Colt?" Becky asked.

"Fran miscarried on the twenty-fifth of November. I know it hasn't been that long and she needs to grieve, but I'm worried about her. Christmas was hard on her. Of course, both of our parents came because it was Christmas and because they wanted to support her... us. But, she just closed everyone out. She's closing me out too.

"Her doctor suggested we get help because she's had depression before. He mentioned a psychiatrist and she hit the roof. I don't know what to do anymore. No matter what I do, it's wrong." He cleared his throat. "Do you have big plans for New Year's?"

"We were going to go skiing tomorrow and then just stay at home on New Year's Eve. Do you want me to come out there and talk to her, Colt? If you do, I'll be there."

"Becky, I don't want to mess up your New Year's plans, but I'm at a loss here. We've always been so happy and now...she just gets farther and farther away. Neither one of us can share how we feel. One minute it looks like there might be a breakthrough and ten minutes later she's looking for a fight."

"I'll be there tomorrow."

"Look, discuss it with Russ before you decide."

"She is my oldest and dearest friend. Russ will understand. We'll go skiing another weekend."

"Let me see if I can get a flight out here for you first. Maybe you could be home by New Year's Eve. Or, maybe Russ would come with you and we'll work something out. Talk it over and I'll check for a flight."

No commercial flights were available. Colt pondered the situation. Then he phoned a local cattle buyer.

"Thompson, what the hell do you want at this time of the night?" Bart Anderson barked.

"Have you got anything lined up for tomorrow morning?"

"Well, it's New Year's Eve tomorrow night."

"Is your plane at the airport?"

"Yes, I went flying today. What's on your mind?"

"My wife had a miscarriage. She's having a pretty rough time, so I'd like to fly her best friend in from Calgary tomorrow. I tried the airlines, but the flights are full. You are my last resort. I don't care how much you charge to fly them here; I'll willing pay if you'll do it for me."

Bart chuckled. "How deep are your pockets?"

"I know you'll be fair and this is really important to me."

"You're asking a lot. It's a long weekend and all," he groused. "But, I like that pretty wife of yours, so I'll do it. What time do you want to leave?"

"Bart, I owe you big time for this. How early can we be in Calgary?"

"I fuelled up when I got in this afternoon, so we can leave here at six o'clock in the morning if you want. That will put us in Calgary by eight or eight-thirty. We'll stop to stretch our legs and have breakfast. We can be back in Swift Current by twelve- thirty or one."

"Thanks, Bart. I'll phone Becky right away... and is it alright if her husband decides to come along?"

"It's a six-passenger, so there's lots of room."

"One more thing, Bart; will you fly them home after the weekend?"

"Gawd! Next you'll be asking for my wallet, too."

"I'm hoping that bringing in her best friend will help Fran. The money is secondary."

"Phone your wife's friend and set it up. We'll be there."

Becky answered as soon as he dialed.

"Can you be at the airport by eight in the morning?" he asked. "A cattle buyer that I deal with has a Beechcraft Bonanza. If you two will meet us at the airport, we can be there by eight thirty tomorrow morning. We'll grab breakfast and head back to Swift Current. We should be back here no later than one o'clock. And he'll fly you home on the second."

"That's terrific. You obviously know people in the right places, Colt."

"He likes my wife!"

"I'm glad he does. Do you have a spare bedroom?"

"Yes, but there's nothing very exciting going on at our house for New Year's. I can get you a good hotel room in town and give you an 'all expenses paid' evening."

"Colt, don't be ridiculous. We'll stay at the farm. I am

excited about this. I haven't seen Frank since the twins were born."

"I can't thank you enough, Becky. I hope you can get through to her."

"We'll be at the airport at eight in the morning." She gave him her cell number so they could contact each other when the plane landed."

Colt phoned Bart and completed their arrangements. Then he walked over to Ellie's place. To his surprise, Ollie was there. They were playing a game of cards and enjoying a drink.

Colt felt guilty about asking her to come to the house by five o'clock in the morning. He asked her to change the sheets in the spare room and if she would make a special New Year's Eve supper. He thought there was a ham in the freezer.

Her eyes were full of questions, but he didn't answer them. He went back to the spare room and finally fell asleep.

His internal alarm woke him half an hour early. He looked at the clothes he'd worn the day before and decided to check in the laundry room. He smiled when he went inside. "Bless you, Ellie!"

He slipped a shirt off a hanger and a clean pair of jeans that she had creased and hung up. He ran upstairs and dressed, then checked on the twins. He dropped a kiss of each one of them, then carried his dirty clothes down to the laundry room before he put a pot of coffee on to brew. He was sipping a cup when Ellie and Ollie came in.

He hugged Ellie. "I don't know what we'd do without you. I'll make all this up to you, once our life gets straightened out. One other thing though; should Frank happen to ask about me, or what I am doing, please don't tell her anything. Don't tell her that I asked you to change the sheets in the spare room or that I asked you to make supper. We had another disagreement last night, and I slept in the spare room again. She may not get up before I'm back and maybe that would be best, in the long run. But, she's not eating enough either and I don't like to see that happening."

Ollie cleared his throat. "Well, maybe Ellie can't ask you what you are doing, but I can. What are you up to, Colt?"

"Ollie, I love that woman upstairs. I've tried everything else; this may be my last chance. I'm bringing in her best friend. I hope she can reach her."

Ollie nodded.

"I'll see you later this afternoon."

Full Circle

CHAPTER TWENTY TWO

It was a beautiful morning to fly. The flight to Calgary was relaxing and when they landed, Colt phoned Becky. They arranged to meet at a restaurant in the airport.

After breakfast, they made their way down to the tarmac and back to Bart's plane. While he did his pre-flight check, Becky, Russ and Colt settled inside. Colt suggested Russ ride up front with Bart so he could get the full view of the trip. Becky and he talked about Frank, the twins, and the miscarriage while they flew to Swift Current.

It was a few minutes after one o'clock when they arrived at the farm. Frank hadn't come downstairs yet. Becky took off her coat and looked at Colt. "I'm going to get her up."

"Becky, don't be surprised if she won't see you."

"I won't let her get away with that. I'll pick the lock or I'll get you and Russ to break the door down. She won't hide from me." She touched Colt's cheek. "She is lucky to have you, Colt. Now, show me the door to your room."

Colt took her up the stairs to the bedroom door and then

left her there. *This has to work! Fran has always turned to Becky. Hopefully, she can get through to her now.*

Becky knocked on the door. "Get up, lazy bones."

There was no response. She pounded on the door. "Frank, let me in! It's Becky and I didn't come all the way from Calgary to have you sleep while I'm here."

She heard footsteps. Frank opened the door cautiously. Her hair was a mess, her eyes were red and swollen. She stared at her friend. "Becky? What are you doing here?"

Becky pushed in and threw her arms around Frank. "It's New Years Eve, silly girl. Russ came with me. We came to see you and those beautiful twins, as well as that wonderful husband of yours. We're here for the weekend, so get up you sleepy head. I don't want to miss a moment of this visit."

Frank clung to her and started to cry. Becky reached back and slammed the door shut, then held her close. "Okay girl, what is going on with you?"

The two friends sank onto the bed and Frank sobbed. Two hours later, Becky had persuaded her to have a shower, fix her hair and get dressed and they walked down the stairs together. Frank was exhausted, but her heart was lighter than it had been for the last month.

Ollie and Ellie were in the kitchen putting the finishing touches on the New Years Eve feast. The aroma of roasting ham filled the kitchen.

Frank looked around the room. "Where are the twins and Colt?"

Ellie smiled. "Colt and Russ went to Swift Current to get snacks and replenish the *happy cupboard*. They took the twins along with them. They'll be back soon."

Frank looked at Becky. "Did you meet Ellie and Ollie?"

Becky nodded. "I met Ollie at the wedding, and Colt told me all about Ellie on the flight back here."

Frank looked puzzled. "Colt flew with you?"

Becky covered her mouth. "Crap...I shouldn't have opened my big yap."

Frank looked at her expectantly. "Well?..."

"He phoned last night and asked if we'd come. He's worried about you, Frank and he knows how close you and I are. That man is crazy about you. He moved heaven and earth to get us here. He even hired a private plane and they were at the Calgary airport at eight o'clock this morning to pick us up."

Frank leaned forward and put her head against Becky's breasts. "I was so nasty to him last night."

"He didn't say anything about that. He just said you wouldn't talk to anyone. He hoped you'd talk to me."

Frank turned around and went up the stairs again. Becky followed her. Frank sat on the bed. She covered her face and tears trickled through her fingers. "I'm such a mess," she sobbed. "We wanted her so much, and I lost her."

"Frank, you are not responsible for the miscarriage. That was out of your hands."

"I'm so tired. I hated Christmas."

"Frank, this is not you. You've been through a lot. Have you talked to your doctor about depression?"

"He wanted me to go to a psychiatrist! I'm not crazy. I just lost a baby."

"Did he say he thought you were 'crazy'?"

"No. But that's why you go to a psychiatrist."

"Frank, you need to change your thinking. Crazy is an uneducated term. Depression is caused by a chemical imbalance in the brain. It's an illness, and people go to a psychiatrist because they're ill, just like they go to a surgeon if they have gall bladder trouble or cancer. The psychiatrist works with the patient to diagnose their problem and prescribes medication to help them heal. You've suffered from depression twice before."

Frank's anger flared. "I didn't go to a psychiatrist. I got over it."

"Both those times your symptoms were mild and you did seem to get over it. But consider how quickly you slipped into the same place when you got pregnant and faced another stressful situation. From a medical point of view, you never really dealt with it before, but now you need to or it could become a serious problem. Before, you walked away from the superficial problems that triggered it. This time it's different; no matter where you go that pain will go with you.

"And you can't walk away from your life here. You can't leave the twins. They need you and you need them. And, Colt will do anything for you. You are the center of his world. I hope you know how much you have been blessed with, Frank."

She forced Frank to look at her. "You need to listen to your doctor, Frank. Get help. Don't ruin your life and the lives of those who are a part of it."

Tears slipped down Frank's cheeks. "I... I don't want to. I just...."

"Wash your face. The guys will be here soon. I want you to see Colt through the eyes of love, not the guilt you feel. Go!"

Frank washed her face and pressed a cold cloth to her eyes. Finally, she came out of the bathroom and looked at Becky. "Let's go downstairs and see if we can do something."

"How about a smile first?"

Frank gave her a wan smile.

"I want to see a real smile. Try again."

Frank smiled. Becky gave her thumbs up and they went down to meet the others.

New Year's Eve was fun at the Thompson household. By the end of the evening, Frank was smiling and when it was time to go to bed, she reached for Colt's hand and led him to the bedroom door.

He tugged her with him to look in on the twins, then they went into the bedroom and Frank locked the door behind them.

She threaded her arms around Colt's neck. "Thank you for bringing Becky here. She always makes me see things in a different light. I've been such a mess and I've taken everything out on you. I'm so sorry."

Colt held her close. "I love you. I love the twins. I loved Cherish. We have to heal and get on with our lives. I know it's only been a month, but I hope we can talk about how we feel and do this together. It's going to take time for both of us."

"Colt," she whispered. "Will you make love to me tonight? And then will you hold me in your arms and fall asleep with me."

Colt kissed her gently. Then he lowered her to the bed. He went to his night table and took out a condom. She helped him put it on and they made gentle, healing love that soothed both of their souls.

When they were finished, Colt wrapped Frank in his arms, pulling her cheek against his chest. "I have missed you so much, hon."

"Do you realize that it was four years ago tonight that we got engaged?" she whispered.

"Yes, it was." He smiled softly and dropped a kiss on her forehead. Then they both drifted off to sleep.

The first of January was a fun filled day. The six of them drove out to the ranch to show Becky and Russ where they were going to build their new home. The sun danced on the snow and it was a winter wonderland. It was late when they got home that evening, but everyone treasured the memory of the day.

Colt touched base with Bart and confirmed the arrangement for him to fly Becky and Russ back to Calgary. Frank and Becky hugged before they left the next morning.

Frank cradled Becky's face in her hands. "Thank you for coming. I needed to see you and get a shot of reality. I've been wallowing in my pain and pushing Colt away. He has tried so hard to support me, but most of the time I haven't let him. You're right. I have so much to be thankful for and I don't want to lose that. I'll go to see my doctor and do what he ever he thinks is best."

"I'm glad to hear that. Keep me posted, okay?" Becky grinned. "I have enjoyed this New Year's immensely and believe me; you'll be seeing more of us. I can't wait to visit you in your new house at the ranch. We'll go riding too."

Colt and Frank waved as the plane took off. They locked hands and walked back to the truck. Colt wrapped his arms around her and pushed her back against the door. "It's wonderful to see you smile again." He kissed her hungrily, arousing passion in both of them.

Frank pulled back and looked into his eyes. "I'll phone Doctor Wilfred tomorrow and ask him to make an appointment with a psychiatrist for me. I can't promise you that I'll never be difficult again. It may happen, but I'll try to recognize what I'm doing."

CHAPTER TWENTY THREE

On January, the first, Brad and Shauna Lee stood in line at the Grande Prairie Airport. Brad's brother and sister-in-law had driven them there from Dawson Creek. Their luggage stood on the floor beside their feet as they said their goodbyes. Shauna Lee paid no attention the janitor who bumped her as he mopped the floor. He looked down, mumbling that he was sorry, as he stepped away when she glanced at him. Everyone was excited about the upcoming wedding and were engaged in animated conversation

Once they were on board, Brad took her hand in his and kissed it. "So was meeting the family too traumatic?"

She smiled at him. "They're wonderful and they made me feel very welcome. Your mom and dad were great."

He chuckled. "I asked Mom if I could sleep with you."

"You didn't!"

"I did. She said it would set a bad example for the others."

"You knew she would say no."

"Yes, but it killed me to be around you all day and not be

able to touch you like this." He slid his hand to her crotch.

She pushed it away. "Someone will see you;" she whispered hoarsely.

"There's a blanket up there. Shall we join the mile-high club?"

Shauna Lee blushed furiously. "Stop it!" she whispered.

He laughed but kept her hand clasped in his, cradled against his thigh.

They changed planes in Edmonton and then flew on to Regina. It was seven o'clock in the evening when they exited the terminal and walked to the pickup. It was a pleasant evening, and Brad noted with satisfaction that it hadn't snowed while they were gone, so he didn't have to sweep off the truck.

It was ten-thirty when they arrived at the house. "It feels good to be home," Brad said. They both sighed with contentment

***

January flew by. Wedding plans took up most of the month.

Shauna Lee, Christina, Frank, and Selena drove to Regina the first weekend in the month and bought their dresses.

Shauna Lee had her heart set on a simple strapless, satin sheath and she found exactly what she was looking for. Instead of a veil, she chose a wide-brimmed bridal hat that featured accents of seed pearls, tulle, and netting.

Frank and Christina's dresses were floor-length royal blue satin sheaths that complemented both of them. Simple satin high-heels were dyed to match them. Selena was darling in a full-skirted white dress that featured a layer of organza and a royal blue sash. The girls were bubbling with excitement when they came home.

When Frank called Patch to ask him how he felt about her inviting her biological father to the wedding, he said he wasn't comfortable with the idea. With a twinge of regret, Frank assured him that she would respect his feelings.

Patch came to Swift Current the following Tuesday and Brad, Colt, Tim, Patch and Sam went to be fitted for suits. Frank and Shauna Lee went with them.

"Isn't this the color of our dresses?" Frank asked as she and Colt looked at royal blue shirts on the rack.

Shauna Lee looked at it closely. "It is," she agreed. "I love that color." She missed Frank's wink at Colt."

That afternoon, when Brad and Shauna Lee were going home, he looked at her with a grin. "Tweetie Bird, is there a hard and fast rule that says you have to have a bunch of penguins standing up there at the altar?"

She smiled. "What would you rather do? Wear blue jeans?"

"Why not?"

"So, are you telling me you would like to wear blue jeans and cowboy hats?"

"It's just a thought."

"Brad, this is your wedding too. My dress is very simple; no frills and lace..."

He laid a finger across her lips. "Don't tell me too much. We don't want any bad luck. And honestly, I don't think you should see what I'm going to wear either. What if that brings bad luck?"

"There is no such thing..."

"Can you guarantee that?"

She shook her head and looked at him. "Brad, I'd marry you in your work pants. I would have eloped. This big wedding is your idea. If you don't want to wear a tux, cancel the order. Just one thing, though, please don't wear blue jeans and chartreuse cowboy shirts. It would look pretty wild in the pictures."

Brad grinned. "And you won't see me until you come up the aisle, right?"

"I'll trust you, but you'll have to coordinate the rest of the guys, too."

He smiled with a devilish twinkle in his eye.

"You already have this all figured out, don't you?"

Patch came to Shauna Lee's firm during the third week of January. Christina sent him into her office.

She was surprised when she looked up to find him there. "Dad, what are you doing here?"

"I'd like to take you to lunch. I need to talk to you."

"I can go with you. What do you want to talk to me about?"

"The wedding."

Shauna Lee groaned. "Dad, please tell me there are no more secrets. I can't deal with that now."

"No, there are no more secrets. But, I have been thinking. I feel kind of bad about not wanting you to invite your f-father."

"It's okay, Dad. It might be best."

"No, it was small of me. If it's not too late, I think you should invite him. Because of him, you are here. I can't claim that right. I put a roof over your head, but it's only by happenstance that I can be called your dad."

"If you truly are comfortable with me asking him, I'd like to."

"Please do it. Now, can I take you for lunch?"

She put on her coat and took his arm. "Can I ask Brad to join us?"

"I already did." His smile was pleased.

The night before the wedding, they had a rehearsal at the church. Afterward, everyone went out for dinner at The Steak House. Brad and Shauna Lee reluctantly parted.

Their wedding day dawned crisp and clear. She got out of bed and wandered into Christina's kitchen. Christina was up already. "So how is the bride this morning?" she asked.

"I'm as happy as a clam! By tonight, I will be Mrs. Tweetie Bird Johnson!"

"Where does this *Tweetie Bird* thing come from?"

"Brad's dad calls his place a bird house. When Brad bought it, his dad said he needed a bird to put in it. Thus, I became Tweetie Bird."

Christina chuckled. "That is cute."

Frank and Selena arrived by nine o'clock. From then on, the morning moved from one appointment to the next.

At one-thirty, Shauna Lee was dressed and ready to go. She knew she looked beautiful in her gown and now, she was impatient to walk down the aisle.

When they arrived at the church, Patch met her in the back room. He was wearing a soft gray pinstriped suit, with a royal blue shirt and a white tie. "Pretty snazzy," she commented. "So, what do the rest of them look like?"

Patch just shrugged and gave her a smile. Frank smirked and Christina turned away.

"You both know! This isn't fair. It's my wedding..."

Christina shook her head as she turned to face her. "No, it's you and Brad's wedding. Not just yours. You'll see him when he sees you."

The organ started playing, Frank walked down the aisle, followed by Christina. Then Selena and Sam made their entrance.

Selena was charmingly precocious, looking at everyone and stopping along the way to preen. She carried a basket of flowers and sprinkled white blossoms as she walked down the aisle.

Sam was adorable in soft gray pinstriped pants and a royal blue shirt with a white satin bow tie at his neck. A small top hat sat on his head and gray and white suspenders looped over his shoulders. He proudly carried a white satin ring pillow.

When the music changed to the wedding march, Patch looked at his daughter. "Are you ready? You're beautiful. Your mom would be proud of you."

As they stepped through the doors, someone perched a top hat on Patch's head. He barely broke stride as they moved and Shauna Lee was so busy looking ahead for Brad that she didn't notice.

Her eyes connected with Brad's and she forgot about what they were wearing until she stopped with Patch at the altar. Her eyes widened. Brad's eyes were twinkling. He was wearing a light gray pinstriped suit, with a royal blue shirt and a white satin tie. On his head, he wore a light gray top hat. Pinned to his jacket was a calla lily that matched the ones in Shauna Lee's bouquet.

He is handsome, she thought. Her eyes slid over Tim and Colt. They both wore light gray pinstriped pants and royal blue shirts with white satin ties. Gray and white suspenders were looped over their shoulders and they both wore top hats.

"I love your outfit," she whispered as she took his hand. "It's sort of like high society in the roaring twenties. My dress and hat fit right in with the theme." She pushed back his jacket to look for suspenders. She wasn't disappointed; they were there. She winked at Brad and he had to squash a chuckle.

The day went flawlessly.

Before the reception, Shauna Lee, and Brad introduced Patch and Bob Matzlan. She held both their hands and said, "Bob, this is my dad, Patch Bergeron. Dad, this is my father, Bob Matzlan." There was a moment of awkwardness as the two men looked at each other.

Brad put a hand on each of their shoulders. "We're happy to have you both here. You're part of Shauna Lee's life. The past is long gone. It would make us happy if you would get to know each other and get along." Patch hesitated and then extended his hand to Bob, who let out his breath slowly and shook it heartily.

It was late that evening when Brad and Shauna Lee got home. He tucked her into the car he had rented for the wedding. He smiled when he opened the passenger door for her. "I wanted to bring my bride home in style."

When they reached the house, he insisted on carrying her

from the car. "I have to carry the new bride over the threshold."

She smiled as she threaded her arms around his neck. "It's a little late, don't you think? I've been over this threshold hundreds of times."

He fumbled to open the door. As he swung it open, he shook his head. "No, you have never been over this threshold, Mrs. Brad Johnson." He let her slip down to stand on the floor. "Welcome home, Shauna Johnson."

He pulled her against him with no regard for crumpling her dress and he kissed her the way he'd wanted to all day. When they came up for breath, he sighed. "Finally! Those little pecks for the crowd drove me crazy."

She eased her hand under his suspenders and pulled them. "I like this look. Whose idea was it?"

"Don't you think I'm that imaginative?" he asked as he picked her up and carried her into the bedroom.

"You are very imaginative, but Frank and Colt were looking at these shirts. I have a feeling..."

"And I have a feeling it's time to initiate this bed, Tweetie Bird Johnson."

CHAPTER TWENTY FOUR

Frank and Colt gathered up the twins and bundled them into the truck. Colt took Sam's top hat, nested it with his and handed them to Frank.

He looked at her carefully. "How are you doing, hon?"

She smiled. "I'm tired now, but it's been a fabulous day. Shauna Lee was gorgeous."

"So were you. You are stunning in that dress."

She reached over and flicked his suspenders. "You guys looked sharp, too. I loved your outfits! Shauna Lee did, too."

When they got home, they undressed the twins and put them to bed. Colt took her hand and led her into the bedroom. He shut the door and reached for her.

"That's the first wedding we've been to since we got married. It brought back memories and reminded me how beautiful you were that day."

"How big I was!"

"Sweetheart, you were beautiful. And yes, you were pregnant but look at the beautiful family we have."

"I know. And I would never change them. But, if we had it to do over, I'd have the courtship, the wedding, and then the twins."

"Does it bother you that we didn't?"

"Not really, but we both got cheated in some ways. You and I never got to do fun things together before we had responsibility. You missed all the special things in the pregnancy journey with the twins. That's why I wanted to have Cherish so badly."

He held her against him, his hand cradling the back of her head. She rested her cheek against his shirt. After a few moments, he slid his hand to the zipper at the back of her dress. He slowly eased it down, then pushed the dress away from her breasts and slid it down off her body.

She smiled at him as she reached for his suspenders. "My grandfather wore suspenders. I never thought of them as being sexy, but they are on you." She pushed them over his shoulders and unbuttoned his pinstriped pants.

They tumbled onto the bed and made passionate love as if it was their wedding night.

The next morning they cuddled in their bed. Colt played with Frank's hair, entwining it in his fingers. "How are you feeling this morning?"

Frank stretched and sat up. She looked at him and smiled. "I feel great."

"It's good to see you feeling better. I'm glad you went to get help."

"Thank you for bringing Becky here. I probably would've been too stubborn to see the psychiatrist otherwise. I could have sunk into a deep depression. I'm sorry I wouldn't listen to you."

He frowned. "You just weren't yourself and it really worried me. I didn't realize that you had been depressed before and I didn't understand what it could do to you."

"It never occurred to me to tell you. It was just part of my life. It happened twice, and it always was when really painful things happened. The first time was when Dad got hurt, and we had to sell the ranch and Martin dumped me, all in a matter of months. That was when I came to work at the ranch. It was the perfect place for me to heal in peace and quiet."

"And the second time?"

Frank looked away. She hesitated.

"Hon, when was that?"

She swallowed hard. "When I realized that I was pregnant with the twins. And... and I knew I loved you and you didn't want to be with me," she whispered.

"Fran..."

"I was a mess. Becky made me see sense that time, too."

"How did Becky help you?"

"Colt..." her eyes shone with tears. "You'll hate this..."

"No, I should know."

"I... I was desperate... I was such a mess... I went to Calgary to see a doctor. I planned to have ...." She covered her face. "I was going to have an abortion. But I just couldn't do it."

Colt jumped out of the bed. His face was white, his fists clenched.

"Please don't hate me, Colt," she pleaded. "It wasn't that I didn't want the baby, but I was such a wreck. I couldn't see how I could look after a child, when I could hardly look after myself. I didn't know I was carrying twins then. I hadn't been to a doctor yet.

"I went to a clinic in Calgary, but I didn't see a doctor there either. I thought of you and how much I loved you. Reason hit me and I couldn't believe I'd even considered an abortion. It was against all of my principles. I ran out of the clinic and went back to Becky's place."

Tears filled his eyes. "I don't hate you, Frank. It kills me to think you were so desperate..."

"It still haunts me. I look at those precious children and think how awful it would have been if I had gone through with it. I couldn't have lived with myself."

A tear slipped down his cheek. "Why didn't you come to me?"

"I should have. I was going, too, even though you'd told me...that you would never...love me. I was going to tell you at the barbecue, but then you announced your engagement to Shauna Lee."

He groaned. "I was such a fool. I nearly cost us everything. And the worst of it is that I had loved you all along."

"Colt, we both made mistakes, but we found our way. The one good thing is that I knew you loved *me* when we got married. I couldn't have handled living with you and thinking you had only married me for the babies."

He walked to her side of the bed, sat down beside her and took her hands. "I've been so happy these past four years. I had no idea how deeply I'd hurt you." He wiped his eyes with his arm.

"I've been happy, too. But I've felt guilty about what I almost did. I think that is why I wanted Cherish so badly. I wanted to share everything about her with you."

"Frank, I have so much to make up to you." He groaned. "A lifetime won't be enough."

She shook her head. "I don't want you to feel like you have to make up for anything. Please, let's just be happy."

He folded her in his arms and held her. He knew he would never see her in the same way again. In his eyes, she was a saint.

Ollie and Ellie had come into the house before they went downstairs. Colt could hear them laughing and chatting and in moments, he could smell coffee brewing. He got up and pulled Frank to her feet. "I think we have to go downstairs."

Ollie laughed when they came down the stairs. "Look who decided to relive the honeymoon morning."

Frank blushed. Colt stopped short and looked at Frank. "We didn't have a honeymoon."

"Then you damned well should," Ollie said.

Ellie poured two cups of coffee and set them on the table. "Come on, you two."

They all sat around the table and talked about the wedding. Ollie chuckled. "It did my heart good to see Patch walk Shauna Lee down the aisle. He was so happy when he came back to the ranch after Christmas."

Colt chuckled. "And Brad isn't out to kill the man anymore. Something big must have happened."

"What did you think of the other guy? The one she introduced as her father, and then she introduced Patch as her dad. What the hell was that about?"

"I think Shauna Lee's life has been far more complicated than any of us can imagine. I wouldn't even dare to guess what happened there, but she and Brad were comfortable with it and Patch and Bob seemed to understand what was going on."

Frank went upstairs to check on the children and Colt chatted with Ollie and Ellie.

"How is she doing?" Ollie asked, motioning upstairs.

"She's doing much better. I'm learning some things that had totally escaped me. My life has been centered on work my whole life. Since we got married, I've been content with my family. It never occurred to me how much Fran and I have missed. We never had a courtship, not even a honeymoon.

"The past four years have been all about the children. It's late, but not too late. I'm going to start spending more time with her, doing things as a couple. I plan to court her now like I would have before we got married, if things had been different. I can't overload you, Ellie, but if we give you blocks of times off; say four or five days at a time, would you be comfortable with being here with the twins over a long weekend?"

"Colt, I can manage the children with no problem. I'm not sure what I would do with that many days off, though."

Ollie grinned. "Well, you can come out to the ranch and spend a few days."

She gave him a teasing look. "You just want me to clean that place up."

Ollie cocked his head and looked at her with a grin. Ellie blushed.

Colt cleared his throat and gave Ollie a pointed look. "Listen here, man. I found her first. Don't steal her out from under me."

Ellie chuckled. "Imagine, two men fighting over me at my age! But, I've already got a boyfriend. He's upstairs with his mom."

She smiled at Colt and then looked at Ollie. "I think I'd enjoy going out to the ranch for a few days. I can beat him at a game of Canasta again."

Colt looked up the stairs. "I want to surprise Fran and do something special for Valentine's Day. I haven't decided what, but if you want too, you can take off today and come back on Wednesday. Fran and I will be fine with the kids."

Ellie's surprise was obvious. She looked at Ollie.

Ollie was smiling from ear to ear. "So, what are you waiting for? As you said, I want another chance to beat you at Canasta."

"Are you sure you want to put up with me for that long?"

Ollie smirked. "Pretty tough job, but I'm willing to give it a try."

Colt didn't miss the look that passed between them. "Just remember, we'll all be moving out to the ranch in the fall, so don't rush into anything you two." He chuckled. "And no twins. Ellie has her hands full already."

Ellie turned scarlet. "Colt!" she sputtered.

When Frank brought the twins downstairs, she was surprised to find that Ellie and Ollie were gone. "Where did they go?" she asked.

"I told Ellie to take time off until Wednesday. She has worked a lot these past six weeks."

"I'm glad you did that. She deserves it. I don't know what

we would have done without her. What is she going to do?"

"She is going out to the ranch with Ollie."

"Oh ho," Frank said with a knowing smile. "I hope we don't lose our nanny."

"I told Ollie not to steal her because I found her first. I also reminded them not to do anything rash. No twins!"

"Colt! You didn't." His amused grin told her he had.

Frank & Colt dressed the children and took them out for a toboggan ride. They spent the morning playing in the snow and everyone came in tired and hungry. After lunch, they put the children down for a nap. Frank and Colt went to their bedroom and lay on the bed.

Colt reached for her hand. "What kind of things do you think we would've done if I'd courted you?"

She rolled over and propped her head on her hand. "I haven't thought about it. What would we have done? What would you have liked to do?"

"Honestly, after my divorce, I just lost myself in work. The only other thing I did was spend time with my race horses; and, in a sense, I made that my work too. I don't know. What would you have wanted to do?"

She eased onto her back and stared at the ceiling. "Well, I used to team rope when I was younger. I wasn't doing that by the time I met you, but I still enjoyed rodeos; even the small ones. Sometimes they were the most fun. And I used to go fly fishing with my dad. I loved to ride horseback for fun, but I loved doing it on the range when I was working, too."

"Did you like going to a show or swimming or hiking or anything like that?"

She sat up and looked at him. "I didn't go to shows. I really didn't date or hang out with girlfriends."

"You didn't date in high school?"

"No, I didn't."

"Did you go swimming?"

"Well, once in a while we went for a picnic at Rochon Sands and we'd swim in Buffalo Lake. A friend of dads had a small boat and he'd pull us around on a tube. Some of the kid's water skied, but I didn't."

"Why."

"I was afraid of deep water." She shook her head. "We used to hike down by the Red Deer River. That was fun, except when you fell on one of the little cactus plants that used to grow on the hills."

Colt chuckled. "I've forgotten some of the things I did. Dad was a farmer, first and foremost, so our life was built around the farm. In the winter, mom and dad curled, but I never did. When I went to high school, I got into high school rodeo; bulldogging steers. I always loved horses and cattle. Obviously I did some of the other kid stuff, but basically we were all workaholics."

"You still are, but you are a great father and a wonderful husband."

"You'll have to teach me how to play."

"I'm not sure that I know how to play either. We'll have to learn together."

Ollie brought Ellie back to the farm early Wednesday afternoon. Later, Colt went over to Ellie's place and told her about his plans for the weekend. She was delighted and assured him that everything would be fine while he and Frank were away.

He had filled Tim in on his plans that morning when they were out in the machine shed. Tim had assured him that he would be around every day while they were gone.

That evening he casually told Frank that he needed to go to Regina the next day, and he suggested that they could spend a night or two there. He raised an eyebrow. "It might be fun if we went to a show and made out."

Her eyes twinkled as she smiled at him. "Hmmm... do you think we can still do that?"

"I'll bet we could teach those young kids a thing or two! Bring a nice dress. We're a day late for Valentine's Day, but I want to take you to a nice place for dinner."

"We celebrated Valentine's Day with the twins last night."

"Ahhh... but this will be a night for lovers. And will you please do me a favor?"

"What is that?"

"Wear the jeans that I bought you for Christmas and your cowboy boots.

They left for Regina early the next morning. On their way into the city, Colt looked at his watch. "I should slip out to the airport now. Tim ordered a part and it's coming in today."

Colt stopped in the parking lot. He grabbed the small carry-on luggage that Frank had packed from the backseat, along with his leather jacket, which he draped over his arm to conceal the carry-on. He took Frank's hand and walked casually into the terminal.

His heart was beating so hard he was certain that she would hear it. He suggested that she wait by the elevator for incoming passengers, while he went to the wicket to check for Tim's part.

Frank looked around while she waited. Colt came back and told her he had to run back to the truck to get a piece of paper he had forgotten, and put the parking stub on the dash so he wouldn't get a ticket.

Halfway out the door, he offered to put her winter jacket in the truck because she had taken it off. She gave it to him and watched him run across the parking lot. She saw him open the truck door and toss her jacket inside. He took something else out of the back and reached to put the parking stub on the dash.

When he came back to meet her, he took her hand. "We have to go up to the next level. We might as well grab something to eat while we wait for the plane to come in."

He guided her through the terminal, taking her through the security check. She looked at him puzzled, but he just emptied his pockets, took off his cowboy boots, watch, ring, belt & buckle and his coat, placed them in the plastic tub and went through the process without question, so she did the same.

When they were putting on their cowboy boots, she whispered, "Why did we have to go through security?"

"It's standard procedure now."

"Yes but..."

"Hon, security is over the top everywhere now, even in these little places." He looked at his watch. "There's a Tim Horton's. Let's stop there. We still have an hour and a half before the plane gets in."

They each had coffee and a muffin. Then they went to the waiting room assigned to the flight that he said they were waiting for.

When they announced the arrival, Frank looked at Colt. "This seems like an odd place to pick up a part for equipment. Are you sure we're not in the wrong area?"

"This is where they told me to come." In a few minutes, people began to arrive through the jet way. Frank was still confused. When the last few people trickled through, Colt got up and went to talk to the woman at the desk. Frank saw him take some papers out of his coat and show them to the attendant.

He engaged her in a serious conversation and then it looked like he signed a few papers. The woman said something to Colt and they both laughed. When Colt came back and sat down, he told her it wouldn't be much longer.

In about ten minutes people with children and elderly people started loading, then First Class passengers. Colt took Frank's hand and pulled her to her feet. She looked confused, but he tucked his arm around her waist and led her to the jet way. He nodded to the attendant and handed her two airline tickets, and then he guided Frank into the corridor.

"Colt, what are you doing?" she whispered, her eyes wide as saucers. "Where are we going?"

"To Kissimmee, Florida."

"What... what are we going to do there?"

"Well, besides what all lovers do, we are going to go to the Silver Spurs Rodeo this weekend."

Colt's courtship had begun.

CHAPTER TWENTY FIVE

On Valentine's Day, Brad came to the office at lunch time and brought Shauna Lee a bouquet of red roses. He also brought a package wrapped in red and covered with ribbons and hearts.

She smiled as she took it. "You are spoiling me."

"It's something simple, but I thought you'd like it."

Shauna Lee opened the package. Her eyes misted as she looked at the framed pictures Brad had nestled in tissue and laid one on top of the other in the box. She lifted the top one out. He had scanned and enlarged the pictures Patch had given her at Christmas.

She ran her finger over the glass frame, touching the smiling faces of her mother and Patch, who was holding her proudly in his arms. She lifted out the second one. It was one of Patch and her mother when they were first married. They were happy and in love. She set the pictures on her desk and turned to him.

"They're your family, sweetheart. They weren't the best

example of parents, but they were your family."

She swallowed hard. "I know that, and now you are my family, and you are teaching me to live life a better way. We'll make sure our children are loved and learn to live life the way you have. They'll never be emotional cripples like me."

He smiled. "Our children?"

She blushed. "That just slipped out."

"Do you want to take it back?"

She looked at him thoughtfully. "No, I want to have your child."

Brad felt like he would burst with joy. He kissed her gently, almost reverently. "Thank you," he whispered. "I wasn't sure you could ever feel that way, after everything you have been through. You never cease to amaze me, Tweetie Bird."

They went out for supper that evening. When they went home and were ready for bed, Shauna Lee took a small package out of her night table drawer, It was wrapped in white and tied with pink and blue ribbons threaded with tiny red hearts.

She sat down on the bed and motioned for him to sit beside her. She put the package in his hand. He smiled as he looked at it. The size and shape gave him no clue to its contents. "It's not much," she said softly.

He released the pink and blue ribbons and loosened the paper. It eased away to reveal a birth control prescription disk. He turned it in his hands and then popped it open. There were five pills left. He looked at her, a question in his eyes. She closed the lid and pointed to the number of refills.

Brad looked closely. 'Refills:00.' He laid it on the bed beside him and turned to her. "What are you telling me, Tweetie Bird?" he asked softly.

"If it's alright with you, I won't get any refills for a while. I'm thirty- eight... my biological clock is winding down. I think we should make a baby as soon as possible. I'll take these last five pills because I don't want to take the chance of messing up my cycle. It could take a while for me to conceive. I've taken birth control pills for a long time."

"Two babies, a boy and a girl?"

"I'm game for two. Even three, if we don't get one of each in the first two tries."

He was smiling gleefully as he pushed her down onto the mattress. "We need to start practicing right now."

***

As February passed, Shauna Lee felt consumed by work. *Swift Current Accounting and Bookkeeping Services* became a hive of activity as income tax season started to gain momentum.

February slipped into March; March slipped into April. By the end of April, Shauna Lee was exhausted. The April workload had required long workdays, even weekends.

Brad's business was growing too, but he had kept the house tidy and cooked meals for them. Still, they missed having time together.

They both sighed with relief after April thirtieth. The first weekend in May, they slept in, luxuriating in the feel of their bodies touching each other, knowing that they didn't have to spring out of bed and rush off to work.

***

February and March and April flew by for Colt and Frank, too. Colt courted her imaginatively. She never knew what he would come up with next.

After the trip to Florida, he took her to a movie theater in Regina so they could make out where no one would know them. At first, it felt awkward, but he teased her until she relaxed and became a willing and eager participant. Before the show was over they left for the privacy of their hotel room.

In March, they flew to Calgary and visited Becky and Russ. The four of them drove to Canmore and into the Kananaskis. The snow was deep along the road and the mountains were spectacular. They stopped at the Nakisa Ski Resort and watched the skiers come down the hill. It was a fun-filled weekend, and Colt and Russ had cemented their friendship.

Their relationship took on a new dimension. They had always loved each other and their sexual chemistry had been undeniable. Colt had always loved her as his wife and Frank had always cherished him as a husband and father, but now their world was expanding. They were learning to have fun together and make new memories as intimate friends, compounding the depth of their loving relationship.

Between trips, they were busy working on plans for the house. They enjoyed the time spent with the twins. In April, they remembered the day Cherish would have been born. Colt comforted Frank as she wept after they planted a flowering plum at the farm.

A couple of weeks later, he surprised her by taking her to horse races in Kentucky. They watched with excitement when his horse ran and even though she placed third from last, it was fun.

In May, the whole family went out to the ranch. To Ollie's delight, Ellie joined them. Colt brought Ollie's mail and left it on the table for him.

Colt and Frank took the quad up to the bench above the main building to inspect the site for the house. They looked at the ranch buildings below.

She reached over and squeezed his hand. "I almost want to pinch myself to make sure this is real."

He leaned his head against hers. "It's real. By Thanksgiving, there'll be a house here. Hopefully, we'll be moved in and we'll celebrate the holiday in it."

They went back to the ranch house for supper. Ollie and Ellie were working in the kitchen while the children entertained themselves with a cat that Patch had rescued.

Colt sat down at the table while Ellie poured him a cup of coffee.

Ollie pointed to an opened envelope on the table. "Take a look at that."

Colt picked it up, noting that the return address was for a legal firm in Vancouver. "Did a long lost relative leave you a fortune?"

"Well, apparently somebody left somebody with something. Read the letter. There has to be some mistake."

Colt drew the folded sheet of paper out of the envelope. He read it and then looked at Ollie.

"Did you sow many wild oats when you were young, old timer?"

Ollie snorted. "Forty-four years ago... how the hell do I remember? No one told me if I did."

Colt smirked as he handed the letter to Frank. "Your past is catching up with you. You've always said you were a rolling stone until you came here."

Frank read the letter. "It's odd that a woman would leave a message in her will, telling you that she had given birth to a son that was yours." She studied the letter. "And it looks like she gave the child up for adoption." She frowned. "This is a cruel thing to do. How would you ever find out where he is or who he is?"

Ollie shook his head. "It says to contact the legal firm for more information." That boy would be forty-four now; a grown man. "He probably has a family. I could be a grandpa and he doesn't even know I exist."

"You are going to call them, aren't you, Ollie?"

"I don't remember a woman by the name of Wanda Ethridge."

"It could be her married name," Ellie said.

"But Wanda... it just doesn't ring a bell."

Frank frowned. "I'm sure she didn't pick your name out of the hat Ollie. It seems like it took them quite a while to track you down. She died eight years ago."

"I'll phone them some time and see what they have to say."

The next day, Colt and Frank went out on horseback to check the pastures. When they reached the top, they swung out of the saddle and sat on a big rock. Colt took her hand.

"How are you doing, hon?"

She knew he wasn't asking how she was enjoying the ride. They had stopped using condoms at the end of March, hoping to conceive again, but so far it had not happened.

"I... there was big blood clots again the day before yesterday. I talked to Mom. She said that happened to her, too, many times. Basically, I miscarry every time it happens."

"You didn't tell me."

"I needed to think. We have the twins. I don't want to ride this roller coaster of hope and despair every month. I planned to talk to you about this before I did anything, but I think I should go back on birth control pills. They worked well when I was with Martin."

"It's your body, hon. You have to do what works best for you, but I'm totally in favor of you going back on birth control pills. We have a busy summer ahead of us and the twins are getting older so we will be doing more with them."

"I was thinking the same thing. Now that we've talked about it, I'll make an appointment with Dr. Wilfred when we get home."

As they rode into the barnyard, Colt looked at Frank. "Are you happy?"

"This has been a wonderful day. I'm totally contented."

When they went into the house, the twins were excited to see them. The four of them sat on the floor and Frank and Colt told them about their day.

Ellie called them for supper and everyone sat at the table. Frank looked at Ollie. "Did you phone those lawyers this afternoon?"

Ollie scooped mashed potatoes onto his plate, and then nodded. "Yes, I did."

"And?"

"It seems that Wanda's will also stipulated, that I wasn't to be contacted about the child until the adoptive father died. He died three years ago. It ticks me off that they kept me in the dark for so many years. I have no idea who she is, but apparently, they have a birth certificate. I asked them to send me a picture of her. They said they would. The crazy thing is I can't be sure I'd recognize her anyway. I never had any long term relationships."

Frank looked at him. "Why didn't you, Ollie?"

He sputtered. "I just never was the settling down kind, especially when I was twenty years old."

By the middle of June, they had the basement poured and the contractor was starting to frame the house. Colt and Frank were spending more time at the ranch with Ellie and the twins. The third week in June, Colt needed more supplies for the contractor.

Patch offered to drive in and bring them back to the ranch if he could stay overnight with Brad and Shauna Lee. He had begun to spend the night at their place whenever he went to Swift Current. Patch liked to garden and he was planting a perennial bed in the back yard for Shauna Lee.

She worked with him when she could and she had discovered that she enjoyed working with plants as well. The shared project was strengthening their relationship, that was something that both of them treasured.

He left right after breakfast the next morning. Colt and Frank worked at the house with the contractor all day. Frank had learned to pound nails side by side with the men and she enjoyed watching the perimeter of the house go up.

That night they were eating supper when the phone rang. Ollie answered it and told Colt that Tim wanted to speak to him. Colt took it in the office, leaving the rest of them talking around the table.

CHAPTER TWENTY SIX

Shauna Lee smiled when Patch came into her office. "What brings you to town today, Dad? You were just here last week."

"Colt and Frank and Ellie and the twins are staying out at the ranch right now. The contractor needs some supplies for the weekend, so I volunteered to come in if I could stay overnight with you. I want to finish up the perennial bed today. I'm excited to see it when it's done. Would you like to go for lunch with me?"

She nodded and reached for her purse.

"Where shall we go?"

She thought for a moment, and then smiled. "We could go to A&W and get a hamburger and something to drink. Then we could go to the park, sit on the bench and eat there. You can tell me how you plan to finish the perennial bed."

"That sounds like a good idea."

As they sat on the bench, ate their hamburgers, and drank a tall glass of root beer, Patch told her about the flowering plum tree he was going to plant in the bed, along with two Red Weigela shrubs to round out the end of it.

Shauna Lee smiled. "It will always be a symbol of our renewed relationship. I'm glad we have made peace and found our way back to each other Dad." She reached out and squeezed his hand. "I love you, you know."

His eyes misted. "I love you, too. I only wish your mom could have lived to know this."

"Maybe she does, Dad. Maybe she has finally brought us together. What are the odds of it happening on its own?"

Patch dropped her off at the office. She hugged him and promised to see him at the house later. When she got out of the truck, she walked to the back and looked at the flowering tree in the box. The pink blossoms were already bursting into bloom. She touched it gently and then waved to Patch as she went inside.

Shauna Lee's heart was happy. That morning she had slipped out and bought a pregnancy test after Christina had come to the office. When she got back, she went straight to the bathroom and used it. Her heart had pounded as she waited the required five minutes before she checked it. She could hardly contain her joy when she saw that it tested positive.

Brad had to be the first to know. She was about to call him when Patch had come into her office. When she returned from lunch, she called Brad's cell. It went to voice mail. She groaned and hung up.

Then she called again. Still no answer! She decided to leave a message. "Hi, daddy. The test was positive! Call me right away."

Brad hadn't called by four o'clock, so she called his cell again. There still was no answer, so she left a message and told him that Patch was at the house and she was going home.

Brad was on his way home from a meeting with Tim at the farm. Shauna Lee had looked into grants available for green energy and discovered that substantial aid was available, so he and Colt had worked out a package deal for ten wind turbines. Three of them were to be installed at the farm.

Tim had made a comment that bothered him. He said a man had dropped by his place the night before, looking for Shauna Lee. When Tim said she didn't live there, the man had said that he knew she did and had shown him a luggage tag that had her name and address on it. Tim had told him that he was wrong and the guy had left in a disgruntled mood.

Brad felt uneasy. "How did some guy get Shauna Lee's luggage tag?" he wondered out loud. He reached for his cell phone and cursed when he realized that he had shut it off. He had messages. They were from Shauna Lee. He listened to the first one. "Hi, Daddy."

Happiness rushed through him. "Daddy! She's pregnant! We're pregnant!"

He stopped at a florist shop and bought the biggest bouquet he could find. He bought a crystal vase to put them in and hurried home.

Shauna Lee had hurried home from the office. She changed into an old pair of sweat pants and a t-shirt. Then she grabbed a pair of cotton gloves, and slid her feet into her runners and went out to join Patch. He had already set in the flowering plum and he was planting the last Weigela bush. She watched while he finished, then helped him shovel bark mulch over the surface of the entire bed.

They stood back to admire their work. "It looks great, Dad." She hugged him and kissed his cheek. "Let's go inside. I'll make some coffee. Brad will be home pretty soon."

"You go make the coffee. I'll put away the tools and clean up here. Then I'll come inside."

Shauna Lee ran inside, tossed her gloves on the bench and slipped out of her shoes. She opened her purse on the counter and grabbed her cell phone, turning it on as she went to the coffee maker.

She was just about to dial when she heard the front door

open. "Brad," she cried as she ran around the corner to meet him in the entry.

She stopped abruptly. A stranger stood in front of her. She couldn't think for a moment. *How... oh, I left the door unlocked for Brad,* she thought.

"Can I help you?" she asked, puzzled.

"You fucking bitch," he snarled.

She recoiled.

"You didn't think I'd find you?"

She stepped backward. "Who... who are you? What are you talking about?" Her finger dialed 911. She left the phone on.

"You think you could fool me? Call yourself whoever you want, those eyes are a dead giveaway."

Shauna Lee backed around the counter, putting it between them. "What are you talking about? I... I don't know you."

"You lying bitch. You put me in jail for getting rid of that little freak. I spent twenty years of my life in that hellhole while you've been running around living the good life."

Fear struck Shauna Lee's heart. Suddenly she realized who he was. She couldn't let him know that she knew; her life might depend on it.

The phone was still on.

"Sir, I have no idea what you're talking about."

"*Sir,*" he snarled. He came around the end of the counter. "You sold my farm you bitch. You stole my life."

"You've got the wrong person."

He rushed at her and swung his fist. It hit her cheek. She sprawled on the floor. He lifted his leg to kick her in the belly.

"No! No!" she screamed. "I'm pregnant. You'll kill my baby."

Patch had just stepped in the back door. He heard Shauna Lee scream. *What the hell is going on?* Then her words registered. *She is pregnant!*

Then he heard a sick laugh. *Who is that?* As he ran down the hall, he saw Brad coming up the steps. He rounded the corner to see a stranger standing over Shauna Lee where she lay on the floor.

The man was laughing crazily. "You're pregnant! You're going to bring another freak into the world." He threw his head back and cackled. "You stupid bitch! You're going to pull the same shit on another sucker? No man will want your freaky spawn. I should let you live, but I came to settle my own score with you. The lucky bastard will never know what I saved him from." He reached into his pocket and in a flash, he had an open blade in his hand.

Everything happened at once. Shauna Lee threw the phone at him as she rolled onto her side. Patch yelled as he launched himself at the man. The stranger turned slightly and drove the blade into Patch's chest.

Brad roared as he came over the counter, the crystal vase raised. He slammed it into the intruder's head. There was a sickening crunch and the man fell to the floor.

Brad reached for Shauna Lee, but she pushed him away as she scrambled to reach Patch.

"Dad!" she sobbed. "Noooo," she screamed. "You can't leave me now."

Police were suddenly everywhere. Brad scrambled to reach Shauna Lee. He dropped down beside her, putting his arms around her. She cradled Patch's head in her lap. Blood seeped out of his mouth. His breathing was labored and irregular, gasping. He opened his eyes and looked at Shauna Lee. "I love you. Take care of my grandch...."

The words faded away with a gurgle and his eyes glazed over.

Shauna Lee keened eerily, her grief unbearable. "He saved my life. He died protecting me and the baby."

A policeman lifted Brad away from her. "Is she pregnant?"

Brad nodded numbly. "We just found out today."

The policeman touched his shoulder with compassion as he asked him to make way for the EMT's.

Brad felt his world crumble as he watched them give her an injection and load a hysterical Shauna Lee onto a stretcher. He fought to go with the ambulance, but the police restrained him. They required his statement before he could leave the scene.

He cursed them roundly, telling them that he had walked into the house to witness a stranger threatening his wife. Her father had charged the man and Brad had vaulted over the counter and hit him over the head with the vase.

Water and flowers were scattered all over the floor. Brad wept as he told them he had brought them home as a gift to celebrate the fact that they'd just learned that they were going to have a baby.

The police asked who they could call that would come and stay with him. Brad looked at him blankly. "You can't stay here alone, sir."

"But Shauna Lee?" Brad asked in confusion.

"She won't be home tonight."

"Then I'm going to her..."

"You need to have someone with you."

Brad gave the police officer Tim's phone number. Tim was there in fifteen minutes. He watched two bodies being carried out. He recognized them both. Patch, and the stranger who had been at his house the night before.

He took out his cell and called the ranch. When Ollie answered, he asked for Colt and told him what had happened.

***

Four months later.

Shauna Lee stood in front of the tree in the perennial bed behind the house. Tears ran down her cheeks as she looked at it. Her hand touched her belly. Patch had died to save her and the baby boy in her womb.

Brad had hit Dave Trutcher from behind and the blow had resulted in the mad man's death. By chance, Shauna Lee had recorded the entire conflict with her cell phone. In the end, that had provided the evidence that answered many questions.

They had determined that Trutcher had been released on parole six months earlier. He had been employed as a janitor at the Grande Prairie Airport. Shauna Lee and Brad deducted that he had recognized Shauna Lee and had stolen her luggage tag. Shauna Lee vaguely remembered that a janitor who was cleaning the floor had bumped into her, but she had been involved in the conversation with Brad's brother and sister-in-law and hadn't really paid any attention to him.

The information on the old tag had led him to Tim's place. When Tim had told him Shauna Lee didn't live there, he probably hadn't believed him.

When Tim had arrived home the next evening, he was surprised to find the back door open. At the time, he hadn't noticed anything missing. Days later he checked the door and could tell it had been picked.

Later still, he remembered that he had left one of the cards from *Swift Current Accounting and Bookkeeping Services* on his table, with miscellaneous other things. Shauna Lee's name was at the bottom of the card.

The police eventually determined that Trutcher had waited outside her office in a stolen car. He'd followed her home, parked the car out of sight and walked to the house. They had found it there later. He had probably watched her working in the back yard with Patch. When she'd come into the house alone, he had made his move.

Brad came out of the house to join his wife. Pain still clouded her eyes. She had been going to counseling for four months, and he knew she would have a long way to go. The shock of her dad's death had been devastating, but the therapy was reaching into other dark corners of her mind too. It would take time, but he was relieved to know that she was on a healing track.

Brad hugged her.

"You were right, you know." She said looking at him.

"I was right about what?"

"I did need help... therapy to help me deal with the past. Your love and support have done so much for me, but I need to deal with a lot of it myself, and I need guidance from someone impartial who can help me face reality."

She picked up Karma and cuddled her as she studied the tree in the perennial bed. "I am discovering that in many ways, emotionally I am still that frightened, eighteen-year-old that I thought I had buried. My whole life has been a facade that I've built to help me cope."

She squeezed his hand. "And you sensed that all along. I just wouldn't accept that I needed help."

"Tweetie Bird, I'm just thankful that you are all right. You were sedated for three days and I was afraid I'd lost you. The trauma of what happened could have been the last straw. I was scared to death."

He caressed her stomach. "And little Patrick in there; I was afraid for him. He was so new, but he's a survivor like his mother. He hung on tight and now he's strong and kicking. Patch will live on through him."

Shauna Lee sighed. "Dad loved me when I was born, then his trust was broken. He couldn't bear the sight of me and I learned to hate him. We didn't see each other for twenty years. Then, against all odds, we met again. We came to terms with our painful past. We learned to forgive and accept, to trust and love each other again. We came *full circle*."

***

The Hand of Fate, Book Three of the Belanger Creek Ranch Series will be available soon.

Check the end of this book for a sneak preview!

***

Thank you for taking time to read *Full Circle, Book Two of the Belanger Creek Ranch Series*. I hope you enjoyed it.

Few people realize how gratifying reviews are to an author and how important they are to the success of a book. Reviews are read by potential readers, who will value your opinion of a book and may decide to buy it (or not) based how on your experience with it.

Writing a review can seem intimidating, *but please do not feel that you can't do it.* Think about *how you felt* about the characters, *what* you liked (or disliked) about the book, and *how* you connected with the story when you were reading it. *Then write it down in simple words.* That is what really counts. Fancy words do not replace simple *honesty* and *enthusiasm,* which are the most compelling ingredients in a review.

Connecting with readers is a heartwarming experience for an author. It reaffirms the value of what we spend hours doing in solitude. *I would love to hear from you and learn a bit about your life.*

If you enjoyed this book, I would be delighted if you could leave a review at any one of the following sites: Goodreads.com, ePrintedbooks.com, Amazon.com, Facebook, Twitter, or my website at **http://gloriaantypowich.com/** If you could post your review on several sites, I would be absolutely thrilled!

Facebook: Gloria Antypowich Author, (Please stop by and like my page!)

Twitter: @gantypowich

Website/Blog: Gloria Antypowich-Romance and Love Stories at **http://gloriaantypowich.com/**

Email: gloria@heartsatrisk.com

I look forward to hearing from you!

AUTHORS NOTES

I have fictitiously used the city of Swift Current, Saskatchewan, Canada and all of the other towns, cities, villages, hamlets or abandoned places on the map that I mentioned in this book. I have done all my research on the area on the internet. I have fictionally used the names of actual businesses that I found in my internet research; (restaurants, fast food places, grocery stores, big box stores, hotels, motels, churches, airports and tourist spots etc.) in fictitious situations in this book.

The Eliminators Show and Shine is an actual event that takes place in Swift Current. I discovered on the internet. It looked like an interesting venue, so I incorporated it into the story in a fictional way. I set it at a different time of the year than it is held in real life because it worked to carry the story forward.

***

The Hand of Fate, Book Three of the Belanger Creek Ranch Series will be available soon.

Here is a sneak preview of the book.

ISBN: Softcover: 978-0-9939166-4-9
E-book: 978-0-9939166-5-6

BOOK THREE CHAPTER ONE

Christina Holmes gathered eighteen-month-old Leanne Johnson in her arms and sat in the rocking chair by the window. Her heart filled with warmth as she snuggled her best friend's daughter against her breast. Christina had learned to accept most of the life's ups and downs, but knowing she could never give birth to a child of her own, was the one disappointment that left a raw spot in her soul.

Leanne's blue eyes brimmed with tears as she pushed away and sat up. She was sucking her thumb as she looked up into Christina's face.

"What's the matter, baby?" Christina asked.

"The poor little tyke is probably tired," Ellie Crampton commented, as she emptied a bottle of 7Up into the fruit juice in a punch bowl. "It's a long drive out to the ranch from Swift Current. Add the excitement of playing with Selena and Sam all afternoon; she's got to be exhausted."

Shauna Lee glanced at the clock on the wall, then, looked lovingly at her small daughter. "You are right Ellie, it's been a long day and she's definitely hungry and tired.

Colt Thompson turned to Brad Johnson, who was mashing a pot of potatoes by the stove. "I swear she was conceived through Immaculate Conception because I don't see any trace of you in her."

Frank Thompson reached across the island where they were all working as they prepared Easter dinner and smacked her husband with a spatula. "Colt!"

"Hey, that stung!" He gave his wife a look of exaggerated pain, and then defended his words. "It's the truth. Look at her; she's a carbon copy of Shauna Lee." Leanne's tiny bone structure, her wispy blonde hair and her big blue eyes fringed by dark eyelashes supported his words.

Shauna Lee looked at Brad and smiled. "Oh, she definitely has his genes! Haven't you noticed how she works her way around, schmoozing to get what she wants? She's just like him; she doesn't take "No" for an answer." Everyone laughed, knowing how tenaciously Brad had pursued her until he'd worn down her every resistance and convinced her that she loved him. She looked at Frank. "Dinner's almost ready, isn't it?"

Tim Bates spoke up as he put bottles of wine on the big country-style table that Christina had just finished setting. "It looks like the boss just needs to finish carving the ham."

"Call Grayson, Ollie and the twins. By the time you get the food on the table, I'll be finished carving the ham."

Tim walked over to the rocking chair and knelt down by Christina. He reached out to brush a finger along Leanne's cheek. "Are you hungry little one?" he asked. The tearful blue eyes brightened as she broke into a big smile and a spate of baby babble. He smiled as he extended his hands and Leanne leaned forward to fall into them. His eyes met Christina's as he took the child. There was a current of understanding between them. He talked to the baby as he stood up and then extended a hand to help Christina get up out of the chair.

While everyone else put the food on the table, Ellie went

to the family room. Grayson McNaughton was watching hockey on TV and Ollie, her 64-year-old husband, was on the floor with the 8-year old Thompson twins playing "ranch". He had built them a barn at Christmas time and now they were "chasing" cows and moving them into the realistic-looking corrals that he'd made to go with it. She smiled.

Selena and Sam had become the grandchildren he would never have — unless, by some miracle, they found his lost son. Possibly, he had grandchildren but they wouldn't know him the way the twins did and after four years of searching, it seemed unlikely that his own son would be found. That was a fact that grated on his mind continuously.

"Dinner is ready." She reached down and ruffled Ollie's graying hair. He looked up at her with smiling eyes. They'd been married for two years, but they had "lived in sin" as Ellie's indignant children had called it, for almost two years before they had made it legal. Ollie had never been married before and he would have married her right away, but while the chemistry and companionship were perfect between them, Ellie had been married for years before and was in no hurry to rush into any permanent relationship at her age. Now she wondered why she'd hesitated, as she couldn't imagine her life without him. The twins jumped up and held out their hands to grasp each of his and tug him to his feet. It had become a ritual, a game they always played and he grunted and groaned as they pulled him to his feet, winking at his wife when the children couldn't see him.

When everyone was seated at the table, Colt honored the occasion by saying grace, giving thanks for this "family" that had come together to share the Easter bounty.

Christina looked around the table, marveling at how they had truly become a family in every way, except for the ties of blood. Four years earlier they had all been mere acquaintances connected by one common thread; Thompson Holdings, Belanger Creek Ranch, and Cantaur Farms

Colt, Frank, and the twins had been the nucleus of it.

Shauna Lee and Brad had met through Colt. Ellie had joined the group as a babysitter for the twins and when they met at the ranch, she and Ollie had connected immediately. Colt had hired Tim to manage Cantaur Farms, and Grayson had joined the crew at Belanger Creek Ranch after Patch Bergeron had died. Christina had worked as Shauna Lee receptionist at Swift Current Accounting and Bookkeeping Services for years, but they'd never had anything more than a business relationship before Shauna Lee and Brad had gotten together. Now all those "strangers" had become a family.

During the past four years common threads of joy and grief, celebration, and tragedy, work, and pleasure, had bound their lives together. The ranch had become the place to meet and share the good times and the sad.

After the dishes had been done, everyone sat around and enjoyed the evening. Grayson went back to the bunkhouse and Tim offered to go down to the old ranch house where Ollie and Ellie lived to get Ollie's prescription pills for acid reflux. He was gone for quite a while and when he got back to the house, he was very distant and unsettled. Christina tried to catch his eye, but he refused to look at her. She finally caught him in the hallway.

"What's up with you, Tim?"

"Nothing," he said brusquely. "I'm going home."

"Tonight?"

"Yes."

"But why?"

He ignored her question. "You can catch a ride back with Brad and Shauna Lee."

"They don't have room for me. They've got the car seats and all the kids' stuff as well as a kennel and Karma."

"They'll make room. I'm getting out of here."

"Tim, what's going on? You've been different ever since you came back from Ollie's…"

"Damn it, Christina. Just leave it alone…"

"But..."

"I said leave it alone. I'm going now. You'll get a ride."

Christina was chilled by the coldness in his attitude. Suddenly he had morphed back into the old Tim, the cold, distant man who had arrived in Swift Current four years earlier. She wanted to shake him, but her instincts told her that something very profound had happened...and he wasn't about to tell her what it was. She couldn't let him leave in this frame of mind. "Tim, I'm coming with you. I..."

He glared at her. "I need some time alone."

"Well, now isn't the time. I'm coming with you."

"I don't need anyone prying right now."

She glared at him. "Prying?"

"Yes, prying. You never can leave things alone."

"Fine, I won't ask any questions, but you're not going alone."

He swore as he turned away. He said an abrupt goodbye to Colt and headed out to his truck.

Shauna Lee looked puzzled. "What's up with him?"

Christina shrugged. "God only knows. It's like something flipped a switch; he's gone right back to being the cold, miserable bastard he was when he first came here."

"Maybe you should just let him go by himself."

Christina shook her head. "He wants me to catch a ride back with you, but something's really wrong. Even Tim wouldn't regress that far in an hour...I'm worried about him."

Christina said a hurried goodbye to everyone and went out to get into Tim's truck, which was idling as he waited. She got in and closed the door.

He scowled at her. "You're so damn stubborn. You should have stayed."

"Just shut up and get on the road. We've got a long drive ahead of us."

He tightened his jaw, throwing her a glare as he put the truck in reverse and backed up. Then he put it into gear and sped out of the yard. They drove in silence. When they were halfway to Maple Creek, it started to snow heavily. Then the wind picked up, whipping it into a blinding blizzard. "What the hell," Tim snarled. "It's almost the end of April. Where does this crap come from?"

Christina said nothing. The visibility became very poor, and he slowed to a crawl as he strained to look into the storm. At one point, he almost missed a curve in the road, his front wheel catching the shoulder. He swore again. The truck inched forward, Tim alert and feeling his way because he could see very little. When they finally reached Maple Creek, it was still a total whiteout. They couldn't see the lights of the town.

"Shit!" Tim exclaimed. "Why the hell didn't you stay at the ranch?"

"And what difference would that have made? It's insane to try to drive in this, whether I'm here or not."

"I'd go on home if you weren't here."

"Then go."

"I don't want to be responsible for having something happen to you." His frustration was evident. "I didn't ask you to come along."

"Hey, buddy, you could have left, but you waited for me. On some level, you wanted my company I sure didn't come because you're charming because you're being a miserable jerk. I came because I felt like I needed to be here for you. So get over yourself. You're stuck with me."

He snorted. "Why would you feel you needed to be here for me? You don't have any responsibility for what happens to me."

"Well, excuse me--I consider you to be a friend. Friends are there for each other."

"I have no friends."

Christina exploded. "You stupid bastard—who do you think all those...."

He slammed on the brakes, reached over and grabbed her coat. "Don't ever call me a bastard again."

She pushed at his hands, but he had a firm grip. His blue eyes were blazing.

"Let go of me," Christina yelled, striking back. He released his hold on her coat and she frantically unhooked her seat belt, opened the truck door and hurled herself out into the storm.

"What are you doing? You can't go out there." He bailed out after her, running to catch her as she floundered through the snowdrifts. He grabbed her by the arm. "Are you trying to commit suicide? You'll get lost and freeze to death."

"Right now that might be a better option than taking a chance on being beaten up in the truck by an ungrateful, hotheaded, maniac."

"I'd never beat you."

"You lost your cool back there, mister, and I don't take kindly to being pushed around."

"I...I...I wouldn't hurt you," he stammered with frustration. He turned back toward the truck, a firm grip on her arm as he led the way. When they reached it, he opened the passenger door to help her get in. He looked into her face in the glow of the interior light. Suddenly he pulled her to him and kissed her angrily.

"Are you crazy?" she gasped, pushing him away. She clamored inside and he slammed the door behind her. She rubbed away the feel of his kiss with her coat sleeve as she glared at him plodding through the snow around the front of the truck.

His mind was in turmoil. What the hell was wrong with him? Why had he kissed her? He stood, staring into the storm for a few seconds before he got in. Then he started the truck and edged onto the highway, squinting against the blinding whiteness as he turned toward Swift Current. Suddenly emergency lights were flashing across the road in front of him. A road block!

Tim swore again as he rolled down his window and Christina noted that she had heard him curse more in the past two hours than she remembered him doing in the past three years. He didn't normally swear. He had when he'd first come to the farm at Cantaur. He'd been cold, angry and bristling with defensiveness. And he'd cursed a lot.

Two policemen approached the truck, bracing themselves against the fury of the storm. "The highway is closed in both directions." The RCMP officer rested his hand against the truck door and peered inside to look at them. "You'll be up against it to find a place to stay for the night. The hotels and motels are full. The restaurants and bars have stayed open, but there's not much room left. There is a small bed and breakfast just up that road behind you and to your right. We've sent two parties there already, but they might be able to make more room."

Frustration oozed out of Tim. "We came from Belanger Creek and it wasn't snowing when we left."

"This storm moved in from Swift Current. There hasn't been any traffic for about an hour and a half. Last reports estimated up to three-foot drifts building in places. I'd advise you to try the B&B. It's the best chance you'll get tonight."

Tim rolled up the window and stared ahead. "Could things get any worse!" He looked across at Christina. "Now what do we do?"

She shook her head. "Well, we can't drive any further, so we'd better try the B&B."

He shifted the truck into reverse and eased backward, then turned onto the adjacent road. The drifts were already hardening and the truck had to fight through the snow in four-wheel drive. They reached the B&B sign and turned into the yard. The lights were a dim haze in the snow. There were three snow-covered vehicles in the yard.

Tim looked at Christina. "He said they'd sent two parties here; there are three cars."

Christina shrugged. "Maybe they have a couch or if nothing else the floor will do. We don't have many choices." She unclasped her seatbelt and opened the door. "Let's go see what they have."

As they stepped onto the porch, the door opened and a tall, slender man stepped into the light to greet them. Tim shuffled uneasily. "The police said you might have a vacancy."

"Uhh...we're fully booked."

Christina bit her lip. "You know, a blanket on the floor will do. We just need a place to stay warm and safe."

"Well...come in and I'll talk to my wife. We have a bed in the attic. We don't use it for the business because it's only a double so it's smaller than most people expect, but seeing this is an emergency...."

"Actually we need two..." Tim growled.

Christina glared at him. "No! If that's what is available, we'll take it."

Tim scowled.

Christina sighed wearily. "For cripes' sake, Tim, it's better than sitting in the truck, freezing. We can't piss each other off any more than we already have tonight. We might as well make up our minds to get a decent rest." She opened her purse. "How much is the room?" She paid, saying "I'm Christina Holmes. Smiley here is Tim Bates."

The man nodded. "This is my wife, Lily and I'm Alvin Bronson. This is a rare storm for this time of the year, but it's not unheard of. It caught a lot of people off guard. We've had a couple of other groups come in tonight. Do you have any luggage?"

"No. I have a small bag in the truck, but I'll sleep in my clothes and get it in the morning," Christina replied.

Lily stepped forward. "That room isn't the warmest. We only use it for the grandkids in the summer. I have a king-sized down filled comforter that'll provide more warmth." When she came back, she handed Tim an extra pillow and the comforter. She handed Christina a pair of long, thermal underwear. "These are mine. We're about the same size so I think they'll fit you and they'll be more comfortable than trying to sleep in your clothes. I'm sorry, but there are no services up there so you'll have to use the washroom down here."

She looked at Tim. "Our son is about your size. He's got a fleece jogging suit here. I'll get it. I'm sure you'll be a lot more comfortable in it than in your jeans and shirt."

Tim started to protest, but Lily cut him off. "I don't want to hear another word. I think you're going to have enough trouble getting comfortable."

Lily came back with a blue jogging suit and handed it to Tim. Alvin led them up the narrow stairs to the room in the attic. After Alvin had left, they looked around the small room. Frost was forming on the single window and they could see wisps of their breath wafting in the chilly air.

Tim glared at Christina. "I guess I get the floor."

"Quit being an ass and get a grip on yourself. There is no need for anyone to sleep on the floor. If you get outside of your narrow mind, I'm sure we are both mature enough to make the best out of this rotten situation. I'm not going to jump away and shriek if your leg touches mine. It's not as if either one of us are interested anything other than sleep and keeping warm."

He stared at her. "Are you suggesting we share the bed?"

"Cripes! Pretend I'm your brother."

"My brother? Then I definitely wouldn't be getting into bed with you. I like him less than I do you."

Christina shook her head. "Screw you. Pretend I'm someone you don't dislike then. What would you do if I were Colt or Brad? You'd damn well get in bed and sleep. I'm going downstairs to change into these long johns and I'll leave my socks on too so you won't be able to accidently touch my skin. I suggest you get into that fleecy thing she gave you and hustle into bed." She went to the door, paused and looked back at him. "Turn off the light so you can't see me when I get back. That way you can pretend it's someone else on the other side of the bed."

When Christina came back, the light was off. She leaned over to touch the end of the bed in the darkness and felt her way along to the far side. She was edging her way to the head of the bed, when her foot hit something and she lost her balance. She gave a muffled gasp as she fell over Tim's body.

Fury, hot and raw, exploded in her chest. "What are you doing down there on the floor?"

"I'm not sleeping in that bed with you. I laid down here so you could just walk in and get into bed when you came back."

"I always sleep on this side of the bed," she hissed.

"How was I to know that?" he huffed as he tried to push her away so he could get out from under her.

She tried to get her balance as she struggled amid the twists of his legs, knees and hips under the quilt.

Finally, he got up on all fours in the tangle of quilt and pushed her up. The room was pitch black, but she felt her way to the foot of the bed, reaching out for the wall. She slid her hand along until she felt the light switch and she flipped it on, bathing the room in shocking light.

Their eyes locked and held. Her fury was tangible, radiating off her with a heat he could feel. Tim looked away first. She walked over and stripped the quilt off him and threw it on the bed, then turned to him, sparks snapping in her eyes.

"You're not sleeping on the floor in this cold room. Stop acting like an adolescent and get in the bed. I don't know what happened to you today, but the man I've come to know as a friend, has regressed into an idiot. Grow up, Tim!"

She switched the light off and felt her way up to the head of the bed; on the wrong side for her. She crawled in and pulled the sheets and the quilt up around her neck, turning on her right side with her back to him. She lay still, waiting to feel his weight settle on the bed. It had seemed like an eternity before it did.

Tim lay on his left side, as close to the edge of the bed as he could get, with his back to her. He was as tense as a board, his senses alert, listening for every breath, every stirring she made. He was shocked, almost angered, when a few minutes later he heard her breathing become a whisper, slow and relaxed and he realized that she was asleep. How could she be asleep already? He shifted gingerly, desperate not to wake her. He was uncomfortable. He usually slept on his back, sprawled across the whole bed. He hadn't shared a bed with anyone since his wife had left him.

His mind was in turmoil. Not only was he in a damnable situation there in the bed, but so many unanswered questions raced through his thoughts. What had he really stumbled upon when he'd gone to Ollie and Ellie's house? Why was that picture laying on the desk in Ollie's office? Seeing it there had shocked him. At first, he'd thought he had to be mistaken, but when he picked it up and looked closely, he knew he'd seen it before. It was his mother.

Then Christina had insisted on coming home with him, and she'd called him a Bastard! The word swirled in his mind. Why couldn't he push it away? He tossed and turned, then finally found refuge in sleep. The warmth of the bed lured him.

Hours later, Christina surfaced slowly, instinctively relaxing into the warmth against her back and the weight encircling her waist. The comfort of it lulled her back into the depths of slumber.

Full Circle

BOOK THREE CHAPTER TWO

That night, the snow had started to fall heavily at around ten o'clock at Belanger Creek Ranch. Shortly after, the relentless winds came, driving in a blinding blizzard. Colt and Brad had driven down to the barn to check on the 200 hundred head of cows with late calves housed in the corrals. The high board shelters on the windward side of the corrals protected them from the brunt of the storm and most of the calves were huddled in the calf shelters.

Ollie and Grayson were already there. They had moved a couple dozen smaller calves inside a covered area because they were newborns and the heavy wet snow would weaken them, promoting scours or pneumonia in the herd.

Ollie voiced Colt's main concern. "This doesn't bode well for the cows and calves that we turned out into the feeding area down by the river.

Colt nodded. "I know. They won't fight against the storm. They'll put their backs into the wind and drift with it. That'll take them down off the hilltops where we've been feeding them, into the shelter of the ravines or clumps of willow."

Ollie's look was sober. "I've seen it happen. If it's bad enough, they'll get down in those narrow sheltered spots and crowd in like sardines in a can. The calves can get trampled pretty easily."

Colt looked into the storm. "The calves in that group are older and stronger, but when 300 cows start to crowd, even the bigger, healthy animals can lose footing and go down."

Ollie nodded. "It depends on how long this lasts. I've seen these storms last for a couple of days. The cattle can get hung up in the willows and suffocate under the drifts that blow over them. I haven't been checking the weather forecast the past couple of days, so have no idea what they are predicting for this one. I didn't even realize it was coming."

Colt looked at Brad. "I didn't either. We were playing cards when it started to snow, but I didn't pay much attention until the wind came up. I just figured it was a quick spring flurry. I should've been more aware."

Ollie brushed the snow off his jacket. "I should have, too. The Cypress Hills can drop some unpredictable surprises on this country."

Colt slapped his gloves against his jeans. "I think this storm actually came in from Swift Current way. There isn't much we can do right now. Even if we were able to ride out there, the cattle would fight us at every turn. Hopefully, this will have blown itself out by dawn and then we'll ride out with the horses. Right now, we're better off to get some sleep and conserve the horses. Can you stick around and give us a hand in the morning, Brad?"

"We won't leave until you get everything straightened out here. Tomorrow is a holiday anyway, and if I need to, I can get one of the installers to go to the shop on Tuesday. Christina will be home, so she'll open the office for Shauna Lee."

Colt looked at Grayson. "Will you help Ollie attach the blade to the tractor in the morning before we ride? Fran will ride out with Brad, you and me. Ollie can follow us with the

Full Circle

tractor and plow the snow off the road so we can drive the truck in if we have any animals that need to be brought home."

Ollie & Grayson nodded in agreement and everyone went their separate ways. At five o'clock, they were up again. Frank and Shauna Lee had breakfast ready and after they'd eaten, Frank left with the men to saddle up.

Shauna Lee could barely see them ride out in the early dawn light and a few minutes later she watched Ollie leave with the tractor, plowing the snow off the road. She watched until he was out of sight, and then turned to clean up the kitchen.

Half an hour later, Colt sighed with relief as they rode into the pasture. "It looks like we lucked out this time. This could have been a disaster. Fortunately, it stayed mild and we only have a foot of snow here. It's so wet and heavy that it won't have piled up in the coulees and ravines the way a dry, cold snow would have, with those strong winds."

Brad nodded in agreement. "We're lucky the wind only lasted a couple of hours."

Colt and Frank rode through the higher end, checking the ravines and willow bluffs as they went. Brad and Grayson rode the lower end of the field, along the river fence and up the east side. Fortunately, no calves had been trampled and no cows were down. They drove the animals back to the feeding areas.

By then Ollie was plowing snow in different sections of the pasture so it would be easier to feed. Colt and Brad went to the feed yard. Brad worked the gate while Colt started the big tractor with the bale buster hooked behind it. He backed up to the stack and loaded one of the 1600 pound bales into the tub and then picked up a second bale with the machine and headed out into the field.

Brad open and closed the gate so no hungry cows could get into the stack yard. He watched with fascination, as the bale buster shredded the bale and augured it out into a long windrow on the ground. When the first bale had been fed, he dropped the second one into the tub and shredded it as well. The cows lined up along the windrows to eat. Colt had made three more trips to different areas of the pasture before he was done feeding.

Frank and Grayson rode their horses among the cows as they ate, watching for any signs of potential problems; an injured foot or leg, a bruised rib causing breathing problems, early stages of pneumonia or scours. Frank's veterinary training alerted her to conditions that might have been missed. She'd quickly learned to count on Grayson's quick eye for problems in the herd and they regularly conferred. . .

After the feeding was finished and the tractor parked back in the feed yard, the four of them mounted up to ride home. Ollie had plowed the drifts out and riding was easier for man and beast. The sun was shining and it was clear that, except where it had drifted in the shaded areas, the snow wouldn't last very long.

Ollie had gone back to the ranch as soon as he'd finished plowing and when they arrived, he was finishing up the chores. They tied their horses to the hitching rail by the barn. Colt and Brad went to help Ollie while Frank and Grayson made a quick tour of the calves. They found no obvious problems, so they took the horses into the barn, unsaddled them and brushed them down. They had turned them into stalls and were giving them each a portion of grain when they heard the quad coming down the hill.

Seconds later, Sam came dashing in the barn door. "Hey, Mom! Ellie and Auntie Shauna Lee are making something to eat at our place. Everyone is supposed to come up there.

"That sounds great. I'll catch a ride back on the quad with you. Dad and the other guys can come in the truck."

"Okay, Mom." They went out and got on the quad. Sam started it, revved it up, and sped up the hill, sending a plume of wet snow and water away from the wheels.

"Sam! You're going to get me soaking wet! Slow down."

"You're wet already, Mom. Didn't you look at your pants and boots?"

She looked down at her clothes. "I am, and I'm cold too."

"How can you be cold? It's nice out and the snow is melting like crazy. Look at the way it's running down the tracks in the road."

"Well buddy...you haven't been out riding since dawn. We've been wading through the snowbanks and walking around looking at the cows and calves. Your turn will come one day and then you'll know what it's like. You'll be chilled to the bone just like we are!"

The quad rolled to a stop at the door and Frank tweaked her son's ear as she got off. "Thanks for the ride, big guy, even if you did soak me again."

The pickup pulled into the yard right behind them and Colt and Brad got out.

"What happened to Grayson and Ollie? They're supposed to come too." Frank asked.

"They're changing into something dry and warm. Then they'll come up."

The smells from the kitchen greeted them when they opened the door. "All of a sudden I'm famished." Colt looked at his watch. "It's no wonder. It's after two o'clock. We were out there for more than eight hours."

Frank and Colt went to their bedroom and took a quick shower to warm up. They put on dry clothes and joined the others in the kitchen. Brad was already there and Shauna Lee was handing him a hot cup of coffee spiked with a shot of Baileys.

"I've got one here for you, too, Frank," she said handing her a hot cup.

"Mm...this is wonderful," she cradled it in her hands, savoring the warmth.

"And me?" Colt asked with a hopeful grin.

"Coming right," Shauna Lee answered. "It sounds like Ollie and Grayson are here now, too," she said hearing the porch door open. "Do you guys want coffee with Baileys in it?"

Grayson said yes, but before Ollie answered, Ellie was pouring a shot of Jack Daniels into a glass for him. Ollie smiled as she handed it to him. "Thanks, love." He said and raised the glass to the others. "This is my poison—it warms you right to the core!"

Everyone sat down at the table and enjoyed a flavorful meal of hot stew and baking powder biscuits. They ate until they were content, then sat and talked about the storm and how fortunate things had turned out.

"I wonder if Tim and Christina got caught in it," Colt said thoughtfully.

"That was strange," Frank commented. "You know, the way he decided to leave so abruptly."

Brad nodded. "Yeah, what the heck happened there, anyway? He was happy and relaxed all day, and then all of a sudden he just did a 180."

Shauna Lee shook her head. "I have no idea. Christina didn't know what was going on either. She was so concerned that she decided to go home with him, even though he didn't want her to."

"Is there something going on between those two?" Colt asked.

Shauna Lee shook her head. "No. They're just friends."

"I've wondered about that" Brad commented. "Lately they're pretty comfortable with each other."

"I've noticed it, too" Frank commented.

Shauna Lee nodded. "Well, I think they've worked out most of their angst by now. He was so bitter when he first came and she really took a dislike to him. Christina always referred to him the 'cold fish.' But they're civil now."

"He has settled in at the farm. I'm really impressed with him," Colt added.

Brad nodded. "He was a great guy when I knew him in the Peace River country. He loved being a farmer and he was a smart businessman. When he got married, everyone who knew them wondered how it had happened. They were like water and oil from the very beginning. I think she thought there were diamonds sparkling in the grain bins and had big ideas about being a rich land owner's wife. The marriage sort of hung together for about eight years, but it was over long before they split.

"When Tim's mother died, it was a big blow to him. His siblings are nothing like him. They're a lot younger and spoiled rotten. He has one brother and he was a cocky, egotistical brat who never did a day of hard work in his life. He gave Tim a bad time when he got old enough to think he could flex his muscles as far as the business went. When his dad died, the farm was worth millions, but they just tore it apart trying to get their hands on all the money. They killed the goose that laid the golden egg and Tim got 'plucked' in the process.

BOOK THREE CHAPTER THREE

Tim awakened slowly, savoring the warmth. A fragrant cloud lay against his cheek, tickling his nose. It smelled like lilacs. He softly blew a tendril from across the tip of his nose. *Hair!*

He became aware of the softness resting against his chest, molding to his hips, his thighs and the leg that intertwined with his. He felt the hip bone beneath his arm as it lay over a curvy waist. He stiffened. *What the hell is she doing?*

Realization flooded through him. No! What the hell was he doing? She was still curled up on her side of the bed. He was the one who was cuddling her, snuggled up as close as he could get, on her side of the bed. Panicked, he listened to the rhythm of her breathing. If he was careful, possibly he could ease his body over onto his own side without waking her up. He inched away carefully.

She stirred and murmured something, stretching her legs gently. Her hand groped, searching for the warmth that had moved away, but she stayed asleep. He edged over slowly

Full Circle

and turned onto his left side again, clinging to the edge of the bed. He exhaled slowly. He'd made it!

His breathing was rapid and he tried to calm it. He couldn't keep his thoughts in line. It felt good to wake up to a warm, soft, fragrant body next to him. He thought he'd put that behind him, but that primal instinct was still there. *Damned women. Always a temptation to a stupid, vulnerable, man.* He lay quietly, thinking about life; his life.

His mother had been the one constant in his life and he'd worshiped her. He thought he knew everything about her, but he didn't know how she figured into Ollie Crampton's life. She always said she didn't have any family, so why was her picture on his desk? He had turned it over and looked at the back of it. It was date-stamped four years ago, just a few months after he'd come to the farm, and it bore the name of a legal firm in Vancouver, B.C. She had died over eight years before.

He rolled onto his back with a sigh and flung his arm across his eyes. *Could Ollie be checking me out? But why? I could understand if Colt had done that before I started working for him, but I was already at the farm when that picture was dated. Ollie and I have talked lots of times over the past four years; we've had some serious conversations about life. Why didn't he say anything about having Mom's picture?*

And why would anyone send a picture of Mom to him? It would have come to Shauna Lee's office, not to Ollie. So what is going on here? Don't they trust me; After Bob Thompson had died last year, Colt sold me his shares in Cantaur Farms. We're partners now, and we haven't had any problems. None of this makes any sense. I've considered those guys to be my friends. I hope I'm not going to get screwed over again.

"You survived the night!" Christina said softly, breaking into his thoughts.

He lowered his arm and looked across at her. His eyes strayed to the curtain of dark hair that spilled onto her pillow and the intoxicating scent of it came back to him. He smiled crookedly. "I see you did, too."

"I was so tired, I just died! And the bed was so warm and comfy." Her fingers plucked at the comforter. "It must have been this feather filled quilt. I'm going to have to get one for home. It was heavenly. Were you warm enough?"

"It was more comfortable than I'd expected it to be. I needed a good sleep."

"So are you in a better frame of mind this morning?"

"A good sleep can't fix everything, Christina, but I'm okay."

"Am I still the enemy, or do you see me as a friend now?" She giggled. "After all we've slept together; that's closer than most friends ever get." Her look turned serious. "I'm a good listener, Tim. I don't break confidences either. I've got my own ugly secrets. But honestly, it probably would help to discuss whatever happened yesterday and get it off your chest. It had to be big to make you do such a 180."

"I don't want to talk about it. I have to figure out what actually happened by myself; what it means to me. I'm going to get up and check the road report." He threw back the blankets and stood up. He looked out the small window, but all he could see was frosted edges and a sea of white. "That doesn't look very promising," he grumbled. He grabbed his jeans and his shirt. "Turn away; I'm going to put on my clothes."

She buried her head under the quilt and waited until he said "Alright, I'm out of here. I'm warning you, it's damned chilly in here. You'd better dress downstairs in the bathroom."

She looked up as he opened the door. He hesitated, then said "Christina…I'm sorry."

"For what?" She grinned. "Oh, you mean for keeping me warm? To be honest, I'd forgotten how good it felt to cuddle with someone."

His jaw slackened, and then his face flushed red.

"Yes, Tim, I know. I woke up earlier. No harm done. Warmth and sleep are basic essentials."

"You are a bitch."

"I know…and you're still a bastard, too. A good sleep can't fix everything."

He slammed the door and went down the stairs. She got up and got dressed. She shivered. The room was cold.

"Good morning," Lily greeted her when she arrived in the kitchen. "Did you sleep well?"

"I was so tired, I just passed out. The bed was warm and toasty. It had to be that marvelous quilt."

"I'm glad the bed worked out alright. Tim said he had a good sleep too, and he seemed a lot more relaxed this morning. Would you like a cup of coffee? Tim went out to get his razor and he's bringing your overnight bag in. He'll have a cup when he comes back."

Christina turned to look when the entry door opened and Tim stepped inside. Their eyes met as he handed her bag to her. She smiled warmly. "Thank you, Tim."

He tried to scowl but didn't quite succeed. "I knew you'd need your hairbrush and I've heard you complain about your morning breath and needing your toothbrush."

"I'm shocked you remembered all that. Obviously a good sleep does improve some things." She winked at him as she turned away and went to the washroom.

When she returned, Tim was sitting at one of the tables in the dining room, drinking coffee. A glance told her that a full cup was waiting for her too, so she joined him. He looked at her and grinned. "Hey, you look pretty good now."

She sat down and took a drink of her coffee. Was he flirting with her, just a bit? No, that couldn't be happening. "Hmm…I've never seen you with a five o'clock shadow before. It's looks kind of rakish on you." She rubbed her hand down her cheek and along her chin.

He looked at her for a long moment. Is she flirting? Get a grip man. That is not happening.

"So, what do you want for breakfast? The B&B package

comes with cold cereal and toast or hot baking powder biscuits and jam or a croissant and a bowl of fresh fruit; your choice."

"I'll have a hot biscuit and jam. I love biscuits." She looked at him curiously. "What are you having? Let me guess; cold cereal and toast."

"How did you know?"

She smiled and gave a shrug. "I'm observant."

The highway was open by ten-thirty that morning and Tim and Christina were on the road as soon as they got word that they could travel. Most of the trip was made in silence, but it wasn't the hostile silence of the previous night's journey from Belanger Creek. It was a companionable silence; two friends traveling together.

About two-thirds of the way home, Tim sighed deeply and looked at her. "About yesterday...when I went down to Ollie's house to get his pills, they weren't in the medicine chest in the bathroom, or on the windowsill by the kitchen sink. They were on the desk in his office."

Christina waited for him to continue, but when he didn't, she said, "Okay. What was so significant about that, Tim?"

He drummed his fingers on the steering wheel, staring ahead, down the road. "My Mom's picture."

"What?"

"It was there on his desk. Just lying there, as if he'd been sitting there looking at it before he'd left."

"But why? I mean are you certain it was her?"

"At first, I thought I imagined it...but I picked it up and studied it. It was taken when she was young; probably in her twenties. There's no doubt that it's her. I've seen it before among her things."

"It doesn't make sense, Tim. How would Ollie get a picture of your mom? And why?"

"I've been asking myself the same thing, and I have no idea why. There was a date-stamped on the back. It was four years ago, in late May, and the name of a legal firm in

Vancouver B.C. was stamped underneath it. I was already at the farm then. I'd been there a few months by that time."

Christina frowned thoughtfully. "And neither Colt nor Ollie has ever mentioned it to you in all this time?"

"No. To be honest, that's what really bothers me about this whole thing. What the hell is going on? Why hasn't anyone mentioned that they knew her or had a picture of her? God, I've come to feel like I was part of the family here; like they are all my close friends. But honestly, Christina, would a family or friends keep something like that from me. And it wasn't shoved away and forgotten in a corner. It was right there in front of his chair. Ellie has to know. How would you feel?"

"So why didn't you ask Ollie about it when you came back up to the house?"

"When I first saw it, I was shocked and I just sat there for a long time, feeling confused. To be honest, I felt betrayed. Then I got mad and I didn't know who I could believe or trust. I just wanted to get out of there."

"Tim, I haven't really known everyone much longer than you have. I've worked for Shauna Lee for years, but until she met Brad, she was nothing more than an employer. I knew she had gone out with Colt before he married Frank, and I'd seen Colt and Bob come into the office, but I didn't really know them on a personal basis. I'd seen Ollie off and on over the years but just in passing.

"But now, I believe in all of them; they are true friends. I...you, too...we've seen it over and over again. They...we... support each other through thick and thin. We're there for each other if things go wrong, we celebrate together when things go well. Everyone works hard, they play together...they're real people. There's something we're missing here."

"But what Christina?" He sighed and looked out the side window. "I'm so tired of having life go sideways on me. I was beginning to settle in, feel a part of things." He thumped the steering wheel with his hand. "And then this happens and now I'm questioning everything again. I can't deal with another disaster."

"Okay, let's try using some logic, instead of emotions. Was your mom still alive when you came here? Somehow I thought your dad died last."

"He did. That's the thing. Mom was gone about six years before Dad, so, why would anyone be sending out her picture four years after he died?"

"Don't assume the worst, Tim. You need talk to Ollie and Colt. You should go back to the ranch as soon as you can and get it all out in the open. If you can wait until next weekend, I'll go with you for support."

His eyes met hers. "You mean you'd do that for me after I've been such a miserable…"

"Bastard? What is it about that word that really gets to you?"

"I am one."

***

Watch for *A Second Chance, Book Four of the Belanger Creek Ranch Series,* coming soon.

If you haven't read *The Second Time Around, Book One of The Belanger Creek Ranch Series* you may be interested it in checking it out. It is the story of Colt Thompson and Frank Lamonte.

Full Circle

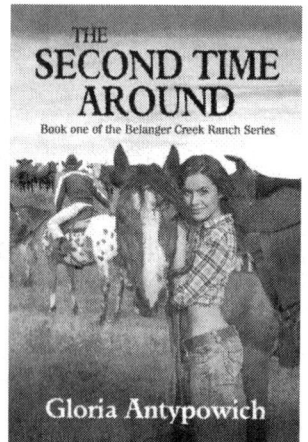

ABOUT THE AUTHOR

Photograph by Suzanne Englund

Gloria Antypowich grew up on a farm and most of her married life has been lived on a ranch. Human relationships fascinate her. Ideas for stories can be found everywhere; overheard conversations in a public place, a couple fighting in a restaurant, a story in the news, even a chance remark in a conversation with a friend. She is enamored with the power of words and she loves to use them to paint images of characters that become so real, they feel like they could be your next door neighbor.

Gloria is an avid reader of several different genres and listens to a wide selection of music. A good game of cards, sharing a laugh with a friend over a glass of wine and spending time with her family are a few of her favorite things to do. She loves to write and says her husband was her inspiration for the heroes in this series of books. He was a cowboy, a rancher — and a lover. Gloria lives with her husband, in the central interior of British Columbia, Canada. They are retired now, but they still have "chemistry".

Made in the USA
Charleston, SC
09 October 2015